"*Kell's Legend* is a [...] fantastic fight scenes. *Kell's Legend* is a novel of power and scope, able to stand as a worthy successor to the Gemmell crown."
Fantasy & Science Fiction Books

"I dived straight in, emerging a couple of days later – with a grin on my face... An engaging, fast-paced cocktail of violence and intrigue that grabs you right from the outset and doesn't let go until you run out of pages."
My Favourite Books

"A bloody, violent, fantastic journey through carnage, terror, and a downright epic tale that makes every zombie movie look bad... Remic is the Tarantino of fantasy, and if that isn't a compliment, then I don't know what is."
Fantasy & SciFi Lovin'

"A blistering read; the pace is frenetic and the action scenes come thick and fast. The fight sequences are often electrifying. *Kell's Legend* is a rip-roaring beast of a novel, a whirlwind of frantic battles and fraught relationships against a bleak background of invasion and enslavement."
Speculative Horizons

ANDY REMIC

Kell's Legend

BOOK ONE OF THE
CLOCKWORK VAMPIRE
CHRONICLES

ANGRY
ROBOT

ANGRY ROBOT
A member of the Osprey Group

Lace Market House,
54-56 High Pavement,
Nottingham
NG1 1HW, UK

www.angryrobotbooks.com
No more heroes

Originally published in the UK by Angry Robot 2009
First American paperback printing 2010

Distributed in the United States by Random House, Inc., New York.

ISBN 978-0-85766-016-9

Printed in the United States of America

9 8 7 6 5 4 3 2 1

This book is dedicated to the man who inspired me to write fantasy in the first place: the late, great David Gemmell.

May he rest well in the Hall of Heroes.

PROLOGUE
Slaughter

"I know you think me sadistic. You are incorrect. When I punish, I punish without pleasure. When I torture, I torture for knowledge, progression, and for truth. And when I kill..." General Graal placed both hands on the icy battlements, staring dream-like to the haze of distant Black Pike Mountains caught shimmering and unreal through the mist: huge, defiant, proud, unconquered. He grinned a narrow, skeletal grin. "Then I kill to feed."

Graal turned, and stared at the kneeling man. Command Colonel Yax-kulkain was forty-eight years old, a seasoned warrior and leader of the Garrison Regiment at Jalder, Falanor's major northern city and trading post connecting east, south and west military supply routes, also known as the Northern T.

Yax-kulkain was hunkered down, fists twitching uncontrollably, staring up into Graal's blue eyes. Pupil dilation told Graal the commander could still understand, despite his paralysis. Graal smiled, a thin-lipped smile with white lips that blended eerily into the near-albino skin of his soft, some would say feminine, face. Running a hand through alabaster hair Graal released a hiss and gave a heavy, pendulous nod. "I see you understand me, colonel."

Yax-kulkain murmured something, an animal sound deep in his throat. He trembled, in his frozen, kneeling position, and with ice crackling his beard, gradually, with incredible force of will, lifted his blue-hued face and snarled up at the conquering general. There came a crack as he forced frozen jaws apart. Ice fell, tinkling from his beard. In rage, the ice-chilled warrior spat, "You will... rot... in hell!"

General Graal turned, staring almost nostalgically across frosted battlements. He spun on his heel, a fast fluid motion, slim blade slamming to cut the command colonel's head from his body. The head rolled, hitting stone flags and cracking a platter of ice. It rocked, and came to a halt, eyes staring blank at the bleak, snow-filled sky.

"I think not," said Graal, staring down the long line of kneeling men, of rigid, frozen soldiers that stretched away down the considerable length of the ice-rimed battlements. "It would appear I am already there." His voice rose in volume to a bellow. "Soldiers of the Army of Iron!" He paused, voice dropping to a guttural growl. "Kill them all."

Like automatons, insects, albino soldiers stepped up with a synchronised rhythm behind the ranks of frozen infantry at Falanor's chief garrison; white hair whipped in the wind, and black armour cut a savage contrast to pale, waxen flesh. Black swords unsheathed, eight hundred oiled whispers of precision steel, and General Graal moved his hand with a casual flick as he turned away. Swords descended, sliced through flesh and fat and bone, and eight hundred heads toppled from twitching shoulders to thud and roll. Because of the frozen flesh, there was no blood. It was a clean slaughter.

Ice-smoke swirled, thickening, flowing in the air from a resplendent and unwary city below, beyond the smashed protection of the garrison stronghold. Buildings spread gracefully and economically up the steep hillside from the broad, half-frozen platter of the Selenau River; and as Graal's odd blue eyes narrowed to nothing more than slits, it was clear the ice-smoke was anything but natural: there were sinister elements at play.

Graal strode down the line of corpses, halting occasionally and stooping to force his finger into the icy stump of a soldier's neck. The swirling smoke thickened. Through this carnage, up the narrow steps to the battlements, glided–

The Harvesters.

They were tall, impossibly tall for men, and wore thin white robes embroidered with fine gold wire and draped over bony, elongated figures. Their faces were flat, oval, hairless, eyes small and black, their noses nothing more than twin vertical slits which hissed with a fast rhythm of palpitation. Their hands were hidden under flapping cuffs and they strode unhurriedly, heads bobbing as they stooped to survey the scene. The ranks of motionless albino soldiers took reverential steps back, and whilst faces did not show fear exactly, the albino warriors of Graal's army revealed a healthy respect. One did not cross the Harvesters. Not if a man valued his soul.

The first halted, peering myopically down at Graal, who folded his arms and smiled without humour. "You are late, Hestalt."

Hestalt nodded, and when he spoke his words were a lazy sigh of wind. "We were preparing the ice-smoke for the city. We had to commune with Nonterrazake. Now, however, the time has come. Are your men ready with their primitive weapons of iron?"

"My soldiers are always prepared," said Graal, unruffled, and he unsheathed his own slender sword. The Harvester did not flinch; instead, a hand appeared from folds of white robe. Each finger was ten or twelve inches long, narrowing to a tapered point of gleaming ivory. The Harvester turned, bent, and plunged all five bone fingers into the corpse of Command Colonel Yax-kulkain. There came a gentle resonance of suction, and Graal watched, mouth tight-lipped, as the body began to deflate, shrivelling, flesh shrinking across the bones beneath.

Hestalt withdrew bone fingers, and leaving a tiny, shrivelled husk in his wake, moved to the next dead soldier of Falanor. Again, his fingers invaded the man's chest, deep into his heart, and the Harvester reaped the Harvest.

Unable to watch this desecration of flesh, General Graal shouted a command which rang down the mist-filled battlements. Ice-smoke eddied around his knees, now, expanding and billowing in exaggerated bursts as he strode towards the steps leading down to the cobbled courtyard. His albino regiment followed in silence, swords unsheathed and ready, and like a tide, with Graal at its spearhead, moved to mammoth oak

gates that opened onto a cobbled central thoroughfare, which in turn led down the steep hillside into
Jalder's central city – into the city's heart.

Two albinos ran forward, slim figures, well balanced
and athletic, graceful and moving with care on ice-
slick cobbles. The oak portals were heaved apart, iron
hinges groaning, and Graal turned glancing back to
the tall stooping figures that moved methodically
along the battlements, draining the dead Falanor garrison of life-force. Like insects, he thought, and made
distant eye contact with Hestalt. The Harvester gave a
single nod: a command. He pointed towards the city...
and his instruction was clear.

Prepare a path.

Ice-smoke gathered in the courtyard, a huge pulsing
globe which spun and built and coalesced with flickers
of dancing silver; suddenly, it surged out through the
gates to flow like airborne mercury into the city beyond, still expanding, still growing, a flood of eerie
silence and cotton-wool death, a plague of drifting ice-
smoke shifting to encompass the unwary city in a
tomb-shroud of blood-oil magick.

ONE
Death-Ice

Kell stood by the window in his low-ceilinged second-storey apartment, and stared with a twinge of melancholy towards the distant mountains. Behind him a fire crackled in the hearth, flames consuming pine, and a pan of thick vegetable broth bubbled on a cast-iron tripod. Kell lifted a stubby mug to his lips and sipped neat liquor with a sigh, feeling alcohol-resin tease down his throat and into his belly, warming him through. He shivered despite the drink, and thought about snow and ice, and the dead cold places of the mountains; the vast canyons, the high lonely ledges, the slopes leading to rocky falls and instant death. Chill memories pierced the winter of his soul, if not his flesh. Sometimes, thought Kell, he would never banish the ice of his past… and those dark days of hunting in the realm of the Black Pikes. Ice lay in his heart. Trapped, like a diamond.

Outside, snow drifted on a gentle breeze, swirling down cobbled streets and dancing patterns into the air. From his vantage point, Kell could watch the market traders by the Selenau River, and to the right, make out the black-brick bulks of huge tanneries, warehouses and the riverside slaughter-houses. Kell remembered with a shudder how dregside stunk to heaven in high summer – that's why he'd got the place cheap. But now... now the claws of winter had closed, they kept the stench at bay.

Kell shivered again, the vision of dancing snow chilling old bones. He turned back to his soup and the fire, and stirred the pan's contents, before leaning forward, hand thumping against the sturdy beam of the mantel. Outside, on the steps, he heard a clatter of boots and swiftly placed his mug on a high shelf beside an ancient clock and beneath the terrifying butterfly blades of Ilanna. Inside the clock, he could see tiny whirring clockwork components; so fine and intricate, a pinnacle of miniature engineering.

The thick plank door shuddered open and Nienna stood in silhouette, beaming, kicking snow from her boots.

"Hello, Grandpa!"

"Nienna." He moved to her and she hugged him, the snow in her long brown hair damping his grey beard. He took a step back, holding her at arm's length. "My, you grow taller by the day, I swear!"

"It's all that fine broth." She peered over his shoulder, inquisitively. "Keeps me fit and strong. What have you cooked today?"

"Come on, take off your coat and you can have a bowl. It's vegetable; beef is still too expensive after the cattle-plague in the summer, although I'm guaranteed a side in two or three weeks. From a friend of a friend, no?" He gave a broad wink.

Removing her coat, Nienna edged to the oak table
and cocked one leg over the bench, straddling it. Kell
placed a hand-carved wooden bowl before her, and
she reached eagerly for the spoon as Kell sliced a loaf
of black nut-bread with a long, curved knife.

"It's good!"

"Might need some more salt."

"No, it's perfect!" She spooned greedily, wolfing her
broth with the eagerness of hunger.

"Well," said Kell, sitting opposite his granddaughter
with a smile which split his wrinkled, bearded face,
making him appear younger than his sixty-two years.
"You shouldn't be so surprised. I *am* the best cook in
Jalder."

"Hmm, maybe, but I think it could do with some
beef," said Nienna, pausing, spoon half raised as she
affected a frown.

Kell grinned. "Ach, but I'm just a poor old soldier.
Couldn't possibly afford that."

"Poor? With a fortune stashed under the floor?"
said Nienna, head down, eyes looking up and glinting
mischievously. "That's what mother says. Mother says
you're a miser and a skinflint, and you hide money in
a secret stash wrapped in your stinky socks under the
boards."

Kell gave a tight smile, some of his humour evaporating. "Your mother always was one for
compliments." He brightened. "Anyway, my girl,
you're the cheeky monkey here! With your tricks and
cheeky words."

"I'm a bit old for you to keep calling me that,
grandpa."

"No, lass, you're still a little girl." He leant forward, and ruffled her hair. She scowled in distaste.

"Grandpa! I am not a girl anymore! I'm nearly seventeen!"

"You'll always be a little girl to me. Now eat your broth."

They ate in silence, the only sound that of fire crackling through logs as the wind outside increased in ferocity, kicking up eddies of snow and howling mournfully along frosted, cobbled streets. Nienna finished her broth, and circled her bowl with the last of the black bread. She sat back, sighing. "Good! Too much salt, but good all the same."

"As I said, the best cook in Jalder."

"Have you ever seen a monkey? Really?" she asked suddenly, displaying a subtle hint of youth.

"Yes. In the deep jungles of the south. It's too cold up here for monkeys; I suppose they're fond of their bananas."

"What's a banana?"

"A soft, yellow fruit."

"Do I really look like one?"

"A fruit, or a monkey?"

She smacked his arm. "You know what I mean!"

"A little," said Kell, finishing his own broth and chewing thoughtfully. His teeth were paining him again. "There is a likeness: the hairy face, the fleas, the fat bottom."

"Grandpa! You don't speak to a lady like that! There's this thing we learnt in school, it's called eti... ettick..."

"Etiquette." He ruffled her hair again. "And when you're grown up, Nienna, then I'll treat you like a grown-up." His smile was infectious. Nienna helped to clean away the bowls. She stood by the window for a few moments, staring out and down towards the distant factories and the market.

"You fought in the south jungles, didn't you, Grandpa?"

Kell felt his mood instantly sour, and he bit his tongue against an angry retort. *The girl doesn't realise*, he chided himself. He took a deep breath. "Yes. That was a long time ago. I was a different person back then."

"What was it like? Fighting, in the army, with King Searlan? It must have been so... romantic!"

Kell snorted. "Romantic? The dung they fill your head with in school these days. There's nothing romantic about watching your friends slaughtered. Nothing heroic about seeing crows on a battlefield squabbling over corpse eyes. No." His voice dropped to a whisper. "Battles are for fools."

"But still," persisted Nienna, "I think I'd like to join the army. My friend Kat says they take women now; or you can join as a nurse, to help with battlefield casualties. They give you good training. We had a command sergeant, he came to the school trying to sign us up. Kat wanted to sign, but I thought I'd talk to you first."

Kell moved across the room, so fast he was a blur. Nienna was shocked. He moved too quickly for a big man, for an old man; it was unreal. He took her shoulders in bear paws with surprising gentleness. And he shook her. "Now you listen to me, Nienna, you have a gift, a rare talent like I've not seen in a long while. The music's in your blood, girl, and I'm sure when the angels hear you sing they'll be green with envy." He took a deep breath, gazing with unconditional love into her eyes. "Listen good, Nienna, and understand an old man. An unknown benefactor has paid your university fees. That person has spared you a lifetime of hardship in the tanneries, or in the factories working weaving machinery so treacherous it'll cut your damn fingers off; and the bastards will let it, rather than stop production. So, girl, you go to your university, and you work like you've never worked before, or I'll kick you so hard from behind, my boot will come out of your mouth."

Nienna lowered her head. "Yes, Grandpa. I'm sorry. It's just…"

"What?" His eyes were dark glowing coals.

"It's just – I'm bored! I'd like some excitement, an adventure! All I ever see is home, and here, and school. And I know I can sing, I know that, but it's not a future filled with excitement, is it? It's not something that's going to boil my blood!"

"Excitement is overrated," growled Kell, turning and moving with a wince to his low leather chair. He slumped, grimacing at the pain in his lower back which nagged more frequently these days, despite the thick, green, stinking unguent applied by old Mrs Graham. "Excitement is the sort of thing that gets a person killed."

"You're such a grump!" Nienna skipped across the room, and tugged on her boots. "I've got to get going. We're having a tour of the university this afternoon. It's a shame the snow has come down so thick; the gardens are said to be awesomely pretty."

"Yes, the winter has come early. Such is the legacy of the Black Pike Mountains." He gazed off, through the wide low window, to a far-distant haze of black and white teeth. The Black Pikes called to him. They always would. They had a splinter of his soul.

"Some of my friends are going to explore the Black Pikes this summer; when they finish their studies, of course."

"Fools," snapped Kell. "The Pikes are more dangerous than anything you could ever imagine."

"You've been there?"

"Three times. And three times I believed I was never coming back." His voice grew quiet, drifting, lost. "I knew I would die, up there. On those dark rocky slopes. It is a miracle I still live, girl!"

"Was that when you were in the army?" She was fishing for stories, again, and he waved her away.

"Go on! Get to your friends; go, enjoy your university tour. And make sure you sing for them! Show them your angel's voice! They will have never heard anything like it."

"I will, Grandpa." Nienna tugged on her coat, and brushed out her long brown hair. "Grandpa?"

"Yes, monkey?"

"I… I nearly told mam, about you, this morning. About coming here, I mean. I do so want to tell her… I hate keeping secrets."

Kell shook his head, face stern. "If you tell her, girl, she will make doubly sure you never see me again. She hates me. Can you understand that?" Nienna nodded, but Kell could see in her eyes she did not have the life experience to truly comprehend the hate his daughter carried for him – like a bad egg in her womb. But one day, he thought savagely, one day she'll learn. We all do.

"Yes, Grandpa. I'll try my best." She opened the door, and a bitter chill swept in on a tide of fresh, tumbling snow. She stepped forward, then paused, and gave a half-turn so he couldn't quite see her face. "Kell?"

"Yes, granddaughter?" He blinked, unused to her calling him by name.

"Thanks for paying my university fees." She leant back, and kissed his cheek, and was gone in a whirl of coat and scarf leaving him standing blushing at the top of the steps. He shook his head, watching her footprints crunch through a fresh fall towards a gentle mist drifting in off the Selenau River.

How had she guessed? he thought. He closed the door, which struggled to fit the frame. He thumped it shut with a bear's fist, and absently slid the heavy bar into place. He moved back to the fireplace, reclaiming his abandoned resin-liquor and taking a heavy slug. Alcohol eased into his veins like an old friend, and wrapped his brain in honey. Kell took a deep breath, moving back to the wide window and sitting on a low bench to watch the bartering traders across a field of flapping stalls. The mist was creeping into the market now, swirling around boots and timber stanchions. Kell gazed at the mountains, the Black Pike Mountains, his eyes distant, remembering the hunt there; as he did, many times in a day.

"Join the army – ha!" he muttered, scowling, and refilled his mug from a clay jug.

* * *

Kell awoke, senses tingling, mouth sour, head fuzzy, and wondered not just what had awoken him, but how in Hell's Teeth he'd fallen asleep? "Damn the grog," he muttered, cursing himself for his weakness and age, and swearing he'd stop the liquor; though knowing, deep in his heart, it was a vow he'd never uphold.

Kell sat up from the window-bench, rubbing his eyes and yawning. He glanced right, but all he saw through the long, low window was mist, thick and white, swirling and coalescing through the streets. He could determine a few muffled stone walls, some snow-slick cobbles, but that was all. A terrible white had expanded to fill the world.

Kell moved to his water barrel and gulped three full flagons, with streams running through his grey beard and staining his cotton shirt. He rubbed his eyes again, head spinning, and turned to watch the mist creeping under his door. Odd, he thought. He glanced up to Ilanna, his axe, hanging over the fireplace. She gleamed, dull black reflecting firelight. Kell turned again, and with a crack the window, nearly the width of the entire room, sheared with a metallic crackling as if it had been placed under great pressure. Mist drifted into the apartment.

In reflex, Kell grabbed a towel, soaked it in his water barrel, and wrapped it over his mouth and nose, tying it behind his head. What are you doing, you crazy old fool? screamed his mind. This is no fire smoke! It will do you no harm! But some deep instinct, some primal intuition guided him and he reached up to tug the long-hafted battle-axe from her restraining brackets. Bolts snapped, and the brackets clattered into the fire…

Ice-smoke swirled across his boots, roved across the room, and smothered the fire. It crackled viciously, then died. Outside, a woman gave a muffled scream; the scream ended in a gurgle.

Kell's eyes narrowed, and he strode to his door – as outside, footsteps moved fast up the ice-slick ascent. Kell twisted to one side. The door rattled, and soundlessly Kell slid the bar out of place. The door was kicked open and two soldiers eased into his apartment carrying black swords; their faces were pale and white, their hair long, braided, and as white as the ice-smoke which had smothered Kell's fire.

Kell grinned at the two men, who separated, spreading apart as Kell backed away several steps. The first man rushed him, sword slashing for his throat but Kell twisted, rolling, his axe thundering in a backhand sweep that caught the albino across the head with blade slicing a two-inch slab from the soldier's unprotected skull. The man stumbled back, white blood spraying through clawing fingers, as the second soldier leapt at Kell. But Kell was ready, and his boot hooked under the bench, lifting it hard and fast into the attacker's path. The soldier stumbled over oak and, double-handed, Kell slammed his axe overhead into the fallen man's back, pinning him to the bench. He writhed, gurgling for a while, then spasmed and lay still. A large pool of white blood spread beneath him. Kell placed his boot on the man's armour and tugged free his axe, frowning. *White blood?* He glanced right, to where the injured soldier, with a quarter of his head missing, lay on a pile of rugs, panting fast.

Kell strode to him. "What's going on, lad?"

"Go to hell," snarled the soldier, strings of saliva and blood drooling from his teeth.

"So, an attack is it?" Kell hefted his axe thoughtfully. Then, his face paled, and his hand came to the water-soaked towel. "What dark magick is this? Who leads you, boy? Tell me now, and I'll spare you." It was a lie, and it felt bad on Kell's tongue. He had no intentions of letting the soldier live.

"I'd rather fucking die, old man!"

"So be it."

The axe struck the albino's head from his shoulders, and Kell turned his back on the twitching corpse showing a cross-section of spine and gristle, his mind sour, mood dropping fast into a brooding bitter pit. This wasn't supposed to be his life. No more killing! He was a retired soldier. An old warrior. He no longer walked the mountains, battle-axe in hand, coated in the blood and gore of the slain. Kell shook his head, mouth grim. But then, the gods mocked him, yes? The gods were fickle; they would see to it any retirement Kell sought was blighted with misery.

Nienna!

"Damn them." Kell moved to the steps, peering out into ice-smoke. He nodded to himself. It had to be blood-oil magick. No natural mist moved like this: organic, like coils of snakes in a bucket. Shivering, Kell moved swiftly down the steps and ice-smoke bit his hands, making him yelp. He ran back up to his apartment and pulled on heavy layers of clothing, a thick hat with fur-lined ear-flaps, and a bulky, bear-skin jerkin which broadened Kell's already considerable width of chest. Finally, Kell pulled on high-quality leather gloves and stepped back into the mist. He moved down wooden stairs and stood on a mixture of snow and cobbles, his face tingling. All around, the mist shrouded him in silence; it was a padded world. The air was muffled. Reduced. Shrunk. Kell strode to a nearby wall, and was reassured by the rough reality of black stone. So, he thought. I'm not a victim of a savage, drunken nightmare after all! He laughed at that. It felt like it.

Head pounding, Kell moved warily down the street towards the market. The cobbled road dropped towards the Selenau River, then curved east in a broad arc and wound up the hill towards rows of expensive villas and Jalder University beyond. Kell reached the edge of the market, and stopped. There was a body on the ground, mist curling around withered, ancient limbs. Frowning, Kell dropped to one knee and reached out. He touched dry, crisp flesh, and cried out, shocked–

Boots thudded at him from the white, and a sword slashed for his head. His axe came up at the last moment, and there was clash of steel. Kell rammed his left fist into the soldier's midriff, heard the woosh of expelled air as the man doubled over. Kell stood, and stamped on the man's head, his heavy boot crushing the albino's skull as more came from the mist and Kell, shock and realisation slamming through him, recognition that he was outnumbered, and his brow furrowed and dark thoughts shot through his brain and his blood was pumping, fired now, a deep pulsing rhythm, and he hadn't wanted this, he'd left this behind and it was back again, drawing him in, drawing him onto the knife edge of–

Murder.

Another sword whistled towards his head, and Kell ducked one shoulder, rolling left, axe whirring fast to embed in flesh. His right elbow shot back into a soldier's face and they were around him, swords and knives gleaming but that made life easier. He grinned. They were all enemy. Kell's mind took a step back and coolness washed his aura. His brain calmed, and he changed with an almost imperceptible *click*. Years fell away like abandoned confetti. He felt the old, dark magick flowing through blood like narcotic honey. He'd fought it. Now it was back. And he welcomed it.

Smoothly, Kell whirled and his axe thundered in an arc trailing white blood droplets. An albino soldier was beheaded, the axe continuing, then reversing suddenly to slam through another's breast-plate, cleaving through steel to shatter the sternum and pierce the pumping white heart within. Kell's fist clubbed a soldier to the ground; he ducked a sword slash, which whistled by his ear, and Ilanna slammed a third albino between the eyes, splitting his head like a fruit. Kell's thick fingers curled around another soldier's throat, and he lifted the lithe albino, legs dangling, and brought him close to his own serene and deadly calm features. He headbutted the soldier, spreading nose across pale white skin, and allowed the figure to flop uselessly to the cobbles. Then Kell was running, pounding through the market dodging husks of dried corpses, his own mouth dry, not with fear, but a terrible and ancient understanding as the extent of the slaughter dawned on him. This wasn't a few rogue brigands. This was a full-scale attack!

And the enemy, with matching armour, were professional, skilled, disciplined, ruthless. Throughout Kell's recent economic slaughter there had been no panic, no retreat. These were a people bred for war. And yet, even so, Kell had a premonition that he had met only the untrained – the frontliners, the new recruits. The expendable.

Sourly, Kell ran on, and stopped by the edge of the market, leaning against the stall of Brask the Baker to regain his breath. The smell of fresh bread twitched Kell's nostrils, and reaching out, he realised the racks of loaves were frozen solid. And so was Brask, down on his knees, hands on the edge of his stall, flesh blue and rigid.

"The bastards," snarled Kell, and calmed his breathing. Unused to running, and suffering the effects of excessive liquor and pipe-smoking, a decade out of the army, ten years sat watching the mountains and the snow, well, Kell was far from battle-fit. He waited for pain to subside, and ignored the flaring twinges of hot knives in his lower-back and knees, in his right elbow and shoulder, an arthritis-legacy from decades wielding a heavy battle-axe and carving lumps of flesh with solid, jarring bone-impact.

The Days of Blood, whispered a corner of his imagination, then cackled at him.

Go to hell!

Kell glanced up, into the mist. No, he corrected himself. Into the smoke. The ice-smoke.

He wasn't far from Jalder University. But it was up-hill, and a damn steep hill at that. Gritting his teeth, face coursing with sweat under his thick hat and heavy clothing, Kell began a fast walk, holding his ribs as he prayed fervently to any gods willing to listen that Nienna was still present in the university grounds… and still alive.

Saark gazed down at her beautiful face, skin soft and coolly radiant in the glow from the snow-piled win-dow-ledge. He lifted his hand and ran it through his long, curled black hair, shining with aromatic oils and the woman smiled up at him, love in her eyes, mouth parting, tongue teasing moist lips. Saark dropped his head, unable to contain himself any longer, unable to hold back the hard hot fiery lust and he kissed her with a passion, tasted sweet honey, sank into her warm depths, savoured her gift, inhaled her scent, im-bibed her perfume, fell deep down into the soft lullaby of their kissing, their cradling, their connection, their joining. His hand moved down her flank and she pressed eagerly against him, moaning deep in her throat, in her chest, an eager, primal animal sound. Saark kissed her harder, more ferociously, feeling the beast inside him rear from the pit of his belly to his throat to encompass his mind and drown everything of reason in a pounding drive of hot blood and lust and the desperate need to fuck.

She stepped from her dress, and from glossy, silken underwear. Saark watched as if in a dream. He removed his jacket, careful not to let the jewels – so recently stolen from this beautiful lady's jewellery box – tinkle, as he draped it over a gold-embroidered chair.

"You are a real man, at last," she breathed, voice husky, and Saark kissed her breasts, tasting her nipples, tongue toying, his voice lost, his mind scattered; how could anybody keep such a gorgeous creature locked in a high cold crenellated tower? But then, her husband was ancient, this woman his prize, a beautiful peasant bought like any other object with favours from an outlying nobleman's villa. He kept her secreted here, a creature denied liberty and sexual congress.

Saark kissed her neck, her throat and her breasts which rose to meet him as she panted in need. He bit her nipples and she groaned, thrusting her naked body onto him. "Why does he keep you locked away, sweetie?" mumbled Saark, and as he murmured his fingers dropped to her cunt, which pressed against his cupping hand, warm, slick, firm, inviting him, urging him to take her... to take her hard...

Both her hands ran through Saark's long, curled black hair. "Because," she hissed, "he knows what a wild cat I'd be if he let me out to play!" She threw Saark to the floor and dropped, straddling him. Saark glanced up as she towered over him, aggressive, powerful, dominant, totally in charge, her jewelled hands on naked, swaying, circling hips, the smile of the jailer etched on her face as she eyed him like a cat eyes a cornered mouse. Saark's gaze slowly strayed, from the sexual cunt-honey dripping from her quivering vulva, to the large rubies on the rings that circled her fingers.

He licked his lips, dry now at the excitement of gems and gold. "I think," he said in all honesty, and without any trace of the subtle cynicism which commanded him and in which he prided himself, "I think this is my lucky day."

It was later. Much later. Weak light sloped through the ice-patterned window. Saark propped himself on one elbow and gazed down at the sultry vixen beside him. She was breathing deep, lost in sleep and a totality of contentment. Gods, thought Saark, with a wry grin, I'm fucking good. In fact, I must be the best.

He ran long fingers from her throat and the gentle hollow there, down her sternum, over her rhythmically heaving breasts, and further down to curl in the rich mound of her pubis. She groaned, lifting her hips to him in unconscious response, and Saark eased his hand away. No. Not now. Not *again*. After all, there was business to attend to. He couldn't afford to get her excited; although, he considered, it was extremely tempting. However. Business was business. Gold was gold. And Saark took his business very seriously.

He stood, and slowly, easily, silently dressed. Finally, he pulled on his long leather cavalry boots, and gazed longingly at the beautiful woman, head thrown back on the bed. Oh, to have stayed there for a whole day and night! They would have enjoyed so many sexual adventures together! But... no.

Saark moved to the mahogany sideboard, and eased open the top drawer. There was money, a small sack of thick gold coins, and these Saark tempted into his pocket. The next drawer held nothing but silken underwear – Saark considered helping himself, but greed for wealth over trophies got the better of him; he didn't want to be too much of a pervert. The third drawer held papers tied together by string. Saark rifled them, looking for bonds, shares or agreements; he found only letters, and cursed. On top of the sideboard he found a long, jewelled dagger, used, he presumed, to open correspondence. It had fine emeralds set in a heavy gold hilt. He pocketed the dagger, and moved to the wardrobe, opening the door with a slow, wary gesture, seeking to avoid the groan of aged wood and tarnished hinges. Swiftly he searched the contents, and at the back he found a satchel. It was locked. Dropping to his knees, he pulled free the jewelled dagger and swiftly sawed through leather straps. Inside, there was a sheath of bonds and Saark whistled silently to himself. He held a small fortune. His smile broadened, for these were Secken & Jalberg; he could cash them at any city in Falanor. Today, Saark realised, was not just a good day. It was probably the first day of a new retirement—

"You… bastard." The words were low, barely more than a growl. Slowly, and still on his knees, Saark turned to see the wavering point of his own slender rapier.

"Now don't be like that, sweetie." He wanted to use her name, but for the life of him, he couldn't remember. Was it Mary-Anne? Karyanne? Hell.

"Don't sweetie me, you pile of horse-shit *thief*."

"Hey, I'm not a thief!"

"And a rapist," she said, eyes gleaming, lips wet with hatred, as they had so very recently been wet with lust.

"Whoa!" Saark held up his hands, and went as if to stand. The rapier stabbed at him, nearly skewering his eye. "What the hell do you mean, Darienne?"

"It's Marianne, idiot! And do you know what the Royal Guard do to rapists when apprehended?" She glanced at his groin, and made a horizontal cutting motion with her free hand.

"Marianne! We had such sweet sex! How can you do this to me? It's despicable!"

"Despicable?" she screeched. "You take advantage of me, then seek to clean me out of every penny I've squirreled away from that old vinegar bastard I call a husband! Do you know what I've had to put up with, marrying the stinking toothless old goat? His acid sour breath? His pawing, hairy hands on my tits? His unwashed, fucking rancid feet!"

Saark managed to get to his feet without losing an eye, and with both hands held in supplication, his voice a soothing lullaby, he searched frantically for a way of escape. "Now, now, listen Marianne, we can both still come out of this smelling of roses…"

"No," she hissed, "I can come out of this smelling of expensive perfume, and satisfied, but you," she jabbed at him again, drawing a shallow line of blood down his cheekbone, "you're coming out of this without your *balls*."

In a swift movement Saark slid free the jewelled dagger, lifted his arm – and froze. The door behind Marianne had opened revealing a tall, lithe warrior with shoulder-length white hair and crimson eyes. The albino stepped forward in a sudden violent movement, and his sword-tip burst from Marianne's chest in a blossom of spurting blood. Marianne's eyes met Saark's. They were filled with confusion and pain and for a moment there was a connection, a symbiosis deeper than words, deeper than souls… she opened her mouth to speak, but a spurt of rich arterial blood flooded out and ran down her breasts, stained her flat toned belly, and dripped with a spattering of rainfall to the warped uneven floor. Marianne toppled over, trapping the albino's sword.

Saark's hand slammed forward, and the jewelled dagger entered the soldier's eye. The albino stumbled back, sitting down heavily. Incredibly, he lifted his hand and pulled free the blade with a *slurp*, letting it tumble to the wooden planks with a deafening clatter.

Saark leapt forward, kicking the soldier in the face and scooped his rapier from Marianne's dead grip. The soldier grappled for his own sword, milk-like blood running from his ruined eye-socket; Saark slammed his sword hard into the soldier's neck, half-severing the head. Saark staggered back, watching milk-blood pump from the limp corpse, and he tripped over Marianne's body, slipping in her blood, hitting the ground hard. His eyes met her glassy orbs. Her face was still, and awesomely beautiful, like frozen china. "Damn you!"

Saark stood, slick with Marianne's warm blood, and moved across the room and, ever the thief, retrieved the jewelled dagger that had saved his life. With rapier tight in his fist, he stepped onto the stairwell and glanced down where ice-smoke drifted lazily. Frowning, Saark descended, and felt the bite of savage cold on his legs. He retreated, and rummaged through the wardrobe, finding heavy furs and leathers. Wrapping himself up, Saark descended again, and stepped warily out onto the cobbled road.

Here, property displayed affluence with open vulgarity, the houses, villas and towers wearing wealth and privilege like jewels. The street was deserted. Even through thick clothing Saark could feel the cold nipping at him, stinging his skin, and he hurried down the street and towards the river – stopping only to gaze at a small child lying face down on the cobbles. Saark moved forward and knelt gingerly by the boy. He prodded the child, then rolled the boy, who was only four or five years old, onto his back and drew back with a gasp. The face and limbs were shrivelled, shrunken, the shirt opened over the boy's heart and deep puncture wounds showing clearly, gleaming under drifting ice-smoke. Saark reached forward and counted five holes, his hand hovering above the wounds. "What did this to you, child?" he whispered, horror suffusing his mind. Then his jaw clenched, his eyes hardened, and he stood, hefting his rapier. "Whatever did this, I'm going to find them, and kill them." Rage swam with his blood. Anger burned his brain. Hatred became his fuel, and death his mistress.

Saark, the outcast.

Saark, the jewel thief!

Once proud, once honourable. No! He had stooped low. He had traded his honour and pride and manhood for a handful of worthless baubles. Saark laughed, his laughter brittle and hollow… like his self-esteem. Yes, he was beautiful; powerful and muscular and dazzlingly handsome. The women fell over themselves to bed him. But deep down... deep down, Saark realised he despised himself.

"Kill them? You will not have to look far, little man," came a soft, ululating voice from the ice-smoke. Saark turned, and there towering over him and wearing snakes of smoke like drifting charms stood the stooped, white-robed figure of a Harvester.

The Harvester's tiny black eyes glowed, and it lifted its hand allowing the sleeve to fall back, revealing five long, bony fingers... pointing at Saark, gesturing to the man's unprotected chest, and the heart, and the pumping blood-sugar within...

Saark took an involuntary step back. A sudden fear ate him.

"Come to me, little one," smiled the Harvester, black eyes glowing. "Come and enjoy your reward."

TWO

A Dark Shroud Falls

Kell reached Jalder University's huge iron gates and stopped, panting, wiping sweat from his eyes. He listened, eyes darting left and right. Screams echoed, distant, muffled by ice-smoke. And more, off to the right, down the hill from where he'd emerged. Kell's teeth clamped tight, muscles standing out along the ridge of his jaw-line; the bastards were murdering everybody! And for what? What petty purpose of slaughter? Invasion? Wealth? Greed? Power? Kell spat, and wiped his mouth with the back of his hand.

I thought I'd left the Days of Blood behind?

I thought my soldiering was done. He smiled, a grim bloodless smile with coffee-stained teeth. Well, laddie, it seems somebody has a different plan for you!

Hoisting his matt-black axe, Kell glanced momentarily at the twin butterfly-shaped blades, like curved wings. It would have been a very dark butterfly: poisonous, deadly, utterly without mercy. This was Kell's bloodbond. The *Ilanna*. Sister of the Soul, a connection wrenched from him by ancient rites and dark blood-oil magick, flowing with his lifeblood, his very essence. Ilanna had many tales to tell. But then, the horror stories of the axe were for another day.

Kell moved warily up a well-kept path. He could barely see past low bushes and winter flowers which lined the walkway beyond neatly trimmed grass. He stopped, as something loomed from the mist: it was a circle of corpses, young women, each a shrivelled dry husk with faces stretched like horror masks, skin brittle like glass. Kell's heart-rate increased and his grip tightened.

If they've hurt Nienna, he thought. If they've hurt Nienna…

He reached the entrance, past more corpses from which he averted his eyes. Up stone steps, he rattled the large oak doors. Locked. Kell's gaze swept the mist, his senses singing to him; they were out there, the soldiers, he could feel them, sense them, smell them. But… Kell frowned. There was something else. Something ancient, stalking the mist.

Shivering with premonition, Kell moved warily around the edges of the building. He found a low window, and using his axe-blade, prised the jamb and struggled inside. It was cool and dark. Ice-smoke swirled around the floor. No candles were lit, and Kell's boots padded across thick rich carpets, taking him past fine displays of silverware and ceiling-high shelving containing an orgy of books. Kell seemed to be in some kind of office, and he reached the door – with its ornate arched frame – and eased out into a carpeted corridor lined with small statues. He listened. Nothing… then a scream, so loud and close-by it rammed Kell's heart into his mouth. He whirled around the nearest corner, to see a young woman on her knees, hands above her face, palms out, skin blue with cold. An albino soldier stood over her, a short knife in his hand. He turned as Kell's eyes fell on him… despite Kell making no sound.

The albino smiled.

Kell launched his axe, which sang across the short expanse and thudded through armour and breast-bone, punching the soldier from his feet to sit, stunned, a huge butterfly cleaving his heart. His mouth opened, and milk-blood ran over pale lips and down his chin. Kell strode forward and crouched before the albino.

"But… you should be powerless against us," whispered the man, eyes blinking rapidly.

"Yeah, laddie?" Kell grasped the axe-haft, put his boot against the soldier's chest, and ripped the weapon free in a shower of waxy blood. "I think you'll find I'm a little different." He bared his teeth in a skull smile. "A little more… *experienced*, shall we say."

Kell turned and crouched by the woman, but she was dead, skin blue, eyes ringed purple. Her tongue protruded, and Kell touched it; it was frozen solid, and he could feel the chill through his gloves.

A distant memory tugged at Kell, then. It was the ice-smoke. He'd seen it, once before, as a young soldier on the Selenau Plains. His unit had come across an old garrison barracks housing King Drefan's men; only they were dead, frozen, eyes glassy, flesh stuck to the stone. As the cavalry squad dismounted and entered the barracks, so tiny wisps of mist had dissipated, despite sunlight shining bright outside. Kell's sergeant, a wide brutal man called Heljar, made the sign of the Protective Wolf, and the inexperienced men amongst the squad imitated him, aware it could do no harm. "Blood-oil magick," Heljar had whispered, and they'd backed from the garrison barracks with boots crunching ice.

Kell rubbed at his beard through leather gloves, and glanced down at his axe. Ilanna. Blessed in blood-oil, she would protect him against ice-smoke, he knew. She would allow him to kill these magick-cursed men. Allow? Kell smiled a bitter smile. Hell, she would encourage it.

Now. Where would Nienna be? The dormitories?

If under attack, where would she run?

Kell, following instinct, following a call of blood, strode through the long corridors and halls of the university building, past corpses and several times past soldiers intent on their search. Up to the second floor, Kell found piles of bodies, all frozen, all arranged as if awaiting… what? What the hell do they want? wondered his confused mind.

A scream. Above.

Kell broke into a run, past lines of bodies laid out with arms by sides, faces serene in cold and death. His hands were tight on Ilanna, his breathing ragged and harsh, and he could sense his granddaughter close by. Up more steps, growing reckless the more he grew frantic with rising fear. Through a dormitory, beds neatly made, wooden chests unopened, and up another tight spiral staircase, taking the steps two at a time, his old legs groaning at him, muscles on fire, joints stabbing him with pain, but all this was washed aside by a surge of adrenalin as Kell slammed into the room–

There were four dead girls, lying on the floor, with long hair seeming to float behind pale chilled faces. Nienna and two others stood, armed with ornamental pikes they'd dragged from the walls during their flight. Before them stood three albino warriors with long white hair, all carrying short swords, their black armour a gleaming contrast to porcelain skin.

The soldiers turned as one, as Kell burst in. With a scream he leapt at them, axe slamming left in a whirr that severed one soldier's sword-arm and left him kneeling, stump spewing milk blood. Nienna leapt forward, thrusting her commandeered pike into an albino's throat but he moved fast, grabbing the weapon and twisting it viciously from Nienna's grip. She stumbled back nursing injured wrists, and watched with mouth open as the skewered albino stubbornly refused to die.

"Magick!" she hissed.

The albino nodded, smiling a smile which disintegrated as Kell's axe cleaved down the centre of his skull and dropped him in an instant. The third soldier turned to flee, but Ilanna sang, smashing through his clavicle. The second strike severed his head with a savage diagonal stroke.

The world froze in sudden impact.

Kell, chest heaving, moved forward. "Are you hurt?"

"Grandpa!" She fell into his arms, her friends coming up close behind, their faces drawn in fear, etched with terror. "It's awful! They stormed the university, started to kill everybody with swords and... and..."

"And magick," whispered a young woman, with short red hair and topaz eyes. "I'm Katrina. Kat to my friends. You are Kell. I've read everything about you, sir, your history, your exploits... your adventures! You are a hero! The hero of Kell's Legend!"

"We've not time for this," growled Kell. "We have to get out of the city. The soldiers are killing everyone!"

Katrina stooped, and hoisted one of the albino's swords. "Normal weapons won't kill them, right?"

Kell nodded. "You catch on fast, girl. The soldiers are blessed – or maybe cursed – with blood-oil magick. Only a suitably blessed and holy weapon can slay them. Either that, or remove their heads."

"Will this kill them?"

"There's only one way to find out."

Nienna and the third young woman, Yolga, armed themselves with the dead soldiers' swords. Kell led them to the spiral stairs, moving cat-like, wary, his senses alert, his aches and pains, arthritis and lumbago all gone. He could sense the women's fear, and that was bad; something dark flitted across his soul, something pure evil settling in Kell's mind. He didn't want the responsibility of these women. They were nothing to him. An inconvenience. He wanted simply to save Nienna. The other two? The other two women could...

I can kill them, if you like.

The thought came not so much as words, but as primitive, primal images, drifting like a shroud across his thoughts. For a decade she had remained silent. But with fresh blood, fresh magick, fresh death, Ilanna had found new life…

"No!"

They halted, and Nienna touched his arm gingerly. "Are you well, Grandpa?"

"Yes," came his strangled reply; and for a moment he gazed at his bloodbond axe with unfathomable horror. The Ilanna was powerful, and evil, and yet – yet he knew without her he would not survive this day. Would not survive this hour. He owed her – *it*, damn it! – owed it his life. He owed it everything…

"I am well," he forced himself to say, words grinding through gritted teeth. "Come. We need to reach the river. We can steal a boat there, attempt to get away from this… horror."

"I think you will find the river frozen," said a low, gentle voice.

The group had emerged like maggots from a wound, spilling from stairs into a long, low hall lined with richly polished furniture gleaming under ice-light from high arched windows. The whole scene appeared grey and silver; a portrait delicately carved in ice.

Kell stopped, mouth a line, mind whirring mechanically. The man was tall, lithe, wearing black armour without insignia. He was albino, like the other soldiers, with long white hair and ashen skin; and yet, yet – Kell frowned, for there was authority there, integral, a part of his core; and something not quite right. This was the leader. Kell did not need to be told. And his eyes were blue. They glittered like sapphires.

"You are?"

"General Graal. This is my army, the Army of Iron, which has forcibly taken and now controls the city of Jalder. We have overrun the garrison, stormed the Summer Palace, subdued the soldiers and population. All with very little loss to my own men. And yet–" He smiled then, teeth bared, and took a step forward, the two soldiers flanking Graal remaining in position so the general was fore-grounded, set apart by his natural authority. "And yet you, old man, are fast becoming a thorn in my side."

Kell, who had been eyeing other corridors which fed the hall in the hope of an easy escape route, eased to his right and checked for enemies. The corridor was empty. He turned, fixing a steel gaze on the general who seemed to be observing Kell with private amusement; or at least, the disdain a piranha reserves for an injured fish.

"I apologise," growled Kell, eyes narrowed, "that I haven't rolled over to die like so many other puppies." His eyes flashed dangerously with a new and concentrated form of hate. "It would seem you caught many of the city-folk by surprise, Graal, with the benefit of blood-oil magick at your disposal. I'm sure this makes you feel like a big cock bastard down at the barracks, Graal, the whore-master, joking about how he killed babes in their beds and soldiers in their sleep. The work of a coward."

Graal was unfazed by insult. He tilted his head, watching Kell, feminine face laced with good humour. "What is your name, soldier?" His words were a lullaby; soft and enticing. *Come to me*, that voice whispered. *Join with me.*

"I am Kell. Remember it well, laddie, 'cause I'm going to carve it on your arse."

"But not today, I fear. Men? Kill them. Kill them all."

The two albino soldiers eased forward, bodies rolling with athletic grace. Kell's eyes narrowed. These men were special, he could tell. They were professional, and deadly. He knew; he'd killed enough during his long, savage lifetime.

The two soldiers split, one moving for Kell, the other for Nienna, Kat and Yolga. They accelerated smoothly, leaping forward and Kell leapt to meet his man, axe slamming down, but the albino had gone, rolling, sword flickering out to score a line across Kell's bearskin-clad bicep that saw the big man stagger back, face like thunder, teeth gritted and axe clamped in both hands.

"A pretty trick, boy."

The albino said nothing, but attacked again, swift, deadly, sword slamming up then twisting, cutting left, right, to be battered aside by the butterfly-blades of Kell's axe. The albino spun, his blade hammering at Kell's neck. Kell's axe slammed the blade aside with a clatter. A reverse thrust sent the bloodbond axe towards the albino's chest, but the man rolled fast and came up, grinning a full-teeth grin.

"You're fast, old man." His voice was like silver.

"Not fast enough," snapped Kell, irate. He was starting to pant, and pain flickered in his chest. Too old, taunted that pain. Far too old for this kind of dance...

The albino leapt, sword slamming at Kell's throat. Kell leant back, steel an inch from his windpipe, and brought his axe up hard. There was a discordant clash. The soldier's sword sailed across the room, clattering from the wall.

"Kell!" came the scream. He whirled, saw instantly Nienna's danger. The three young women were backing away, swords raised, the second albino warrior bearing down on them, toying with them. But his stance changed; now, he meant business. Even as Kell watched, the man's sword flickered out and Nienna, face contorted, lashed out clumsily with her commandeered sword; it was batted aside, and on the reverse sweep the albino's blade cut deep across Yolga's belly. Cloth parted, skin and muscle opened, and the young woman's intestines spilled out. She fell to her knees, face white, lips mouthing wordless, her guts in her hands. Blood spilled across complex-patterned carpet. "No!" screamed Nienna, and attacked with a savage ferocity that belied her size and age. And as the albino's sword slashed at her throat, in slow-motion, an unnervingly accurate killing stroke, Kell heaved his axe with all his might. The weapon flew, end over end making a deep thrumming sound. It embedded so far through the albino that both blades appeared through his chest. With spine severed, he dropped instantly, flopping spastically on the ground where he began to leak.

Kell whirled back, eyes sweeping the room. The first soldier had regained his sword. Of Graal, there was no sign. The man, eyes locked on his dead comrade, fixed his gaze on Kell. The look was not comforting, and the arrogant smile was gone. He stalked towards the old warrior who realised–

Bastard, he thought. He'd thrown his axe.

Kell backed away.

You should never throw your axe.

"Graal said nothing about a swift death," snapped the albino, and Kell read in those crimson eyes a need for cruelty and torture. Here was a man with medical instruments in his pack; here was a man who enjoyed watching life-light die like the fall of a deviant sun.

Kell held up his hands, bearded face smiling easily. "I have no weapon." Although this was a lie: he had his Svian sheathed beneath his left arm, a narrow blade, but little use against a sword.

The albino drew square, and Kell, backing away, kept his hands held in supplication.

"Your point is?"

"It's hardly a fair fight, laddie. I thought you were a soldier, not a butcher?"

"We all have our hobbies," said the albino with a delicate smile.

Nienna's sword entered his neck, clumsily but effectively, from behind, finally embedding in his right lung. The albino coughed, twisted, and went down on one knee all at the same time. His sword lashed out in a reverse sweep, but Nienna skipped back, bloodied steel slipping from her fingers.

The albino coughed again, a heavy gurgling cough, and felt blood bubbling and frothing in his damaged lung. He felt the world swim. There was no pain. No, he thought. This wasn't how it should end. He felt tingling blood-magick in his veins, and his fingers twitched at the intercourse. He dropped to his other knee. Blood welled in his throat, filled his mouth like vomit, and spilled down his black armour making it gleam. His head swam, as if he'd imbibed alcohol, injected blood-oil, merged with the vachine. He tried to speak, as he toppled to the carpet, and his eyes traced the complex patterns he found there. Darkness was coming. And weight. It was pressing down on him. He glanced up, unable to move, to see boots. He strained, more white blood pooling like strands of thick saliva from his open maw. Kell was standing, his axe, blades stained with blood and tiny flutters of torn flesh, held loose in one hand, resting on the carpet. Kell's head was lowered, and to the albino his eyes looked darker than dark; they appeared as pools of ink falling away into infinity. Kell lifted his axe. The albino soldier tried to shout, and he squirmed on the carpet in some final primitive instinct; a testament to an organism's need to survive.

Ilanna swept down. The albino was still.

Kell turned, glanced at Nienna. She was cradling Yolga's head and the girl was mumbling, face ashen, clothes ruined by her own arterial gore. The other girl, Kat, was standing to one side, eyes wide, mouth hung loose. As Kell watched, Yolga spasmed and died in Nienna's arms.

"Why?" screamed Nienna, head snapping up, anger burning in the glare she threw at Kell.

Kell shrugged wearily, and gathered up one of the albino's swords. This one was different. The steel was black, and intricately inlaid with fine crimson runes. He had seen this sort of work before. It was said the metal was etched with blood-oil; blessed, in fact, by the darkness: by vachine religion. Kell ripped free the albino's leather sheath, and looped it over his shoulders. He sheathed the sword smoothly and moved to Nienna.

"Get your sword. We need to move."

"I asked you – *why*?"

"And my answer is *because*. I don't know, girl. Maybe the gods mock us. The world is evil. Men are evil. Yolga was in the wrong place at the wrong damn time, but you are alive, and Kat is alive, so pick up your sword and follow me. That is," he smiled a nasty smile, "if you still want to live."

Nienna moved to the fallen soldier. She took hold of her embedded sword, and tugged at it until it finally gave; it squelched from the corpse. She shuddered, tears running down her cheeks, and followed Kell to the corridor. Kat put her hand on Nienna's shoulder, but the young woman shrugged off the intimacy, displacing friendship.

"How do you feel?"

Nienna snorted a laugh. "I think I've lost my faith in the gods."

"I lost mine a long time ago," said Kat, eyes tortured. Nienna stared at her friend.

"Why?"

"Now is not the time." Kat hoisted her own stolen sword. "You did well, Nienna. I froze. Seeing Yolga like that…" She took a deep breath, and patted her friend once more. "Honest. You did brilliant. You… saved us all."

"How so?"

"That soldier would have killed your grandpa. Without a weapon, he was just meat."

Nienna looked at her friend oddly, then transferred her gaze back to Kell, whose eyes were sweeping the long, majestic hall. He glanced back, bloodied axe in his great huge paws. And with his thick grey beard and the bulk of his bearskin, for a moment in time, a sliver of half-glimpsed reality, he appeared to be natural in that skin. A warrior. No, more. A bestial and primitive ghost.

"Follow me," he said, breaking the spell. "And stay silent. Or we'll all be dead."

Nienna nodded, and with Kat in tow, they followed Kell out to the hall.

Saark stared, transfixed, as the Harvester stooped and bobbed, striding forward with a rhythmical, swinging gait, ice-smoke trailing from its robes, black eyes like glossy coals drawing Saark into a world of sweetness and joy and uplifting mercy—

Come to me, angel.

Come to me, holy one.

Let me savour your blood.

Let me take you on the final journey.

Let me taste your life…

The long, bony fingers reached for Saark, who stood with every muscle tense, his body thrumming like the string on a mandolin. Saark's eyes flickered, saw the hooded man creeping up behind the Harvester even as those long points of white reached for Saark's chest and his shirt seemed to peel away and five white-hot needles scorched his skin and he opened his mouth to scream as he felt flesh melt but there was no sound and no words and no control and pain slapped Saark like a helve to the skull, stunning him, his legs going weak as an ice-wind whipped across his soul–

The hooded man screamed a battle-cry and charged, a large meat-cleaver held clear above his head, his bearded face, red and bitten savagely by the ice-smoke, contorted into a mask of frenzy.

The Harvester turned, smooth, unhurried, and as the cleaver lashed down the Harvester's arm lifted in a sudden acceleration, and the cleaver bounced from bone with a clack and spun off, lost from the man's flexing hands. The Harvester's finger slammed out, puncturing the man's chest above his heart. He screamed.

Saark fell to his knees, choking, coughing, and re-leased from the spell, grappled wildly at his burning, melting chest. He glanced down, at five deep welts in his skin, deep purple sores surrounded by concentric circles of heavy bruising. Saark continued to cough, as if slammed in the heart by a sledgehammer, and he watched helpless as the Harvester lifted the brave attacker high into the air kicking and screaming, impaled by the heart on five spears of bone. Body thrashing, the man screamed and screamed and Saark's eyes widened as he watched the man sucked and shrivelled, arms and legs cracking, contorting, snapping at impossible angles as the skin of his face was drawn and shrivelled until it was a dry, useless, eyeless, husk.

The corpse hit the ground with a rattle; like bones in a paper bag.

The Harvester turned back to Saark, flat oval face leering at him. Thin lips opened revealing a black interior ringed with row after row of tiny teeth.

Saark grunted, rolled onto his hands and knees and accelerated into a sprint faster than any man had a right to. He powered away, chest on fire, heart pounding a tattoo in his ears, mouth Harmattan dry, bladder leaking piss in squirts down his legs. Down long alleys he fled, with no sounds of pursuit. He turned, and almost choked. The Harvester was pounding after him, so close and silent Saark almost fell on his face with shock. He slammed right, twisting down a narrow alleyway, dropping ever downwards towards the river. He skidded on icy cobbles, turned again, and again, ducking into narrow spaces between carts and stalls and wagons, squeezing past boxes, and suddenly shoulder-charging a door to his left and barging through a deserted house, past still bubbling pans and up narrow stairs to the roof—

He halted, listening.

Nothing.

His terrified eyes roved the staircase below, and he moved to the window and stared down into the street. Had he lost it? He tried to calm his breathing, and climbing out of the window, he reached up to the eaves of the house and with frozen fingers, ice-smoke swirling around his boots, he grunted, hoisting himself up onto slick slate tiles. Carefully, Saark climbed to the ridge-line and without waiting moved swiftly along the house apex, leaping a narrow alleyway with a glimpse of dark cobbled streets encased in ice below. Scary, yes, but not as heart-wrenchingly terrifying as the creature that pursued him; the monster that sucked life and blood and fluid from bodies, the beast that drank out people's souls. Saark shuddered.

What hell has overtaken the world? he thought. What law did I break, to be so cursed?

From house to house, from roof to roof, Saark leapt and slithered, many times nearly falling to cobbles and stalls far below. Through drifting mist he ran, a rooftop ghost, a midnight vagabond; only this time he was on no simple errand of theft.

This time, Saark ran for his life. And for his soul.

"Wait."

Kell's hushed whisper, despite its low tone, carried with surprising clarity. Nienna and Kat froze instantly in place. Both young women were walking a high-rope, skating thin ice, breathing the tension of the besieged and sundered city. Again and again they passed corpses, shrivelled husks, sometimes piles of men, women, heaps of disjointed child corpses, huddled together as if for warmth; in reality, all they craved was a chance at life.

Kell lowered his hand, half-turned, gestured for the girls to join him. They scampered down the cobbled road, gloved hands holding cloth over the freezing skin of their faces, swords sheathed at waists more as tokens than real weapons. Both girls understood that in real world combat, their lives hung by a thread. And the thread was named Kell.

"See," he hissed, gesturing towards the Selenau River, flowing like ink beneath swirling tendrils of ice-smoke. "The enemy have a foothold here; now it'll be damn impossible to steal a boat."

Nienna watched the albino soldiers, streams of them in their hundreds, marching down the waterfront. Many dragged prisoners, some kicking and screaming. These, they locked in huge iron cages which had been erected beside the sluggish wide river. Many dragged corpses, and these they piled in heaps as if... Nienna frowned. As if they were waiting for something?

Nienna's eyes searched as far as the false horizon. Sometimes, ice-smoke parted and she got a good glimpse down a length of the river. Huge black and red brick factories lined the water; they were mainly dye-works, slaughterhouses and tanneries. The sort of place which Nienna had been destined to work before her "nameless benefactor" stepped in with university fees. Huge iron cranes stretched across the river for loading and unloading cargo. Wide pipes disgorged chemical effluence, dyes and slaughterhouse blood and offal into the river. Even in winter, the place stank to high heaven; in summer, vomit lined the water-front from unwary travellers.

Kat edged forward, and crouched beside Kell. She met the old warrior's gaze and he had to admire her edge. "What about another way out of the city? There's too many of the bastards here." She spat on the ground.

"They will have the gates covered. This whole situation stinks, Kat. I've seen this sort of... slaughter, before. The Army of Iron don't want anybody getting out; they don't want anybody to spoil their master plan. If somebody was to get word to King Leanoric, for example..."

"That is our mission!" said Katrina.

"No, girl. Our mission is to stay alive. Anything else – that comes later."

In truth, Kell still felt deeply uneasy. What sort of conquering army simply committed murder and atrocity? It didn't make sense. Slaughter all the bakers, who would bake bread for the soldiers? Murder the whores and dancers, who then to provide entertainment? Soldiers marched on their stomachs, and fought best when happy. Only an insane general went on a pointless rampage. Kell had seen it once before, during the Days of Blood. Bad days. Bad months. Kell's mouth was dry at the thought. Bitter, like the plague.

The Days of Blood…

A dark whisper. In his soul.

A splinter. Of hatred. Of remorse.

You took part, Kell. You killed them all, Kell.

Visions echoed. Slashes of flashback. Crimson and shimmering. Diagonal slices, echoes of a time of horror. Screams. Writhing. Slaughter. Whimpering. Steel sawing methodically through flesh and bone. Worms eating skin. Eating eyes. Blood running in streams down stone gutters. Running in rivers. And soldiers, faces twisted with bloodlust, insanity, naked and smeared with blood, with piss and shit, with vomit, capering down streets with swords and knives, adorning their bodies with trophies from victims… hands, eyes, ears, genitalia…

Kell swooned, felt sick. He forced away the terrible visions and rubbed a gloved hand through his thick beard. "Damn you all to hell," he muttered, a terrible heaviness sinking through him, from brain to stomach, a heavy metal weight dragging his soul down to his boots and leaking out with the piss and the blood.

"You look ill." Kat placed a hand on his broad, bear-clad shoulder.

"No, girl, I am fine," he breathed, shuddering. And added, under his breath, "on the day that I die." Then louder, "Come. I can see a tunnel under the tannery."

"That's an evil place," said Kat, pulling back. "My little brother used to collect the piss-pots used in the tannery; he caught a terrible disease from there; he died. I swore I would never go inside such a place."

"It's that, or die yourself," said Kell, not unkindly.

Kat nodded, and followed Kell and Nienna down the street, all three crouching low, moving slowly, weapons at the ready and eyes alert. As they approached the tunnel, an incredible stench eased out to meet them: a mixture of gore and fat, dog-shit, piss, and the slop-solution of animal brains used in the bating process. Kell forced his way inside, treading through a thick sludge and coming up grooved and worn brick steps into a room hung with hides still to be stripped of hair, gore and fat. They swung, eerily, on blood-dried hooks. There were perhaps a hundred skins waiting for the treatment that would eventually lead to water-skins, armour, scabbards and boots. Kell stepped over channels running thick with disgorged brains.

"What is that?" gagged Nienna.

"When the skins arrive, they need to be scraped free of dried fat and flesh. The tanners then soak skins in vats mixed with animal brains, and knead it with dog-shit to make it soft." He grinned at Nienna, face demonic in the gloomy light where shadows from gently swinging skins cast eerie shapes over his bearded features. "Now you can see why you were so lucky to be accepted into the university, girl. This is not a place for children."

"Yet a place where children work," said Kat, voice icy.

"As you say."

They moved warily between swinging skins, the two women flinching at the brush of hairy hides still strung with black flesh and long flaps of thick yellow fat. At one point Kat slipped, and Nienna grabbed her, hoisting her away from a channel filled with oozing mashed animal brains and coagulated blood.

"This is purgatory," said Nienna, voice soft.

Kat turned away, and was sick.

As Kell emerged from the wall of hung skins, so he froze, eyes narrowing, head turning left and right. Before him stood perhaps twenty large vats, four with fires still burning beneath their copper bases. This was where excess flesh and hide strips were left to rot for months on end in water, before being boiled to make hide glue. If nothing else, this place stunk the worst of all and Kell was glad of the cloth he held over his mouth.

Then Kell turned, frowning, and strode towards a vat containing the foul-smelling broth and hoisted his axe. "Are you coming out, or do I come in axe-first?"

"Whoa, hold yourself there, old fellow," came an educated voice, and from the shadows slipped a tall, athletic man. Nienna watched him, and found herself immediately attracted; something the dandy was no-doubt used to. His face was very finely chiselled, his hair black, curled, oiled back, neat above a trimmed moustache and long sideburns that were currently the height of fashion amongst nobles. He wore a rich blue shirt, dark trews, high cavalry boots and a short, expensive, fur-lined leather cloak. He had expensive rings on his fingers, a clash of diamonds and rubies. His eyes were a dazzling blue, even in this gloomy, murky, hellish place. He had what Nienna liked to call a smiling face.

Kat snorted. Nienna was about to laugh as well, so ridiculous did the nobleman look in this evil-smelling tannery from hell; until she saw his sword. This, too, had a faint air of the ridiculous, until she married it to his posture. Only then did she consider the broad shoulders, the narrow hips, the subtle stance of an experienced warrior. Nienna chided herself. This man, she realised, had been underestimated many times.

"Why are you skulking back there, fool?"

"Skulking? *Skulking*? Old horse, my name is Saark, and Saark does not skulk. And as for fool, I take such a jibe as I presume you intend; in utter good humour and jest at such a sorry situation and predicament in which we find ourselves cursed."

"Pretty words," snorted Kell, turning back to Nienna and Kat. He turned back, and realised Saark was close. Too close. The rapier touched Kell's throat and there was a long, frozen moment of tension.

"Pretty enough to get me inside your guard," said Saark, voice soft, containing a hint of menace.

"I think we fight the same enemy," said Kell, eyes locked to Saark.

"Me also!" Saark stepped back and sheathed his blade. He held out his hand. "I am Saark."

"You already said."

"I believe it's such a fine name, it deserves saying twice."

Kell grunted. "I am Kell. This is Nienna, my grand-daughter, and her friend Kat. We were thinking of stealing a boat. Getting the hell away from this invaded charnel house of a city."

Saark nodded, moving close to Nienna and Kat. "Well, hello there, ladies." Both young women blushed, and Saark laughed, a tinkling of music, his eyes roving up and down their young frames.

"Saark!" snapped Kell. "There are more important things at play, here. Like the impending threat on our lives, for one."

Saark made a tutting sound in the back of his throat, and surveyed his surroundings. And yet, despite his smile, his fine clothes, his finer words, Nienna could see the tension in this man; like an actor on the stage, playing a part he'd rehearsed a thousand times before, Saark was enjoying his performance. But he was hampered, by an emotion which chipped away at the edges of his mask.

Fear.

It lurked in his eyes, in his stance, in a delicate trembling of his hand. Nienna noticed. She enjoyed people-watching. She was good at it.

Saark took a deep breath. "How did you know I was here?"

"I could smell you."

"*Smell me*?" Saark grinned then, shaking his head. His face was pained. "I cannot believe you could smell me amidst this stench. I like to think I have better grooming habits."

Kell had moved to a window, was standing back from the wooden shutters and watching soldiers down by the river. He turned and eyed Saark warily. "It was your perfume."

"Aaah! Eau du Petale. The very finest, the most excitingly exquisite…"

"Save it. We're moving. We can escape via the pipe which dumps tannin and slop out into the river. If we head down into the cellars, I'm sure…"

"Wait." Saark brushed past Kell and stood, one manicured hand on the shutters, the other on the hilt of his rapier. Suddenly, Saark's foppish appearance didn't seem quite so ridiculous.

"What is it?"

"The carriage. I know it."

Kell gazed out. A carriage had drawn alongside a cage full of weeping prisoners; all women. The carriage was black, glossy, and had an intricate crest painted on the door. The horses stomped and chewed at their bits, disturbed either by the stench of the tanneries or the moans of the women. The driver fought to keep the four beasts under control and their hooves clattered on ice-rimed cobbles.

"Well, I know *him*," snarled Kell, as General Graal stalked towards the carriage and folded his arms. His armour gleamed. He ran a hand through his long white hair, an animal preening. "He's the bastard in charge of this army. He called it the Army of Iron."

"You know that one?" Saark met Kell's gaze.

"The bastard sent a couple of his soldiers to kill me and the girls."

"He was far from successful, I see."

"I don't die easy," said Kell.

"I'm sure you don't, old horse." Saark smiled, and turned back to the distant performance. The carriage door was opened by a lackey, and a man stepped down. He was dressed in furs, and held a cloth over his face against the chill of ice-smoke, which was dissipating even as they watched – its job now done. The man had shoulder length black hair, which gleamed.

"Who is he?" said Kell.

"That," said Saark, staring hard at Kell, "is Dagon Trelltongue."

"The king's advisor?"

Saark nodded. "King Leanoric's most trusted man. He is, shall we say, the king's regent when the king is away on business."

"What about Alloria?"

"The queen?" Saark smiled. "I see, Kell, you have little schooling in nobility, or in royalty. It would be unseemly for a woman to rule in the king's absence; you would have her meeting with common-folk? Doing business with captains and generals? I think not."

"Why," said Kell, ruffled, "would Trelltongue be here? Now?"

Saark transferred his gaze back to the two men beside the carriage. "A good question, my new and aged and ragged friend. However, much as I would love to make his acquaintance at this moment in time, I fear your escape plan to be sound – and immediately necessary. Would you like to lead the way, Kell, to this pipe of disgorging effluence?"

Kell hoisted his axe, looked at Nienna and Kat, then tensed, crouching a little, at what appeared behind the two women.

"What is it?" hissed Nienna, and turned…

From the hanging wall of skins, moving leisurely, gracefully, came a Harvester. Its flat oval face seemed emotionless, but the small black eyes, coals in a snow-man's face, searched across the room. Vertical slits hissed with air, and the creature seemed to be… sniffing. The Harvester gave a grimace that may have been a smile.

"I followed you. Across the city." The voice was a dawdling, lazy roll, like big ocean waves on a fused beach.

Saark drew his rapier, and gestured to the two women to move. He took a deep breath, and watched as the Harvester lifted a hand. The embroidered robe fell away leaving five long, pointed fingers of bone…

"I thought I explained, sweetie. You're just not my type." But terror lay beyond Saark's words, and as he and Kell separated, Kell loosening his shoulders, axe swinging gently, Saark muttered from the corner of his mouth, "Watch the fingers. That's how they suck the life from your body."

Kell nodded, as the blast of terror hit him. He stood, stunned by the ferocity of fear which wormed through his mind. He saw himself, lying in a hole in the ground, worms eating his eyes, his skin, his lungs, his heart.

Come to me, came the words in his head. A song. A lullaby. A call stronger than life itself.

Come to me, little one.

I will make the pain go away.

The Harvester drifted forward, and with a scream Saark attacked, rapier moving with incredible speed; a lazy backward gesture slapped Saark a full twenty feet across the tannery, where he landed, rolling fast, to slam against a vat with a groan.

Five bone fingers lifted.

Moved, towards Kell's heart.

And with tears on his cheeks, the old soldier seemed to welcome them…

THREE
A Taste of Clockwork

Anukis awoke feeling drowsy; but then, the ever-present tiredness, like a lead-weight in her heart, in her soul, was something she had grown to endure over the years, something which she knew would never leave her because... because of what she was. She stretched languorously under thick goose-down covers, her long, curled, yellow hair cascading across plump pillows, her slender white limbs reaching out as if calling silently across the centuries for forgiveness.

Anukis glanced at the clock on the far wall. It was long, smooth, black like granite. Through a glass pane she could see tiny intricate cogs and wheels, spinning, turning, teeth mating neatly as micro-gears clicked into place. A pendulum swung, and a soft *tick tick tick* echoed through the room. Anukis's eyes stared at the clock, loving it and hating it at the same time. She loved it because her father, Kradek-ka, had made the clock; and just like his father before him, he had been one of the finest Watchmakers in Silva Valley, his hands steady, precise, incredibly accurate with machining and assembly; his eye had been keen, not just with the precision of his trade, but with the delicate understanding of materials and what was perfect for any machine job. But it had been his mind that set him apart, indeed, highlighted him as a genius. Anu's grandfather had accelerated and pioneered the art of watch-making, turning what had once been a relatively simple art of mechanical time-keeping into something more... advanced. This way, Kradek-ka had upheld the family traditions, and helped to save, to prolong, and to advance their race. The vachine.

Anukis rubbed at her eyes, then stood, gasping a little at the cool air in the room. Naked, goose-bumps ran up and down her arms and she hurried into a thick silk gown which fell to her ankles. She moved to a porcelain bowl and washed, her long, dainty fingers, easing water into her eyes, then carefully, into her mouth. She rubbed at her teeth, cold water stinging, then moved to the window of her high tower, gazing out over Silva Valley, eyes scanning the high mountain ridges which enclosed the huge tiered city like predator wings around a victim.

Anukis smiled. A victim. How apt.

Maybe they'll come for me today, she thought. Maybe not.

A prisoner of the High Engineer Episcopate since her father had died (had been murdered, she thought hollowly), she was not allowed out from a small collection of rooms in this high tower suite. However, what the high-ranking religious Engineers and Major Cardinals did not realise, was that Anukis was not a pure *oil-blood* like the majority of the city population lying under a fresh fall of snow below, pretty and crystalline, a pastel portrait from her high window.

The smile faded from Anukis's face.

No. She was far from pure. She carried the impurity seed within her. Which meant she could not drink blood-oil. Could not mate with the magick. Could not... feed, as a normal vachine would feed.

Anu could never enjoy the thrill of the hunt.

There came a knock at the door, and a maid entered carrying a small silver bowl which she placed by Anukis's bed. With head bent low, she retreated, closing the door on silent hinges, hinges Anukis herself had oiled for the purpose of freedom. Anu moved to the bowl, glanced down at the tiny, coin-sized pool of blood-oil that floated there, crimson, and yet at the same time streaked with rainbow oils. This was the food of the vachine. Their fuel. That which made them unholy.

Anukis could not drink blood-oil. In its refined state, such as this, it poisoned her, and made her violently sick. She would be ill for weeks. To the Watchmakers, the Major Bishops, the Engineers, this was heresy, a mockery of their machine religion; punishable by exile, or more probably, death. Anu's father had gone to great pains to protect his daughter for long years, hiding her away, dealing with the amoral Blacklippers of the south and their illegal import of Karakan Red, as it was known. Only this unrefined, common source – fresh from the vein – would, or could, sustain Anukis. And, she was sure, it was this subterfuge which had led to her father's untimely death...

A face flashed in her mind. Vashell! Tall, athletic, powerful, tiny brass fangs poking over his lower lip. He was prodigal, a powerhouse of physical perfection and one of the youngest ever Engineer Priests to have achieved such a rank. Destined for greatness. Destined for leadership! One day, he would achieve the exalted rank of Major Cardinal; maybe even Watchmaker itself!

He had asked Anukis to marry him on two occasions, and both times her father had rejected Vashell's advances, fearing that for Anukis to marry was for Anukis to die. But she saw the way Vashell looked at her. When he smiled, she glimpsed the tiny cogs and wheels inside his head, saw the glint of molten gold swirling in his eyes. He was true and pure vachine; a wholesome, blood-oil servant to the Vachine Religion. Vashell, a spoilt prince, an upstart royal, had got everything he ever wanted. And, she knew with a shudder, he would never stop until he possessed Anukis.

And... then that happens? She smiled sadly to herself.

Well, she would have to kill him. Or failing that, kill herself.

Far better death than what the Engineers would do to her if they discovered her tainted flesh.

Anukis opened the window and a cold wind gusted in, chilling her with a gasp and a smile. Far below, the sweeping granite roads shone under fresh snow, most of which had been swept into piles along the edges of the neat, gleaming thoroughfares. Buildings staggered away, maybe six or seven storeys in height, and all built from smooth white marble mined from the Black Pike Mountains. The architecture was stunning to behold, every joint precise. Arches and flutes, carvings and ornate buttresses, many inlaid with precious stones to decorate even the most bare of Silva Valley's buildings – gifts from the all-giving Pikes. And the city itself was huge; it drifted away down the valley, mountains rearing like guardians to either side, for as far as Anukis could see. And her eyesight was brilliant. Her father had made sure of that.

The scent of snow came in to her, and she inhaled, savouring the cold. The vachine had a love affair with cold, but Anukis, being impure and contaminated, preferred a little warmth. This, again, was a secret she had to jealously guard. If the Engineers discovered what she was… and the things she did when darkness fell…

Despite its well-oiled silence, Anukis caught the sound of the door opening. She also sensed the change in pressure within the room. Her eyes shone silver with tears and still gazing out over her beloved city, the one which her grandfather, and father, had given so much to advance, she said without turning, her voice a monotone, "What can I do for you, Vashell?"

"Anukis, I would speak with you." His voice was soft, simple, almost submissive in its tone. But Anukis was not fooled; she had heard him chastise servants on many occasions, watched in horror as he beat them to death, or kicked them till they bled from savage wounds. He could change at the flick of a brass switch. He could turn to murder like a metal hawk drops on its prey…

"I am still in mourning. There is little to say."

"Look at me, Anu. Please?"

Anukis turned, and wiped away a tear which had run down one cheek. With the tiniest of clicking sounds, she forced a smile to her face. Ultimately, her father would want her to live. Not sacrifice herself needlessly for the sake of sadness, or misery, or impurity. She took a deep breath. "I'm looking, Vashell. You have picked a bad time to intrude on my thoughts. And I am barely dressed. This is an unfortunate time to receive company. But then, if the High Engineer Episcopate keeps me a prisoner, I suppose my body is theirs to do with as they please…"

"Hush!" Vashell stepped forward, but stopped as Anukis shrank back, cowering almost, on the window-seat. "If anybody hears you speak so, your life will be forfeit! They will drain your blood-oil. You will be husked!" For a vachine, there was no greater shame.

"Why would you care?" Her voice turned harsh, all the bitterness at her father's death, all the poison at being kept prisoner rising to bubble like venom on her tongue. "You are a party to all this, Vashell! You said, twice, that you loved me. And twice you asked my father for the gift of marriage. Yet you stand by the Engineers whilst they keep me locked here," and now her eyes darkened, the gold swirling in their pupils turning almost crimson in her flush of anger, "and you collude in the capture of my sister."

Vashell swallowed, and despite his mighty physical prowess, he edged uneasily from one polished boot to the next. "Shabis is fine, Anu. You know that. The Engineers are taking care of her. She is well."

"She is a young girl, Vashell, whose father has just died and whose sister has been imprisoned. When can I see her?"

"It will be arranged."

Anukis jumped down from the window-seat and strode to Vashell, gazing up at him. He was more than a head taller than the slender female, and she herself was nearly six feet in height. "You said that a week ago," she snarled, staring up into his eyes. Vashell squirmed.

"It is not easy to arrange."

"You are an Engineer Priest! You can do anything!"

"Not this." His voice dropped an octave. "You have no idea what you ask. So many in the High Council outrank me." He took a deep breath. "But... I will see what I can do. I promise."

"On your blood-oil soul?"

"Yes, on my eternal soul."

Anukis turned her back on him, moved to the window. She gazed across the city, but the beauty was now lost on her; decayed. A sudden wave of hate slammed through her, like a tsunami of ice against a frozen, volcanic beach. She would see it destroyed! She would see the Silva Valley decimated, and laid to a terrible waste...

"You came here to ask me, didn't you?"

"I can help you, Anu."

"By marrying me?"

"Yes! If you become the wife of an Engineer Priest, you will be sacrosanct. The Engineers cannot keep you prisoner! It would go against the Oak Testament. You know that."

"And yet, still I choose to say no."

Anukis felt Vashell stiffen, without turning to look. She allowed herself a small smile. This was one thing she could deny him. But when he spoke again, the smile slowly drained from her face like bronze from a melting pot.

"Listen carefully, pretty one, when I say this. For I will speak only once. Your father was found guilty of heresy by the Patriarch; I do not know what happened to him, but we both know, without seeing the corpse, that he is dead. The Engineers wanted you and your sister dead, also; I am all that stands between the two of you, and the Eternal Pyre. So, think very carefully before offering a facetious answer... because, if I choose to withdraw favour, the last of your worries will be your separation from your sister."

Vashell swept from the apartment, door slamming in his wake so hard it rattled the oak frame. Dust trickled from between well-machined stones. Echoes bounced down the stairwell.

Shivering, Anukis turned and stared at the elegantly carved portal, then back out over the city. She shivered again, and this time it was nothing to do with the cold. Above her, her father's clock ticked, every second reminding her of a melting life.

Anukis licked ice-cold lips.

She thought about blood.

And that which was denied her.

Tonight. Tonight, she would visit the Blacklippers.

The sun set over the mountains casting long crimson shadows against granite walkways. Anukis listened, acute hearing placing guards down in the tower entry. She could hear muted conversation, the flare of a lit pipe, the laughter of a crude rude joke. Anukis pulled on her ankle-length black gown, belted the waist, and lifted the hood to obscure her golden hair and pastel features.

She moved to a heavy cabinet beside the door, lifted it with ease, carrying it across a thick rug and tilting it to wedge under the door handle. Moving back to the window, she watched the sun's weak, crimson rays finally die like spread fingers over the jagged peaks of the Black Pikes; then she leapt lightly onto the window seat and prised open the portal.

An ice wind whipped inside. Anukis climbed out, finding narrow handholds in the marble and stone, and easing herself over the awesome drop. "Don't look down," she murmured, but just couldn't help herself. It was a long fall to hard granite ruts polished smooth by brass wheels. Anukis eased herself along the narrow crack, moving only one hand, or one boot, at a time, so she always had three points of contact. The wind snapped at her with teeth. Away from the window, darkness fell like molten velvet. Anukis felt totally isolated. Alone.

For perilous minutes she eased herself around the flank of the tower, to where she'd discovered a worn vertical rut. Above, tiles converged into a marble trough which had grown a leak, probably a hundred or more years previous. This in turn had allowed water to groove the marble facade, giving slightly deeper handholds, almost like steps, down which Anukis could climb several storeys to a sloping ridge of tiles.

Several times she almost slipped; once, gasping, she swung away from the wall and her boots scrabbled on marble as sweat stung her eyes, and she felt a fingernail crack. But she calmed her breathing, stopped her panicked kicking, and hauled herself up on bloody fingertips, regaining her handhold, saving her life.

Down, she eased, an inch at a time, as the wind mocked her with brutal laughter.

Below, Silva Valley spread away, some sections well lit, others deep dark pits of intimidation. Despite Watchmaker rule, not every vachine was equal; a complex religious hierarchy existed which sometimes led to murder and civil unrest. Royal torture was delivered for gross acts of sacrilege, but the vachine were powerful, proud, and physically superior. The illegals took some ruling. Only the Machine God kept them sane.

Anukis hit the tiles lightly and dropped to a crouch. Her eyes scanned, swirling with gold, finding the patrolling Engineer Deacons and their minions and watching them as she had watched from her cell window. With care, she eased across sloping tiles on her carefully plotted route, and dropped down to a second storey balcony. She knocked a plant-pot, which clattered, and swiftly she scaled the rails, hung, and dropped to a lower balcony as light emerged above her, muttering voices casting curses on the wind.

Anukis landed on the smooth granite road, and checked herself. Tugging her hood tight, she hurried down the dark street, winding downhill to the Brass Docks.

Silva Valley was just that, a valley; but at its heart, a dissection, lay the Silva River, which emerged from a complex core of caves and vast subterranean tunnel systems beneath the Black Pike Mountains, and named the Deshi Caves. In his youth, Anukis's father Kradek-ka had explored the tunnels in detail, had been part of several professional vachine expeditions to map the labyrinth beneath the mountains. But something odd had occurred which the more religious of the vachine called *bo-adesh*. Occasionally, the tunnels moved, altered, shifted within the infrastructure of the mountain vaults. Some said it was down to blood-oil magick; some said the Black Pike Mountains were alive, had been alive longer than Man, and were in contempt of vachine deviation and intrusion. Whatever, many of the under-mountain routes were mapped and used for travel on long brass barges, or even to reach other distant valleys; but some were prohibited. Dangerous. Death to those who travelled...

In those early days of exploration, many had been lost to the Deshi Caves. Anukis remembered long cold evenings, sitting on her father's knee, staring into dancing flames as he recounted some of his travels, how they used blood-oil markers on the stone, ropes under the water, magick fires by which to see. And still many had died; hundreds had died, lost, drowned, or simply vanished. Sometimes, an empty brass barge would drift from the mist of an early morning, a single bell chiming. Empty. No signs of struggle. It had been Kradek-ka's view that terrible beasts lived under the Black Pike Mountains; creatures nobody had ever before seen... or at least, seen and lived thereof to speak.

Anukis shivered; and not just with the cold.

She stopped at an intersection, easing into shadows beyond the pooled light from a swinging brass lamp. Two guards passed and stopped beneath the yellow orb, lighting long pipes and exchanging pleasantries. Anu watched them carefully; these weren't real Engineer Deacons; they didn't have the shaved heads and facial tattoos of the Royal; but they were as near as damn it. And certainly authorised to kill Anukis beyond curfew. She smiled, her smile a crescent in a bloodless face. And the reason for curfew?

The vachine were running out of blood-oil.

The vachine had bled the cattle dry...

Oh, the irony!

The guards moved on, and so did Anukis, loping across the road and delving into more darkness. Down she strode, cloak pulled tight, breath emerging in short gasps of dragon smoke.

She rounded a corner, and the Silva River opened before her, vast, wide, and glass-still at the base of the Silva Valley. Buildings staggered in staccato leaps far down the steep descent before her, right to the ebony water's edge. Anukis hurried on, down narrow back-streets of this vast and beautiful city, down ill-advised routes. Three times she spotted thieves before they spotted her, and circumnavigated their positions. Even so, she knew, she would have needed no weapon to deal with their kind. Outcast. Impure...

Like me, she realised.

But then, despite her disabilities, she was... special.

Her father had made sure of that.

Anukis reached the long flanks of the Brass Docks and halted, a few feet from the water, listening to the lilting slap against brass jetties. She waited patiently, searching out more guards; finally, she moved down a wide curving walkway which followed the crescent of the Silva River towards... The Black Pikes. And the Mouth, which disgorged ice-pure mineral-rich waters from deep beneath echoing mountain halls. She felt the Breath before she saw the river's ominous exit; it emerged, hissing and singing sometimes, to wash cool mineral-scented air over those who stood within five hundred yards. Anukis walked into the breeze, which tugged annoyingly at her hood, and stopped by the Brass Docks warehouse block. She glanced right, where huge brass and bronze freighters bobbed at anchor, trade vessels and smaller navy vehicles, many unmanned and silent, some showing tiny yellow glows from fat-oil lamps. Carefully, she stepped down a narrow alley and entered a maze, skilfully negotiating a complex route which led her to a steep, dark stairwell.

From the depths, a cold breeze blew, and Anu skipped down slick granite, slowing as she reached the bottom. The crossbow appeared before the Blacklipper, strung and tensioned, and his teeth gleamed behind the black-tainted scarring of his lips.

"Going somewhere, my pretty?"

"I have business with Preyshan."

The Blacklipper moved from the shadows, and she saw he was what they called a Deep Blood; not only his lips were stained black from the powerful narcotic, even the veins beneath his skin had taken the taint, showing a diffused map of web-strands beneath his pale white skin. Anukis shuddered inside; he had to be close to death to look like this. Ready for the Voyage of the Soul.

Seeing the shudder, the man smiled. "Don't you be worrying about me, pretty one. I've had a good life. My Paradise awaits."

"One filled with blood-oil?"

The crossbow jerked towards her, and his eyes narrowed. "One such as you shouldn't readily condemn, pretty, outcast vachine."

Only she wasn't an outcast.

Because – they didn't know... yet.

And if the Watchmakers discovered her impurity?

She heard they had special chambers for just such occurrences.

Anukis shuddered, and squeezed past the leering Blacklipper, feeling his fetid rigor-mortis breath on her face, his body pressed close to her own, its muscles surprisingly iron-hard beneath his web-traced skin. She hurried on, down more and more steps, and deep into a maze of brass-walled corridors which eventually gave out to smooth-hewn tunnels, some flooded. Several times Blacklippers challenged her, and several times Anukis used her magick card. The name: Preyshan. One of the three kings of the Blacklippers.

As she entered the maze beneath the Silva River, so she could discern a distant booming sound. It was said to be the noise made by the souls of the drowned, banging on the river bed for spiritual release. Anukis moved on, hand touching the smooth wall where lode-veins of crystals and blood-red mineral deposits could be traced, glittering, in the glow of irregularly placed fat-lamps.

The corridor ended in an iron gate. She gave her name, and the gate swung open revealing a long, low chamber filled with perhaps fifty men, and only a handful of women. Many were Blacklippers, some from the south, over the mountains; Falanor couriers who had sworn an oath to keep from using blood-oil and its deviants in order to turn huge profits smuggling. Money, not blood-oil, was their own particular narcotic.

"Anu!" boomed Preyshan, striding forward, towering over the vachine and beaming her a generous smile. His lips were jet black, riddled with blood-oil, his eyes blue and wide. He wore a bushy black beard, and his size was prodigious beneath cheap market clothing. "So long since you last visited! How is your father?"

"My father is dead," said Anukis, voice soft, her eyes lowered to the ground lest she fill with tears and betray her weakness here, of all places. "I think the Engineers murdered him." Preyshan reached out, a huge, black-nailed hand cupping her chin and lifting her eyes to his, where there came a spark of connection.

"Truly, Anukis, I am sorry. He was a great man."

"And now he's a dead man."

"You have escaped their machinations?"

"For now. But I must return. I have come for..." She did not say it. Could not say it. But Preyshan understood; after all, the only vachine who visited Preyshan and his underground minions were those in need of the impure, and the illegal, Karakan Red. Smuggled in from beyond Black Pike. Fresh blood.

Preyshan gestured, and could sense the need in Anukis. A man ran forward with a small brass cylinder. He passed it to Anukis, who took it gratefully and unscrewed the top. Carefully, she consumed a small amount of the contents, and the Red glistened on her lips. As Preyshan watched, the blood shone against tiny, elongated canines of the female vachine before him, and he caught a sense of movement deep within her mouth; of whirring wheels, tiny cogs meshing and integrating, balancer shafts lifting, rotating cylinders and pumping pistons. He smiled, and it was a dry smile.

Paradoxical, thought the large Blacklipper, that as the vachine feed from man, so here, and now, in an ironic twist of fate and science, so men feed from the vachine to become Blacklipper. A twisted symbiosis? Ha! He could debate the philosophy all night.

Anukis gave a deep, drawn-out breath. Gold clouds, like golden oil, swirled in her eyes. She glanced up, a swift movement, lethargy gone as energy infused her, as blood infused her. "I'll need to take more," she said, quietly.

Preyshan nodded. "Why not stay here, with us? You will be safe here, Anu. You know that."

For an instant she saw the longing in the big man's eyes, but then it was gone, a neat mask replaced, the portcullis gate closed. Anukis licked her lips, tracing the last of the Red and swallowing. Inside, she felt greased. Oiled. Whole again.

"I cannot. The Engineers have Shabis..."

Preyshan nodded, and taking the woman's elbow, guided her to one side of the low chamber. Here, where a breeze blew in from deep subterranean mountain tunnels, where they could not be overheard, Preyshan leant against the wall and interlaced his fingers.

"If you stay, Anukis, I will fetch Shabis for you."

"How–"

He reached out, placed a finger against her lips. "You vachine are powerful, yes. But you do not understand my heritage; or my history." His eyes glittered. "The Engineers hold no fear, for me. Nor does Vashell."

Anukis shook her head. "If I allowed you to do this, I would place you all in great jeopardy. Your whole world…"

"I know this. We know this. Our existence is a dangerous one at best. But still…" He touched her arm. "You know I would do this for you. For your father, the great man, but mainly… for you."

"I understand." Anukis stepped forward, reached up on tip-toe, and kissed him on his black necrotic lips. "You are a great man, Preyshan. I am lucky to be… loved, by such as you."

Preyshan opened his mouth to speak, but his eyes narrowed, shifting over Anukis's shoulder.

"Breach!" screamed a voice, followed by a metallic screech and a twanging sound as five crossbows disgorged industrial quarrels. Three vachine, tall, athletic, hands curved into gleaming metal claws, skin peeled back from faces revealing long, curved steel fangs bared and growling, screaming, leapt from the tunnel. Crossbow bolts riddled them, and one vachine was punched back, slamming the wall, body a torn and twitching marionette of tattered flesh and twisted, bent gears; savaged clockwork. The others leapt amongst the men in great bounds, claws slashing left and right sending severed limbs flying, and long fangs descending on throats, ripping out windpipes in a sudden harsh attack. Swords hissed from sheaths as the two vachine paused, hunkered on all fours like beasts, heads rotating, eyes glittering, tiny cogs and wheels humming in their skulls. The Blacklippers converged, sword and axes drawn, spears held in clammy hands, faces grim with a need to kill these invaders—

Preyshan ran forward, his own sword held in one great paw, his face merciless in the cold glow of brass lamps. The vachine leapt, fangs tearing at arms and throats in a mad flurry of ripping flesh and savagery and inhuman speed; swords slammed, spears stabbed, and Preyshan, as if with some primeval instinct, turned back towards the iron gates – open, now, with this sudden breach of violence.

His soul fell from his world.

In the tunnel, more vachine eyes glittered. And with a roar they flooded the chamber, ten, twenty, fifty of the clockwork vampires, bowling over and through the Blacklippers ripping at flesh tearing heads from bodies steel fangs and brass claws tearing easily through unprotected flesh and succulent raw bone…

Preyshan skidded, turned, sprinted back towards Anukis who stood, shocked, mind not registering what her eyes could see. "We've got to get out of here!" he screamed at her, pounding across stone, but as he reached her he faltered, and his eyes met hers, and there was confusion there, and sudden pain, and he glanced down at the brass blade emerging from his chest. Blood bubbled around the wound, and his mouth opened allowing blood to roll through his thick beard. He reached out towards Anukis, and their fingers met, but Preyshan carried on falling to the floor and hit with a heavy slap. He lay still.

Anukis fell to her knees amidst the sounds of slaughter, tears on her pale cheeks, and she stroked Preyshan's beard. Gradually, a presence drifted through her confusion, and into her consciousness. Sobbing, she glanced up.

Vashell smiled, placed his boot on Preyshan's back, and pulled free his short brass sword, weighing the weapon thoughtfully.

"What a surprise, finding you here in this den of iniquity. And I see, you've drank your fill of Karakan Red. And left none for me? Tut tut, sweetheart." He shook his head, eyes mocking. "No wonder you could never marry me, Anukis." He squared his shoulders. Took a deep breath through fangs stuck with torn flesh. "I see now, with your impurity, with your taint, with your fucking sacrilege, how we could never be compatible."

"Damn you, Vashell! What brought you here? Why kill these–"

"Blacklippers? Why? You ask me why?" He pressed the heavy brass blade against Anukis's throat and lifted her, panting, from her knees using the point. "Because, my darling, they are illegal smugglers. Because, sweetheart, they undermine our core vachine society. And because, my beautiful little Anukis, they are the unholy, the impure, and the damned."

He glanced over his shoulder, to where savage vachine warriors had finished off the last of the Blacklippers in a bout of savagery that had sprayed the walls with blood. The chamber was littered with mangled corpses. The vachine started a low, metallic keening, and with fangs prominent, savoured the kill.

Vashell leant close. His breath was sweet. "Just like you," he said.

FOUR
Canker

Kell drifted in a world of darkness, a sea of dark oil, lantern oil, fish oil, blood-oil, unrefined, a tar mess like offal and the thick syrup from which butchers fashioned their tasty black puddings... and his eyes closed, and opened, in a languid breath for this was a dream and he knew it was a dream, and as a dream it could not be real. But if it was not real, why the hell was Ilanna so damned cold in his hands?

You must let me in, she said.

Her voice was cool, a metallic sigh, the voice of bees in their hive, the voice of ants in their nest, and Kell shivered and felt fear, not the adrenalin fear of a sudden bar brawl, nor the terrifying heart-gripping fear of hanging from high places, boots trying to scrabble on ice-slippery rock, sure as hell that when you fell the rocks and jagged natural spikes and the mountain herself would have no mercy, no pity, just a hard fast cold death. No, this fear was different, strange, an educated fear; this was the fear of knowledge; this was the fear of loss. This was Ilanna, the bloodbond axe, and she was in control. But more than that. She knew she was in control, and that she would always win the battle.

No, said Kell, scowling, fists clenching hard. He breathed her in; breathed in her metal, the musk of her iron-oil, the stench of old blood clinging like a parasite to her haft, her blades, her edge. He breathed in the perfume of the axe. The aroma of death. The corpse-breath of Ilanna.

But you must, she pleaded, *I am Ilanna, I am the honey in your soul, I am the butter on your bread, the sugar in your apple. I make you whole, Kell. I bring out the best in you, I bring out the warrior in you.*

No, he snarled. You bring out the killer in me.

That's what you always wanted, she said.

I never wanted what you had to offer.

You lie! If I was flesh and blood and bone you would have been in my bed quicker than a drunk husband after a whore. But I am steel, with sharp blades and a taste for blood. And you took what I had to offer, Kell, my sweet, you took my gift of darkness, my gift of violence, and you saved your own life. But there is a price, a price for everything, and you know you must let me free, out into the world again.

Kell laughed. "Must?" Words like "must" ring sour in my head like corked wine; they crack my skull with their… he savoured the word, instruction. What if I climbed the highest Black Pike peak, Ilanna? Dropped you into a crevasse, one of the mile deep pits guaranteed never to see anybody but the most foolhardy explorers? You'd be fucked then, my lass, would you not? Kell grinned to himself. Never again a taste of blood. Never again the splinter of bone. Just darkness, ice, the drip of water, the passing of centuries.

So you wish to die, Kell? Her voice was a beautiful lullaby, so musical in better times happier times it would
have lulled Kell to his bed. Often Kell had pictured the
woman behind the voice. He corrected himself. The
demon behind the voice, for Ilanna was anything but
human, a thousand leagues from mortal. He pictured
her as tall, beautiful, elegant; but also haughty, arrogant, filled with a self-love that made her despise all
others. A cruel woman, then. And a deadly foe.

I do not wish to die, he said, and the words shamed
him.

The Harvester is a terrible, deadly enemy, Ilanna said,
and Kell felt the axe vibrating in his fingers, growing
hot *with a million tiny judders. You cannot kill it, so do not
ever try. Even I could not sever his head, crush his bones. The
best you can do is slow him down, for every cell in his alien
body is infused with blood-oil magick. He is a creature of
blood, and nothing mortal can break him.*

How do I slow him?

*He is tall, off-balance; a creature of mechanical motion.
Aim for his knees, strike his knees and ankles with all your
might. You may buy yourself a minute at best. But be quick,
Kell.* Her voice rose to a shriek as their sliver of time,
their slice of twisted reality started to accelerate in
sudden violence into the real–

World.

The bone tubes slammed for Kell's heart and he
rolled, fast, slamming the ground and coming up,
teeth bared in a grimace, axe clenched tight to his
breast. The Harvester chuckled, frame bobbing as he
turned on Kell who charged, axe swinging for the
Harvester's chest. The creature made no move to

protect itself, but instead attacked, clawed hands lashing out at Kell who altered his strike at the last moment, his charge turning into a low roll as the axe swept for the Harvester's knees... there came a crunch, a compression of bone, and the Harvester shrieked and buckled, toppling like a sack of dry twigs and Kell was up and running, pushing Nienna and Kat along towards the stunned figure of Saark, who was crawling to his knees, clutching his head. Blood tricked from a cut at his temple, and he looked ashen, about to be sick.

"Is it dead?" breathed Nienna, and they all glanced back.

Across the gloom of the tannery, the Harvester rose to its feet and turned to face them. Its eyes burned like tiny black holes of hatred. It pointed at Kell, and started forward, and the group ran between huge tankers, rusted and smeared with shit, making the girls gag and vomit. Down a brick slope they ran, and Kell pointed with his axe, in silence, almost afraid to speak. There was a wide tunnel, which led out and down...

"I can't crawl in there!" wailed Nienna.

"You'll have to, chipmunk," said Saark, flashing Nienna a smile she did not understand, and jumped in, shit and chemicals splashing up his leggings, staining his silk shirt, mixing with blood, and vomit and rendering his dandy imagery a bad comedy. The opening wasn't as wide as it first looked, and Kell leapt in, splashing forward, with the girls following reluctantly. They stooped, squeezing into the waste pipe, Kell leading and Saark taking up the rear, his rapier out, his eyes dark.

The Harvester stopped, making a soft keening sound. Ice-smoke drifted from the cuffs of its robe, and it watched the four people vanish. In silence it turned and stalked from the tannery.

The waste pipe led down, beneath the tannery and into a narrow black-brick sewer filled with waste. Kell dropped in, scratching the skin of his hands and shins and belly, then helped Nienna and Kat to climb down the rugged, crumbling brickwork. He turned, squinting at distant light, as a cursing Saark dropped down beside him.

"Thanks for the help," he said, tone openly sardonic.

"Don't mention it."

"Damn! Would you look at this silk shirt? I'll never be able to get it clean. Do you know how much it cost? It's the finest weave, from the Silk-Blenders of Vor... they wear these in Leanoric's Court!"

"There are more important things than silk shirts, Saark."

"Don't be ridiculous. Do you know how many women this shirt has wooed? How many tapered fingers have stroked its flank? It's like a magick key. First it unlocks the heart; then it unlocks the chastity belt."

"Grandpa, what's a chastity belt?" came Nienna's voice from the gloom.

Kell threw Saark a dark look. "Nothing, don't listen to the pampered shit-streaked fool. Follow me. We need to move fast."

They splashed through thick, swirling waste, trying hard not to think about the guts and offal, dyes and dogshit which made up the slurry. At one point Nienna brushed against a dead cat, half-submerged, and she screamed, her hand coming up to cover her mouth. Her body heaved, frail frame wracking with disgust, and Kat comforted her, holding her close, as they continued to wade forward. There wasn't time to stop; no time for weakness. The Harvester might be waiting at the other end of the tunnel.

The tunnel was long, dropping at several stages on its way down to the Selenau River. Occasionally vertical venting tunnels, narrow fist-wide apertures, rose up through brick and stone and promised tantalising glimpses of the outside world.

Kat screamed, suddenly going down on one knee. Slop rose up to her chin and she spluttered, eyes closed, face twisted in disgust. "Nienna," she wailed, but Kell surged back to her, pushing Nienna up ahead to Saark, who was muttering dark oaths, his face smeared with guts and old blood. It was even stronger than Saark's perfume.

"What's wrong?" snapped Kell.

"I twisted my ankle."

"Can you walk?"

"I don't know."

"Walk or die," said Kell, voice low, eyes glittering.

Kat forced herself up, wincing, and leaning on Kell's shoulder she limped after Nienna and Saark. She was stunned by the iron in the old man's muscles, but equally stunned by the icy turn of his attitude.

Would he have left me? she thought.

The Hero of Jangir Field?

The Black Axeman of Drennach?

She ground her teeth, thinking of her life, of the bitterness, of the failures, of the people who had left, and more importantly, the people who had returned. Of course he would leave her, she thought, and a particular lode of bitterness ran through her heart. That's why he came back, instead of letting Nienna help her friend. If she'd broken her ankle, slowed them down, made excessive noise... she looked up at his grey beard, the wide, stocky set of his shoulders, the huge bearskin which made him seem more animal than human. Well, she thought. She was pretty sure his long knife would have slid through her ribs, ending the problem, negating the threat.

She shivered, as a chill breeze caressed her soul.

And for the first time she looked at Kell not as an old man; but as a killer.

Saark had stopped, hand held out towards the others. He turned, eyes meeting Kell's. "It's the river," he said.

Kell nodded, pushing to the front. The noise of fast flowing water invaded the tunnel egress, and he watched the circle of light, drifting with ice-smoke, for quite some time. He edged forward, took a good grip on his axe, and peered outside.

Slop and effluence dropped down through a series of concrete channels, and fell under a timber platform and into the Selenau River. Here, the river took a tight turn, narrowing between two rock walls and raging over several clumps of stone, white and frothing, and charging off through the city. The timber platform was based on rock, then edged out on stilts over the river, the wood dark and oil-slick with preservative. Several drums and barrels stood at one end, and a small, calm off-shoot of concrete-hemmed water housed five small boats on a simulated canal.

Saark was beside him. "We take a boat?"

"Seems like a good idea, lad."

"Let's do it."

"Wait." Kell placed a hand on Saark's chest. "That… thing, a Harvester it's called; it was keen to suck our blood, yes?"

Saark nodded.

"Chances are, it's out there. We need to move fast, Saark. No mistakes. Be ready with that pretty little sword."

Again, Saark nodded, and the group waded out into grey light, the sky filled with wisps and curls of ice-smoke, thinner now, but still reducing visibility over a hundred yard range. Kell was scanning left and right as they scrambled down icy concrete ramps, past where the sludge from the tannery pipes fell. Then his boots hit the wooden platform with a thud, and he stood, a huge bear, arms high, axe held before his chest as his gaze swept the world.

Nienna and Kat slid down the concrete ramps on their bottoms, followed by Saark, his poise perfect, fine clothing ruined by dyes and shit. His sword was in his fist, and his eyes were narrowed, focused, searching…

Kell moved to a boat, and hacked through the knot with his axe blade. Taking the rope in one fist, he ushered the girls and Saark, who had turned, towards the end of the timber platform lost in mist – from which drifted the Harvester, eyes glowing, five bony fingers pointing towards the group.

"Get in," growled Kell.

Saark took the girls, and they leapt into the boat, cracking ice around the vessel in the still-water channel. The currents tugged, and Saark leaned forward, grasping the platform. "Get in, Kell," he snapped. But Kell had turned, and rolled his mighty shoulders as the Harvester accelerated, frame bobbing as it moved fast towards him, a high-pitched keening coming from its flat, oval nostrils. Kell sprinted, and leapt, axe lashing out but the Harvester moved, fast, rolling away from the blades, bony fingers lashing out. Kell's axe cut back on a reverse stroke, slamming the arm away, and he skidded on icy wood, righting himself. The Harvester lowered its head towards him.

"You will die a long, painful death, little man."

"Show me, laddie," snarled Kell, head low, shoulders lifted, powerful, as the Harvester attacked. His axe lashed out, was knocked aside but he ducked, whirled a low circle with Ilanna singing through cold air to slam fast at the Harvester's legs... it stepped back and the axe turned, coming up over Kell's head in a glittering arc as he stepped in, and the blades smashed down at the Harvester's shoulders. There came a sound, like snapping wood, the blades were savagely deflected to the right dragging Kell off-balance. A fist hit Kell in the ribs, and he hit the ground on the way down. The Harvester's fingers slammed at his heart, but he rolled, Ilanna cutting an arc to smash the extended fingers, trapping them in the wood, embedding both bony fingers and axe in the platform.

Kell climbed to his feet, clutching his ribs, and the Harvester tugged at its trapped fingers, making a low

but high-pitched growling sound. Its head snapped
up, black eyes scowling at Kell who reached under his
jerkin and pulled out his Svian knife. He leapt forward, knife slashing for the Harvester's throat, blade
cutting white flesh that parted like fish-meat, but no
blood came out no scream emerged and the Harvester
slapped a back-handed blow against Kell sending him
rolling across the platform.

"Get in the boat!" screamed Saark. The current was
pulling at them more viciously, and ice crackled in a
flurry of shots.

Kell climbed to his feet, bearded face filled with a
dark, controlled fury. He watched the Harvester rip its
fingers free with a splintering of torn wood, and
Ilanna fell to the platform with a slap. The Harvester
stood tall, flexing its undamaged fingers. Kell swallowed. The blades should have amputated; instead,
there was no mark. His gaze lifted to the slit throat,
but the fish-flesh had knitted together, and was whole
again.

Kell knew, now. There was blood-oil magick here;
he could not kill this creature. Ilanna had been right,
and this sickened him.

He ran, and the Harvester leapt at him with a hiss,
fingers slashing for his heart. But Kell ducked, turned
his run into a slide on icy wood, under the Harvester's
flashing bone talons to grasp his axe. Arms pumping,
he sprinted for the boat even as Saark's grip finally
lost its battle and the boat slid out along the still water,
crackling ice, to join the flow of the raging torrent.
Kell leapt, landing heavily in the boat which rocked
madly for a moment. Then he stood, staring back at

the Harvester as he replaced his Svian in its sheath beneath his left arm, and they were whisked away into thickening mist.

"A good effort," said Saark, smiling kindly at Kell. "If the bastard had been human, it'd now be dead."

"But it's not," growled Kell, slumping down and taking the boat's oars. "And that makes me want to puke. Come on, let's get out of this godsforsaken city. It gives me the shits."

General Graal led the way to the elevated tower room, presenting the broad target of his back to Dagon Trelltongue.

Dagon, a tall but slender man with shoulder-length grey hair and small eyes, wearing the finest silk and wool fashion-clothing of the south, felt keenly the presence of the delicate sword at his waist, the jewelled knife under his arm and the poison in the vial at his hip-belt. He swallowed, dry spit in a dry mouth. He could kill Graal, a swift piercing of sword through lungs, watch the general's blood bubble onto the rich carpets they now walked. Dagon could send the Army of Iron back north, with no leader, no hope, no fire; he could save the coming war, save his friend, lord, and King, Leanoric – and indeed, all the people of Falanor.

Dagon's eyes narrowed. Bastards!

No. They would pay. They would suffer.

Damn them all.

They entered a large chamber, once one of Jalder's finest council offices. Thick carpets kept chill from stone flags, the walls were plastered and painted white, and the whole room was decorated with dark wood, inlaid with gold. Fine works of art hung at intervals around the chamber; discreet. Many comfort couches were set apart, amidst desks and stone pedestals showing several of Falanor's heroes. Dagon had been here before, on many occasions, usually on business for King Leanoric. Now, there was a more sombre, and chilling, atmosphere.

Graal reached a long, lacquered desk and turned, suddenly, a swift movement. His long white hair drifted around his face for a moment, bright blue eyes fixing on Dagon who swallowed, seeing the smile on Graal's face, knowing that Graal had read his thoughts, had presented his broad back as a test, a free shot, a target; and Dagon also knew this man was a mighty warrior. If he'd dared to attack, to try and save his people… well, he would now be dead.

"A brandy?"

"No, I shouldn't," came Dagon's rich voice. He was a born orator, but here, in this company, he felt like a child. All his richly rehearsed speeches crumbled in the air like the stench of warm cabbage.

"I appreciate the, ah, ice-smoke is not to everybody's liking. It chills the bones. Go on, Dagon, you have made a long journey to visit, a long journey to –" he laughed softly – "save your life. A little brandy cannot hurt. It is distilled from peaches from King Leanoric's own orchards, I believe."

Dagon took a glass, and his eyes reflected in Leanoric's crest carved skilfully into the faceted crystal surface. He drank deep, and observed Graal watching his trembling fingers, his nervous tongue, and he finished the brandy, felt warmth flood him, felt alcohol tingle his brain giving him just a little courage.

"So you will tell me everything?" said Graal, sipping at his own drink. Dagon saw the man's fingers were long, tapered, even the finger-nails white. His gaze moved up to blue eyes fixed on him. Strange, that they were blue, thought Dagon. He watched. Graal did not blink.

"Yes," croaked Dagon, eventually, feeling weak at the knees, full in the bladder, frightened to his very core.

"Numbers of infantry, cavalry, archers, pikemen? Where the divisions are stationed? The names of their division generals? Brigadier generals? Numbers of horses, supply chains, military routes through Falanor, everything?"

"Yes."

"And of course," said Graal, moving to Dagon, stooping a little to peer closer into the official's eyes, "Leanoric. They say he is a great battle king. That he cannot be beaten on the field. He has shown, endlessly, that he has a brilliant mind, a tactician without compare. He is strong, handsome, commands respect and honour from his soldiers. Is all this correct?"

"It is… my lord."

"I am a general, not a lord," snapped Graal, crushing his crystal glass. It shattered, long jagged shards slicing Graal's hand, thick brandy flowing over the wounds and dripping, mixed with normal red blood into the carpet. Graal did not flinch, did not even look at the wound, but retained his connection with Dagon.

"Yes, general," whispered Dagon.

"There is one more thing."

"General?" Dagon's voice was little more than a whisper.

"Alloria. Leanoric's queen. The mother of his two boys. She is his backbone, is she not? His love, his life, his strength. I want to know where she is, where she travels in the winter, who her maids of honour are, and which hand she uses to wipe her arse."

"Alloria? But... I agreed to instruct you in armies, military strategy, and to speak of Leanoric..."

Graal's hand snapped out, taking Dagon by the throat. Shards of crystal, embedded in Graal's flesh, pierced Dagon's skin and he squealed, legs kicking as Graal lifted him off the ground. "You will tell me everything. Leanoric is a worthy adversary; but if I remove his reason for life, diverge his thoughts by taking his queen then I have a powerful bartering tool, I have, shall we say, a strategy our tactician will appreciate. I cannot afford to lose time on this..." he smiled, almost sardonically, "invasion. You understand, Trelltongue?"

"Ye-es," he managed, throat weeping blood.

Graal dropped Dagon to the carpet, turned, and languorously poured himself another brandy. His head came up as something drifted through the doorway, and Dagon's breath caught in his throat as he watched the Harvester approach. He had seen them at work, seen them drain the corpses of women, and children. These creatures filled him with a terror straight from a deep primeval pit; a terror so awesome he could barely vocalise.

"Hestalt. There is a problem?"

The Harvester nodded, black eyes turning on Dagon and burning through the king's advisor. Graal waved his lacerated hand, "Don't mind him, he is of no consequence." Graal began picking shards from his flesh, some as long as two inches. He did not wince. "What's wrong?"

"The man. The *hero*. Kell."

"He still lives?"

"More than that. He has been a… thorn, in my side. He has escaped."

"Send a squad. They'll catch up with one old man."

"No, Graal. He is more dangerous than you could comprehend… and it stems from his axe. I know a bloodbond weapon when I see one. Graal, he must be dealt with immediately. You understand?"

Graal rubbed at his chin, eyes distant. "He was there? During the Days of Blood? If he is in possession of a bloodbond weapon he must surely have experienced those days; one way or another." Graal's eyes glittered. His splintered hand was forgotten. "There is immense power in such a weapon. Power we can use, yes?"

The Harvester nodded. "Send a canker."

Graal frowned. "A little excessive, my friend."

"I want him stopped. His life extinguished. Now!"

Graal gave a single nod. It was rare he'd seen a Harvester so ruffled. He walked to the window, wondering if there was some unwritten bond here; some information to which he was not privy. Graal signalled to an albino soldier, who disappeared. Dagon Trelltongue used the time to pull himself to his feet, removing a tissue from one pocket and dabbing at his bleeding throat. He could feel the flesh, bruised, swollen, punctured, and he knew he would struggle to speak for the next few days.

Distantly, there came a sound, savage, brutal, a snarling like a big cat only this noise was twisted, and merged with metal. Dagon shivered involuntarily, and found General Graal's eyes locked to him again. The general was smiling, and gestured idly to the doorway. "A canker," he said, by way of explanation, as six soldiers pushed a cage through high, ornately-carved double-doors.

Dagon felt piss running down his legs as his eyes fastened on the cage, and he was unable to tear his gaze free from the vision.

It was big, the size of a lion, but there the resemblance ended. Once, it had been human. Now it raged on all fours, pale white skin bulging with muscle and tufts of white and grey fur. Its forehead stretched right back, mouth five times the size of a human maw, the skull opened right up, split horizontal like a melon and with huge curved fangs dropping down below the chin like razor-spikes. Everywhere across the creature's body lay open wounds, crimson, rimmed with yellow fat, like the open, frozen flesh of the necrotic, and inside Dagon could see tiny wheels spinning, gears meshing, shafts moving and shifting like, like...

Like clockwork, he realised.

Dagon blinked, and tried to swallow. He could not.

The creature snarled, shrieked and launched at the cage wall. Huge bars squealed, one rattling, and the creature sat back on its haunches with its strange open head, its twisted high-set eyes, one higher than the other, staring at Dagon for a moment and sending a spear of ice straight to his heart. Inside that skull he saw more clockwork, gears and levers stepping up and down, tiny wheels spinning. He fancied, if he listened carefully, he could hear the gentle, background *tick tick tick* of a clock.

"What is it?" he whispered.

"A canker," repeated Graal, moving over to the cage and putting his hand inside. Dagon wanted to scream *Don't do that, it'll rip your fucking hand off!* But he did not. He stared, in a terrible, dazed silence. "When vachine are young, little more than babes, they go to the Engineer's Palace for certain, necessary, modifications. However, the vachine flesh is occasionally temperamental, and suffers, shall we say, a setback. The muscle, bone and clockwork do not meld, do not integrate, and as the vachine grows so it loses humanity, loses emotions, loses empathy, and becomes something less than vachine. It twists, its body corrupting, its growth becoming an eternal battle between flesh and clockwork, each component vying for supremacy, each internal war filling the new-grown canker with awesome pain, and hatred, and, sadly, insanity. Eventually, one or the other – the flesh, or the clockwork – will win the battle and the canker will die. Until that point, we use them for hunting impure vachine. The Heretics, the Blasphemers, and the Blacklippers."

Graal turned, then. His words had been soft, a recounting of Engineer Council Lore, the Oak Testament, and he blinked as if awaking from a dream. "This is Zalherion. Once, he was my brother.

The vachine process was good to me. But not, I fear, to him."

The canker moved forward, and licked at Graal's hand like a dog would its master. The canker growled, then, head turning, its eyes fixed again on Dagon and Graal gave a laugh, a sweet sound, his blue eyes sparkling. "No, not him, Zal. We have another one for you." The canker growled, a distorted lion-sound, and with a squeal of bolts Graal opened the cage.

The canker leapt out, brass claws gouging rich carpets. It moved with an awesome power and feline grace despite its twisted frame and open wounds, towering over the men, even the Harvester, and gazing down at Graal with something akin to love.

Graal's head turned, and the Harvester moved forward, eyes closing, five bone fingers reaching out towards the canker. It growled, backed away a step, hunkered down. Then a moment later, it stood and sprinted from the room leaving grooves in the stone.

"What did you do?" whispered Dagon, aware that if he survived this encounter, and the one soon to follow, it would be a miracle of life over insanity; of luck over probability.

"The Harvester imprinted an image of Kell inside the canker's mind. Now, Zal will not stop until Kell is dead."

Dagon lowered his head. Tears ran down his cheeks.

The small boat sped down the river, but eventually the banks widened and the urgency and violent rocking slowed. Nienna sat, stunned, huddled close to Kat for warmth, and also the mental strength of friendship.

She had watched her grandpa, Old Kell, fight the Harvester in something like a dream state, aware at any moment that the creature might smash him from existence, suck the life from his shell with those long razor bone fingers... and yet it was like she was watching a play on a stage, because, to see her grandpa fight was unreal, surreal, something that just wasn't right. He was an old man. He cooked soup. He told her stories. He moaned about his back. He moaned about the price of fish at the market. It wasn't right.

"Are you well?" asked Kat, hugging her briefly.

Nienna looked up into Kat's blood-spattered, toxin-splashed face, and nodded, giving a little smile. She took a deep breath. "Yes, Kat. I think. Just. Everything has been crazy. Wild! I can't believe Grandpa is so... deadly."

Kat, remembering her companion's perceived savagery back in the tunnel, her cold realisation that Kell would leave her to die, said nothing, simply nodded. An ice-veil dropped over her heart, smothering another little piece of her humanity with bitter cynicism.

"We'll be all right," said Nienna, mistaking Kat's inner turmoil and total fear – not at the world outside, but at the man in the boat. "We'll get through this, you'll see. We'll go to university. Everything will be all right."

Kat gave a small, bitter laugh. "Yeah, Nienna? You, with your sheltered upbringing, your loving mother, your doting grandpa, all caring for you and holding you and being there for you. I never had any of that." Her voice was astringent. Filled with acid. "I've been alone in this world, alone, for such a very long time, sweet little pampered Nienna. I fought every step of the way just to gain entry to Jalder University; I lied, I cheated, I stole, in order to try and crawl up from the stinking gutter, to make a better life for myself, a better future. Nobody has ever been there for me, Nienna."

"What about your aunt? The one who raised you after you parents died? The one who baked you bread, and washed your clothes, and braided your hair with beads?"

Kat gave another laugh, and gazed off along the frozen river banks. The trees were full of snow, the air full of mist from the fields, and they were leaving the city fast behind, the Selanau River carrying them south. "My aunt? She never existed. I used to live in taverns, haylofts, anywhere I could find. I would sneak into merchant's houses and use their baths, steal clothes from servants, steal bread from the ovens and soup from bubbling pans. I was a ghost. A thief. An expert thief." She laughed again, tears running down her cheeks. "I've always been alone, Nienna. Always been a fighter. Now... it's gone, isn't it? The university? Life in Jalder? All I fought to build, it has been taken away with a click of some dictator's scabby fingers."

"I'm there for you, now," said Nienna, voice small, and hugged Kat.

"Everybody leaves me in the end," she said.

"No! I will be there for you. Forever! Until we die."

"Until we die?"

Nienna squeezed her friend, took her hands, pressed her cold skin, her frozen fingers, and hugged her like the sister she'd never had. "I swear on my soul," she whispered.

The boat ride had slowed, and within a couple of hours they finally left the clinging veils of ice-smoke and mist behind. A new world opened before them, fresh and bright as they drifted from wreaths of haze into a landscape of rolling fields crisp with frost and patches of snow. Large hills lined the horizon, many thick with great scars of conifer forest, junipers, yews and blue spruce, great green and white swathes that stretched in crescents across the undulating hillsides peppered with teeth of rock and littered with pink and magenta winter heather giving bright splashes of colour.

Eventually Kell guided the boat to the banks of the river lined with towering silver fir, and they cruised for a while in silence, each huddled in their own damp clothing, stinking from the tannery, lost in thought at the recent, savage events that had overtaken Jalder.

"There," said Saark, pointing.

Kell nodded, spotting the small stone cottage backed by yews, and guided the boat towards a shingle beach where he leapt out into the shallows and dragged the boat up the shingle with a grunt. He stood, axe in pink chilled hands, as the others jumped free and Saark joined him, rapier out, searching for any possible enemy.

"You think they'll follow us here?" said Saark.

"Have you *ever* seen a creature like that Harvester?"

"No."

"Me neither. I've no idea what they'll do, my friend. But for now, at least, we've put a good twenty miles between us and the… madness in Jalder." At his words, he saw Nienna shudder and he moved to her, placing his arm around her shoulders. "Come on, Nienna. We'll build a fire." He hugged her.

"I was thinking. Of mam."

Kell frowned. "She'd gone to work at Keenan's Farm, yes? To work on the pottery?"

Nienna nodded, face frightened.

"That's eight miles out of the city," said Kell, soothingly. "She'll be fine. Trust me. The enemy want the garrison; it's not worth their effort scouring the countryside for every little farmstead."

Nienna gave another nod, but Kell could see she wasn't convinced.

They approached the stone cottage warily. It was single storey, simple in construction with a thatched roof. No smoke came from the chimney, and no livestock scattered in the yard as was normal for these modest but cosy dwellings.

"It's deserted," said Saark, kicking a bucket which clattered across the mud.

Kell threw him a dark scowl, and moved to the entrance. "What's the matter? You sorry there are no serving wenches at hand to see to your every petty whim?"

Saark shrugged, and stood, a hand on one hip, his rapier pointing at the ground. He plucked at a tattered, stained cuff. "Well, I'm sorry there are no serving wenches sat on my hand, Kell old horse. It's been commented in social circles how I can supply the most exquisite of pleasures to even the most buxom pigs with a face like a horse arse." He smiled, showing neat teeth. "I have a certain way with female flesh. And with male flesh, come to think of it."

"Keep your thoughts to yourself," said Kell darkly, "or you'll have a way with my fist," and he entered the cottage. He emerged a moment later, and gestured them inside. They stepped in. The floor was flagged with stone, and a table and several chairs, old, battered but expertly crafted, stood in one room. A kitchen bench ran down one entire wall containing wooden plates and cups, and a large jug. The second room contained a huge bed, still scattered with old blankets. Saark peered in, and tutted.

"What's the matter now?" snapped Kell.

"No silk sheets," smiled Saark, and rubbed at weary eyes. He yawned, and stretched. "Still, it's good enough for tonight. I'm going to take a nap."

"No you're not," said Kell, turning to face him across the long table.

"Excuse me?"

"I said," growled Kell, "you're not going to put down your head and leave all the work to us. We need wood for the fire, water for the pot, and I spied a vegetable patch outside with cabbages and potatoes. They need to be pulled from the frozen soil and scrubbed clean."

"I'm sure you'll get on just wonderfully with such menial labour," smiled Saark, Kell's anger apparently lost on him. "It is, of course, no job for a nobleman and dandy of such high repute."

"Are you hungry?"

"Of course! But alas, I cannot cook, have never chopped wood, and my lower back is a tad sore from all my romantic endeavours. Alas, your jobs, valiant and necessary as they are, are beyond a simple cox-comb like myself." Saark turned, as if to enter the mouldy bedroom.

"If you don't work, you don't eat," said Kell, voice low.

"Excuse me?"

"Is there a problem with your hearing? Something, perhaps, that needs cleaning out with the blade of my axe?"

Saark scowled. "I may be a sexual athlete, and I may dress in silks so expensive the likes of you could not afford them even if you worked a thousand years; but I will not be threatened, Kell, and don't you ever doubt my skill with a blade."

"I don't doubt your skill with a blade, boy, just the skill with your brain. Get out there, and chop some wood, or I swear I'll kick you down to the river like an old stinking dog and drown you."

There was a moment of tension, then Saark re-laxed, and smiled. He crossed to the doorway, both young women watching him in silence, and he turned and gave Kell a nod. "As you wish, old man. But I'd do something about that sexual tension; it's eating you up, and alas, turning you into a cantan-kerous ill-tempered bore." His eyes flickered to Kat, lingered for a moment, then he gave a narrow smile and left.

Within moments, they heard the chopping of wood. Saark had obviously found the wood shed.

Nienna crossed to her grandpa, and touched his arm. "He means no harm," she said. "It's just his way."

"Pah!" snapped Kell. "I know his sort; I saw plenty of them in Vor and Fawkrin. He takes, like a parasite, and never gives. There are too many like him, even in Jalder. They have spread north like a plague."

"Not any longer," said Kat, eyes haunted. "The albino soldiers killed them all." She took the jug from the long bench and left, heading down to the river for water. Kell sighed, and placed Ilanna on the table with a gentle motion. He took Nienna by both shoulders, and looked into her eyes, deep into her eyes, until she blushed and turned away.

"You did well, girl."

"In the university?"

"All of it," said Kell. "You were strong, brave, fearless. You haven't been moaning and whining," he glanced outside, his insinuation obvious, "and you have proved yourself in battle." He smiled then, a kindly smile, and Nienna's old grandpa returned. "Funny, you said you wanted an adventure. Well, you've brought us that, little Nienna." He ruffled her hair, and she gave a laugh, but it faded, twisted, and ended awkwardly.

This was not a day for laughter.

Kat washed herself as best she could, then filled her jug at the river, and carrying it back towards the stone cottage she stopped, observing Saark work. He had tied back his long, dark curls, and stripped off his shirt revealing a lean and well-muscled torso. He had broad shoulders tapering to narrow hips, and although he claimed never to chop wood, he did so with an expert stroke, his balance perfect, every swing striking true to split logs into halves, quarters and eighths ready for the fire.

Kat watched him for a while, the sway of his body, the squirming of muscles under pale white skin, and the serenity of his handsome face in its focus, and concentration. No, she decided; not a handsome face, but a beautiful face. Saark was stunning. Almost feminine in his delicacy, his symmetry. Kat licked her lips.

He turned, then, sweat glistening on his body despite the chill, and he waved her towards him. Slowly, she approached, eyes down now, feeling suddenly shy and not understanding why.

"Hello, my pretty," he said with a wide friendly smile. "Would it be possible to quench my thirst?"

"Sir?"

"The water," he laughed, "can I have a drink?"

Kat nodded, and Saark took the jug, taking great gulps, water running down his chest through shining sweat. She saw his chest had the same curled, dark hair as his head, and as he lowered the jug he grinned at her, eyes glittering.

"Do you like what you see?"

"What do you mean?"

"You were watching me. Whilst I chopped wood."

"I was not!"

"How old are you, girl?"

"I'm eighteen. I'm a woman, not a girl."

Saark looked her up and down, eyes widening. "Well, I can see that, my pretty." His voice deepened. "You are all woman."

"Have you finished with the jug?"

Grinning again, Saark handed it back and Kat turned to leave.

"You can sleep with me tonight, if you like? I'll keep you warm against the ice and the snow; keep you safe against the bad men in the dark."

"The only bad man in the dark would be you," snapped Kat, without turning, and stalked back towards the cottage, her cheeks flushed red. But she was smiling as she walked.

Kell lit a fire, and within an hour warmth had filled the cottage. Darkness fell outside, and night brought with it a storm of snow and hail, which rattled off the windows as a mournful wind howled through the yew trees out back.

Nienna and Kat cooked a large pot of stew, thick with cabbage and potatoes, and plenty of salt which Kell found in a cupboard along with dried herbs, thyme and rosemary, which they added for flavour. They sat around the table, eating. All had cleaned themselves as best they could in the ice-cold river, and Nienna found some old clothes in a chest in the bedroom. Despite being cold, and smelling mildly of damp, they were far superior to the stained items which had suffered the tannery. Each in turn changed, burning old clothes on the fire and pulling on woollen trews and rough cotton shirts. Saark went last, and when Nienna handed him the thick trousers and shirt he held them at arm's length, his distaste apparent.

"What would you like me to do with these?" he asked Nienna.

She gave a short laugh. "Put them on, idiot!"

"Are you sure? I thought they were for cleaning out the pigs." He glanced over at Kell and grimaced. "I see you've settled comfortably into your new wardrobe, old horse."

"These clothes are fine," Kell said gruffly, not looking up.

"Not itchy at all?"

Kell glanced up from his stew. "Not for me," he said. "But you may find them a little rough, what with your baby-soft skin, manicured hands and cream-softened arse."

"Ha! These are the clothes of the peasant. I'll not wear them."

"Then you'll stink of dog-shit, old brains and cattle-fat for the next week."

Saark considered this. "You sure they don't itch?" he asked. "There's nothing worse than a peasant's fleas. Except, maybe, a whore's syphilis!" He laughed at his joke, and carried the clothes through to the bedroom with Kell staring after him, eyes glowing embers.

The door closed, then opened again. "Any chance one of you young ladies could help me dress? You know how tiresome this can be for us fine noble types."

"I'll do it," said Kell, pushing back his chair which scraped against the stone floor.

"Ach, that's all right, big man. I… I think I can manage."

Saark disappeared, and Kell returned to his stew, complementing Nienna and Kat on their cooking.

When they'd finished eating, Nienna said, "Grandpa?"

"Yes, monkey?"

"Will the…" she seemed to be fighting with her thoughts, "will those albino soldiers come after us? This far from Jalder?"

"No, girl," said Kell. "They took the garrison, then the city. If they do intend to invade Falanor further, then the logical route is to head south down the Great North Road. After all, King Leanoric built it for transporting his troops." He smiled, and it was grim. "It's ironic, however, that I think he envisioned his own soldiers using it. Not the enemy."

"Where did those albino men come from?" said Kat. She was leaning back, hands stretched towards the fire, belly full and at least savouring a little contentment.

"From the north, past the Black Pike Mountains. I saw them once; they have a huge civilisation there."

"Why does nobody in Jalder speak of them? Why is there no trade?"

Kell shrugged. "The paths across the mountains are treacherous indeed. For most of the year impassable, even; certainly impossible for an army to travel. This Army of Iron must have found a new route, something to which I am not privy."

"Is it true there are tunnels under the Black Pikes?"

Kell nodded. "Many. And more treacherous than the mountain trails, of that I am certain." His eyes were distant, now, as if reliving ancient days. "I've seen many a man die in the Black Pikes. The mountains take no prisoners."

"You speak as if they live?"

"Maybe they do," said Kell, rubbing wearily at his eyes. "Maybe they do."

Saark chose that moment to make his grand entrance, and he grinned, giving a twirl by the bedroom door. "I look like you people, now," he said, tying back his long curls.

"You said they were clothes for a peasant," pointed out Kell.

"Exactly," smiled Saark. "Is there any more stew? I'm famished."

"You've already had two bowls," said Kat.

"I'm a growing lad who needs his energy." He winked at her, and sat down, ladling more stew into his bowl. "By all the gods, this stinks of cabbage."

"You can always go hungry, lad," said Kell.

"No, no, I'm starting to enjoy the… ahh, cabbage flavour. It's certainly an acquired taste, but I think, in maybe a year or two, I might just get used to it."

After the girls were asleep, Saark waved a small flask at Kell. "Drink, old horse?"

"Stop calling me old horse. I ain't that old."

"Ach, so you won't be wanting this whisky, aged fifteen years in oak vats, will you?"

"Maybe just a drop," conceded Kell. "To warm against the winter chill." He took the flask, drank deeply, and handed it back to Saark, smacking his lips. "By all the gods, that's a fine drop." He eyed Saark. "Must have cost a pretty penny."

"Stolen by my own fair hand."

"'The World despises a thief, leste he undermyne Mighty Kings'," quoted Kell, staring hard at Saark. "I kind of echo that sentiment, laddie."

"All fine and well, when you have money in your purse. Ask those without. The merchant who shared his produce won't be needing it; the albino soldiers killed him and his wife."

"And I suppose you had just... ravished her?"

Saark snorted laughter, and took another drink. "Ravished? Come come, Kell, we are both men of the world. You can speak to me as one man to another. Yes, I fucked her. And what a pretty piece of quim she was, too. Never have I tasted such succulent honey."

Kell's eyes hardened, fists clenching. "You have very little respect for women, lad."

Saark considered this. "Well, they have very little respect for me. Now, listen Kell." He leant forward, firelight dancing in his dark eyes. "We need to decide what we're going to do next. You know, as I, the Army of Iron will head south. We have but a few days; they will consolidate their position, leave their own garrison in command of Jalder, and travel the Great North Road. We need to be gone from here by then; their scouts will spread out, and will certainly find us. We are easy to spot." He thought. "Well, you are."

Kell nodded, and when he replied his voice was cool. He found it hard to hide his distaste for the popinjay. Kell was a simple man who wore emotions on his face, and on his fists. He told it like it was. "What do you have in mind, Saark?"

"Much as it pains me to say this, for there is little actual personal profit in it for me, but... we should ride south. We should warn King Leanoric. It is the right thing to do."

Kell picked up a sharp bread knife, toyed with it between his fingers. He seemed uneasy. "Surely, the king already knows? His northern capital has been sundered."

"Maybe. Maybe not. If the Army of Iron surprises Leanoric... well, they can plough through Falanor like a knife through a sleeping man's eyeball. Our armies would topple. People enslaved. All that kind of tiresome business of Empire. Could you live with that on your conscience, Kell?"

"You're a fine one to speak of conscience."

"For a cuckolded husband? No. For the slaughter of an entire population? Use your head, Kell. And anyway... there may be a warm spot in the Hall of Heroes for somebody who does the Heroic Thing." He winked. "One must always try and please the gods. Just in case."

"You're a worm, Saark."

"Maybe. But a man needs all the help he can get. We must warn Leanoric. He will need to gather the Eagle Divisions; if surprised, he could be sorely routed. What life then for a dandy on a mission?"

Kell nodded, and his eyes met Saark's. "You are from the south, aren't you lad?"

"Yes. Hard to hide the Iopian burr."

"Have you met the king?"

"Once," said Saark, his voice dropping soft, eyes becoming dreamy. "Many moons ago, old horse."

The fire was burning low. Outside, the wind howled and hail rattled in bursts against the windows like a smash of arrows. Kell came awake, one arm cold,

head foggy. The whisky had done him few favours. It
rarely did.

What had woken him?

Kell sat up, from where he lay before the fire. He
could hear Nienna's rhythmical snoring in the bedroom. Across from him, Saark turned in his sleep, but
did not wake. Kell stood, and reached for his axe, then
crouched beside Saark and shook him.

"Mmm?"

"Shh. I heard something."

"Probably a rat."

"There are no rats. I checked."

"Probably a chicken." He shook off Kell's grip. "Let
me go back to sleep."

"Might be an albino soldier with a dagger for your
throat," whispered Kell in Saark's ear.

Saark rolled over, pulled on his boots, and drew his
rapier. "You are the fun soul of any party, Kell, you
know that? Shit then. Let's go check it out."

"Wake the girls."

"Why? Women are best left asleep after the night's
work is done, in my opinion."

"We may need to leave fast."

Saark moved to the bedroom, woke the girls and
watched without embarrassment as they dressed in
the gloom, leaning against the doorway, his eyes lin-
gering on breasts. Kell moved to the front door and
stopped. He stared at the wooden planks, which rattled in the wind; outside, hail bombarded the world
and Kell tilted his head, frowning, eyes narrowing,
then was suddenly moving, twisting, diving aside at
high speed as the door – including torn hinges and

wrenched locks – imploded with a squeal and crash, the whole thing slamming across the room and missing Kell by inches, to crash into the far wall where it exploded into chunks and splinters. Kell lifted his axe, Saark whirled around, face drawn, sword high, and there in the entrance stood... the canker, Zalherion. It growled, a low metallic sound underlain with a thrashing of delicate brass gears.

"What the hell–" hissed Saark.

The canker leapt, its bulk smashing stones from the door surround as Kell rolled right, axe thundering in an arc to slam flesh with a thump and spray of bright blood; Saark's rapier slashed the creature's flank, carving a long razor-line down bulging muscle and the creature roared, head thrashing as it turned, bulky and huge in the room as it stomped chairs to tinder. Saark whirled. To Nienna and Kat, he hissed, "Out the window! Run down to the boat, now, as if your lives depend on it!"

He leapt as the canker turned on him, and a great paw on the end of a bent, angled, barely human arm snapped at him. Talons tore three shallow jagged lines across his clothing, hurling him across the room upside down to thud the wall and hit the floor, tangled and groaning. Kell's axe, Ilanna, slammed at the creature's spine, blades embedding in flesh. He tore his axe free as the canker screamed, rearing up, head smashing the ceiling and bringing down thick plaster and several cracked wooden beams. Grimly, Kell wrenched free his axe, took a step back for balance and weighting, and hammered it again as if chopping wood. Blades bit flesh, muscle, and several small brass gears were flung free of the canker, tinkling as they scattered across the stone floor.

The creature turned on Kell, huge open maw filled with gnashing clockwork and drooling thick crimson pus. It howled, and charged at him in the confined space, and Kell scrambled back, twisting to avoid the swipe of massive talons at the end of a human arm, his axe coming up to deflect a second blow, ducking a third swipe which hit the fireplace behind him, cracking stones with sheer force of impact.

Kell looked deep into the canker's eyes. The rage there was indescribable... the pain, the suffering, the anguish, the hatred. He swallowed hard as its shoulders tensed, and Kell realised it was going to crush him against the stone of the cottage wall with sheer bulk and weight – and he didn't have room to swing Ilanna! There was nothing he could do.

FIVE
The Church of Blessed Engineers

Anukis awoke slowly, as if from a long, bad dream. She could taste blood, and two of her teeth were smashed. She reached into her mouth and plucked the tiny pieces of bone free, wincing, wanting to cry, but forcing back the piercing pain and ignoring the fire. She had more urgent matters to consider.

Coughing, Anukis sat up and opened her eyes. She was naked, wrists chained, and the room was illuminated by a dim light. However, her superior vachine eyes kicked in with a tiny background whirr of clockwork, and her eyes enhanced the ambient light. She was in a cell. It was a good cell, a clean cell; precise, and fashioned totally from metal.

Anukis looked about. The floor was steel, ridged for grip, and sporting channels no-doubt to carry away blood and the water used to sluice out the honey from the tortured. The walls were black iron, rusted in patches, the ceiling brass and set with tiny squares to allow entry for distant daylight.

Anukis stood, testing her body, checking how much damage had been done. The vachine had beat her; oh,

how they enjoyed their sport, slamming the impure
with fists and boots, but no teeth – no, Vashell had not
allowed them to rip her apart with fangs and claws.

Not yet, anyway.

Anukis endured her savage beating; it lasted maybe
an hour. She recognised it had gone on long after she
had lost consciousness. Slowly, now, she checked her
way through her bones, searching for breaks; there
was a mild fracture in her left shoulder blade, and she
winced as she rolled it, ignoring the torn and protest-
ing muscles, the impact bruises, but going deep,
analysing the pain within. One finger was snapped,
on her left hand – ironically, her wedding ring finger.
I suppose Vashell won't be asking me to marry him
anymore, she thought, and felt a hysterical giggle
welling in her breast which she quashed savagely. No.
Not here. You cannot lose your mind here. Because
to lose your mind is to...

Die.

Such a simple word. An effortless concept. The natural order of all things: to live, and to die. Only the
vachine were different, for they had introduced a
third state with their hybrid watchmaking technology... as created by her grandfather, and refined,
accelerated and implemented by her father Kradek-
ka. It was a state of life which was partially removed
from life; not death, no, not exactly. But only a sidestep away from the long dark journey.

Anukis realised two ribs were cracked, and she bit
her tongue against the pain as she shifted her weight.
She ran her hands over her naked, pale skin, up and
down her legs, over her hips and belly, stroking her

flanks, searching for tears in flesh and damage to muscle and tendon within. Finally, satisfied, Anukis walked around her cell, hands tracing contours on the walls and pausing, occasionally, at odd-shaped slots and sockets. These were for the mobile torture devices of the Engineers and Cardinals. She had heard of such things; but never witnessed. With a cold chill she grasped her position, and understood with clarity that her opportunity might come sooner than she realised.

Anukis moved to the cell door for analysis. It was brass, thick and very, very heavy, a solid slab with only a hand-sized portal through which to feed prisoners. Anu's fingers traced the join between door and the metal wall – it was precise, as befitted a religion and culture of engineers and metal craftsmen.

As she stood, she heard a lock mechanism whirr and took a hurried step back. The door swung inwards, silently, and a figure was outlined. It was the athletic figure of Vashell, the light source behind him, his features hidden in darkness and shadow.

"Have you come to gloat, bastard?"

His fist lashed out, slamming Anukis's face and dropping her to the floor. He stepped forward, and his boot smashed her face, stamped on her chest, and as she lay, stunned, bleeding, he stamped on her head.

Vashell pulled off a pair of gloves and moved, sitting on her bed, reclining a little, hands clasped around one armoured knee. He smiled, his brass fangs poking over his lower lip, and his eyes were dark, oil-filled, glittering first with resentment, then with amusement at Anukis's pain.

She lay, wheezing, head spinning, and it took many minutes for the effects of the blows to subside. Finally, she sat up, coughed up blood which ran down her breasts and pooled in her lap, in her crotch, an ersatz moon-bleeding.

"Ten years ago we played in my father's garden," he said. "We ran through the long grass, and you giggled, and your hair shone in the winter sun. We walked down to the river, sat watching the savage fast waters filled with ice-melt from beneath the Black Pikes; and I held you, and you told me you loved me, and that one day we would be together."

"No."

"Yes."

"Your memories are twisted, Vashell. It didn't happen like that." She coughed, holding her breast, blood staining her chin like a horror puppet. "You chased me. I struggled. I asked for you to leave me alone!"

"Liar!" he surged to his feet, face contorted into a vachine snarl. Inside his mouth, gears stepped and wheels spun.

Anu was crying as she looked up at him. "Vashell," she said, gently, "I never said I loved you, I never loved you. You saw what you wanted to see. You pursued me for a decade, and never once did I give you reason to believe I returned your love; I was careful, because you were an Engineer Priest, and I knew to anger you would be fatal."

Vashell subsided, and sat again, staring at her, his expression unreadable. "I loved you," he said, simply.

"You captured me, had me beaten. Just now, you kicked me like a dog. How can you sit there and say you loved me?"

"You betrayed me!" he snarled, spittle flying from his fangs. "You made me a fucking mockery amongst the Engineers; you have undermined my authority, lowered my rank, and you sit there and wonder why I strike you? That is my *right*, fucker. You have earned the beating, and much, much more. You are impure. Bad blood. A Heretic. No true vachine would have led an Engineer Priest on such a pretty dance."

"I led you nowhere! You are a fool, Vashell. Weak and stupid, brutal and savage. What could I possibly see in you to love? And you know what the worst thing is?" Her voice dropped, her face lowered, and her eyes were dark, staring up at him, submissive, subservient, and yet totally in control at the same time. "If I, a simple ill-blood, would not join you as your wife, would not mother your children, then what pure-blood vachine would ever touch your corrupt and deviated shell?"

Vashell did not reply in words, only in actions. He knelt by her, looking down at her pale white flesh, her slender limbs, her feminine curves, and with his clenched fist, claws curled tight, he pounded her face again and again, and took her head in his hands and rammed it against the floor, and even as she lay, bleeding, head spinning, not even understanding what hit her so mercilessly, so he suddenly halted and rocked back on his heels, crying a little, tears on his cheeks. He leant forward, low, and kissed her smashed lips, her blood running into his mouth like the finest

Karakan import; he kissed her, his tongue sliding between her lips and his hand moving down her throat,
over her breasts, stroking her belly, dipping between
her legs to play for a while as she lay, panting, chest
rising and falling in rapid beats, and she finally
coughed, eyes flickering open…

"Get *off* me!" she screamed, and Vashell rocked
back, stood and swiftly left the cell. The door slammed
shut, and Anukis was left, crying and alone, battered
and bleeding, abused and frightened, on the cell floor.

Kill me now, she thought. For I am nothing more
than a slave.

A female vachine entered after a day of bad dreams,
and with a bowl of water and a rag, cleaned the blood
from Anukis's body with gentle strokes and soothing
clucks. Anu opened her eyes, watched the vachine,
an ugly specimen where the clockwork had become
mildly disjointed, misaligned, and merged with the
flesh of her face so that gears and cogs were openly
visible against her cheeks, on her tongue, inside her
bone-twisted forehead; whilst she was still vachine, it
was considered vulgar to have such a show. And yet
like any disease, this was totally uncontrollable.

"There you go, little lady," said the woman.

"Thank you," said Anukis.

"Soon have you good as new."

"What's your name?"

The vachine smiled. "I am Perella. I've been as-
signed by Torto, one of the five Watchmakers, to tend
you during your stay."

"Where am I?"

"The Engineer's Palace, of course."

Anukis groaned. When you entered the Engineer's Palace, as one such as she, it was a rarity you left. At least, not with the same number of limbs, cogs or brain platters.

"Do not fret," said Perella, kindly. "I'm sure everything will be all right."

"You are kind." Anu's voice was stiff. "But can I ask, do you know why I'm here? I am impure. I cannot take blood-oil. I am a Heretic." She bowed her head, accepting her shame.

"To me, you are just another vachine." Perella smiled. "It is my understanding that your... condition, comes through no fault of your own. It's a simple unmeshing, something over which you have no control – despite what religious fanatics might believe. Shh. Someone approaches."

Footsteps slapped the metal walkway, and Vashell appeared. He smiled warmly at Anukis. "It is good to see you well."

"What?" she snarled. "You beat me unconscious and arrive to make pleasantries? Go to your grave, Vashell, and enjoy the worms eating your eyes."

Vashell made a gesture, and Perella hurried from the room. Vashell's face darkened, and only then did she see the collar and lead he carried. He moved forward, fastened the collar around her throat and wound twin clanking chains around his gloved gauntlet. "Come with me. We're going for a walk."

"You would parade me naked?"

"Heretics deserve no dignity," he said.

Anu snarled then, a vachine sound, and her fangs lengthened showing the gleam of brass. Vashell laughed, and tugged on the chains making Anukis stumble; she righted herself with difficulty, through her broken bruised frame, and he dragged her out into the corridor where the metal grille walkway dug viciously into her naked feet.

Anu's face burned red as Vashell led her like a dog, tugging occasionally as if for his own amusement. They moved away from the prison block, and back to the hub of the Engineer's Palace. As they approached from the prison arm so they passed more and more vachine, and several Engineers and Cardinals who stared at Anukis with distaste, some with open hatred, baring fangs in a show of aggressive challenge. Anu kept her head high, meeting the gaze of every pureblood, challenging them, snarling back with her own hatred and loathing.

At the hub central there was a high domed ceiling of brass, and a huge circular desk fashioned from a single mammoth block of silver-quartz and polished into smooth perfection, gleaming, beautiful, and sculpted with fine chisels into a thousand different scenes of vachine history, and vachine victory. Behind this circular symbol sat the bulk of the Engineers and their subordinates, Engineer Priests, working on intricate machinery, individual workstations full of delicate hand tools and machine tools, some powered by burning oil, some by the energy and pulse of silver-quartz which was mined, with great loss of life, by the albinos deep beneath the Black Pike Mountains. Silver-quartz was one of the three fabled ingredients of the vachine. The timing mechanism of a vachine's heart; and indeed, his soul.

Vashell stopped before the huge silver bank, and grinned at the other Engineers, obviously displaying his prize with pride. The sentiment was clear; what he had failed to dominate by love and marriage, he now dominated by fear and violence. This would gain him respect after his perceived darkening at Anu's newly discovered impure status. He had been right. She had made a fool of him.

The Engineers to a man – for they were all male – set down delicate tools with care and stood. There were nearly three hundred of them; the core of vachine society trained highly in the arts of clockwork and the magick of blood-oil. Anu's eyes swept along the ranks, ranging across short and tall Engineers and Engineer Priests alike, all wearing silver religious insignia on their shoulders, all focused with looks of hatred at this woman, this half-pure, the daughter of one who had, once, been great. Kradek-ka. The Watchmaker.

"See?" bellowed Vashell, pulling the chains tight so his superior height caused Anu to stand up on tiptoe, straining, the veins and muscles of her throat standing out. "The one who shamed me! Now, she walks as my slave. Until I see fit to dispose of her."

The Engineers were staring, eyes narrowed, and began to hiss, the noise filling the domed chamber as steel and brass fangs slid from jaw sheaths and they narrowed eyes at the impure; but more than that. A high-ranking impure who had shamed an Engineer Priest. This was not done.

And then, standing there, naked and chained before the Engineers, Anukis realised the full extent of her slavery. Desolation swamped her. This was not going to be a simple case of torture and execution. No. Not only Vashell's pride and vachine honour were on trial here; the whole of the Engineer culture felt cheated, abused, despoiled, and Anu realised with a lead heart that they would force her to live as long as possible... and make her suffer humiliation, degradation, and pain greater than any impure had ever suffered.

Anu shivered, goose-bumps running along her flesh, and Vashell pulled her tight before his Engineer brethren and his fangs grew long, and suddenly a hushed silence flowed through the chamber and Vashell's head dropped, his fangs plunging into Anu's neck, into her artery, and he sucked out her blood and lifted her, like a ragdoll in his powerful arms as he drank her, drank her impurity, and Anu grew limp, dizzy, and lying naked in Vashell's abusive embrace she slipped away into welcome darkness.

The rhythm danced through her. It pumped through every blood vessel, every vein, every artery, to her heart. It pumped, an echo to her own heart, a heartbeat doppelganger chasing through haemoglobin and the rainbow thick mix of blood-oil and alien blood and her mind was transfused with confusion, like a spider spinning a web over glass, and as she awoke her mouth was full of fur, her eyes sticky with blood, her ears pounding with an ocean, waves crashing a bone beach of despair and she coughed, and choked, spluttered, her eyes forced open through stickiness and she stared down at silk sheets.

Anukis coughed again, phlegm spattering the fine white silk, and she groaned, pain slamming her from every angle. She stared straight ahead, at the rock wall filled with lodes of minor silver-quartz thread, and realised with a start she was *in* the mountain...

She rolled, and sat up, her golden curls cascading down her back. She had been washed, shampooed, scrubbed of blood and dirt, and now she wore a light cotton gown that did little to protect her vulnerability. Her hand came up, touched her neck, caressed the dual puncture marks.

He bit me, she thought, eyes narrowing.

The ultimate disgust, from one vachine to another.

The ultimate rape. An implied and direct insult; of superior blood over toxic blood. No vachine bit another. It was not done.

Winter sunlight sleeted through long, low windows at the edge of the room, and Anukis eased her feet over the edge of the bed, feeling tender, feeling sore, feeling battered and bruised and weak. She filled up with self loathing and spat on the fine thick red carpets. "The bastard."

She stood, trembling, limbs frail, and tottered across to a marble stand containing a brass jug. She poured herself a little water, and drank. It made her feel sick.

Before her, through the window, she could see the spread of Silva Valley. It was beautiful, serene, a pastel painting of perfect civilisation, vast and finely sculpted, a culture at its peak. Where am I? she thought, and the answer came easily enough. This was a mountain villa, and obviously belonged to Vashell's parents. They were rich. They were Engineers. They were royalty.

The mountain villas were built at the summit of the rising city, up at the head of the valley in premium sites for exaggerated architecture, and using the mountain itself as a base. These villas overlooked the vachine world, and commanded the greatest views one could buy in Silva Valley.

Anukis stood for a while, watching the view. It was morning, and the vachine world was coming awake. She could see thousands of vachine on the streets below, buying, selling, transporting goods. If she stretched, she could just determine the bulk of the Engineer's Palace to the left, and a curved walkway leading to a dark mouth. A steady stream of vachine queued along the snake of the path, many carrying bundles in their arms. These were inventions, or broken mechanisms they wished fixing. Some came with requests for the Engineers. Some came with information.

Anukis smoothed her hands down her cotton flanks, and thought of Shabis, her younger sister. Shabis was true vachine, no impure blood ran through her veins, greasing her cogs and wheels, and Anukis knew that even her own sister knew not of her impure nature. Only Kradek-ka had been party to the secret; and they both guarded it fervently. After all, if word got out, she would forfeit with her life.

Anukis smiled, for what felt the first time in a century. She thought of Shabis, young Shabis, only sixteen years old, long beautiful golden curls, taller than Anukis, more slender, her limbs delicate and regal. Her eyes were dark, her face a little more pointed; she was a stunning Vachine Goddess!

The smile fell from Anu's face. If Shabis still lived…

There came the tiniest of clicks. Vashell stood there. He wore full battle armour, and a dazzling array of weapons. His boots were polished, his head held high, his face and eyes unreadable. Then he smiled, and moved forward, standing beside Anukis to stare out over Silva Valley and the jewelled contents of the vachine empire.

"I cannot believe it came to this," said Vashell. His voice sounded, genuinely, hurt.

"Go away, and die quietly," whispered Anukis.

Vashell turned, and took her hands in his own. He held her gently, but there was no illusion there for Anukis; she knew damn well how brutal he could be. His gentility was an affectation. His humbleness a façade.

"If you had asked me our futures three months ago, I would have been so sure, so adamant, that we would be wed, and living a life of rich royalty. We were the perfect match, Anukis."

"You abused me," she hissed, looking at him then, her eyes flashing dark. "In front of the Engineers and Priests! You took my blood, you humiliated me, you beat me. You are a canker, Vashell; maybe not visibly so, not in the open flesh, but deep in your heart your clockwork has deformed and twisted, and even now has eaten that part of you which was human."

Vashell stood, stunned by the insult. To call a vachine a canker was… unthinkable.

He took a deep breath, and Anukis watched him master his anger; his fury.

"I can make this right," he said.

"An utter impossibility."

"I still love you."

Anukis stood, and turned back to face the Silva Valley. Still, Vashell held her hands and she felt his grip grow tight, holding her, refusing to allow her a simple freedom.

"The only person you love is yourself," said Anukis.

"Listen to me." There was urgency in his voice. "You were caught red-handed with the Blacklipper king himself. You were witnessed drinking Karakan Red. We had been staking out the lair for months, tracing Preyshan's suppliers – and then you stumbled in screaming out your impure status. It was all I could do to stop the Engineers slaughtering you where you stood... and believe me, I put my own life on the line in those few moments out there under the Brass Docks. Since then, I have been observed, closely watched by the Watchmakers to see how I'd react, to see how I treated you. Don't you understand, Anukis? If I had not behaved the way I did, both our lives would have been forfeit! We would never have escaped the claws of Silva Valley! But now... now I have a *plan*."

"Explain to me your plan." Her voice was low. Still she did not face Vashell. Her anger went beyond speech.

"Since the humiliation inside the Engineer's Palace, it is believed I have broken you, and brought you here as my sexual plaything, until I grow tired, until I murder you and send your corpse back to the Engineer's Palace for dissection. Now, their watch has grown lax. I feel the trails of blood-oil magick weaken with every passing second, every heartbeat. Within a few days we will be free, and can leave this place. Together. If you so wish."

"What of Shabis?"

"She will come with us! You must believe me, Anukis. It has all been an act! I love you dearly; more than life itself. I have been working to secure our freedom, to sneak us from under the vachine net."

Anukis turned, and looked into his eyes, and chewed her lip.

"You mean this?"

"Yes," he said. "Kiss me."

"What?"

"Kiss me. Show me what I am missing."

Anukis frowned, and it felt wrong, Vashell's words felt wrong and they came crashing down inside her brain. Why would a High Born Royal, an Engineer Priest with all the makings of earning a future rank of Watchmaker give up everything for her? Her own lack of self-esteem bit her, and bit her hard.

"I don't know whether to trust you," she said, her voice low, trembling. "You did terrible things to me, Vashell. You tore out my heart, you humiliated me; you took away what vestiges of pride still remained!"

"No." He shook his head. "Your pride was already gone. I saved your life. It's that simple. You know I speak the truth. You know how we are watched. And now, I can save both you, and your sister, if you only trust me. You took that physical beating from me; and

I was observed. It was an evil necessity. Now I have only love for you." He moved close, shushing her, lips tickling her ear, and slowly his mouth moved around and he kissed her and his kiss was gentle, loving, his hands running through her hair, gently, over her body and she squirmed under his grip, a mixture of lust, and love, and confusion, and hatred, all running and combining with her fear and uncertainty and he kissed her, and she kissed him back, and she fell into him, fell into his world and he hugged her, his face over her shoulder, and his fangs eased free of brass jaw sheaths and Vashell closed his eyes, face a rapture of love and contentment.

He came to her that night, and in the darkness and the glow of molten lanterns she loosened her cotton robe which slipped from perfect, bruised shoulders. Vashell stood, his eyes wide, basking in her beauty, basking in her slender vachine warmth, and he stepped forward and his hands moved out, rested lightly on her lips and she smiled up at him, and he smiled back, and love was in his eyes as he gave a low growl of lust and pushed her back to the bed. He kissed her, his hands on her flesh, his claws tracing grooves down her curves, and Anukis moaned as she gave herself to him, fucked him, partially from want, partially to save her life, and to save her sister, and confusion raged through her and only later did she wonder about the love in his eyes. Was it his, or simply the reflection of her own?

Anukis had a dream. She dreamt of Kradek-ka. He was tall, and powerful, a noble Watchmaker in full vachine battledress. He stood over her, then sat down, cross-legged before her, his swords scraping the floor. A fire burned, an old wood fire, traditional, smoke trailing embers into the air. Flames glittered in his swirling gold eyes.

"Anukis?" he said gently.

"Father!" She fell into his arms and he held her, his powerful arms encircled her and she cried, cried tears of gold and blood, and she knew then that everything would be fine, the world would be good, and Anukis would not have to face the horrors of the world alone. "I've missed you so much, Daddy. I've been so alone and so terrified without you."

"You need to listen to me, girl." His voice was gentle, despite his size. "I am in… a curious place. I think I may be dead."

"How did you come to my dreams?"

"I do not know, girl. What I do know is your position. They have found out, yes?"

"It was horrible," she wept.

He wiped away her tears. Firelight glinted on his silver fangs. Out of all the vachine, every single one of the eighty thousand strong population in Silva Valley, Kradek-ka was the only creature who could take pure silver. Normally, silver would disrupt every other element of clockwork, twist every ounce of silver-quartz, dislocate every heartbeat rhythm; but not with Kradek-ka. He was a mystery to the Engineers. A conundrum to other Watchmakers, and even to the Patriarch Himself.

"I have advice for you."

"Tell me what to do."

"Marry Vashell."

"What?"

"It is your greatest chance of survival. And I want to see you live, Anukis. I want to see you live so very, very much."

She awoke, and the room was warm; it smelt of oil. It smelt of the narcotic, blood-oil.

Vashell was there, naked beside the bed. His erection was magnificent to behold, his balls inset with tiny gears, the smallest of spinning toothed cogs which ground and whirred, and all reflecting the light from a hundred burning candles.

Anukis lay back, panting, her golden curls highlighting her pale frame.

"I wanted you so much," he said.

"I love you, Vashell," she said, remembering the fear in her father's eyes. The lie tripped easily from her tongue. It was a lie of existence. A lie of endurance. A lie of survival; for if she survived, she could find her father, and save her sister.

"And I you." He touched her, his hands on her breasts, her hips, sliding smooth into her slick cunt, and she closed her eyes and allowed him to take her, again, and again, and again, the only sound his panting, and the tiny *tick tick tick* of his clockwork inside her.

"Shabis!"

Shabis ran across the room, bare feet curling in thick carpets, and fell into Anu's arms. "Nuky," she said, nuzzling her older sister, and they held each other, breathing one another's natural scent, feeling the flow of sisterly love, of a bond greater than all else.

Shabis pulled back, tears coursing her cheeks. "How are you?"

Anu glanced to Vashell over her shoulder. "I am well. I am in love! How are you? Have the Engineers harmed you? Are you well?"

"I am fine," laughed Shabis. "I have been treated like royalty. Spoilt, really. You look happy, Anukis; although battered a little." She glanced over her shoulder at Vashell. "He told me about you, kept me informed about your health. I am so glad you two are in love! It will be a marriage made perfect, and your children will be beautiful!" She giggled, pulling Anukis to the bed. She turned, and waved Vashell away. He departed.

"Truly, have they looked after you?"

"They have," said Shabis, and kissed Anu's cheek. "And you?"

Anu's face went hard. "I have been condemned, Shabis. I have been treated worse than any dog, worse than any canker." She pulled away, stood, walked to the splendid view. It had begun to snow in Silva Valley, and a thick fall muffled the world.

"What do you mean?"

Shabis was behind her. Holding her. Concern shone in her eyes.

"Vashell beat me. He hurt me, Shabis. He hurt me bad. He paraded me like a slave before the Engineers. Then he… he took my blood." She heard a hiss of intaken breath. "He drank from me, Shabis. He drank from my veins, made my impurity whole, for all to see. Then he… he took me. Physically. Carnally. I had little choice if I wanted to save both of us."

She fell silent, brooding, watching the snow. Somehow, Silva Valley had again lost its beauty, its charm. It was a perfect pastel painting, framed by silver-quartz and yet to Anukis, now, after everything that had happened, it was a vision of hell. Worse. Of a canker-riddled cancer hell.

"What will you do?" Shabis's voice was barely more than a whisper.

"I have a plan!" Anu took Shabis, and shook her with passion. "I will kill Vashell. And we will flee. We will leave Silva Valley, we will leave this world for good. Cross the Black Pike Mountains; make a new life."

"But what of the vachine?" said Shabis, softly. "What if the clockwork becomes faulty? Who will fix us?"

"I have some skill," said Anu, eyeing her sister, sensing the fear, the lode of cowardice that ran through her like an earthquake fault in the world mantle. "Don't you understand, Shabis, they killed our father! We are alone now. Alone in the world."

"Killed... no! They did not! He still lives! He is on a journey under Black Pike, he will be back in a few months."

"And you believe them?"

"Why should I not?"

"What else have they told you?"

"Nothing! Anu, you're frightening me. Stop it!"

"I'm sorry, little one. Sweet Shabis, we must leave this place. I want you to be ready. Do you understand?"

"Yes. I understand."

Anu shook her, and Shabis's hair fell, tousled. "You're hurting me!"

"This is serious, Little One. Do you understand?"

"Yes! Anu, yes!"

"Good."

There came a hiatus. Shabis played with her hair, and they both watched the snow. Eventually, Shabis said, "Anu?"

"Sister?"

"How will you kill him? Vashell, I mean?"

"I have a secret weapon."

"What is that?"

Anu's eyes glowed dark. "You will see."

Night had fallen. Anu was awoken by a savage blow across her face, which broke her nose and left her choking on a gush of blood down her throat. She rolled instinctively, momentarily blinded, covering her face, her claws out and slashing a wild vicious arc, but connecting with nothing. After a few moments she could see, and she stood, naked, blood covering her breasts, to see Vashell holding a pick-axe helve. It was stained with her blood. His eyes shone.

"What is this?" she snarled, fear touching the edges of her heart.

"Show me your secret weapon! Come on, Anukis, show me how you intend to kill me! Show me now."

Anu backed away, and Vashell moved around the bed.

"Where's Shabis? What have you done with my sister?"

"Shabis?" Vashell smiled, and from the gloom, in the glow of the candles, Shabis appeared. She was smiling, a broad smile. Her hands came up, rested, interlacing over Vashell's shoulder. Her hips were staggered, her stance commanding.

"What are you doing?" said Anu. She felt understanding flood from her soul.

"Vashell is mine, bitch. He will marry me. He told me what you did to him; how you tried to poison him with your impure blood. You are a canker, Anu, diseased, toxic, not a true vachine. You will rot in hell."

Anu stood, mouth open, pain pounding through her head, her crushed nose stinging, and stared with utter, total disbelief at the scene before her. Her jaws clacked shut, and she watched Vashell turn, kiss Shabis, sliding his tongue into her mouth.

"He will never marry you," said Anu, eventually.

"Liar! We are betrothed. The Watchmakers will conduct the ceremony in three weeks' time. You lied about him taking you; you lied to make him more evil in my mind, so when the time came for you to kill him I would help. Vashell is filled with honour; he would never stoop to fuck an impure." She snarled the word, fangs ejecting a little. Her dark eyes were narrowed, and Anu could not believe what she was seeing. She could not comprehend the hatred emanating from her sister. She did not understand.

Vashell ran his hand down Shabis's flank, stroking her, and said, softly, "Kill her, Shabis. Kill Anukis."

Growling, Shabis ejected claws and fangs with tiny slithers of steel and brass. She dropped to a crouch, and moved around the bed, eyes narrowed and fixed on her sister, face full of hatred, her tongue licking lips in the anticipation of fresh blood...

"No," said Anu, voice near hysteria. "Shabis! Don't do this! Vashell lies!"

"Spoken just like an impure," snapped Shabis, and with a feral vachine snarl, leapt at her lifeblood.

SIX
Toxic Blood

Kell tensed as the canker lowered its head, muscles rigid, a low metal buzzing growl coming from its wide open head and loose flapping jaws; and he stared into that gaping maw, stared into those eyes and shuddered as his past life – and more importantly, more hauntingly, the Days of Blood – flashed through his mind and he felt regret and self-loathing, and a despair that he hadn't put things right, hadn't found forgiveness and sanctuary from others, and more importantly, for himself...

The canker howled, rearing up. More dust and stones poured from the destroyed ceiling. A huge cross-member dropped, clunking against the canker which hit the ground under huge weight, snarling and snapping, and through the falling dust Kell saw Saark, his blade buried deep in the canker's flank and Saark screamed, "The roof's coming down! We've got to get out!"

Kell nodded, slammed his axe into the canker's head with a thud which brought another bout of thrashing and snarling, then he squeezed around the edges of the wall and sprinted, as more stones and timber toppled around him, diving out of the doorway and hitting the snow on his belly with a violent exhalation of air. Behind, the cottage screamed like a wounded beast, shaking its head in agony; and the roof caved in.

Saark was there, black with dust, dragging Kell to his feet. "I don't think it will stop the bastard."

Kell took a deep breath. Snow drifted around him, like ash in the night. He turned, staring at the cottage which seemed to rise, then settle, a great dying bear. For a second it was still, then somewhere deep within started to shift and stones, rubble, timber, all started to move and rise and Saark was already running towards the shingle beach and the boat, where Nienna and Kat urged them on. Kell followed, wincing at pains in his ribs, his shoulder, his head, his knees, and he felt suddenly old, and weary, battered and bettered, and he stumbled down onto the shingle as behind them, with a terrible sadistic roar the canker emerged from the detritus in a shower of stones.

The heavens grumbled, and distantly lightning flickered a web. Thunder growled, a beast in a storm cage behind bars of ignition, and heavy hail pounded the shingle around Kell as he heaved the boat down the beach, axe cleaving the securing rope, and leapt in, rocking the vessel.

They moved away from the bank, as the canker orientated.

"It can't see us," whispered Saark. "Shh." He placed a finger on lips.

As they drifted away, they watched the canker, seemingly confused; then its head lifted, huge open maw searching the skies, and it turned and its head lowered and it charged across cobbles and mud and snow straight in their direction...

Nienna gave a gasp.

"It's fine," breathed Saark, throat dry with fear. "The river will stop the bastard."

The canker reached the edge of the rampant water and without breaking stride leapt, body elongating into an almost elegant, feline dive. It hit the black river, rippled by hailstones, and went under the surface. It was gone immediately.

Kell stood, rocking the boat, and hefted his axe.

"Surely not," snapped Saark, lifting his own blade and peering wildly about their totally vulnerable position.

"It's under there," snarled Kell. "Be ready."

Silence fell, like a veil. Hail scattered across the river like pebbles. More thunder rumbled, mountains fighting, and lighting lit the scene through storm clouds and sleet.

"It was sent, wasn't it?" said Saark, gazing at the dark river.

"Yes," said Kell, eyes searching.

"How did it find us?"

"It followed your petal-stench perfume, lad."

"Hah! More like the stench from your fish-laden pants."

Calm descended.

They waited, tense.

The boat suddenly rocked and there came a slam from beneath; it swayed violently, turning around in the current. Something glided beneath them, snapping the oars with easy cracks; broken toothpicks.

"I don't like this!" wailed Nienna.

"Shut up," growled Kell. "Take out your swords. If you see anything at all, stab it in the eyes."

The boat was slammed with tremendous force from beneath, lifting out of the water, then slapping down again and spinning, turning, all sense of direction lost now, gone now, in the turbulent storm. The boat was hammered again, and it shuddered, timbers creaked, and a long crack appeared across the stern.

"We need to get back on land!" shouted Saark.

"We have no oars," said Kell, voice calm, axe rigid in steel-steady hands. "We will have to kill it."

Abruptly the canker emerged, mighty jaws ripping free the prow of the boat and Saark ran with a scream, sword raised, as the canker released the boat and lunged, grabbing his leg and dragging him backwards, his body thumping from the boat's prow and disappearing suddenly over the edge…

Everything was still.

The river surged, and the water levelled.

"Saark!" screamed Katrina. But the man was gone.

With a curse Kell dropped his axe to the floor of the boat, and leapt into the black river. He was encompassed immediately, swamped by darkness, by a raging thunder, merging with the gathered filth of Falanor's major northern city. Down he plunged, unable to see Saark, unable to find the canker. He swam down with powerful strokes, and withdrew his Svian from beneath his arm; down here, Ilanna would be useless. What a warrior needed was a short sharp stabbing weapon...

Where is he? screamed Kell's mind.

His lungs began to burn.

He thrashed, turning, round and around, but everything was black. He felt panic creep into him like crawling ivy; he had scant seconds before the canker drowned Saark, and that was providing the beast hadn't ripped him apart with tooth and claw.

Kell was saved by the lightning. It crackled overhead, above the boat, and for an instant the churning river was lit by incandescent flashes. Kell saw the canker, dragging Saark down, and powered after them, Svian between his teeth, straggled hair and beard flowing behind him. He found them in the darkness, and his blade slashed down, he felt it enter flesh, grind in cogs, felt the canker lashing out and he was knocked back, and everything was a confusion of bubbles and madness and darkness and something was beside him, huge and cold, a wall of smoothness that slid past and Kell felt, more than saw, Saark slide up beside him. He grabbed the unconscious man, his very lungs filled with molten lava as he kicked out, boots striking the smooth, gliding wall and propelling him to the surface...

Lighting crackled again, a maze of angular arcs transforming the sky into a circuit. Kell looked down, and saw a battle raging beneath the river, between the canker, all claws and disjointed fangs, and a huge, silent, black eel. It must have been fifty yards long, its body the diameter of three men, its head a huge triangular wedge with row after row of sharp teeth. It had encircled the canker, was crushing the thrashing beast, its head snapping down, teeth tearing flesh repeatedly. Kell thought he saw trails of blood like confetti streamers in the black; then he burst from the surface, lungs heaving in air, Saark limp under one arm, and looked for the boat.

It had gone, slammed down the river without oars on powerful currents and a rage of mountain snowmelt.

Kell cursed, and half swam, half dragged Saark through the water, angling towards the high banks. He stopped, shivering now, teeth chattering, bobbing under the high earth walls too high to climb. He moved on, still dragging Saark's leaden weight through the darkness, through ice-filled waters, until the banks dropped and wearily Kell rolled onto a frozen, muddy slope, dragging Saark up behind him, and he lay for a while, breath panting like dragon smoke, head dizzy with flashing lights.

Eventually, the cold bit him and Kell roused himself. He shook Saark, who groaned as he came awake, coughing out streamers of black water. Eventually, he stared around, confused.

"What happened?"

"The creature dragged you under. I dove in after you. I'm pretty damn sure you're not worth it."

"Charming, Kell. You would whisk away the pants from any farmer's daughter without hindrance. Where's the boat?"

"Gone."

"Where are we?"

"Do I look like a fucking mapmaker?"

"Actually, old horse, you do, rather."

Something surged from the river nearby, a huge black coil, then submerged with a mighty splash. In its wake, the canker, or more precisely, half of the canker, floated for a few moments, bobbing, torn, trailing strings of tendon and jagged gristle, before gradually sinking out of sight.

"At least that's one problem sorted," said Saark, voice strangled. He reached down, rolling up his trews. Puncture holes lined his shins and knees, bleeding, and he prodded them with a wince. "I hope I'm not poisoned."

"It's dead. For now." Kell climbed to his feet. He sheathed his Svian and cursed. His axe, Ilanna, was on the boat. Gone. Kell ran hands through his wet hair and shivered again. Snow began to fall, just to add to his chilled and frozen mood.

Saark had found something in one of the puncture wounds, and with a tiny schlup pulled free a fang. "Ugh!" he said, staring at the brass tooth. "The dirty, dirty bastard." He flung it out into the river. "Ugh."

"We need to find Nienna," said Kell.

"And Kat," said Saark, glancing up at the old man.

"And Kat," agreed Kell. "Come on."

"Whoa! Wait up, maybe you're in the mood for running cross-country in the dark, covered in ice; I'm going to die if I stay out here much longer. And you too, by the looks of it. You're turning blue!"

"I've crossed the Black Pike Mountains," growled Kell. "It takes more than the fucking cold to kill me."

"And that was… how many years ago? Look at you, man, you're shivering harder than a pirate ship in a squall. We need fire, and we need dry clothes. Come on. These lowlands are populated; we'll find somewhere."

They walked, Saark limping, roughly following the course of the river until a thick evergreen woodland of Jack Pine and Red Cedar forced them inland. Trudging across snow and frozen tufts of grass, they circled the woods and eventually came upon a small crofter's hut, barely four walls and a roof, six feet by six feet, to be used during emergencies. With thanks they fell inside, forcing the door shut against wind and snow. As was the woodland way, a fire had already been laid by the last occupant and Kell found a flint and tinder on a high shelf. His shaking hands lit a fire, and both men huddled round the flames as they grew from baby demons. Eventually, what seemed an age, the small hut filled with heat and they peeled off wet clothing, hanging items on hooks around the walls to dry, until they sat in pants and boots, hands outstretched to the flames, faces grim.

"What I'd give for a large whisky," said Kell, watching steam rise from their clothes.

"What I'd give for a fat whore."

"Do you ever think about anything other than sex?"

"Sometimes," said Saark, and turned, staring into the flames. "Sometimes, in distant dreams, I think of honour, of loyalty, and of friendship; I think of love, of family, of happy children, a doting wife. All the good things in life, my friend. And then I remember who I am, and the things I did, and I am simply thankful for a fat whore sitting on my face. You?"

"Me what?"

"I gave you a potted history. Now it's your turn. You're a hero, right?"

"You make the word 'hero' sound like 'arsehole'."

"Not at all." Saark grinned, then, his melancholy dropping like a hawk from the heavens. "I heard a poem about you, once. 'Kell's Legend', it was called. That's you, right? You're the character of legend?"

"You make 'character' sound like 'arsehole'."

"Very droll. Come on, Kell. It was a good poem."

"Ha! A curse on all poets! May they catch the pox and have ugly children."

"This poem was a good one," persisted Saark. "Proper hero stuff. Had a decent rhyme as well. Foot-tapping stuff, when recited in a tavern by men with harps and honey-beer and the glint of wonder in their eyes."

Kell drew his Svian blade. His eyes glowed and he pointed at Saark in the close proximity. "Don't even fucking think about it. All poets should be gutted like fish, their entrails strung out to dry, then made to compose ballads about how they feel with the bastard suffering. A curse on them!"

Saark sang, voice soft, hand held out to ward off Kell's knife should he make a strike:

"Kell waded through life on a river of blood,
His axe in his hands, dreams misunderstood,
In Moonlake and Skulkra he fought with the best
This hero of old, this hero obsessed,
This hero turned champion of King Searlan
Defiant and worthy a merciless man."

Kell snorted. "Poets make a joy out of slaughter, the academic smug self-satisfying bastards. I am ashamed to be a part of that song! Bah!" Kell frowned darkly. "And you! You sing like a drunkard. I can sing better than that, and I sound like a fart from a donkey's arse... and I'm proud of it! A man should only sing when he's a belly full of whisky, a fist full of money, and the idea of a fight in his head. You can keep your cursed poetry, Saark, you idiot. A bad case of gonorrhoea on you all! Death to all poets!"

"Death to all poets?" chuckled Saark, and relaxed as Kell sheathed his long, silver-bladed Svian. "A little harsh, I find, for simply extending the oral tradition and entertaining fellow man. But was it true? The stuff in the poem? The Saga?"

"No."

"Not even some of it?"

"Well, the bastards spelt my name right. Listen, Saark, we need to go after Nienna and Kat. They could end up miles away. Leagues! They could be in danger even as we sit here, wasting our breath like a whore wastes her hard-earned coin."

"We'll die if we go back to the storm." Saark's voice was soft.

"Where's your courage, man?"

"Hiding behind my need to stay alive. Kell, you're no use to her dead. Wait till the sun's up; then we'll search."

"No. I am going now!" He stood and reached for his wet clothes.

Saark sang:

"And brave Kell marched out through the snow,
  His dullard brain he left behind,
  He took with him a mighty bow,
  His thumb up his arse and shit in his mind."

Kell paused. Stared hard at Saark, who shrugged, and threw another chunk of wood on the fire. "You're being irrational, my friend. I may dress like an idiot, but I know when to live, and when to die. Now is not the time to die."

Kell sighed, a deep sigh of resignation, and returned to the fire. He sat, staring into flickering flames.

"Say it," said Saark.

"What?"

"Admit that I'm right."

"You're right."

"See, that wasn't too painful, eh, old horse?"

"But I'll tell you something, Saark. If anything happens to Nienna, then I'll blame you; and it'll take more than fucking poetry to remove my axe from your fat split head."

Saark laughed, and slapped Kell on the back. "What a truly grumpy old bastard you are, eh? You remind me of my dad."

"If I was your dad, I'd kill myself."

"And if I was your son, I'd help you. Listen, enough of this banter; we need to get some sleep. I have a strange feeling tomorrow's going to be a hard day. Call me extreme, but it can't get any worse."

"A hard day?" scoffed Kell. "Harder than yesterday? That seems unlikely. However, young man, I will take your advice, even though it pains me to listen to somebody with the wardrobe sense of a travelling chicken."

"At least that beast... at least it was dead, in the river. It was dead, wasn't it?"

"It was a canker."

"A what?"

"A canker. That's what it was."

"How do you know that?"

"I saw one. Once. Halfway up a mountain in the Black Pikes; it tried to kill us."

"What happened?"

"It slipped on ice. Fell six thousand feet onto rocks like spears." Kell's eyes gleamed, misted, distant, unreadable. He coughed. "So put that Dog Gemdog gem in your poem, laddie. Because the canker, well, it's a vachine creation. And there are more of the bastards where that one came from."

Saark shivered, and scowled hard at Kell. "Well, thanks for that cheerful nocturnal nugget, just before I try and sleep. Sweet dreams to you as well, you old goat!"

The boat spun out of control through the blackness and Nienna screamed, clinging to Kat. "What do we do?"

"We row!"

"The oars were smashed!"

The two girls looked frantically for something to use as a paddle, but only Kell's axe caught Nienna's eye and she stooped, picking up the weapon. She expected a dead-weight, impossible to lift, but it was surprisingly light despite its size. She hefted the weapon, and it glowed, warm for a moment, in her hands. Or had she imagined that?

"You can't paddle with that," snapped Kat.

"I was thinking more of hitting it into the beast's head."

"If it comes back," said Kat.

They both thought of Saark, and Kell, under the freezing river, fighting the huge beast. They shivered, and neither dared to wonder what the outcome would be.

The boat spun around again, and bounced from a rotting tree-trunk, invisible in the darkness. The river grew wider, more shallow, and they found themselves rushing through a minefield of rocks, the river gushing and pounding all around.

"What do we do?" shouted Kat over the torrent.

"I don't know!"

Both girls moved to the boat's stern, and with four hands on the tiller, tried to steer the boat in towards the shore. Amazingly, it began to work, and they bounced and skimmed down the fast flow and towards an overhanging shoreline in the gloom... with a crunch, the boat beached on ice and stones, and Nienna leapt out as she had seen Kell do, holding his axe, and tried to drag the boat up the beach. She did not have the strength. Kat jumped out and they both tried, but the boat was dragged backwards by wild currents and within seconds was lost in the raging darkness.

Snow fell.

The girls retreated a short distance into the woods, but stopped, spooked by the complete and utter darkness. A carpet of pine needles were soft underfoot, and the heady smell of resin filled the air.

"This is creepy," whispered Nienna.

Kat nodded, but Nienna couldn't discern the movement; by mutual consent, their hands found one another and they walked deeper into the forest, pushed on by a fear of the canker that outweighed a fear of the dark. They stared up at the massive boles of towering Silver Firs, and a violent darkness above which signified the sky. Random flakes drifted down through the trees, but at least here there was no wind; only a still calm.

"Will that creature come back, do you think?" asked Kat.

"I have Kell's axe," said Nienna, by way of reply.

"Kell and Saark couldn't kill it," said Kat.

Nienna did not answer.

They stopped, their footsteps crunching pine needles. All around lay the broken carcass shapes of dead-wood; ahead, a criss-crossing of fallen trees blocked their path, and cursing and moaning, they dragged themselves beneath the low barricade to stand, again, in a tiny clearing.

"Look," said Nienna. "There was a fire."

They ran forward, to where a ring of stones surrounded glowing embers. Kat searched about, finding dead wood to get the blaze going, and they fed twigs into the embers, waiting for them to ignite before piling on thicker branches. Soon they had the fire roaring, and they warmed their hands and feet by the flames, revelling in their good fortune.

"Who do you think was here?" asked Nienna.

"Woodsmen, I should think," said Kat. "But they'll be long gone. A fire can burn low like that for a couple of days." She took a stick, and poked around in the fire. Flames crackled, and sparks flew out, like tiny fireflies, sparkling into the air. Around them, the chill of the forest, the smell of cold and rotting vegetation, filled their senses.

"What are we going to do, Kat?" said Nienna eventually, voicing that which they were both thinking.

"I don't know. Kell will find us."

"Maybe he…" She left it unsaid.

"I've read about your grandfather," said Kat, staring into the fire. "He's a survivor. He's a… killer."

"No he's not. He's my grandpa." Nienna scowled, then glanced at Kat. "What do you mean? A killer?"

"His legend," said Kat, avoiding Nienna's gaze. "You'll see. He'll come looking for us. For you, I mean."

"He'll come for both of us!" snapped Nienna, frowning at the tone Kat employed. "He's an honourable man! An old soldier! He would always do the right thing."

Kat said nothing.

"Well well well," came a strange voice from the trees. It was a twisted voice, full of friendly humour and yet mocking at the same time. "What have we got here?"

Both girls leapt up, and Nienna lifted the axe. From the gloom of the forest emerged six men, drifting slowly from the black. They were a rag-tag bunch, dressed in little more than rags and stained, matted furs. They wore heavy scuffed boots and carried tarnished swords; two men hefted fine yew longbows.

"What do you want?" snarled Kat.

The man who spoke was tall and lean, his face pock-marked, his eyes large and innocent. His hair was long and dark, tied back beneath a deerstalker hat with furred edges. He was grinning at the two young women, showing a missing tooth.

"We don't want anything, me sweets. You've made yourself comfortable in our camp, is all."

"Are you robbers?"

The man held his hands apart, and he carried no weapons. "Tsch, just because I lives in the forest, me sweets, doesn't make me a robber. Has been a hard time for us all I think. This winter is a harsh one, for sure. Only now, we were out hunting for meat." He gestured, to where one of the forest-men carried a pole containing two dead hares. "Pickings are lean," he said, eyes narrowing, but then he smiled again. "Don't let us worry you. You got the fire going; that's got to be worth a mouthful of rabbit meat."

Kat nodded, and the men moved around easily, leaning weapons against trees with two of them sitting by the fire, holding out chilled hands. The leader seated himself and gestured to Nienna and Kat, still standing, to have a seat.

"I won't bite, me sweets. Honest. Come and sit your-self down here. Keep yourself warm. You both looks like you'll die from the cold! I'm Barras, and I'd wager you're a long way from your homes. City girls, are ye?"

"From Jalder," said Nienna, and Kat kicked her on the ankle. Nienna threw her a dark look.

"Jalder's a fine city," said Barras, smiling broadly, friendly, as one of his companions began to skin and gut the rabbits. "I have a lot of good friends who live there. Well, people I owe money to, anyways."

"It was overrun! By an army. An army of albinos!" hissed Nienna, her eyes wide.

Barras rubbed at his chin with a rasping sound. "Is that so ways? That would be bad news, if I hadn't owed so much silver to the Hatchet Man."

"Who's the Hatchet Man?" asked Kat, intrigued.

"Runs the gambling dens. When you don't pay, he cuts off your hands with a hatchet. Chop!" He roared with laughter, as one of his men brought a large pan of water and set it on the fire. Barras leaned forward, then, his lips pouting as he considered a question. Almost instinctively, Kat leaned forward to listen; but Nienna found her hands tightening on Ilanna. Something wasn't right. The atmosphere felt… just wrong.

Nienna glanced about. And it hit her. All of the men still wore weapons. They had removed some for show; but they still wore short swords. They were behaving like they were winding down, making camp, but nobody skinned a rabbit with a sword sheathed at his side. Or was she simply looking for trouble where none should be found? She stared at Barras. His face was filthy, yes, but honest. Why not trust him? He was a simple woodsman enduring a harsh winter… surely they would have a house or cottage nearby. A wife? Three children to feed?

Barras edged a little closer. He licked his lips. "What's your name, me sweets?"

"Kat."

"I was a-wondering, Kat, if you taste as good as you look?"

There came a moment of silence, and both Nienna and Kat surged to their feet but one of the woodsmen had circled behind and a club cracked Nienna's skull, sending her sprawling sideways, fingers losing grip on

Ilanna, and two men grabbed Kat, bearing her to the ground where she screamed, until one punched her, a heavy blow that silenced her in an instant.

Nienna's last sight was of Barras, lifting Ilanna and frowning a little as his eyes scanned the delicate faded runes along the black haft. He shook his head, then stared at Nienna in a curious way; before a second vicious blow from behind rendered her unconscious.

Nienna awoke to pain, pain in her fingers, hands, and running like fiery trails along her forearms and biceps, to end like pits of coal deep within her shoulders. She moaned, and her eyes flickered open. Her head pounded. A sour taste filled her mouth, and she realised she had vomited down her shirt.

She was moving, swaying, and at first she thought it a reaction to being hit over the back of the head. Then she realised the awful truth; she was tied up, and hung from the branch of a tree. She scowled, anger charging to the front of her mind. Bastards, trussing her up like a chicken! She heard laughter, and shouting, the crackle of the fire, and as she gently moved around on her length of rope she saw Kat. She was in a state of undress. Six men had ripped free her shirt and trousers, and she stood in her underwear and boots, a long stick in her hands, face a curious mix of hatred and fear as the men spread out, surrounding her, and she jabbed at them with a stick.

"Watching them, me sweets?"

Nienna looked down, saw Barras standing close to her, not looking at her, but watching the spectacle with Kat.

"Let us go," she said.

"Why? We're going to have a pretty fun with you two for, oh, I'd say the next month. You can get a lot of use out of a young woman like yourself; you have so much stamina, so much passion, so much anger. But, finally, when we've fucked you, and beaten you, and broken your spirit worse than any high-bred stallion, when you no longer scream during orgasm, when you no longer scratch at faces and pull at hair… when your spirit is gone, me sweet little doll, then, and only then, do we slit your throats."

Nienna stared down at the man, tasting vomit, and wondering how she could kill him. His words frightened her more than anything she had had ever heard, or ever seen; worse than the albino army, worse than any canker. For here, and now, this was personal, not just an invasion, and this man was evil, a total corruption of the human shell. She was still stunned that she had not been able to see it. To smell it. It was a sobering life experience.

"How could you do that to us?" she asked, in a small voice.

Barras glanced up, then reached out, his hand creeping up the inside of her trouser leg. His fingers were rough on her skin. She squirmed, but he was stronger than he looked; he grinned as his fingers groped her inner thigh, her soft flesh, her young flesh, and his eyes were old and dark and deeply malevolent.

"Not everybody in this world has the same morals as you, little honey. You little rich girls; well, you deserve every fucking you get."

The men, laughing, got the stick from Kat and bore her to the ground. One kissed her, and when she bit his tongue in a spurt of bright blood he slapped her hard, across the face, then again with the back of his hand. Blood trickled from her nose and she lay, stunned, fingers clenching and unclenching. The man pulled free her vest revealing small, firm, breasts. He squeezed them, one in each hand, to the cackling of his companions…

"Call them off," said Nienna, voice so dry she could hardly speak.

"Why, me sweets?"

"You saw the axe," said Nienna, voice turning hard. "It's Ilanna."

Barras narrowed his eyes then, scowling at her. "Where did you hear such a name?"

"It's true," she hissed. "It's my grandfather's axe. He's coming. Soon. He will kill you all."

"What's his name?"

"You know his name, you heap of horse-shit."

"Speak his *name*!" snarled the woodsman.

"He is Kell, and he will eat your heart," said Nienna.

This impelled Barras to move, and cursing (cursing himself, he knew he had seen the axe before), he stepped forward to talk to the woodsmen; but something happened, a blur of action so fast he blinked, and only as a splatter of blood slapped across his face and dirt-streaked stubble did he leap into action…

The creature slammed across the clearing from the darkness of the trees in an instant, picking one man up in huge jaws, lifting the man high at the waist and crunching through him through his muscle and bones

and spinal column and he screamed, gods he
screamed so hard, so bad, as the canker shook him
and gears spun and wheels clicked and turned and
gears made tiny *click click tick tock* noises, and it threw
him away like a bone into the forest.

Barras ran forward, screaming, his sword raised…

The canker whipped around, a blur, and leapt, biting off the woodsman's head in a single giant snap.

His body stood for a moment, still holding a tarnished sword, an arc of blood painting a streak across
the forest in a gradually decreasing spiral. Then a
knee buckled; the fountain of blood soaked the pine
needle carpet, and the body crumpled like a deflated
balloon.

Nienna struggled against her ropes, and she could
see Kat crying, pulling on her vest and trews.

"Kat! Over here! Get the axe!"

The remaining four woodsmen had grouped together, pooling weapons. With a scream, and as a unit
that displayed previous military experience, they
charged across the fire at the canker which growled,
hunkering down, crimson eyes watching the charge
with interest, as a cat watches a disembowelled mouse
squirm.

Kat grabbed the axe and, still sobbing, half crawled,
half ran towards Nienna. She swung at the rope,
missed, then swung again and the sharp blades of
Ilanna sliced through with consummate ease. Nienna
hit the ground, and Kat helped her get the ropes from
her wrists to the backing track of screams, thuds, gur-
gles, and most disturbingly, the solid crunches of
impact, of gristle, of snapping bones.

The girls half hoped the woodsmen had won; but then, they'd have to face the prospect of rape and murder.

But what would happen with the canker?

Kat pulled on her boots, and something smashed off into the forest, a woodsman, picked up by the canker, slamming an axe into its back again and again and again as it charged through the forest with his legs in its jaws. There came the smash and crack of breaking wood. A gurgle. Another crack; this time of bone.

Nienna and Kat stood, shivering, wondering what to do.

Slowly, the canker emerged from the gloom, lit only by the flames of the fire. Blood soaked its white fur, and congealed gore interfered with fine cogs and gears, splashed up its uneven, distended eyes. Skin and torn bowel were caught in long streamers between its claws, and it made a low churning sound as if about to be violently sick...

"Back away," mumbled Kat, as Nienna hefted the axe and they started to retreat into the forest.

Nienna stood on a branch, which snapped.

The canker turned, slowly, red eyes watching them.

"Is it going to charge?"

"I don't know."

"Don't move!"

"It's already seen us!"

"Stop talking!"

"You're talking as well!"

They stopped. The canker stopped. They eyed each other, over perhaps fifty yards. Then, with a wide grin – which looked like the creature had peeled the top of its head right off – it let out a howl, a howl to the fire, to the forest, to the moon, and lowered its head with a grinding snarl and with a shift of gears, a mechanical grind of cogs, the canker leapt at the girls...

SEVEN
The Watchmakers

"Don't do this," said Anu, backing away, her face an image of horror as Shabis's fangs gleamed, her claws flexed and she leapt. Anu somersaulted backwards, away from the attack, landed lightly, and as Shabis leapt again, claws tearing the carpet, oil gleaming in her eyes, so Anu leapt, kicked off from the wall and flipped over Shabis's head. She landed in a crouch, unwilling to reveal her own killing tools, unwilling to fight her sister.

"Shabis!"

Shabis whirled, mad now. "You will die, bitch!"

"With what poison has he filled your head? What lies?"

Shabis charged, claws swiping for Anu's throat. Anu swayed back, brass and steel a hair's-breadth from her windpipe, then punched her sister in the chest, slamming her back almost horizontally where she hit the carpet on her face and coughed, clutching her chest, pain slamming violent through heart and gears and clockwork...

Anu's eyes lifted to Vashell. "Call her off."

Vashell backed away, tongue wetting his lips. She could see the bulge in his armoured pants. He was getting a thrill out of this: out of watching two sisters fight to the death.

"Stop her!" shrieked Anu, as Shabis crawled to her feet, the corners of her mouth blood-flecked.

"No," he said, voice barely more than a growl. "This is the final trial. Don't you see? This is the final... entertainment. A repayment, if you like, for all the pain and suffering you have caused. Shabis." Shabis looked at him, the rage in her eyes flickering to love. "If you kill her, then we will marry, we will spend a glorious eternity together; you will never have to work again, we will languish in a blood-oil rapture; just you and I, my love."

Shabis turned to Anu, head low, eyes dark. She let out a snarl and charged at Anukis who was crying, great tears flowing down her cheeks, soaking her golden curls, and Shabis leapt like a tiger, both sets of vachine claws coming together to crush Anu's head and Anu swayed, ejecting a single claw which swiped down, sideways, as Shabis sailed past. There came a tiny *flash*, an almost unheard grinding sound, and Shabis hit the ground hard, rolling, wailing, her clawed fingers coming up to her face where blood and blood-oil mingled, leaking from her severed... fangs.

Anu had cut out Shabis's fangs. The ultimate symbol of the vachine.

"No!" wailed Shabis, blood-oil pumping as the cogs in her head, in her heart, ejected precious blood-oil. "What have you done to me, Anukis?" She climbed to her feet, ran to Vashell, who put out his arms to comfort her as she sobbed, her blood-oil leaking into his clothing and his eyes lifted to read Anukis who stood, face bleak, as she retracted her single claw.

"Now you need another assassin," said Anu, triumph in her eyes.

Vashell nodded. "You are correct." With a savage shove, he pushed Shabis away, drew his brass sword, and with a swift hard horizontal swipe, cut Shabis's head from her body. Blood and blood-oil spurted, hitting the ceiling, drenching the walls and bed in a twisting shower of sudden ferocity. Shabis's head hit the sodden carpet, eyes wide, mouth open in shock, pretty features stained. Anu could see the clockwork in her severed neck, between the fat and the muscle, the veins and the bone, nestled and intricate, bonded, and it was all still spinning happily, now slowing, as cogs could not mesh and a primary shaft failed in its delicate spin. Shabis's eyes closed, and her separated body folded slowly to the carpet, as if deflating. Her vachine aborted. Shabis died.

"No!" screamed Anu, running forward, dropping to her knees beside the corpse of her sister. Her head snapped up. "You will die for this!" she raged.

"Show me." Vashell still held his sword; it was a special blade, specifically designed for slaying vachine; for the killing of their own kind. It had a multi-layered blade, and carried a disruptive charge. It wasn't so much sharp as... created to cut through clockwork.

Anu's eyes narrowed. "You are a V Hunter?" she said.

"Yes." He smiled. It was a sickly smile, half pride, half... something else. Amongst the vachine, the V

Hunters were despised; it was a rank handed out by the Watchmakers, and a V Hunter's sole role was to hunt down and exterminate rogue vachine... to cleanse and, essentially, betray their own. Amongst the population they were feared and loathed. Their identities were kept secret, so they could work undercover throughout Silva Valley. They reported directly back to the Watchmakers, and indeed the Patriarch, and answered to no Engineer.

"You have been hunting me all this time?"

Vashell laughed, and sheathed his sword. He turned, running hands through his hair drenched in the blood-oil of Shabis. He turned back, and stared down at Anu. "Don't be so naive. What would I want with you, pretty little plaything?"

"What *do* you want, then?"

"I want something much more precious. I want your father, Anukis. I want Kradek-ka. He has gone; fled. Left you to suffer, along with... that." He stared, a snarl, at Shabis's corpse. "Now, you will take me to him. By all that is holy, by all the relics of our ancestors, you will take me to Kradek-ka."

Anukis overcame her fear, and snarled with fangs ejecting, and leapt; Vashell dropped his shoulder, and with an awesome blow backhanded Anukis across the room where she hit the wall, cracking plaster, and hit the floor on her head, crumpling into a heap. She groaned, broken, and her eyes flickered open.

"I'll leave you to clean up the corpse," said Vashell, and leaving footprints in Shabis's blood, he stalked from the room.

Anu stared for long, agonising moments, her eyes seeming to meet those of her dead sister. Tears rolled down her cheeks, her body slumped to the ground, and her eyes closed as she welcomed the oblivion of pain and darkness.

It began as a ball. A tight ball; white, pure, hot like a sun. And that ball was anger, and hatred, and rage so pure, so hot, that it engulfed everything, it engulfed her concept of family and name and honour and duty and love and spread, covering the city and the valley and the Black Pike Mountains; finally it overtook the world, and the sun, and the stars, and the galaxy and everything broiled in that tiny hot plasma of rage and Anu's eyes flickered open and it was dark, and cool, and she was thankful.

She lay on a steel bench. She was dressed in plain clothes, and boots. She looked down, and started, and started to weep. Her vachine claws had been removed, the ends of her bloody fingers blunt stumps. She reached up, and winced as she felt the holes where her fangs should have been. Inside her, she felt the heavy *tick tick tick* of clockwork, in her head and in her breast; and she cursed Vashell, and cursed the Engineers, for they had taken away her weapons and she would rather be dead. It was what they once did to criminals before the Justice Laws, and just before a death-sentence was meted out. It was the lowest form of aberration. The lowest form of dishonour; beyond, even, the transformation to canker. Even a canker had fangs.

Winter sunshine bled in through a high window, and Vashell emerged smugly through a door. He wore subtle vachine battledress, skin-armour, they called it, beneath woollen trousers and a thick shirt and cloak. His weapons, also, were hidden. His eyes shone.

"Get up."

"No."

"Get up!" He ejected a claw, and held it to her eye. "Anukis, I will take you apart limb by limb, orb by orb, tooth by tooth. I will massacre you, but your clock-work, your mongrel vachine status, will keep you alive. We know Kradek-ka made you special; you think us fools? You think the Engineers haven't been inside you? Examined every cog, every wheel, every tiny shaft and pump? Kradek-ka did some very special things to you, Anukis, technology we didn't even know existed. First, we were going to kill you. It was fitting. You are an abomination. But then a specialist discovered... the advanced technology, inside of you. You will help me find Kradek-ka. I promise you this."

"I don't know where to look," she said, voice low, staring at the razor tip of Vashell's claw.

"I have a start point. But first, I want to show you something."

Vashell tugged on a thin golden lead, almost transparent, and scaled with a strange quartz mesh; sometimes, it could be seen, rippling like liquid stone; other times it was completely invisible, depending on how it caught the light. Anukis felt the jolt, and realised it was connected to her throat. Another humiliation. Another vachine slight.

Vashell tugged, and Anukis was forced to stand. She growled, tried to eject her fangs by instinct but only pain flowed through her jaws. She wept then, standing there on the leash. She wept for her freedom; but more, she wept for her dead sister, wept for her lost father.

"Follow me."

Anukis had little choice.

"Where is this?"

"Deep. Within the Engineer's Palace."

"I did not know these corridors, and these rooms, existed."

"Why should you? Even Kradek-ka would not tell you everything. After all," he smiled, eyes dark, filled with an inner humour, "you are female."

The corridors were long, and the more they delved into the Engineer's Palace, the deeper they penetrated, conversely, the more bare and more undecorated it became. Gone were carpets, silk hangings, works of oil-art. Instead, bare metal, rusted in places, became the norm. Deeper they travelled, Anukis trotting a little to keep up with Vashell's long stride.

They walked for an hour. Behind some doors they heard grinding noises, deep and penetrating; behind others jolts of enormous power like strikes of lightning. Behind others, they heard rhythmical thumping, or the squeal of metal on metal. Yet more were deadly silent beyond, and for some reason, these were the worst for Anukis. Her imagination could create Engineer horrors worse than anything they could show her.

Vashell stopped, and Anukis nearly ran into him. She was lost in thought, drowning in dreams. She pulled up tight, and he looked down, his look arrogant, his eyes mocking, and she thought:

One day, I will see you weep.

One day, I will watch you beg, and squirm, in the dirt, like a maggot.

One day, Vashell. You will see.

"We are here," he said.

"Where?"

"The Maternity Hall. Your father's creation."

"Maternity Hall? I have never heard of this." A cold dread began to rise slowly through her, and Vashell pushed at the solid metal door, grey and unmarked, and Anukis found herself led into a huge, vacuous chamber which stretched off further than the eye could see. It was filled with booths and benches, and the air was infused with the cries of babes.

Goose-bumps ran up and down Anu's spine. She stood, stock still, her eyes taking in the bleak, grey place.

She walked forward, as far as her leash would allow, and Vashell tugged her to a halt. Obedience. She stared at benches, where babes lay, squirming, their cries ignored as Engineers worked on them. In the booths which drifted away she could see what looked like medical operations taking place. Many of the babes were silent, obviously drugged. Around some, a cluster of Engineers worked frantically. Every now and again, a buzz filled the air, or a click, or a whine.

Anu stared up at Vashell. "What are they doing?" she whispered.

"Welcome to Birth," said Vashell. "You don't think the vachine create themselves, do you? Every single vachine is a work of art, a sculpture of science and engineering; every vachine is created from a baby template, the fresh meat brought here shortly after birth to have the correct clockwork construct grafted, added, injected, implanted, and from thence the true vachine can grow and meld and begin to function."

"So… we all begin as human?"

"Yes."

"But we feed from human blood! The refined mix of blood-oil! That makes us… little more than cannibals!"

Vashell shrugged, and smiled. "Blood of my blood," he said, sardonically. "I find it hard to believe Kradek-ka never explained it to you. He kept you in a bubble, Anukis. He created this; this structure, this schedule, he elevated the systems of clockwork integration to make us better, superior, to elevate us above a normal impure flesh. With vachine integration we are the perfect species. Can you not see this, Anukis? This is your family's life work. This is the creation of the vachine."

Anu sagged, leaning against Vashell, her mind spinning as she watched a thousand babies undergoing vachine integration. She saw scalpels carving through flesh, through baby chests and into hearts, replacing organic components with clockwork, replacing valves and arteries with gears and tubes. Babies cried, squealed, and their wails were hushed by pads held over mouths until they lost consciousness. Blood trickled into slots and was carried away to be further refined and fed back into Blood Refineries in order to create the blood-oil pool.

"We are vampires," said Vashell, staring down at Anu who was pale and grey, a shadow of her former self. "Machine vampires. We feed on the human shell; revel, in our total superiority."

"What we're doing is *wrong*," snarled Anu.

"Why? The creation of a superior species?" Vashell laughed. "Your naivety both astounds and amuses me. Here, the rich noble daughter, blood-line of our very own vachine creators – and you do not even understand the basics?"

A babe squealed and there was a chopping sound. Anu saw the flash of a silver blade. The tiny head rolled into a chute and was sucked away. The corpse was thrown into a bag, and an Engineer moved to a distant cart and slung the body aboard, along with all the other medical waste.

"So," said Anu, fighting for air, "every babe that is born, here in Silva Valley, it comes here? It comes to be formed into vachine?"

"Yes. But more than Silva; the vachine have spread, Anu. We are breeding soldiers in other valleys. We are growing strong! We grow mighty! Our time for domination, for expansion, for Empire, is close."

"But–" said Anu.

Vashell frowned. "What do you mean?"

"Something is wrong," said Anu, with primitive intuition. "What's going on, Vashell? What's happening here?"

"We need to find Kradek-ka." He scowled. He would say no more.

For an hour Vashell dragged Anukis through the Maternity Hall, and she saw things so barbaric she wouldn't have believed them possible. The babies were operated on, implanted with clockwork technology – in their hearts, in their brains, in their jaws, in their hands. Even at such a young age they were given weapons of death, using blood-oil magic, clockwork, and liquid brass and gold, silver-quartz and polonium, in order to control and power and time the mechanisms of the vachine.

"How many work?" she said, at last, exhausted.

"I do not understand?"

"How many babes... become vachine? Successfully?"

"Fifty five in a hundred successfully make it through the – shall we say, medical procedures. Fifty five in a hundred accept the clockwork, accept the fangs, and can grow and meld and adapt and think of themselves as true machine."

"What about the others?"

"Most die," said Vashell, sadly. "This is a great loss; if we could improve the rate of melding, our army would be much larger; we could advance so much more quickly."

"And?"

"The cankers?" Vashell laughed. "They have their uses."

"Take me away from this place," said Anu, tears on her cheeks, fire in her part-clockwork heart.

"As you wish. I thought you needed to know, to understand, before we set out on our quest."

"Quest?"

"To find your father. He was working on a refined technology. In trials he had pushed acceptance from fifty-five to ninety-five in a hundred; we barely lost any babes. You see, Anu, why we need to find him? If you help me, if we pull this off for the Watchmakers, for the whole of vachine-kind, then you will be saving hundreds, thousands of lives, every year. You understand?"

"You bastard."

"Why so?"

"You have played me like a jaralga hand. I must help you. I must help end this atrocity."

"Your father's atrocity," corrected Vashell.

"Yes," she said, face ashen, voice like the tomb.

Anukis walked down long corridors of stone. She walked down long tunnels of metal. She became disorientated by it all; by the directions, the elevations, the dips and curves and banks, the smells of hot oil and cold metal. In weakness, she resigned herself. She was a puppet now, a creature to be controlled by Vashell. He had taken away her gifts, taken away her special gifts. She felt hollow. Abused. In pain. But more... she felt less than vachine, less than human, a limbo creature of neither one world or the next. She was a shadow; a shadow, mocked by shadows. Tears welled within her, but she would not let them come. No, she thought. I will be strong. Despite everything, despite my weakness, despite my abuse, I will be strong. I need my strength. I will need it as I hunt down my... father.

"Good girl," soothed Vashell, misunderstanding her compliance, and keeping her leash tight in his gloved fist. Anukis did not struggle, did not pull, did not fight her taming.

She smiled inwardly, although her face was stone. She was beyond the displaying of hatred. And when she killed him, when she massacred Vashell, as she knew, coldly, deep down in her breast and heart and soul that she would, it would be a long and painful death. It would be an absolution. A penance. An act of purifying like nothing the Engineers had before witnessed.

They walked, boots padding.

"Where are we going?" she asked, eventually.

"You will see."

Gradually, the stone and metal walls started to show signs of the Engineers; symbols replaced numbers, and decorations became evident as the wall design became not just more opulent, but more instructive. Anukis found herself staring at the designs on the wall, the artwork, the very shape of the stones. Many were fashioned into toothed cogs, gears of stone, and the whole corridor began to twist with design as the stone gave way to metal, gave way to brass and gold, laced with silver-quartz mortar. Slowly, the walls changed, became more than walls, became machines, mechanisms, clockwork, and Anukis recognised that this was no longer a corridor, but a living breathing working machine and the Engineer's Palace was more than just a building: it was a live thing, with a pulse of quartz and a heart of gold.

"Stop."

Vashell held something, what looked like a tiny circle of bone, up to a mechanism beside a blank metal door. There came several hisses, of oiled metal on metal, as the object in his hand slid out pins and integrated with the machine. The portal opened, but in the manner of nothing Anukis had ever seen; it was a series of curves, oiled and gleaming, which curled around one another, twisted like coils as the door didn't just open, it unpeeled.

They stepped through, into a working engine.

The room was crammed with a giant mechanism of clockwork, a machine made up of thousands and thousands of smaller machines. Brass and gold gleamed everywhere. Cogs turned, integrated, shafts spun, steam hissed from tiny nozzles, brass pistons beat vertically, horizontally, diagonally, and everywhere Anukis looked there were a hundred movements, of rockers and cams, valves and pistons, and she shivered for it reminded her of the clockwork she had watched inserted into babies... only on a much, much larger scale; a vast scale. A terrible scale.

Vashell led her forward, through a natural tunnel amidst the heart of the vast machine which stretched above them for as far as the eye could see, away into darkness. She could smell hot oil, and the sweet narcoleptic essence of blood-oil. And another smell... a metallic undertone, acidic, insectile, the metal perfume of a million moving parts.

Vashell's boots stamped to a halt, muffled against the brass floor, and Anukis looked up, blinking in the poor golden light. There was a simple metal bench, and behind it sat a woman. Her hands toyed with a complex mechanism, which moved and spun and gyrated and morphed, even as her hands moved endlessly around and within the machine. It was like watching a doctor performing high-speed surgery inside an organism, a living, beating, functioning organism. Anu looked to the woman's face. It was perfect and distorted at the same time. She seemed to wear a brass mask, which glittered dully.

"Hello, Daughter of Vachine," said the woman, smiling, her eyes shining, her hands still constantly merging and integrating with the almost organic clockwork. "My name is Sa. I am Watchmaker."

Anukis could not hide her amazement; nor her distaste.

The Watchmakers were clinically paranoid, in Anu's opinion. They never walked amongst the people, instead hiding away in the Engineer's Palace and issuing orders many of the vachine population found detached from the real world, divorced from the society in which a modern vachine lived, operated, ate and drank.

"You have abused me," said Anu, simply.

"We have strengthened you," said Sa.

"What do you want of me?" said Anu.

"We have a problem," smiled Sa, her golden brass eyes kindly, her fangs peeking just a little above the lip of her mask. She was beautiful, Anu realised, in a vachine way. Despite her lack of stature, despite an athletic and powerful appearance, Anu realised this small dark-skinned woman exuded energy and she noted Vashell's subservient stance. An ironic reversal, considering the behaviour she'd witnessed back in her cell: it had been a stage-act, just for her benefit. Anukis scowled. She was a pawn. Manipulated. Played for a fool. A tool in somebody else's workbox.

"You need my father," said Anu, voice now cold, eyes hardening.

"Our problem goes far, far deeper than your father," said Sa, head tilting to one side. Still her hands played, sinking into a mist of spinning gears and wheels. "It is the blood-oil."

"What about it?"

"We are running dry," said Sa, watching Anukis carefully. "As you know, to the north we have the Fields, out past the Organic Flatlands. But the cattle are dying, have ceased to breed, and our refined blood-oil supplies are nearly exhausted. We have sent a scouting force south, beyond the Black Pike Mountains; they are searching out new possibilities for fresh cattle."

Anu gave a single nod.

"Do you understand the implications of what I am saying?"

"If the blood runs out, it cannot be refined into blood-oil; then the vachine will begin to seize. And die."

"Yes. This is a threat to our civilisation, Anukis. But more than that, the Blood Refineries your father helped build... to develop and engineer. They have contracted, shall we say, a fault. Something endemic to his math, his engineering, his blood-oil magick, and subsequently an element only he can put right. Kradek-ka was a genius." She said it low; with ultimate respect. "He was Watchmaker."

"What happens if the Refineries fail?"

Sa smiled, but there was no humour there. "We will return to a state of hunting and savagery. But how can eighty thousand vachine satiate their blood-oil lust? We will devolve, Anukis. Our society will become decadent, will crumble, will fade as we turn on one another, revert back to clans and tribes. It does not even bear thinking about. The dark ages of our civilisation were a bloody, evil time, where we fed upon ourselves, upon each other. Now, we are fed by the blood of others. Our population is fed by cattle, bred for the purpose. The age-old war with the albinos from under the mountain, all that is in the past. We conquered, we dominated, they became our slaves — and all because of our culture, our civilisation, our evolution! I cannot allow this be taken away. I cannot let this hierarchy, this religion, fail."

"I am impure-blood," said Anukis, voice low. Her eyes were fixed on Sa. "You have cast me out from your vachine world. Why should I care if you perish? Vashell has abused me, humiliated me, murdered my sister, and I am cast out by my own people because of a twist of genetics over which I had no control. I hate to be crude, Sa, but you meat-fuckers can suffer and die for all I care."

Sa smiled. Her eyes glittered behind her mask. "Did your father ever tell you about the origin of the cankers, sweet Anukis?"

"What do you mean?"

"Cankers are... Kradek-ka's greatest achievement. They are, shall we say, a method of utilising waste product. They are bred, and nurtured, deformities; a mish-mash of twisted clockwork and flesh, and put simply, the insane end-product of when a vachine goes bad. We keep them apart from vachine society; so you know the term, I am sure, as insult. But you have never seen the end product." She took a deep breath. "However..."

The pause hurt Anukis. She could not describe why she felt such a sudden, indescribable terror, but she did. Her eyes grew wide. Palpitations riddled her clockwork breast. Her hands clenched together, and fear tasted like bad oil in her mouth.

"What are you saying?" she said.

Sa stood, and placed her fluid clockwork machine on the bench. She walked around its outskirts, hand trailing a sparkle of clockwork slivers, gold dust, blood-oil. She stood before Anukis, looking up into the pretty woman's beaten face, deformed now by the removal of vachine fangs. She stood on tip-toe and kissed Anukis, her tongue slipping into her mouth, fangs ejecting and biting Anukis's lower lip, a vampire bite, a tasting, a savouring, a gentle taking of blood...

Sa stood down. Anukis's blood sat on her lips, in her fangs, and their eyes were connected and Anukis, finally, understood. Her hate fell, crushed. Her anger was crumpled like a paper ball. Her sense of revenge lay, stabbed and bleeding, dying, dead.

"You will help us find Kradek-ka. You will help us repair the Blood Refineries."

Anukis nodded, weakly. "Yes," she said.

"There are some things far worse than death," Sa said. Then turned to Vashell. "Show her the Canker-Pits on your way out. Only then will she truly understand the limits of her... future potential. And the extremes of her father's twisted genius."

"Yes, Watchmaker." Vashell bowed, and dragged Anukis on her leash.

* * *

Alloria, Queen of Falanor, sat in the Autumn Palace looking out over the staggered flower fields. Colours blazed, and the trees were filled with angry orange and russet browns, the bright fire of summer's betrayal by autumn and a final fiery challenge to the approaching winter.

She sighed, and walked along a low wall, pulling her silk shawl a little tighter about her shoulders as her eyes swept the riot of colours stretching out, and down, in a huge two-league drop from the Autumn Palace to the floodfields beyond. Distantly, she could see workers tending the fields; and to the left, woodsmen cleared a section of forest using ox to drag log-laden carts back to the palace in readiness for the harsh snows which always troubled this part of the country.

"There you are!"

Mary ran along the neatly paved walkway and gave a low curtsy to her queen. Alloria grinned, and the two women embraced, the young woman – Alloria's hand-maiden for the past year – nuzzling the older woman and drinking in her rich perfume, and the more subtle, underlying scent of soap-scrubbed skin and expensive moisturiser.

Mary pulled back, and gazed at the Queen of Falanor. Thirty years old, tall, elegant, athletic, with a shock mane of black hair like a rich waterfall, now tied back tightly, but wild and untamed when allowed to run free without a savage and vigorous brushing. Her skin was flawless, and very pale; beautiful in its sculpture as well as translucency. Her eyes were green, and sparkled green fire when she laughed. When

Alloria moved, it was with the natural grace of nobility, of birth, of breeding, and yet her character flowed with kindness, a lack of arrogance, and a generosity which ennobled her to the Falanor population. She was not just a queen, but a champion of the poor. She was not just queen by birth or marriage, but by popular consent; she was a woman of the people.

"You are cold," said Mary. "Let me bring you a thicker shawl."

"No, Mary, I am fine."

Mary gazed out over the splendour of fire ranged before them. It was getting late, the sun sinking low, and most of the workers were finalising their work and walking in groups along pathways through distant crops. "The winter is coming," she said, and gave an almost exaggerated shudder.

"I forgot," smiled Alloria, touching Mary's shoulder. "You hate the ice."

"Yes. It reminds me too much of childhood."

"Never fear. In a week Leanoric will have finished his training, and the volunteer regiments will be standing down for winter leave; he will meet us back at Iopia Palace and there will be a great feast. Fires and fireworks will burn and sparkle for a week; then, then you will feel warm, my Mary."

Mary nodded, still very close to Alloria. "I will never be as warm as when I am with you, my queen," she said, voice little more than a whisper.

Alloria smiled, and placed a finger on Mary's lips. "Shh, little one. This is not the place for such conversation. Come, walk with me back to my chambers;

I've had a wonderful blue frall-silk dress delivered, and was wondering how well it will fit."

They walked, arm in arm, along stone and marble paved walkways, between sculpted stone pillars and under roof-trellises filled with roses and winter honeysuckle. Scents filled the air, and Alloria closed her eyes, wishing she was back with her husband, her king, her lover, her hero. She smiled, picturing his smile, feeling his hands on her body. She shivered, then, as a ghost walked over her grave.

"What's the matter?"

"Nothing. I am just thinking of Leanoric. I miss him."

"He is a fine husband," said Mary. "Such strength! One day, perhaps, I will find such a man."

"Erran has been watching you, I think."

"My lady!" Mary blushed furiously and lowered her eyes. "I fear you are mistaken."

"Not so. I have seen him watching you, watching the way you walk, the sway of your hips, the rising of your breast when you have run an errand. I think he is in love."

Erran was the Captain of the Guard at the Autumn Palace, thirty-two years old, single, muscular, attractive in a dark, flashing way. He was gallant, noble, and one of the finest swordsmen in Leanoric's Legions; hence his placement of trust in protecting Queen Alloria.

"You jest," Mary said, eventually.

"Come, let us ask him!"

"No, Alloria!" gasped Mary, and Alloria let out a giggle, breaking away from the younger woman and running up a flight of marble steps. At the summit two guards stood to attention carrying long spears tipped by savage barbs. They stared, eyes ahead, as Alloria approached and swept between them, skirts hissing over inlaid gems in the gold-banded floor.

"Erran! Erran!"

He arrived in a few heartbeats, at a run, hand on sword-hilt. "Yes, my queen?"

"Do not worry, there is no alarm. I have a simple question for you."

Mary arrived, panting a little, and Alloria saw Erran's eyes drift longingly over Mary, then flicker back to her face, a question in his eyes, a sense of duty restored. "I will do my best, my queen."

"No," whispered Mary.

"I wondered if you'd found replacement guards for the two men taken sick last week? It leaves us with a force of only eighteen in the palace grounds."

"Word has been sent to the nearest town, my queen. Replacements are riding even as we speak from the local garrison. I have the captain's personal guarantee that he sent two of his finest men."

"Good! When will they arrive?"

"Later this evening, I believe," said Erran, with a smile of reassurance. "Have faith in those who serve you, my queen."

"I do, Erran. I do." Her smile was dazzling and she moved towards her chambers beneath arches of alabaster, steel and marble. Behind, the bloated shimmering sun was sinking over the horizon, and near-horizontal beams cast a rich ruby ambience throughout the Autumn Palace. Mary followed, a hand on Alloria's arm, her face flushed red.

Erran stood stiffly to attention. "My queen," he said.

"Oh, one more thing." She turned, suddenly. "Mary here is feeling a little flushed, a little tired. I wondered if you might walk with her, out in the gardens? Give her maybe an hour of your time? She would greatly appreciate it."

"I would… be honoured, my queen. But I am on duty."

"I am taking you off duty."

Erran gave a crooked smile. "And who would do my job whilst I walk in the gardens?"

"Oh hush, there are guards everywhere, man, and I am but a few heartbeats away. I have lungs, do I not? And I was trained by Elias, Leanoric's Sword-Champion. I am not as fragile as many people assume." She grinned, her eyes twinkling. "I could beat you, I'd wager."

Erran smiled broadly. "I know this, my queen," he said. "I have seen you best three of my men with a blade. The humiliation stung my pride like a horse-whip! But–"

"No buts. This is a direct order," said the queen. "And I would hate to inform Leanoric you disobeyed a direct order."

Erran snapped a salute. "As you wish, Queen Alloria." He turned, and smiled at Mary, who seemed suddenly incapable of speech. "If you would like to follow me, my lady? I will escort you for fresh air."

Mary nodded, threw a scowl at Alloria, and departed, her silk slippers silent on marble steps.

Alone now, Alloria entered her chambers and closed the doors. She loved to be alone, without guards or hand-maidens, without servants or lackeys. She knew attendance came with her position, and this made her crave solitude even more... except at night, in the cold dark hours, when she would cry out for Leanoric, missing him terribly, missing their two sons, Oliver and Alexander, aged twelve and fourteen, who were travelling with their father learning the Art of Warcraft.

No. In the darkness, Mary would come and climb into bed with Alloria, and they would hold each other, sharing warmth, sharing the simple comfort of human contact, and Alloria knew that Mary loved her, knew that Mary loved her in a way slightly accelerated from the contact and comfort Alloria craved, and that Mary treasured those nights they spent, only thin layers of silk and cotton between their firm, sleep-warmed bodies. But Alloria belonged to Leanoric, her king, her one true love, her hero and soldier and lover and father and husband, a man, a real true strong man, who...

The image flashed like lightning, piercing in her mind.

The Betrayal.

She stumbled a little, righted herself, and gasping ran to a stand and poured water into a goblet. She drank, greedily, then slapped the cup down, panting, cursing herself for having a memory, or at least, having a memory of those terrible days and weeks when she had–

No, don't say it, don't even think of it...

it did not happen; it was a dream, a bad dream.

Why had she done such a terrible thing to the man she loved? Her husband? The father of her children?

And he had forgiven her. Her smile was cracked as she looked at herself in the silver mirror. Her eyes had lost their green fire. She blinked away tears, found inner strength, and reached towards a tiny stone jar. Her hand paused over the jar, which was intricately decorated with ancient battle scenes and heroes from Falanor's long turbulent history.

"No." Her word seemed loud, and cracked, in the echoing empty chamber, despite the proliferation of hanging silks and furs and the many tapestries which adorned walls, again depicting the history of Falanor.

Her hand moved away from the jar and hovered, uncertainly, for a moment; she felt weakness flood her, rising from her toes to her brain like the sweep of an Elder wand, and her hand snaked out, knocked the lid clumsily from the jar which clattered to the marble table-top. Alloria refrained from cursing, and didn't look inside the jar, simply wetting her finger and dipping it into the dark blue powder therein. She stared at her green eyes in the mirror as she rubbed the powder under her tongue, instantly enjoying the relaxing honey of blue karissia entering her blood, entering her mind, and she knew it was weakness and a certain specific horror from her past that made her indulge in this rare drug, and that was no excuse, but it was something she had come to rely on during the old days and the bad days when things had seemed so unclear and seemed to go so wrong. Blue karissia pulsed in her, flowed with her heartbeat, and the world swayed and quickly Alloria slipped from her shawl and dress and climbed into bed to fall instantly asleep, her dreams filled with colour and beauty and an enveloping blue.

Alloria woke to darkness, and the world felt wrong. She could taste the bitter after-effects of the narcotic, and wondered how long she had been under its spell. An hour? Three hours? She sat up, disorientated and feeling mildly nauseous. She shivered, and stepping from her bed pulled on a long silk gown, kicked her feet into thick slippers and found the water jug. She drank greedily, the dehydrated drink of the blue, and only then did a flood of questions tumble into her gradually awakening mind...

Why had the lanterns not been lit? In her chambers, and also outside, on the paved walkways? Normally the garden would be filled with globes of light. Alloria found it hard to believe the lightsmiths had been remiss in their duty.

Warily, she moved to the doors of her chamber and opened one a crack. Outside, a velvet silence rolled through the Autumn Palace. Alloria listened for the familiar footsteps of guards, the distant clink of armour. She heard nothing. She opened her mouth to call out, and closed it again, changing her mind.

Where was Erran? And the other guards? During the hours of darkness she usually had two men posted outside her sleep chambers. Where were they? It was unthinkable they would be away from their post.

Her eyes scanned the black, and goosebumps ran up and down her flesh. Something was wrong; deeply wrong. She could feel it in her blood and bones. Slowly, she eased the door shut. She had a short sword, nicknamed a glade blade, back by the bed. She crept away, back, and padded across the floor. She winced as she drew the blade, for it whispered, oiled steel on leather, but she felt better with the sword in her hands. She knew how to use it; how to defend herself; although she had never been called upon, in reality, to kill, and somewhere deep in her subconscious she wondered how she would respond to the necessity.

She stood, in the darkness, uncertain of what to do.

Then a voice broke the silence; it was cool, clear, and way too arrogant. "What are you going to do with the sword, sweet little Queen Alloria?"

She tensed, poised for attack, tracing the voice that was *in the room, gods, he was in the room and with her and where was Erran, where were the guards? Would she have to fight the intruder alone?*

Fear flooded her.

"Who are you?" Her voice was stone. Ice.

Something moved in the darkness, and Alloria lifted her sword, a swift movement, or so she thought. In retrospect, it was probably hampered by the drugs she'd taken to help her sleep; to help alleviate the nightmares.

"I am here to help."

"Who are you?"

"My name is Graal. I have travelled a long way for you, my queen." He stepped into a pool of light filtering through high windows; he was tall, athletic, and moved with grace. He had long white hair and blue eyes blackened by the night. His face was beautiful, and Queen Alloria found herself paralysed by the effect. He carried no weapon.

"My guards are nearby," she said, voice quieter than she would have liked.

"Your guards are all dead," sighed General Graal. As if emphasising his point, and with perfect timing, something huge moved outside, crunching wood, gouging marble, and settled with a grunt. It was big, Alloria could sense that; and primitive. It grunted when it breathed, its shadow a crazy dance on a far wall.

What are you? she thought, with a shudder.

What is happening here?

Graal approached, and the sword flickered up with a hiss, but he carried on moving and stepped within her reach, batting the blade aside with a consummate ease that shamed her. She tried to withdraw the weapon, to stab at him, but he held the blade and then he held her jaw, and fear flushed through her like an emetic.

"Where is Mary?" she said.

"Alas, nearly everyone is dead."

"No!"

"All dead."

"Erran?"

"All dead, my sweetness. It is you we have come for; and your... drug taking has made it so easy. So sweet." Alloria fell from the world, then, fell and fell and only recovered when she realised Graal was removing her clothes.

"What are you doing?" she shrieked. Outside, the huge creature shifted again, cracking timber.

"Alas, this is a necessary consequence of war."

She started to fight, but Graal was too strong, and he punched her, suddenly, viciously, and she lay stunned half on the bed, her gown hitched high, her cold pale loins exposed in the gloom.

Without passion Graal fucked her, raped her, and she cried and her tears soaked into the bed sheets and as Graal rose to ejaculation so his head lowered, incisors ejecting, and he bit her neck and she screamed and he tasted her blood, drank her as with a grunt he came, and she felt warmth inside her and blood pumping from her, and everything made her sick and weak and weeping; she turned, and vomited on the bed, and conversely, this seemed to give Graal some pleasure; some form of satisfaction.

He pulled up his breeches, his childmaker pale and thin and glittering with complex gold and brass wires in the spilling light from the moon. Emphatically, he licked Alloria's blood from his vachine fangs.

"My husband will hunt you down for this," snarled Alloria, eyes narrowed, fingers plugging the twin wounds in her neck. Hatred was a real thing in her core, a toxic scorpion wild in her breast.

"I hope so," said Graal, and gestured, to where Mary was held in a tight embrace by an albino warrior. She was bound, gagged, her eyes wide. She had seen everything. Graal smiled, a crooked smile full of malice. "See she is released near to Leanoric's camp. It will provide… interesting results, I feel."

"What are you doing?" hissed Alloria.

A sword pressed against her throat, and she whimpered, and Graal leant in close. He kissed her lips, passionately, with love, and she was too frightened to pull away. She could still feel his seed, warm inside her, and with shame she feared him, but more, with guilt she feared the cold darkness of death.

"I am laying a trail," he said, and gestured. Mary, the sweet little one who had attended Alloria so honourably, was dragged by her hair from the room. Blood streaked her face, her breast and her loins. She had not been treated well.

"He will kill you," hissed Alloria. "He will kill you all!"

"We will see," said Graal, and struck a savage blow which knocked her to the bed; then to the floor. Darkness flooded in, and she remembered no more.

EIGHT
Stone Lion Woods

The canker leapt with a howl, and the girls hunkered in terror. It landed, and with a blink they realised they weren't the target. One of the woodsmen was still alive, groaning softly, and had lifted his sword and rolled, groan turning to a snarl at the sight of the canker... which stooped, suddenly, and with a crunch, bit off his head.

Kat eased through dead pine needles, through the rotting forest underlay as the canker ate the corpse noisily. It tore long strips of meat from his thighs and bones with crunches and rips, and then from the man's broad arse, huge lumps which glistened. It swallowed them down in a fast, slick gobble.

They both crouched, watching the canker. Nienna felt herself shivering, and they scavenged around for what torn items lay at their feet. As they dressed in rags, so Kat stood on a dead branch, which cracked. The canker lifted its head from its feast, blood rimed around the massive open jaws, and stringing from its twisted teeth. Nienna saw, suddenly, that this was a different creature from back at the cottage. The mouth

was smaller, more lop-sided to the left, the teeth like
blackened steel stumps, which bludgeoned meat
rather than sliced it. It was also slimmer, less bulky
than the first canker they'd witnessed, and with a
start, Nienna saw it had breasts, small and rounded,
hanging down between its stumpy front legs; the nipples gleaming like polished iron, aureoles of copper,
and within the frighteningly thin translucent skin tiny
pistons worked.

It was a woman, Nienna realised, and this, somehow, made the cankers a thousand times worse. One
thing to be a monster; but to be a monster created
from a human shell? To think that through a series of
twisted decisions, of incorrect choices, of random bad
luck, one could end up... like *that*?

"Gods," she hissed, and the canker tilted its head,
focusing on her and Kat as if for the first time. Its tiny
gold-flecked eyes narrowed, and raising its head, it
bellowed up into the dark night forest in something
akin to pain...

Not waiting to see if it attacked, Nienna and Kat
turned and ran, sprinting as fast as they could, tearing
down forest lanes and leaping fallen trunks, ducking
under thick branches, as all around the snow continued to pepper the forest innards and the cold stillness
invaded them, their bodies and their minds, threatening with icy chill...

Breaking branches told them they were being
pursued. Nienna glanced back to see the canker
wedge between two boles of trees that must have
been a hundred years old apiece; it roared again, a
terrifying squealing bass sound that echoed off

through the forest, through the trees which swayed high up as if in hissing appreciation of the gladiatorial hunt taking place within.

With a grunt, and the cracking of wood, the canker broke through the trees. They fell, toppling from high above, crashing through branches and other smaller trees and bringing a whole mass of forest down in a howling crunching terrifying clump.

Nienna and Kat were running, pine needles peppering their hair from above as trees fell and whipped. The canker howled again, and continued to crash after them, clumsy in its passion.

"Thick woods," panted Nienna, face streaked with sweat and covered by numerous tiny scratches.

"What?"

"Head for thick woods; the trees will stop the canker. Slow it down!"

Kat nodded, and they veered left. The canker altered its course, crashing and smashing, thumping and tearing its way through the forest like a whirlwind. Soon, the trees grew more closely placed, but this plan didn't work as well as Nienna and Kat anticipated; for one thing, the more dense sections of forest were the younger sections of forest. The older, thicker trunks were more widely spaced; they had conquered their territory, their particular arena of forest floor, and at their bases where little sunlight reached were simple carpets of pine and discarded branches. Here, now, in the midst of entanglements was where new trees fought for supremacy, for height, for sunlight, and Nienna realised with a pang of horror that the canker ploughed through such trees with ease. There was no halting it…

"I've got to stop!" wailed Kat.

"What is it?"

"My feet, they're cut to ribbons!"

Darkness poured into the thick forest, like from a jug. That was the second downside, Nienna realised, acknowledging her own error of judgement with a sour grimace. The thicker the woods, the more dark and terrifyingly cloying it was. With bigger trees, at least some light, and snow, crept through. Here it was just icy and dark, with little ambient light

Kat stopped, and Nienna stopped beside her. They stood still, listening to the canker falter, and halt; a bellow rent the air, and they heard the deformed beast sniffing.

"Maybe it won't see us," said Kat, voice trembling. She shuffled closer to Nienna, and they held each other in the caliginous interior. They could not even make out one another's faces.

"Yes."

The canker, snuffling and grunting, came closer. Now they could hear the tiny, metallic undercurrent of vachine noise; the click of gears, the whistle of pistons, the spinning of cogs.

"What the hell is it?" said Kat.

"Shh."

Even now, it came closer, and closer, and both girls held in screams and prayed, prayed for a miracle as their feet bled and they shivered, sweat turning to ice on their trembling flesh…

Something huge moved above them and Nienna felt a great presence in the trees, as if a giant stalked the forest and the canker growled, screamed, and leapt, and there were sounds of scuffling, of claws scrabbling wood and jaws clashing with metallic crunches and then a mammoth, deafening, final *thud*. The forest shook, as if by a giant's fist.

Silence curled like smoke.

Nienna and Kat, both trembling, looked at one another.

What happened?

To the canker, but also… out there?

There came a series of sudden hisses, and clanks, and then silence again. Whatever had happened to the canker it had been immediate, and final. Some giant predator? A bear, maybe? Nienna shook her head at her internal monologue. No. A bear couldn't have killed the – thing – that pursued them. So what, then?

"Come on, let's move," whispered Kat.

Something huge and terrible reared above them in the darkness, smashing branches and whole trunks in its ascent and making Kat scream out loud, all sense of self-preservation vanished as primeval terror took over and the dark shadow reared above, and roared, suddenly, violently, a deep and massive bass roar without the twisted undercurrents of the canker…

"I know where we are," hissed Nienna, clutching Kat in the shade.

"Where?" she wept.

"Stone Lion Woods," whispered Nienna, her mind filled with horror.

"I'm telling you," said Saark, "it's crazy to head out into the snow!"

"Well, I'm going, aren't I."

Kell opened the door, and stepped out into the storm. It had lessened now, and small flakes tumbled turning the forest clearing into a haze. Kell's eyes swept the dark trees.

"Get your sword."

Saark reappeared in his damp clothes, grumbling, and stood beside the immobile form of Kell in the snow. "What's the matter now, you old goat? Forgot your gold teeth? Left your hernia cushion? Maybe you need a good hard shit?"

Kell turned on him, eyes wide, flared in anger. "Shut up, idiot! There's something in the trees."

Saark was about to offer further sarcastic comment, but then he, too, sensed more than heard the movement. He turned his back on the small hut and faced the trees, rapier lifting, eyes narrowing.

Kell drew his Svian from under his arm, and cursed the loss of his axe. He felt it deeply; not just because it was a weapon, and he needed such a weapon now. But because the axe was… his. Ilanna. His.

"Hell's teeth," muttered Saark, as the albino soldiers edged carefully from the trees, gliding like pale ghosts, their armour shining in shafts of moonlight tumbling between snow-clouds.

"I count ten," said Kell, delicately.

"Eight," said Saark.

"Two archers, just inside the trees, off to the right."

"By the gods, you have good eyesight! I see them!"

"Horse-shit. I wish I had my axe."

"I wish I had a fast horse."

"Very heroic."

"Not much use for dead heroes in these parts."

The albino soldiers spread out, crimson eyes locked on the two men. Kell stepped away from Saark, mind settling into a zone for combat; and yet, deep down, Kell knew he would have struggled even with his axe. With a long knife? Even one as deadly as the Svian? And with his bad knees, and cracked ribs, and god only knew what other arthritic agonies were waiting to trip him up?

He grimaced, without humour. Damn. It wasn't looking good.

"Drop your weapons," said the albino lieutenant.

"Kiss my arse," snarled Kell.

"Superb: weaponless *and* an idiot," said Saark, eyes fixed on the soldiers.

"You can always run back through the woods and jump in the river."

"Now that is a good idea."

They stood, tense, waiting for an attack. The lieutenant of the albino soldiers was wary; Kell could see it in his eyes. He wasn't fooled by an old man and a dandy dressed in villager's clothing. He could see Saark's hair, the cut of his stance, the quality of his rapier. There were too many factors of contrast, and the albino was cautious. This showed experience.

"Ready?" muttered Kell... as something huge, and hissing, with gears crunching and hot breath steaming slammed from the trees and into the midst of the albino soldiers, rending and tearing, ripping and smashing, causing an instant sudden confusion and panic, and the albinos wheeled in perfect formation, swords rising, attacking without battle cries but with a superb efficiency, a cold and calculating precision which spoke more of butchery than soldiering... swords slammed the canker, and two sets of arrows flashed from the trees, embedding in the canker's flanks. Rather than wound the creature, or slow it, it sent the canker into a violent rage and it whirled, grabbing an albino and ripping him apart to scatter torn legs spewing milk blood in one direction, and a still screaming torso and head in the other. More arrows thudded the canker's flanks, and it reared, pawing the air with deformed arms, hands ending in glinting metal claws, and fangs slid from its jaws as its vampire vachine side emerged and it leapt on a soldier, fangs sinking in, drinking up milky blood and then choking, sitting backwards as swords hacked at its cogs and heavily muscled flesh and it spat out the milk, reached out and grasped an albino by the head, to pull his head clean off trailing spinal column and clinging tendons which *pop pop popped* as they dangled and swung like ripped cloth.

"This is our invitation to leave, I feel," muttered Saark.

"Into the woods," said Kell. "I'll wager they've got horses nearby."

As the savage battle raged, so Kell and Saark edged for the trees, then ran for it, tense and awaiting the slam of sudden arrows in backs. They made the tree-line, cold, snow-filled, silent, and behind them howls and grunts bellowed, and swords clanged from clockwork as the canker spun and danced in a twisted spastic fury.

"There." Kell pointed.

They moved through the trees, the sounds of battle fading behind; within minutes the noises were muffled, like a dream from another world.

A group of horses were tethered to a tree by a small circle of logs. Kell untied the reins, and taking four mounts they spurred the remaining creatures and mounted two black geldings, leading the other two along a narrow forest deer-trail.

"Which way?" said Saark.

"Away from the canker."

"A good choice of direction, I feel."

"Seems the wisest, at the moment."

"A thought occurs, Kell."

"What's that?"

"That creature back there. It was different to the last, the one ripped apart in the river. There are… two of the beasts, at least. Yes?"

"Observant, aren't you, laddie?"

"I try," grinned Saark, in the dark of the snow-locked forest. "What I'm trying to say is that, if there are two, maybe you were right, maybe there will be more. And they are not the sort of beasts we can fight with peasant's sword and axe."

"Under the Black Pike Mountains, Saark," Kell's voice was a grim monotone, "there are thousands of these creatures. I saw them. A long, long time ago."

They rode in silence.

Eventually, Saark said, "So, to all intents and purposes, there could be an essentially endless supply of these ugly bastards?"

"Yes."

"Well. That's put a dampener on things, old horse." He followed as Kell switched direction, heading deeper into the forest. Now, the sounds of battle, all sounds in fact, had vanished. Only a woolly silence greeted them. Above, the trees swayed, whispering, false promises murmured in dreams. "By the way, which way are we going?"

"Towards Nienna."

"And you know this because?"

"Trust me."

"Seriously, Kell. How can you know?"

"She has my axe. I can feel it. I am drawn to it."

Saark stared at Kell in the murk. One of the geldings whinnied, and Kell leaned forward, stroking his head, calming him. "There, boy. Shh," he said.

"He's not a dog, Kell."

"Do you ever stop yakking?"

"What's that supposed to mean?"

"Back in Jalder, a neighbour of mind had a shitty yakking little bastard of a dog. All damn night, yak yak yak, with barely a word from the woman to chastise the beast. Many times, the little bastard yakked all night; so one summer, fatigued by lack of sleep, and in a temper I admit, I took down my axe, went around to my neighbour, and cut off her dog's head."

"Is this a sophisticated parable?"

"The moral of my story," growled Kell, "is that dogs that yak all night tend towards decapitation. When I'm annoyed."

"Proving you are no animal lover, I'd wager. What happened to the neighbour?"

"I broke her nose."

"You're an unfriendly sort, aren't you, Kell?"

"I have my moments."

"Was the yakking dog some veiled reference to my own delicate tongue?"

"Not so much your tongue, more your over-use of said appendage."

"Ahh. I will seek to be quiet, then."

"A good move, I feel."

They eased through the night, listening with care for the canker, or even a squad of albino soldiers; neither men were sure who would be victorious, only that the battle would be vicious and long and bloody, and could not end without some form of death.

Suddenly, Saark started to laugh, and quelled his guffaws. Silence rolled back in, like oily smoke.

"Something amuse you, my friend?"

"Yes."

"Like to share it?"

"That damn canker, attacking its own men. I thought they were on the same side? What a deficient brainless bastard! Laid into them as if they were the enemy; as if it had a personal vendetta."

"Maybe it did," said Kell, voice low. "What I saw of them, they had few morals or intelligence as to who or what they slaughtered. They were basic, primitive, feral; humans who had devolved, been twisted back by blood-oil magick."

"Humans?" said Saark, stunned. "They were once men?"

"A savage end, is it not?"

"As savage as it gets," said Saark, shivering. "Listen, old man – how do you know all this?"

"I was in the army. A long time ago. Things… happened. We ended up, stranded, in the Black Pike Mountains and had to find our way home. It was a long, treacherous march over high ice-filled pathways no wider than a man's waist. Only three survived the journey."

"Out of how many?"

Kell's eyes gleamed in darkness. "We started with a full company," he said.

"Gods! A hundred men? What did you eat out there?"

"You wouldn't want to know."

"Trust me, I would."

"You're like an over-eager puppy, sticking your snout into everything. One day, you'll do it to something sharp, and end up without a nose."

"I still want to know. A nose has limited use, in my opinion."

Kell chuckled. "I think you are a little insane, my friend."

"In this world, aren't we all?"

Kell shrugged.

"Go on then; the suspense is killing me."

"We ate each other," said Kell, simply.

Saark rode in silence for a while, digesting this information. Eventually, he said, "Which bit?"

"Which bit what?"

"Which bit did you eat?"

Kell stared at Saark, who was leaning forward over the pommel of his stolen horse, keen for information, eager for the tale. "Why would you need to know? Writing another stanza for the Saga of Kell's Legend?"

"Maybe. Go on. I'm interested." He sighed. "And in this short, brutal, sexually absent existence, your stories are about the best thing I can get."

"Charming. Well, we'd start off with his arse, the rump – largest piece of meat there is on a man. Then thighs, calves, biceps. Cut off the meat, cook it if you have fire; eat it raw if you don't."

"Wasn't it... just... utterly disgusting?"

"Yes."

"I think I'd rather starve," said Saark, primly, leaning back in his saddle, as if he'd gleaned every atom of information required.

"You've never been in that situation," said Kell, voice an exhalation. "You don't know what it's like, dying, chipped at by the howling wind, men sliding from ledges and screaming to their deaths; or worse, falling hundreds of feet, breaking legs and spines, then calling out to us for help for hours and hours, screaming out names, their voices following us through the passes, first begging, then angry and cursing, hurling abuse, threatening us and our families; and gradually, over a period of hours as their words drifted like smoke after us down long, long valleys, they would become subdued, feeble, eaten by the cold. It was an awful way to die."

"Is there a good one?"

"There are better ways."

"I disagree, old horse. When you're dead, you're dead."

"I knew a man, they called him the Weasel, worked for Leanoric in the, shall we say, torturing business. I got drunk with him one night in a tavern to the south of here, in the port-city of Hagersberg, to the west of Gollothrim. He reckoned he could keep a man alive, in exquisite pain, for over a month. He reckoned he could make a man plead for death; cry like a baby, curse and beg and promise with only the sweet release of death his reward. This Weasel reckoned, aye, that he could break a man – mentally. He said it was a game, played between torturer and victim, a bit like a cat chasing a mouse, only the cat was using information and observation and the nuances of psychology to determine how best to torture his victims. The Weasel said he could turn men insane."

"You didn't like him much, then?"

"Nah," said Kell, as they finally broke from the trees and stood the geldings under the light of a yellow moon. Clouds whipped overhead, carrying their loads of snow and hail. A chill wind mocked them. "I cut off his head, out in the mud."

"So you were taking a moral standpoint? I applaud that, in this diseased and violent age. Men like the Weasel don't deserve to breathe our sweet, pure air, the torturing bastard villainous scum. You did the right thing, mark my words. You did the honourable thing."

"It was nothing like that," said Kell. He looked at Saark then, and appeared younger; infinitely more dangerous. "I was simply drunk," he said, and tugged at the gelding's reins, and headed towards another copse of trees over the brow of a hill.

Saark kicked his own mount after Kell, muttering under his breath.

* * *

The sun crept over the horizon, as if afraid. Tendrils of light pierced the dense woodland, and Kell and Saark had a break, tethering horses and searching through saddlebags confident, at least for the moment, that they had shaken their pursuers. More snow was falling, thick flakes tumbling lazy, and Kell grunted in appreciation. "It will help hide our tracks," he said, fighting with the tight leather straps on a saddlebag.

"I thought the canker hunted by smell? Lions in the far south hunt by smell; by all accounts, they're impossible to shake."

Kell said nothing. Opening the saddlebags, the two men searched the albinos' equipment, finding tinder and flint, dry rations, some kind of dried red-brown meat, probably horse or pig, herbs and salt, and even a little whisky. Saark took a long draught, and smacked his lips. "By the balls of the gods, that's a fine dram."

Kell took a long drink, and the whisky felt good in his throat, warm in his belly, honey in his mind. "Too good," he said. "Take it away before I quaff the lot." He gazed back, at the thickly falling snow.

"The question is," said Saark, drinking another mouthful of whisky, "do we make camp?"

"No. Nienna is in danger. If the albino soldiers find her, they'll kill her. We can eat as we ride."

"You're a hard taskmaster, Kell."

"I am no master of yours. You are free to ride away at any moment."

"Your gratitude overwhelms me."

"I wasn't the one pissing about on the bed of a river, flapping like an injured fish."

"I acknowledge you saved my life, and for that I am eternally grateful; but Kell, we have been through some savage times, surely my friendship means something? For me, it's erudite honour to ride with the Legend, to perhaps, in the future, have my own exploits recounted by skilled bards on flute and mandolin, tales spun high with ungulas of perfume as Kell and Saark fill in the last few chapters of high adventure in the mighty Saga!" He grinned.

"Horse-shit." Kell glared at Saark. "I ain't allowing no more chapters of any damn bard's exaggerated tales. I just want my granddaughter back. You understand, little man?"

Saark held up his hands. "Hey, hey, I was only trying to impress on you the importance of your celebrity, and how a happy helper like myself, if incorporated into said story, would obviously become incredibly celebrated, wealthy, and desired by more loose women than his thighs could cope with."

Kell mounted his horse, ripped a piece of dried meat in his teeth. He set off down a narrow trail, ducking under snow-laden branches. "Is that all you want from life, Saark? Money and a woman's open legs?"

"There is little more of worth. Unless you count whisky, and maybe a refined tobacco."

"You are vermin, Saark. What about the glint of sunlight in a child's hair? The gurgle of a newborn babe? The thrill of riding an unbroken stallion? The brittle glow of a newly forged sword?"

"What of them? I prefer ten bottles of grog, a plump pair of dangling breasts on a willing, screaming, slick, hot wench, a winning bet on some fighting dogs, and maybe a second woman, for when the first wench grows happily exhausted. One woman was never enough! Not for this feisty sexual adventurer."

Kell looked back, into Saark's eyes. "You lie," he said.

"How so?"

"I can read you. You have behaved like that, in the past, giving in to your base needs, your carnal lusts; but there is a core of honour in your soul, Saark. I can see it there. Read it, as a monk reads a vellum scroll. That's why you're still with me." He smiled, his humour dry, bitter like amaranth. "It's not about women, wet and willing, nor the drink. You wish to warn King Leanoric; you wish to do the right thing."

Saark stared hard at Kell, for what seemed like minutes, then snapped, "You're wrong, old man." His humour evaporated. His banter dissolved. "The only thing left in my core is a maggot, gorging on the rotten remains. I drink, I fuck, I gamble, and that's all I do. Don't think you can see into my soul; my soul is more black and twisted than you could ever believe."

"As you wish," said Kell, and kicked his horse ahead, scouting the trail, his Svian drawn, a short albino sword by his hip on the saddle sheath. And ahead, Kell smiled to himself; finally, he had got to Saark. Finally, he had shut the dandy popinjay's mouth!

Saark rode in sullen silence, analysing his exchange with Kell. And in bitterness he knew, knew Kell was close to the bone with his analysis and he hated himself for it. How he wished he had no honour, no desire to do the right thing. Yes, he drank, but always to a certain limit. He was careful. And yes, he would be the first to admit he was weak to the point of village idiot by a flash of moist lips, or the glimpse of smooth thigh on a pretty girl. Or even an ugly girl. Thin, fat, short, tall, red, brown, black or blonde, light skinned, freckled, huge breasts or flat; twice he'd slept with buxom black wenches from the far west, across Traitor's Sea, pirate stock with thick braided hair and odd accents and smeared with coconut oil... he grew hard just thinking of them, their rich laughter, strong hands, their sheer unadulterated willingness... he shivered. Focused. On snow. Trees. Finding Nienna. Reaching Leanoric.

Up ahead, Kell had stopped. The gelding stamped snow.

Saark reined behind, slowing the other two horses, and loosened his rapier. "Problem?"

"This fellow doesn't want to proceed."

Saark looked closer in the gloom of the silent woods. The gelding had ears laid back flat against its head. The beast's eyes were wide, and it stamped again, skittish. Kell leaned forward, stroking ears and muzzle, and making soothing noises.

"Maybe there's a canker nearby."

"Not even funny," said Kell.

"He can sense *something*."

"I think," said Kell, eyes narrowing, "this is Stone Lion Woods."

Saark considered this. "That's bad," he said. "I've heard ghastly things about this place. That it's... haunted."

"Dung. It's dense woodland full of ancient trees. Nothing more."

"I heard stories. Of monsters."

"Tales told by frightened drunks!"

"Yes, but look at the horses." Now, all four had begun to shiver, and with coaxing words they managed another twenty hoof-beats before Kell and Saark were forced to dismount and stroke muzzles, attempting to calm them.

"Something's really spooking the animals."

"Yes. Come on, we'll walk awhile."

They moved on, perhaps a hundred yards before Kell suddenly stopped. Saark could read by his body language something was wrong: he had seen something up ahead. And he didn't like it…

"What is it… oh." Saark stared at the statue, and his jaw dropped. It was thirty feet high, towering up between the trees. It was old, older than the woodland, pitted and battered by the elements of a thousand years, sections covered in moss and weeds, lichens and fungi; and yet still it stared down with a menacing air, a violent dominance.

"What's it supposed to be?" questioned Saark, tilting his head.

"A stone lion, perhaps?" muttered Kell. "Hence, Stone Lion Woods."

"I've never seen a lion look like that," said Saark. "In fact, I've never seen a lion. Not in the flesh. Apparently, they are terrifying, and stink like the sulphur arse-breath of a cess-pit."

"It is a lion," said Kell, voice low, filled with respect. "Only it's twisted, deformed, reared up on hind legs.

Look at the mane. Look at the craftsmanship in the sculpted stonework."

"I'm more interested in whether it'll topple on us. Look at those cracks!"

The two men watched the statue, a hint of awe in their eyes, hands stroking the skittish horses, calming the beasts with soothing murmurs. A little snow had filtered through the canopy of Stone Lion Woods, and sat on the statue, shining almost silver in the gloom. The effect was ghostly, ethereal, and Saark shivered.

"I don't like it here. The rumours speak of terrible beasts. Ghosts. Hobgoblins. Were-dragons."

"Horse-shit. Come on. I feel my axe; she's getting close."

Saark looked oddly at Kell. "You can really sense the weapon?"

"Aye. We are linked. She's a bloodbond weapon, and that means we are joined, in some strange way I cannot explain, nor understand."

"A bloodbond. I have heard of such things." Saark closed his mouth, reluctant to speak more. The tales and legends of bloodbond magick were dark and fearful indeed: stories used to frighten little children. Like the Legend of Dake the Axeman; he was huge and shaggy, with the grey skin of a corpse and glowing red eyes. Dake would creep down the chimney of bad little boys and cut off their hands and feet in the night. If they were really bad, Dake would take the child with him, back to the Tower of Corpses where he'd hang the child in a cage from the outside wall and let Grey Eagles eat their flesh. Even now, Saark remembered his father scaring him with such stories when he'd been a bad boy: when he'd slapped his sister, or stolen one of his mother's fresh-baked pastries.

For years, such nightmares had been erased from Saark's memory. Now, especially in this caliginous and eerie place, watched over by a twisted stone statue, the horror of those dark tales from childhood crept back into Saark's sparking imagination. He remembered all too clear huddling under thick blankets watching the twitching shadows on the walls... waiting for Dake the Axeman to come for him.

"Are you all right?" said Kell.

"I was just... thinking of my childhood."

"Were they happy times, aye?" said Kell.

Saark pictured running into the house holding a kite he'd made to find his father swinging from a high rafter by the neck, his face purple, one eye hanging on his cheek. There was dried blood around his mouth, his tongue stuck out like some obscene cardboard imitation. Taking a bread knife, he'd cut down the dead man and sat with him, rocking his head, holding his stiffening hands until his mother arrived home... with the city bailiffs, ready to repossess their family home. There had been no sympathy. A day later, they were walking the streets.

"Happy, yes," said Saark, banishing the memories like extinguishing a candle. Strange, he thought. To resurrect them here, now. He'd locked them away in a deep, hidden place for decades. Saark coughed, and tugged at the horses. "Come on. Let's move. This place gives me the shits."

"You sure you're well?" asked Kell. He appeared concerned. "You looked, for a moment there, like you'd seen a ghost."

Saark pictured his father, swinging. "Maybe I did," he said, voice little more than a whisper; then he was gone, striding down a wide, twisting trail and Kell tugged his own mount forward. The gelding gave a small whinny of protest, and moved reluctantly.

"That's not good," muttered Kell, sensing a change in Saark's mood. "Not good at all."

They moved through the woods, deep into gloom for an hour, gradually picking a route over roots and branches, through a mixture of junipers, Jack Pine and Tsugas, through rotting leaves from towering twisted oaks and thick needle carpets from clusters of Red Cedar. The woods were old here, ancient, gnarled and crooked, and huge beyond anything Saark had ever witnessed.

Reaching a natural clearing, Saark halted and gazed at the array of statues, his mouth dropping open. There were seven, arranged in a weird natural circle as if the trees themselves were wary to set root and branch near these twisted effigies.

"What," he said, "are those?"

"The Seven Demons," said Kell, quietly. He placed a hand on Saark's shoulder. "Best move quietly, lad. We don't want to upset them."

"What do you mean by that?"

"Blood-magick is an old beast, no matter what the vachine think. It goes back thousands of years. When you've travelled as much as I, you learn a few things, you see a few things; and you begin to understand when to keep your head down."

"You've been here before?"

"Yes."

"So, is this place haunted, then?"

"Worse, laddie, so let's just be quiet, move quickly, get to Nienna and hope we don't upset anything."

"That sounds ominous."

"It can only get worse, trust me. The Stone Lion Woods didn't garner their savage reputation through idle banter, drunken discourse or the loose tongue of a happy mistress." Kell grinned at Saark, and at his contradiction. He could see it in Saark's eyes... you've conned me, thought Saark. Kell shrugged. "Follow me close, lad. And keep your puppy yelps to yourself."

They moved through the circle of statues. Some were big, incredibly old, unrecognisable in their shape or form, weathered, battered, broken, and covered in fungus and moss. Two of the statues were man-sized, a stone representation of twisted, unfathomable monsters; a third was a man, tall and proud, regal almost; another was a lion, and another... something else entirely. A final statue was small, only knee high, and reminded Saark of a deformed embryo, only a touch bigger, and stood on hind legs with joints reversed like those of a dog. He shivered. He felt curiously sick.

They plunged back into the woods, Kell following his senses, although Saark wondered if Kell was crazy and simply navigating a random path. Regularly Saark checked his back-trail, for albino soldiers, or worse, the cankers which seemed to be hunting them. They walked all day, sometimes slowing to squeeze through narrow sections of tangled branches, and leading the skittish horses with care.

The night fell early, and again the two warriors came upon a circle of seven statues at dusk. Saark began to get twitchy, jumping at lengthening shadows as the trees crowded in, gnarled and crooked, limbs reaching over them, towards them, brushing at faces and clothing, dropping their lodes of snow to the woodland carpet.

Kell stopped. "We'll leave the horses here," he said. They were beside a narrow cross-roads, trails probably formed by wild deer, badgers and boars.

Saark nodded. "Is Nicnna close?"

"Ilanna is close. I'm hoping the girl is with her."

"You mean your granddaughter."

Kell stared at Saark. "That's what I said."

They carried on, on foot, until they came to a long corridor in the thick woodland; it was almost rectangular and walled with evergreen leaves and pine branches, holly and juniper and hemlock entwined with honeysuckle and creepers. The air was thick with resin and woodland perfume, cloying, a heady aroma, and Nienna and Kat were both seated on a thick fallen log.

"Nienna," said Kell, his voice low, barely more than a growl. His eyes fixed on Ilanna, resting beside the girl; and then transferred back as she turned. Her face was frightened, skin tight, eyes wide; she mouthed at Kell, and he frowned, trying to make out the words.

Saark crept up beside Kell, crouched at the edge of the leaf corridor. He frowned. "What's she trying to say?"

His words, although quiet, reverberated down the natural sound channel. Nienna stood up suddenly and grasped Kell's axe in tiny hands, turning away from the men towards a distant clearing, rich in its greenery. Something began to click, like pebbles dropped on boulders, and Kell stood and launched himself down the corridor towards the two girls... beyond, almost out of sight but hinted at, it rose hugely from the ground, earth and dead leaves and brown pine needles tumbling around the *thing* as it detached from the woodland floor and huge grey limbs unfolded to reveal fists, each the size of a man, and twisted limbs only barely reminiscent of the lion it had once represented...

"It's a Stone Lion," shrieked Nienna as Kell reached her, took her in his hands, shook her.

"Are you injured?"

"No! It saved us! Saved me and Kat from the canker!"

A noise began to *thrum* through the woods. It was ancient, if a noise could be such a thing, primeval, not really words but music, a song, a song made from stone and wood and fire, and it rose in pitch and volume until it was a roar and Kell glanced back, saw the fear in Saark's eyes, could hear the whinny of their tied horses struggling at tethers and he took his axe, his Ilanna, and she melted into his hands like warm soft female flesh, and she was there with him and his agitation and fear fled and Kell was whole again, a total being and he realised, in that crazy snapshot of time how his addiction and his need was rooted deep down in his skull, his bones, his blood, his soul, and Ilanna was his saviour; and more, also his curse.

"It said it would kill you," hissed Nienna, her eyes not on Kell but the creature still rising from the earth at the end of the tunnel. "It said we were protected by the forest, because of our… innocence. But it knew you would come, you and Saark; it said you were defiled. Abused. You were not creatures of the Stone Lion Woods. It said it would eat you, like it ate the canker…"

"Go to Saark," said Kell, his face grim, and grabbed Kat, pushing her after Nienna and both girls fled along the green corridor. A cold wind blew, filled with the smell of ice and leaves, of rotting branches, of sap, of mouldy pines and wild mushrooms and onions.

Kell grasped Ilanna, and faced the Stone Lion.

Its roar died down, and it stooped low, stepping into the corridor. It was five times the height of a man, twisted, a merged and joined creation of stone and wood, earth and trees, and primal quartz; it was a carved thing, a live thing, a demon of the deep woods, a spirit of the darkness, and its face, despite being a worn weathered blur of stone and wood, looked down at Kell and he could have sworn it was grinning.

He glanced back. Tightened his grip on his axe. "Saark!" he roared. "Get to the horses! Get the girls out of here!"

Saark nodded, and they fled.

Kell turned back, faced the Stone Lion. It growled, a long, low, permanently mewling sound, and took a few tentative steps, as if testing its legs worked. It lowered its head then, spine crackling, and roared at Kell with a hot blast scream which stank of rotting wood, sulphur, onions and death.

Kell's beard whipped about him, and he ground his teeth, face dropping into a snarl.

Give me your blood, said Ilanna. Her voice was sweet music in his mind, but Kell steeled himself, for he knew the deception, knew how this thing worked; he had been tricked before, had been used before by Ilanna... and it had led to terrifying results.

"You know I cannot."

You will *not!*

"I remember the last time," he muttered, as the Stone Lion took another step forward on twisted legs, sizing him up, its eyes falling on the axe in his hands, its head tilting to one side, almost... inquisitive.

It's going to crush me, he thought.

How can I fight something that... big?

It will be different this time, promised Ilanna. *I will be good. I promise you. I will smash this puny creature of blood-oil magick, of the forest and the soil. I will not... abuse you, Kell. I know I injured your mind, and your pride. It will be different this time!*

"No."

The Stone Lion charged, the ground thundering, and Kell stood his ground, axe raised, eyes narrowed, mouth a grim, sour, dry line and it smashed towards him, and at the last moment he rolled, felt the Stone Lion's huge bulk slam past and the axe sliced one leg, a butterfly blade exiting with chunks of stone and wood splinters. Kell's shoulder hit the earth, he rammed the wall of the green lane, was spun around by the incredible force, and with a grunt he gained his feet, watched the Stone Lion stumble, skid, turn, and lower its head towards him. He hefted Ilanna, moving

to the centre of the trail, studying the way the Stone
Lion carried itself; he'd injured it, damaged it in some
way, but it had not screamed. There was no blood.
Now, in silence, it advanced, more slowly, and its huge
long arms came thumping towards Kell and he
swayed back, fast, a stone-like fist whirring a hand's-
breadth from his face and his axe slammed the arm
but glanced off, nearly wrenching Kell's arms from
sockets. He skipped back avoiding another blow, then
the Stone Lion surged forward and Kell was backing
away, his axe ringing from arms and fists as he deflected blow after blow, his own arms jarring with
every strike of the axe-blade, but the Stone Lion was
tough, its skin like stone and Kell realised its legs were
its weakness; he ducked a whirling appendage, then
rolled under its reach towards the thick trunk-like
legs. Ilanna sang in his scarred hands as he cut chunks
from the Stone Lion's twisted timber shins, embedded
one butterfly blade in a thigh with a clunk and
wrested it free as the Stone Lion caught him in the
chest with a blow, accelerating him down the green
lane to tumble, and lie on his chest, panting, before
scrambling to his feet and lifting his axe with a grimace.

The Stone Lion was gazing down at itself, at its
damaged legs. It looked up, glared at him, and let out
a high-pitched roar that made Kell shudder. But he
stood his ground, and glimpsed a thick yellow liquid
oozing from the cuts and slices he'd inflicted. The
Stone Lion took a step forward, then went down on
one knee. It stood again, grasping the lane to heave
itself up.

Kell decided this was the right moment.

He turned and ran, stampeding through leaves and dead pine, listening for pursuit from the massive creature of legend. As he reached a thick section of woodland he risked a glance back, but the Stone Lion still stood its ground, glaring at him, its chest... heaving? Heaving, or laughing. Kell was unsure which. Then he blinked, and realised the wounds he had so skilfully inflicted were healing, the thick yellow liquid had hardened, formed a shell over the cuts like hardening sap.

Kell fell into the woodland; only then did he hear the pursuit, the thump thump thump of a heavy pendulous charge, and the ground was shaking beneath him and fear filled him up like a jug. He realised he could not kill it... unless he gave control to Ilanna. He scowled. That would only happen over his dead body.

Run! If he could reach the horses, he could outrun the Stone Lion. Perhaps.

He charged on, branches slamming his face and arms, the Stone Lion in pursuit. He reached the crossroads where they'd tethered the horses, and for a second was flooded with relief, for Saark and the young women were nowhere to be seen; they had fled, were gone, were safe. His sacrifice had bought them time. Only, now... he frowned. All the horses were gone. Which meant he was... on foot.

"Saark, you dandy bastard!"

A roar echoed through the trees behind, and Kell cast about; Saark had headed south, as they'd discussed, to reach King Leanoric, warn him of events in

Jalder. Kell sprinted down the trail but the recent fighting, lack of sleep, and the curse of age and inactivity hit him like a cobble. He faltered within a hundred yards, was streaming with sweat after two. The Stone Lion still pursued. It ceased its bestial roar, but Kell could hear the thump of heavy steps... how could he not? He grimaced.

"Horse-dung," he muttered. He was going to die here.

Ahead, through heavy snow, the trees grew thinner and a fantasy entertained Kell; maybe he was by the edge of Stone Lion Woods? Maybe there was a boundary to the Stone Lion's territory, beyond which it could not pursue? Blood-oil magick worked like that, sometimes...

But there was no guarantee.

Kell laboured on, and could hear the Stone Lion growing closer, and closer, a dark shadow behind, a black ghost in the trees. Kell stopped, wheezing, red lights dancing in his brain. He hawked, and spat a lump of phlegm to the woodland floor.

A high roar, bestial, like a choking woman, made him jump and surge forward... as growls up ahead made him skid to a halt, confused. Through the trees, Kell saw the shape of a canker. Something died inside him. He was trapped. By all the gods! Trapped!

"Not good."

His eyes narrowed, as the first canker was joined by two more, all three different shapes and sizes, but each with a wide-open head showing cogs and gears clicking and moving. Kell glanced back. The Stone Lion was there, advancing on him. He could see its legs now, and no wounds were visible… it had completely healed.

Kell sprinted, axe tight in sweat-slippery hands, and the cankers saw him; with spastic jerks of deformed and bloated heads, they let out vicious, triumphant growls and howls and thuds of accelerating, deviated twisted clockwork with bunched muscles run through with lodes of silver-quartz, and with snarls they leapt to the attack… and in a whirling chaos of confusion, with the Stone Lion roaring behind, and the smell of hot canker oil in his nostrils, Kell narrowed his eyes and lifted his axe in the eerie snow-brightened woodland where snow flurries drifted and swirled, and as panic detonated around him he leapt at the cankers and brought the singing, glinting blades of Ilanna around in a savage downward sweep…

NINE
Army North

Leanoric sat his charger on the hill just outside the ruins of Old Valantrium, and thought about his father. To the northeast, he could see the distant gleaming spires of Valantrium, one of Falanor's richest, most awe-inspiring cities, constructed by the finest architects and builders in the land, its streets paved with marble painstakingly hewn from the Black Pike Mines in the south-west of the staggering and awe-inspiring mountain range.

What would your father do? he thought, and despair settled over him like a cloak.

Leanoric turned his charger, gazing west. He could just make out the gleaming cobbles of the Great North Road, which some called his finest creation. A single, wide avenue, it ran for nearly sixty leagues through hills and valleys, through forests and moorland, dissecting the country and linking Falanor's capital city Vor in the south, with the major northern university city of Jalder. The Great North Road was an artery of trade and guaranteed protection, patrolled by Leanoric's soldiers. It had been successful in banishing thieves, solitary highwaymen and outlaw brigands, sending them either further north into the savage inhospitable hell of the Black Pike Mountains, or south, across the seas to worry other lands.

What would your father do?

Leanoric rubbed his stubble, evidence of three days in the saddle, and turned his charger again, scanning for his own scouts due back from Old Skulkra and Corleth.

The rumour, delivered by an old merchant on a half-dead horse, had sent prickles of fear lacerating Leanoric's spine and scalp.

Invasion!

Jalder, invaded!

Leanoric smiled, a bitter careful smile, and placed his Eagle Divisions in his mind; he had twin regiments of eight hundred men each camped on Corlath Moor, three days march from Jalder; he had a further battalion of four hundred men stationed at the Black Pike Mines at the west of the range, maybe a week's march, longer if the coming snows were heavy. Further north, he had a brigade of sixteen hundred infantry near Old Skulkra, and close to them a division of five thousand led by the wily old Division General, Terrakon. And another brigade to the east of Valantrium Moor, on manoeuvres.

Within two weeks he could muster another four brigades from the south of Vor, and descend on Jalder with nearly twenty thousand men – the entire Army of Falanor. Twenty thousand heavily armed, battle-trained soldiers, infantry, cavalry, pikemen. But… but what if this was nothing more than the ravings of some drunken, insane old merchant? Some bastard high on blue karissia, frothing at mouth and veins, and with his speculative fear putting into action the slow mechanical wheels of an entire army's mobilisation?

It had not escaped Leanoric that winter was coming, and thousands of soldiers were looking to return to their homesteads. Leanoric had already delayed leave by three days; every hour, he felt their frustration growing, accelerating. If he didn't release his northern armies soon, they could become trapped by snow as the Great North Road became more and more impassable. Then, Leanoric risked insubordination, desertion, and worse.

Leanoric ground his teeth, sighed, and tried to relax. If only his scouts would bring news!

It was a bad joke, nothing more, he told himself. The garrison at Jalder was more than able to cope with raiding brigands from the Black Pike Mountains; with outlaws, rogue Blacklippers and the occasional band of forest thugs.

Leanoric considered the old merchant, who even now was being tended by Leanoric's physicians in his own royal tent. The man could no longer speak, his skin burned and peeling as if half cooked over a fire. Eyes wide, the man – they still had not established a name – had ridden in on a horse which promptly collapsed and died, ridden to death, iron-shoes down to the hoof, foam ripe on mouth and nostrils. The tortured merchant had babbled, incoherently at first, then delivered his news in fits and starts between wails for mercy and cries for the king to spare his life. It had been... Leanoric searched for a word... he sighed, and ran a hand through his short, curled golden hair. It had been distressing, he thought.

So. What would his father have done?

Leanoric considered the former king, dead now the last fifteen years. After a lifetime as Battle King, a warrior without peer, huge and fast and fearless, a man to walk the mountains with, a man with whom to hunt lions, Searlan, King of Falanor, at the age of fifty six had been thrown from his horse and broke his neck and lower spine. He'd hung on grimly for three days as specialist physicians and the skilled University Surgeon, Malen-sa, tended him; but eventually the life-light, the will to live, had faded from his eyes as his paralysed limbs lay limp, unmoving, and understanding sank as if through a sponge to penetrate his brain. He would never walk again, never ride a horse, never hunt, dance, make love, fight. In those last few days, as realisation dawned, Searlan had lost the will to live; and had died. The physicians said, eventually, after much consultation, that death had occurred through internal bleeding. Leanoric knew this to be untrue; it had been his own blade that pierced his father's heart, at Searlan's request, one stormy night as Leanoric sat by the bedside holding back tears.

"Son, I will never walk again."

"You will, father," said Leanoric, taking the old man's hands.

"No. I understand my fate. I understand the reality of the situation; I have seen these injuries on the battlefield so many, many times. Now my turn has come." He smiled, but the smile shifted to a wince, then a gritting of teeth as he fought the pain.

"Can you still not feel your toes?"

"I can feel my heart beating, and move my lips, but my fingers, my toes and my cock all remain out of my control." He laughed again, although he struggled to perform even that simple function. "I am lucky I can still talk to you, my son. Lucky indeed."

Leanoric squeezed his fingers, although there was no movement there, no return pressure.

"I love you, father."

Searlan smiled. "You've been a good boy, Leanoric. You've made me proud, every single day of my life. From the moment the midwife brought you squealing from your mother's cut womb, covered in blood and mucus, your tiny face scrunched up in a ball and your piss carving an arc across the room – to this moment, here and now, there has been nothing but joy."

"There will be more joy," said Leanoric. Tears filled his eyes. His throat hurt with unspent sorrow.

"No. My time in this world is done."

"Let me fetch mother."

"No!" The word was like a stinging slap, and stopped Leanoric as he rose from the stool. "No." More gentle, this time. "I cannot say my farewell to her; it would break my heart, and hers too. It must be this way. It must be death in sleep."

Leanoric stared hard into his father's eyes.

"I cannot."

"You will."

"I cannot, father."

"You will, boy. Because I love you, and you love me, and you know this is the thing that must be done. I would ruffle your hair, if I could; even that simple pleasure is denied me."

"I cannot!" Now, he allowed tears to roll down his cheeks. Leanoric, rarely bested in battle, the son of the great Battle King who had led a charge against the Western Gradillians, suffering a short-sword blow to the head which cracked his skull allowing shards to poke free – and never uttered a whimper. Now, he allowed his fear and anguish to roll down cheeks from eyes far too unused to crying.

"Let it out, son," said Searlan, kindly. "Never be afraid to cry. I know I used to tell you the opposite," he coughed a laugh, "but I was making you strong, preparing your for kingship. You understand, boy, what I ask of you? It is not just for me; it is for all of you, and for Falanor. The land needs a strong king, a leader of men. Not a dribbling old fool in a chair, unable to wipe his arse, unable to ride into battle."

Leanoric looked into his father's eyes. He could find no words.

"Take the thin dagger, from the chest behind you. I have a wound, here on my chest, from fencing with Elias a few days ago; by gods, that man is fast, he will be a Sword-Champion one day! I want you to pierce my heart, through the wound. Then plug it using cotton, don't let blood spray anywhere. It will look like I died in my sleep; that my heart stopped beating."

"I cannot do that to you, father. I cannot..." he tasted the word, "I cannot murder you."

"Foolish pup!" he raged. "Have you not listened to a single word I said? Be strong, damn you, or I will get one of the serving maids to do it, if you have not the mettle."

Leanoric stood, unable to speak, and took the dagger as instructed. He took a cotton cloth, and placed it over his father's heart. Then, looking down into the old man's eyes, he watched Searlan smile, and mouth the words, "Do it," and he pressed down, his teeth grinding, his jaw locked, his muscles tensed as Searlan spasmed, gritted his teeth, and with a massive force of will did not cry out, did not weep, did not make any other sound than a whispered… "Thank you."

Leanoric cleaned the blade, replaced it on the chest, cleaned his father's wound using a sponge and water, and replaced the old bandage over Elias's original sword strike. Then, slowly, his hands refusing to work properly, he pulled the covers back over Searlan's body. Gently, he reached down and closed his father's eyes, silently thanking him for being a hero, a great king – but most of all, the perfect father.

Now, sitting atop his charger with the weight of the country across his own bowed shoulders, Leanoric took a deep breath and wiped away a tear at the memory. I hope, he thought, I will have such courage at the time of my own death.

A horse galloped towards him. It was Elias, Sword-Champion of Falanor and Leanoric's right-hand man, general, tactician and adviser. Elias saluted, and rode in close. "One of your scouts is approaching, yonder."

"From Jalder?"

"No, he wears the livery of the Autumn Palace."

"Alloria?" Leanoric frowned; it was rare Alloria troubled him when out with the army. She would only send a rider if there was… an emergency. Coldness and dread swept through him.

The horse, heavily lathered, ran into camp and Leanoric, with Elias close behind, spurred his mount towards the rider. Soldiers helped the rider dismount, and as the person practically fell from the saddle it was with shock they realised it was a woman, in a tattered, torn, bloodstained dress. She wore the livery colours of the Autumn Palace; but beneath that, she wore defeat and desolation.

"Gods, it's Mary, Alloria's maid!" She looked up, and dirt and despair were ingrained in her skin, and in her eyes. She saluted the king, and dropped to one knee, head bowed, weeping, although no tears flowed. The horror of past hours had bled her dry.

"King," she said, words burbling, body shaking, "I bring bad news."

Leanoric leapt from his horse, and turned to the nearest soldier. "Man, go and get a physician! And you man," he pointed to another, "bring her water." He rushed forward, caught Mary as she went to topple, and found himself cradling the pretty young woman, her face filthy, blood in her eyelashes.

"Who did this to you?"

"The soldiers came," she sobbed, "oh, sire, it was terrible, and Alloria…"

The soldier returned with water, and Leanoric forced down his panic, despite the look in Mary's eyes which made him falter, made a splinter of ice drive straight through his heart. In a strangled voice, he said, "Go on, Mary, what of Alloria?"

"Great king, there has been… an attack. On the Autumn Palace."

"By the gods," growled Elias.

"What of Alloria?" repeated Leanoric, voice quiet, a strange calm fluttering over his heart, his soul. He knew it could not be good. He knew, intrinsically, that his life was about to change for ever.

"She has been taken," said Mary, averting her eyes, staring at the ground.

"By whom?"

"He had white, pale skin. Long white hair. Bright blue eyes that mocked us. He said he was part of the Army of Iron. He said his men had taken the garrison at Jalder... And..."

"Go on, woman!" Leanoric's eyes were burning with fury.

"He has taken Alloria with him."

"What was his name?" said Leanoric, voice emotionless.

"Graal. General Graal."

Leanoric turned to Elias, but the man shook his head. He returned to the shivering form of Mary, and she glanced up at him, pain in her face, in her eyes, then looked away.

"There is more?" said Leanoric, softly.

"Yes. But for you alone. Can we go to your tent?"

Leanoric stood, picking up Mary in his arms and bearing her swiftly through the camp. Fires burned, and he could smell soup, and stew. Men were laughing, bantering, and leapt to their feet saluting at his rapid approach. He ignored them all.

Elias pulled back the tent flaps, and Leanoric laid Mary on a low bed of furs and silk. She coughed, and Elias closed the tent flaps, offering the woman another mug of water which she thankfully accepted.

"Can we speak in private?" said Mary.

Leanoric nodded, their eyes met, and Elias departed. Alone now, with shadows lengthening outside, Mary reached up to Leanoric, put her hand on his shoulder, her eyes haunted in a curious reversal, from subject to monarch, from young to old, from naïve to wise.

"Did they hurt her?" snapped Leanoric. "Tell me! What did they do to her?"

Mary opened her mouth, and some tiny intuition made her close it again. What if, she wondered, Graal's abuse of the queen made her a less than valuable commodity? Maybe, and as she looked into Leanoric's eyes she felt a terrible guilt at her thoughts, but maybe if she told him the truth, told the king of the violent rape by General Graal, maybe he would not want her back at all. After all, it was only a few short years since Alloria's betrayal...

"He... bit her," said Mary, finally.

Leanoric stared at her, without understanding. "What do you mean? He *bit* her?"

"I know it sounds... strange. Metal teeth came out from his mouth, long metal teeth, and he bit Alloria in the throat and drank her blood." Mary closed her mouth, confused now, aware she sounded like a mad woman. She risked a glance at Leanoric. "Graal said he had taken Jalder, he had taken Jangir, and would march on the capital, on Vor. He said if you stood in his way, he would kill Alloria."

"Do you know where he has taken her?" Leanoric's voice was frighteningly soft.

"Yes. She has been sent to a place called Silva Valley, in the heart of the Black Pike Mountains. Graal said it was the home of the Army of Iron. What are you going to do, Leanoric? Will you rescue Alloria? Will you stand against this man who drinks blood?"

Leanoric stood, and turned his back on Mary, his soul cold. He opened the tent flap, ushered in a physician and stepped out into fast-falling dusk. Around the camp laughter still fluttered, and Leanoric had a terrible premonition. Soon, there would be little to laugh about.

"What is it?" said Elias, stepping close.

"Walk with me."

They strode through the camp, past the outlying ruins of Old Valantrium and up a nearby hill on which a beacon fire had been lit. Leanoric pushed a fast pace, and reaching the top, he finally turned to Elias, his face streaked with sweat, his eyes hard now as events tumbled around him, fluttering like ashes, and he set a rigid course through his confused mind. He knew what he had to do.

Jangir had a garrison brigade posting of sixteen hundred men. If Mary was right, if it had been taken… and if Graal had infiltrated as far as the Autumn Palace, and therefore had men in Vorgeth Forest, and could even now be marching with his army on Vorgeth, Fawkrin, or further east to Skulkra and Old Skulkra… Leanoric's mind spun.

How could he not know?

How could he not realise his country was under attack? Infested, even.

"What are we going to do?" said Elias.

Leanoric gave a grim smile that had nothing to do with humour. He pulled on his battle-greaves. In a voice resonant of his father, he said, "Old friend, we are going to war."

Standing there, as the sky streaked with red and violet, as he watched his world, his country, his beloved Falanor die under a blanket of darkness, Leanoric outlined his plan to his general, and his friend.

"These bastards have come from the north, taken Jalder, and taken Jangir. So their forces amass to the west of the Great North Road, somewhere around Corleth Moor, maybe Northern Vorgeth; this makes sense, these damn places are desolate, haunted, and people try not to go there because of the twisted history of Jangir Field. A good place to hide an army, is what I'm thinking."

"What then?"

"I have a brigade at Gollothrim, and a division here at Valantrium. We can pull our battalion down from the Black Pike Mines, and we have a brigade near Old Skulkra. If we can surround the bastards, hit them from each flank and make sure the Black Pike infantry emerge from the north... well, we can rout them, Elias. They'll think the whole damn world has descended on them."

"We need more information," said Elias, warily. "The size of the enemy force. Exact locations. Does this Graal have heavy cavalry, spears, archers? Are his men disciplined, and do they bring siege weapons?"

"There is little time, Elias. If we don't act immediately I guarantee we will be too late. This Graal is a snake; he is striking hard and fast, and taking no prisoners. We did not see him coming. It is a perfect invasion."

"Still, I advise despatching scouts. Three to each camp with your plans following separate routes, in case any rider is captured; we can code the messages, and pick hardy men for the task. I'll also arrange for local spies to scour Corleth Moor; we can send message by pigeon. I have a trusted network in the north."

Leanoric nodded. "With a little more information, and time, we can encompass them. I still only half believe Mary! Who would dare such an outrage? Who would dare the wrath of my entire army?" With twenty thousand men at his disposal, this made Leanoric perhaps the most powerful warlord between the four Mountain Worlds.

Elias considered their plan, rubbing his stubbled chin, his lined face focused with concentration. Internally, he analysed different angles, considered different options; he could see what King Leanoric said made sense, made complete sense; yet still it sat bad with him, an uneasy ally, a false lover, a cuckolded husband, a friend behind his back with a knife in his trembling fist.

"Consider," said Elias, voice as quiet as ever, and as he spoke his hand came to rest on the hilt of his scabbarded sword – a blade no other man alive had touched. "This General Graal cannot be a foolish man. And yet he marches halfway across Falanor to steal the queen; why? What does he gain?"

"He makes me chase him."

Elias nodded. "Possible. Either chase him, or to undermine your confidence. Maybe both. And yet he has already, so we believe, conquered two major cities with substantial garrisons. So he either has a mighty force to be reckoned with, or…"

"He's using blood-oil magick," said Leanoric, uneasy.

"Yes. You must seek counsel on this."

"There is little time. If I do not muster the Eagle Divisions immediately, the entrapment may not work. Then we'd be forced to fall back…" his mind worked fast. "To Old Skulkra. It is a perfect battleground. And I have a… tactic my father spoke of, decades ago."

"But if Graal uses the old magick, your plan will not work anyway," said Elias. "You know what I'm thinking?"

"The Graverobber," said Leanoric, voice sober, voice filled with dread. "I fear he will kill me on sight."

"I will go," said Elias.

"No, I have another job for you."

Elias raised his eyebrows, but said nothing. He knew his king would speak in good time.

Leanoric pursed his lips, lifted his hands to his face, fingers steepled, pressed against his chin. Then he sighed, and it was a sigh of sadness, of somebody who was lost. He spoke, but he would not meet his friend's gaze.

"What I ask of you, Elias, I have no right to ask."

"You have every right. You are king."

"No. I ask this on a personal level. Let us put aside rank, and nobility, for just one moment. What I ask of you, is… almost certain death. But I must ask anyway."

Elias bowed his head. "Anything, my king," he said, voice gentle.

"I would ask you to travel to the Silva Valley." Leanoric paused, as if by leaving the words unspoken, he would not have to condemn his general, would not have to murder his friend. He sighed. He met Elias's gaze, and their eyes locked, in honour and truth and friendship and brotherhood. "I would ask to you find and rescue Alloria."

"It would be my honour," said Elias, without pause for breath.

"I recognise–"

"No." Elias held up a hand. Leanoric stopped. "Do not say it. I am a man of the world, and if I may point out, far more seasoned a warrior than you." He smiled to take the sting from his words. "I trained with your father, and I admired your father; but I love his son more. And I love my queen. I will do this, Leanoric, but feel no burden of guilt. I do it gladly, of my own free will."

Leanoric grasped Elias, a warrior's grip, wrist to wrist, and beamed him a smile; a grim smile, but a smile nonetheless.

"I will save the country; but you must save my heart-blood. You must find my wife."

"It will be an honour, my friend."

"Bring her back to me, Elias."

Elias smiled. "That, or die trying," he said.

After thirty minutes, Elias was ready to depart. He had a swift black stallion, compact saddlebags and his trusted sword by his hip. He looked down at Leanoric, and the few men gathered.

"Ride swift," said Leanoric.

"Die young," replied Elias.

"Not this time, Elias."

"As you wish."

"Bring her back to me."

"I'll see what I can do, my liege."

He touched heels to flanks. The stallion, a fine, proud, unbroken beast of nineteen hands, needed little encouragement, and with a snort of violence galloped off down a wide cart track, and towards the distance snake of grey: the Great North Road.

Leanoric watched for long, long minutes, long after Elias, his Sword-Champion, had vanished from view. He listened to the night air, to the hiss of the wind, and fancied he could smell snow approaching.

Grayfell, one of Leanoric's trusted brigadier generals, glanced off into the gloom. "There's a storm coming," said the short, gruff soldier, rubbing at his neatly trimmed grey beard. His eyes of piercing yellow met Leanoric's, and the king gave a curt nod.

"That's what I am afraid of," he said.

As dawn broke, Elias stopped by a fringe of woodland and surveyed the Great North Road. It glittered in weak dawn light, wreathed with curls of mist, cobbles gleaming like grey and black pearls. For long minutes the king's Sword-Champion watched, listening, observing, analysing, wondering. He eased out from cover, and within minutes allowed the stallion his lead so that he galloped along the cobbles, hoof-beats clattering through the early morning air.

Elias rode hard, all day, pausing only in the early afternoon to allow his horse a long cool drink by a still lake. As he stood, stretching his back and working through a variety of stretching exercises taught to cavalry riders, which he usually reserved for before battle, a few eddies of snow drifted around him and he gazed off to the distant northern hills, and saw the white gathering eagerly like icing on a cake. Cursing, Elias continued north, sometimes running the stallion on smooth grass alongside the hard cobbles, sometimes dismounting and walking the beast. He knew in his heart this was going to be a long journey; a test of stamina, and endurance, as well as strength and bravery. Still, Elias thought grimly, he was up for the task.

That night, camping beneath a stand of Blue Spruce, wrapped in his thick fur roll, Elias came awake as snow brushed his face. His eyes stared up at thick tree boughs ensconced in needles, interlaced above him, rich perfume filling his senses, and beyond at an inky, violet sky. Snowfall increased, and with it a sinking in Elias's breast. The enemy, with Alloria as prisoner, had a good head start. Snow would slow them down; but it would also slow him. He could only pray they were travelling by cart, or on foot; but he doubted it. They'd kidnapped the Queen of Falanor; they would be riding fast horses, hard, to put as much distance between Falanor's Eagle Divisions and their reckless prize. Once they hit the Black Pike Mountains, Elias knew he was doomed. The range was treacherous, the valleys and narrow passes a labyrinth, and once inside their enclosing wings Elias would have lost the queen… and even if he did manage to navigate to this Silva Valley, what would he find there? A waiting army? A division of grinning soldiers? Damn, he thought. He had to catch up with them before the Black Pikes. He had to rescue his queen before she entered the death-maze...

He started before dawn, filled with a rising panic, and an increased level of frustration.

Elias pushed the stallion hard, too hard he knew, and just after noon as more snow fell muffling hoof-beats on the Great North Road, he spied a village and guided his mount from the cobbles, bearing east down a frozen, rutted track. However, a hundred yards from the collection of rag-tag huddled cottages, he halted. His stallion snorted, stamping the snow.

Something was wrong, he could feel it, and a cold wind blew, ruffling his high collar and making him shiver. Unconsciously, he loosened his sword in its scabbard as his gaze scanned from left to right, then back.

Nothing moved. No chickens clucked in the yards, no children squealed, no people walked the street, or stood on corners with pipes and gossip. Elias narrowed his eyes, and dismounted. Feeling foolish, and yet at the same time fuelling his sense of necessity, he drew his sword and dropped his mount's reins. He advanced on the deserted village, sword at waist-height, head scanning for enemy...

And who are the enemy, mocked his subconscious?

The Army of Iron? Halting in its mighty conquest of Falanor to annihilate one tiny, insignificant village?

The answer was yes.

Elias stopped at the head of the main street, and gazed out, and down, across frozen mud and fresh new drifts of snow, at the corpses which littered the thoroughfare. Elias squinted. He'd thought of them as corpses, but as he peered closer, now that he thought about it, they seemed more like...

"Gods!" he hissed, skin freezing on his bones, blood chilling in his veins, eyes wide, lips narrow, sword gripped unnaturally tight. "What in the Nine Hells has caused this?"

He stopped by an old man, face down, frame shrivelled, skin little more than parchment shell over brittle narrow bones. Elias dropped to one knee, crunching fresh snow, and rolled the old man onto his back... only to cry out, stumbling back as he realised it wasn't the corpse of an old man at all, but a young woman, her flesh melted away, skin pulled back over her grinning skull like some parody of decrepitude and death.

Elias stalked down the street, his horror rising, his hatred rising, his rage and anger fuelled to a white-hot furnace by what he saw. And he knew; knew without truly understanding the intricacies of blood-oil magick that this this was a result of the dark art; the old art.

"Bastards," he said, shaking his head, gazing down at children, shrivelled husks, still holding hands. Their faces were far from platters of serenity; they had died in terrible pain, without honour, without dignity, and Elias stared and stared and cursed and spat to one side of the street.

"Is this what Graal has in store for us?" he muttered, considering this Army of Iron and its white-haired general.

Back down the street, a scream rent the air, and it took Elias long slack moments to realise it was his horse. He turned and ran, skidding on ice as he rounded two low-walled cottages, their doors barely high enough to allow a child entry.

The horse was on its side, in the street, quivering as if in the throes of epilepsy. Mist curled in tendrils at boot-height and Elias narrowed his eyes, approaching warily, searching left and right for signs of the enemy. Had it been struck by an arrow? Or something more sinister? He was ashamed to notice that his hands shook.

"A fine beast," came a soft, lilting voice, mature and yet... deranged, to Elias's ears. "Such a shame the source is poor, toxic you understand, for purposes of refinement. Otherwise, we might not have to harvest you."

Elias whirled, sword flashing up, to see a tall creature in thin white robes, delicately embroidered in gold and blue. But it was the face that sent shivers down Elias's spine, and had the hairs on his neck crackling like thin ice over a deep pond. The face was flat, oval, hairless, and incredibly pale. Small black eyes watched Elias with what he considered to be intelligence, and the nose was little more than slits in pale skin. The creature, for this was no man, breathed fast, hissing and hissing and sending more shudders to wrack Elias's body as it suddenly moved towards him, bobbing as it walked, a display which would have been almost comical if it wasn't for the aura of death and the stench of putrefaction which seemed to pervade the creature and its surroundings with every living, breathing pore...

"What are you?" breathed Elias, words barely more than a whisper.

The creature came close. "I am a Harvester, boy. And you are Elias."

"How could you know that?"

"I know many things," said the Harvester, and lifted its hand, the sleeve of its robe falling back to reveal long, bony fingers. "I know you are the friend of King Leanoric. I know you seek his Queen, Alloria, taken by the vile Watchmaker Graal... but all in time, my son, all in time, for you are prime fodder, are you not? And you have information which may aid our cause. Come, come to me..."

Elias leapt, but even as he leapt ice-smoke poured from the Harvester, from its tiny black eyes and open mouth, from its fingers and very core and it slammed Elias, dropping him in a moment, sword frozen to the skin of his fingers, body convulsing and juddering, spastic fits wracking him with a violence he could not have believed possible...

"Let's take away your pretty toy," said the Harvester, stepping close, and Elias saw the skin stripped from his fingers leaving several with nothing more than bone and a few strips of dangling, pink flesh. And as Elias dropped into a descent of terror and disbelief, and pain and raw burning agony, he could still hear the Harvester talking as it worked, and remembered those five bony fingers hovering over his heart... "Come to me now, boy, come to the Harvester, we'll look after you, we'll take you to the Watchmaker and you'll have such a pretty time, you'll have the time of your life..."

* * *

Elias opened his eyes. It was dark, and cold, and wooden walls surrounded him. For a terrible long moment he thought he was in a coffin, buried alive beneath fetid soil with worms struggling to ease through cracks and eat his eyes as he still breathed... a scream welled in his throat, bubbling through phlegm as his hands slapped out, thudding against wood...

"Where am I?" he croaked, realising he was terribly dehydrated, blinking, coughing, and he sat up and realised he wasn't in a box, but a cart, and it bumped over rough ground and he stared down at his hand where two fingers were nothing more than torn and shattered bone, and he screamed, even though there was no pain, he screamed and his screams echoed out through the darkness...

"Quiet!" snapped a soldier, his sword prodding Elias in the chest and forcing him back to his rump in the cart.

Elias said nothing, but cradled his wounded hand and gazed around through veils of red sweet nausea. Darkness and mist filled his vision, and through the vapour like ghosts walked soldiers, ten, a hundred, a thousand, and each one had a pale face and crimson eyes and white hair; their armour was black, and Elias leant forward and vomited into his own lap, and stared for a long time at strings of saliva and puke as he rewound his brain and played through the meeting with... the Harvester? So. He had found the army. But how long had he been unconscious? How far from Leanoric was he now? He could have travelled a hundred miles, or a thousand. No, he thought to himself, staring again at his flesh-stripped fingers. Realisation struck him worse than any axe blow to the back of the head.

His hand was crippled; a deformed relic.

He could no longer hold a sword.

Tears ran down his face then, and all dignity and pride fled him. He knew, deep down, that all men feared something more than all else; each man had a breaking point, whether it be cancer, loss of sight, the death of children or parents. But for Elias, Sword-Champion of Falanor, it was a loss of his right to swordsmanship.

Random images flickered through his mind, and he realised he was delirious.

He was a boy again, practising with a wooden blade...

He was a man, teaching his own children the art of the sword...

He was standing, shivering, behind the curtains as Leanoric killed his father, King Searlan...

Time flowed like black honey; with no meaning. The cart stopped and he was given bread and water, but did nothing more than vomit when it hit his stomach. A harsh voice snapped, "Leave him, if he dies, he dies."

"No. Graal will have the entire fucking army flogged!"

"Damn that Harvester; if he'd done his job a'right, we wouldn't be having these problems." There came a curse in another, guttural, almost mechanical language, and harsh hands with smooth skin forced more water down his throat. This, Elias managed to retain, and after another few miles bouncing in the cart, which he now realised was drawn by two pale, milk-skinned geldings, they halted and Elias was dragged from the platform, his hands bound tight behind his back with thin gold wire which bit his skin and made him cry out… it felt like he was being eaten by insects. Glancing back, he watched the wire moving constantly, with tiny blades, like tiny teeth, all made of copper and brass and continually sawing.

Elias was forced through the camp. They were on high moorland. Trees formed a solid black wall to the north. Above, the stars were obscured by bunching snow-clouds. Mist swirled around his boots. His hand throbbed, fingers stinging him like nothing on earth; and tears still flowed like acid down his cheeks. How had he been taken so easily?

Elias grimaced. If this was the sort of magick they were using, if an icy blast could take out the best Sword-Champion of Falanor in a few seconds of confusion, of utter cold, then this new threat, this new menace, this terrible foe was going to roll over Leanoric's Eagle Divisions like a hot knife through butter.

We're doomed, he realised.

I must get to the king. I must warn the king!

Elias was dropped to the ground, and he realised he was prostrate within a circle of men. He looked up, around at their faces which showed no empathy, no emotion, and then a black armoured warrior, tall and elegant, wearing a black helm obscuring his long, flowing white hair, turned and gazed at him.

"You are Elias," he said. "The Sword-Champion of Falanor."

"I am!" Pride flared in his breast. They could torture him, but he would not talk. He spat at the soldier. "Damn you, what do you horse-fuckers want?"

"I know you think me sadistic," spoke the soldier, looking up at the sky. "You are incorrect. When I punish, I punish without pleasure. When I torture, I torture for knowledge, progression, and for truth. And when I kill... I kill to feed."

"Then kill me, and be done with it!" snarled Elias, fury rising. He tried to surge up, to attack this arrogant albino, but only then did he realise hands pinned his soldiers, holding him to the ground.

"No," said Graal, dropping to one knee and staring into Elias's face. "Today is not your day. This time, it is not your time." He half-turned. "Bring her."

Queen Alloria was dragged, kicking and struggling, to the centre of the circle. She was beaten, her face bloodied, her arms tied behind her back with wire, blood covering her bare arms and wrists and hands. But she did not cry. She held her head high, eyes fierce, and she spat at Graal as she was thrown to the heather. She struggled to her knees and glared at her captors, glared at the albino soldiers around.

"Elias?" she hissed, almost disbelievingly, voice filled with an agony of recognition.

"I came to find you," smiled Elias. "Leanoric sent me. Even now he musters the Army of Falanor. We will wipe this pale-skinned scum from the face of the world!"

"You don't understand," said Alloria, eyes filled with tears.

"Hush now," said Graal, and kicked her in the head, a movement of gentle contrast as he sent her spinning violently to the heather, stunned, blood leaking from smashed lips, mouth opening and closing from the sudden shock of the blow.

Elias looked up. "I'll kill you, fucker," he said.

"Later, later," said Graal, waving the Sword-Champion into silence. "I had bad news this morning. It would appear my... brother, is dead." Graal's crimson eyes were locked to Elias. Elias smiled.

"Good. I hope the maggot suffered."

"He suffered, my boy. He was a twisted vachine, you see. A canker. A creature who could not absorb the clockwork, whose body betrayed his heritage, a living rejection constantly at war with his own internal machinery." Graal sighed. "But I see you don't understand; I see you need... an education."

Graal stood, and waved beyond the circle of soldiers. A handcart was dragged by four men, and aboard it lay... Elias, knelt, was stunned by the vision, his eyes wide, failing to recognise, or at least comprehend, what they saw. It was big, a twisted lion-shape, with pale white skin, tufts of white and grey fur, a huge head split wide with long curved fangs of razor-brass. The body was torn open in places, and Elias could see fine machinery moving inside, tiny wheels, miniature pistons. Elias coughed, and tilted his head, failing to comprehend.

The stench washed over him. Elias vomited on the heather.

Graal moved to the carcass, in two pieces, and placed a hand on bloated flesh. He looked almost fondly into small dark eyes, lifeless now, despite the moving machinery inside the canker's flesh. "Dead, but not dead. Alive, but not alive. Poor Zalherion. Poor Zal. You never thought it would be this way, did you? You never thought it would be like this."

Graal turned, and pointed at the ground. The flat of a blade slammed Elias's head, and he went down with a grunt. Stars spun. He opened his eyes, and heard a sound of hammering as stakes were driven deep into the frozen earth. His hands and legs were staked out, and as he came round he began to struggle. "What are you doing?" he screamed, voice rimed with panic. "What the hell is going on?"

"You will help us," said Graal, voice cool.

"What do you want to know?" panted Elias.

"Not that way. You see," Graal turned, and moved back to the cart. Drawing his sword, he slit the dead canker, his brother, from groin to throat. Skin and muscle peeled back as if the carcass had been un-zipped, intestines and organs tumbled out, most merged with tiny intricate machinery, still moving pistons, still spinning gears. Some parts had tiny legs, and they began to walk rhythmically, like the ticking of clockwork, across the heather... "You see," continued Graal, "when a canker dies, then usually the machine within him dies at the same time. But at times a phenomenon occurs which we do not understand; the machinery becomes parasitical and self sustaining... it lives on after the death of the host, and can be transferred to another living creature. Watch."

"No!" hissed Elias, voice barely a whisper.

"Watch this, it's unique," said Graal, smiling, stepping back as machinery moved across the heather towards Elias's staked out figure.

Pistons whirred, accelerating, as if sensing new blood, new flesh. Gears clicked in quick succession. Wheels spun and golden wires writhed like snakes, flowing through the heather until they reached Elias and crawled up his body as he began to scream, and shout, struggle and kick and thrash but the wires edged up his skin, up his hands and feet and arms and legs, worming under his clothing and dragging behind them small intricate units, machine devices, all clicking and whirring and stepping gears. Wire crawled over his face like a mask, and Elias screamed like a woman, but the wires wriggled into his mouth and wormed up his nose, they squirmed into his eyes making him thrash all the more, screams suddenly halting, a cold silence echoing across the moors as the first machinery unit arrived, scampered up his cheek and wedged into his mouth amidst muffled cries. It forced itself into him, down his throat, cutting off his airways and, subsequently, noises of pain. More machinery arrived, and tiny sharp scalpels sliced the flesh of Elias's belly, opening his stomach wide and amidst spurts of blood and coils of bowel, with tiny brass limbs and pincers they dragged themselves inside him to feed and to merge and to join with his flesh in a union of muscle and artery and machine...

"They're so independent," said Graal, unable to disguise his wonder. "Even as Watchmaker, I do not understand. It is a miracle! A true and awe-inspiring sight, to stand here, mortal, bowed, subservient, and observe this sentience! This metal life! It is a privilege not bestowed by the Oak Testament."

Around him in the mist, albino soldiers stood uneasily, eyes wide, watching the staked out figure of
Elias squirm, their faces forced into neutrality as the
metal-wreathed man, now seemingly more machine
than human, thrashed and struggled, kicking and
wriggling, and thrashing with such violence they
thought he might tear off his own arms and legs...

Alloria opened her eyes, face-down on the heather,
and turned, watching Elias consumed by metal, by
wire and pistons, by gears and cogs. The clockwork
ate into Elias, severing and savouring his flesh like ripe
fruit, entering him, raping him, melding him, joining
him, and Alloria watched with all blood flushed from
pale cheeks, unable to speak, unable to scream, unable to vomit, as Graal stood amiably by and revelled
in the clockwork creating a second-hand vachine.

TEN
Jajor Falls

Kell met the canker head on, both snarling, both leaping through witch-light on the snow-laden woodland. They hammered together, canker claws clashing a hair's-breadth from Kell's face as his axe slammed the beast's neck, and he felt blades bite through thick corded muscle and into whirling clockwork deep within; their bodies thumped together and all was madness; even as they collided, Kell's free hand grasping a huge claw-spiked canker paw, something huge and dark sailed over their heads and the Stone Lion landed snarling, elongated face stretching to roar and with fangs clashing, it collided with the two cankers, and the three figures smashed together, claws raking, teeth gnashing, and blood and wheels went spinning off into the undergrowth. One canker kicked back, crouched, then leapt atop the Stone Lion, fangs fastening on its head. With a massive crunch it bit the Stone Lion's head in two, pulling back, claws fixed in the Stone Lion's torso as it shook its prize like a dog with a bone and the Stone Lion went down on one knee; but even as the canker chewed, spitting out chunks of wood and stone, so the Stone Lion's fist whirred up, over, and down with a *whump* that shook the woodland and crushed the canker into a mewling heap, spine broken, and claws flexed and ripped out its lungs in a bloody spray of mechanical parts and still pumping organs. The Stone Lion smacked the second canker against a tree, as Kell hit the ground, Ilanna embedded in the canker's neck, but a high shriek filled the woodland and the canker turned from Kell, leaping on the Stone Lion's back as its companion attacked the Stone Lion from the front, and both fastened huge jaws on the Stone Lion which spun in a fast circle, long arms flailing, trying to dislodge the beasts from its body.

Kell sat down heavily with a grunt, all energy flushed from him. He pulled out his Svian half-heartedly and watched the raging battle as the Stone Lion charged trees, crushing the cankers against ancient oaks, and the feral twisted vachine deviants retaliated with brass claws, opening holes in the Stone Lion's belly to allow molten fungus to pour free…

Wearily, drained, saddened, Kell rolled his shoulders and neck, only now realising the muscles he had strained, the joints impacted, the huge bruises and many lacerations to his skin. He felt like a pit-fighter after twelve bouts, each one knocking another chunk from his prowess, as well as his sanity. He laughed a little, then, as the roaring went on, and for a few minutes Kell had a ringside seat in the most savage battle he had ever seen.

The two remaining cankers were gradually chewing the Stone Lion to death, cutting chunks from it, attempting to get another premium hold for that final, terminal great bite. Even with half its head missing, the Stone Lion was putting up a good fight, pounding huge fists and claws into the cankers to accompanying shrieks of mis-meshed gears and the thump of compressing flesh. All the time, the wounded canker with no lungs and a broken spine paddled aimlessly in the dead leaves, making a strange mewling sound, not so much expelled air but the pathetic squeaking of a winding-down clock. Kell saw dark blood-oil pump out in a few savage spurts, and eventually the wounded canker was still.

"At least they fucking *die*," murmured Kell, eyes narrow, wary, observing the final performance.

The Stone Lion accelerated backwards, hammering a tree and finally dislodging the clinging canker. It stamped down on the canker's head, pushing it deep under the earth as the remainder of heavily muscled body flopped like a rag-doll, and it turned, searching out the final beast... which bounded to the attack, ducking low under a swipe and catching the Stone Lion in the throat with its fangs, ripping out a huge section of stone- and wood-flesh to reveal narrow tubes, like vines, within. The Stone Lion dropped to one knee, and slammed the canker with a fist, a blow that propelled it into a tree where it snapped a rear leg with a brittle loud crack that echoed through the woodland.

The Stone Lion settled slowly to the ground, forming almost a heap of what now appeared nothing more than an outcropping of stone and ancient wood. It seemed to give a huge sigh, and Kell watched the great, ancient creature die on the woodland carpet. Despite its savagery, he felt almost sad.

The canker trapped under the earth by Stone Lion finally stopped struggling, with Kell's axe poking from the rigid, corded muscles of its throat. Kell stood, walking numbly through the carnage, to place his boot on the carcass and tug free Ilanna.

He turned, staring at the final canker. It growled at him, a feral sound of hatred, and tried to stand. Instead, it fell back in pain and whimpering. Something metallic squeaked in a rhythmical manner.

Kell hefted his axe, and strode to the canker which glared. It lunged, and he dodged back, then planted his axe blade in its neck. He rocked the blade free and blood-oil spurted, along with several coils of wire. Kell hefted Ilanna again, dodged another swipe of canker claws, and with the second strike decapitated the beast.

Blood gushed for a while, then slowed to a trickle. Kell could see the gleam of parts inside the neck, but each cog and wheel was curiously formed, as if kinked, and each piston was bowed or bent, each gear buckled. Kell shook his head; he didn't understand such things. Looking around, he grasped a handful of dead leaves and started cleaning the twin axe blades.

"Old horse! Why didn't you wait for us? You've had all the fun!"

Kell glanced up, gradually, to see Saark leading his horse amidst the flesh and clockwork debris. The clearing – the creatures had smashed the trees into a clearing – appeared as a minor battlefield. Blood gleamed everywhere. The ground was littered with brass and steel clockwork mechanisms.

Kell said nothing.

"It's fine," Saark called back through the trees. "Kell's heroically battled three cankers and the Stone Lion, and managed to kill them all!"

Saark stopped before Kell, who watched Nienna and Kat appear, faces shocked by the carnage. The horses were skittish, and they tied them to a tree by the edge of the battle and moved to Kell. Nienna hugged him, and he smiled then, but his eyes never left Saark.

"I injured the Stone Lion," he said. "Then I ran. But there was no horse for me." There was a dark gleam in Kell's eye, a suggestion of violence in his stance, and Saark noticed Kell did not lower his axe.

"We left a horse for you, old boy," said Saark, voice lowering, humour evaporating. "Didn't we, girls?"

"We left your horse," said Kat, smiling uncertainly, not understanding the tension in the air.

"We did, grandfather," said Nienna, putting her hand on Kell's torn bearskin. "I saw Saark tie the creature myself. He is not to blame if it escaped."

Saark held his hands wide. "An accident, Kell. What, you think I'd leave you to die back there?"

Kell shrugged, and turned his back on the three, gazing off through the trees. His emotions raged, but he took a deep breath, calming himself.

Once, said Ilanna, in his mind, in his soul, *you would have killed him for that.*

I would have questioned him.

No. He would already be dead.

That was in the bad days! he stormed. When I was so drunk on the whisky I didn't know what I was doing. Those were evil days, Ilanna, and you used to fuel me, used to feed me, used to push me towards violence every step of the way, only so you could taste blood yourself, you depraved fucking whore!

Kell turned and faced Saark, and forced a smile. "I apologise," he said, as their eyes locked. "I mistrust too easily. There is a thing called a Fool's Knot – the slightest pressure, and it slips. But of course, you would never use such a thing on me."

Saark grinned. "Of course not, Kell! In fact, I have only now just heard of such a knot, this very moment you mentioned it. Now. We are all exhausted, the girls are frightened, hungry, in a fiery agony of chafing from riding, and I fancy I saw evidence of civilisation only a few short leagues from this very spot."

"What kind of evidence?"

"Traps. Trappers never stray too far from home. Come on, Kell! Think of it! Comfy beds, whisky, hot beef stew, and if we're lucky," he lowered his voice, leaning in close, "a couple of willing buxom wenches apiece!"

"Show me the way," said Kell, and frowned. Saark confused him; he wanted to believe the man, but his intuition told him to plant his axe in Saark's head the first chance that arose. "If it was just me and you, I'd say no. I have a feeling the albino army is moving south; chasing us, effectively. It will destroy every damn town and village it hits, raiding for supplies and destroying buildings in the army's wake so their enemies can't make use. I have seen this before."

"But think of the girls," said Saark, voice lower, playing to Kell's weakness. "Think of Nienna.

Frightened half to death, chased by horrible creatures, forced to fight for her life; she told me she and Kat were captured by evil woodsmen, who proceeded to—"

"Tell me they didn't!" Kell gripped his axe tight, eyes slamming over to Nienna.

"No, no, calm down, Kell. The girls have their integrity. But it was only a matter of time; that Stone Lion you so effectively slew..." Saark peered at the dead creature, frowning, "Gods, did you cut off half its head? Anyway, that Stone Lion rescued them. The woodsmen were attacked by a canker, and the Stone Lion killed the canker. Saved their lives, but damn near frightened them to death! They need time to relax, Kell. They need normality."

"And you need an ale," said Kell, staring hard at Saark.

"I admit, I am a man of simple pleasures."

"Let's move, then."

Kell and Saark walked to where Nienna knelt, examining an intricate piece of machinery. "I don't understand," she said, looking up at the two men. "Are they just monsters? They have... this thing inside them. At school once the teacher took an old clock apart, and it looked like this, with wheels and cogs and spinning parts; only this looks... bigger, stronger, as if it would power a much larger clock."

"It powered something more dangerous than a clock," said Kell, rolling his neck with cracks of released tension.

I can tell you what it is, said Ilanna.

Go on.

It is an Insanity Engine, invented by the forefathers of Leerdek-ka and Kradek-ka, then further refined by those Engineers. We saw creatures powered by these machines under the Black Pike Mountains.

Kell's face coloured, and he ground his teeth. Never mention that, he snarled. Understand? If you ever bring up Pike Halls again, I will cast you into the river! Do you understand me, bitch?

You are still ashamed, then? Ilanna's voice, so beautiful and musical, was little more than a whisper.

Aye. I am still ashamed. Now leave me be; I have two frightened girls to attend to.

They rode in silence through the remainder of the day until evening drew close, and finally emerged from the dense woodland of Stone Lion Woods. Saark scouted ahead, checking for signs of the Army of Iron; or indeed, cankers or any other creature that might take a fancy to the small travelling party.

Kell, Nienna and Kat stood by the edge of the woods, looking out over snowy fields and hills. Saark had been right: distant, a few lights shone, lanterns lit against the fast encroaching darkness.

"I'm sorry," said Kell, at last, facing them.

"What for?" asked Kat, eyes wide.

"For leaving you, on the boat. It was foolish. I should have stayed with you. I should have known when I jumped that you'd be swept away and have to fend for yourselves. That was... foolish of me."

"But Saark would have died," said Kat.

Kell gave a little shrug. "And you two nearly died... and worse, according to Saark. Those woodsmen; I knew them. They were savage creatures indeed, and if the canker hadn't come you would still be there, singing a high sweet tune with skin hanging in strips from your backs and arses." He saw their eyes, wide and pale, and coughed, taking a deep breath. "Sorry. Listen. You stay with me from now on. You understand?"

"Saark will look after us, as well," said Kat, face round and innocent in the failing light. The moon had risen, a pale orb the colour of dead flesh, as the sun painted the low western horizon a dazzling violet.

"Be careful with Saark," warned Kell.

"Don't you trust him?" asked Nienna, surprised.

"I do not know the man," said Kell, simply. "He joined us in the tannery; aye, I saved his life, but that was just me being... human. Instinct. I curse it!" He gave a bitter laugh. "They write poems about you for less, so it would seem."

"He is totally trustworthy," said Kat, nodding to herself, eyes distant. "I know it. In my heart."

"In your heart, lass?" Kell smiled a knowing smile. "I've seen the way he looks at you. And you have, too. But I warn you; don't trust Saark, and especially not like that. He has enjoyed a hundred women before you, and he'll have a hundred women after."

Kat flushed red. "I am waiting for the right man to marry! I am not... for sale, Kell. Saark can look all he wants, I know his ilk, and I know what I want in a man. Yes, Saark is handsome; never have I seen such hair on a man! And he has the gift of the silver tongue, in more ways than one, I'd wager..." Nienna giggled, "but I am proud of my virtue. I know a good man is out there, waiting for me. I do not need your… fatherhood." She narrowed her eyes. "I can look after myself."

"As you wish," said Kell curtly, returning his sweeping gaze to the snowy fields. "But know this. Saark is not a man of honour. He will come for your flesh."

"A man of honour? And I suppose you are as well–"

"What's that supposed to mean?" snapped Nienna, glaring at Kat. "That's my grandpa you're speaking to. The hero of Kell's Legend! Don't you know your contemporary history? Your battle-lore? He saved the battle at Crake's Wall, turned the tide of savages in the Southern Jungles!" Anger flushed her cheeks red. Her fists were clenched.

Kat looked sideways at Kell, who continued to stare across the fields. "It's fine, Nienna," he said, voice little more than a whisper. Then, to Kat, "You're talking about back at the tannery, aren't you lass?"

Kat nodded.

Kell continued, "Yes. I was brutal, brutal and merciless towards you, and I shocked you into movement, into action! If you'd lingered on your injuries, on your fear, you could have killed us all. I could not allow you, even as a friend of Nienna, to be responsible for her death. I would not allow it!" He turned, stared at his granddaughter with a mix of love, regret, and nostalgia. He smiled then. "I would cross the world for you, my little monkey. I would fight an army for you. I would kill an entire city for you. Nobody will get close to you again, this I swear, by the blood-oil of Ilanna."

Nienna moved forward, took his hand, snuggled in close to him. "You don't have to do all that, grandfather." Her voice was small, a child again, nestling against the only father figure she had ever known.

"But I would," he growled. "No canker will get close. I'll cut out the bastard's throat."

"Saark's coming."

They watched him approach, walking his horse with care over snowy undulations. He was smiling, which was a good sign; at least the Army of Iron hadn't rolled through destroying everything in its path. For a long, hopeful moment Kell prayed he was mistaken, prayed to any gods that would listen that he was wrong; but a sourness overtook his soul, and he fell into a bitter brooding.

"There's an inn, with rooms. I've booked us three." He glanced at Kell. "Wouldn't like to put up with your snoring again, old horse. No offence meant."

"None taken; I am equally horrified by the stench of your feet."

"My feet! I am aghast with horror! Oh the ignominy! And to think, we risked mutilation and death to come back for you with a horse. Old boy, we should have left you to eat fried canker steaks for the next week; maybe then you would have learnt manners."

Kell pushed past Saark, leading his own horse. "That's an impossibility, lad. A man like me… well, I'm too honest. A farmer. A peasant. Manners are the reserve of gentry; those with money, those born with silver on their tongue…" Saark smiled, inclining his head to the compliment, "… and equally those with a brush up their arse, shit in their brains, a decadent stench of bad perfume on their crotch, and a sister who's really their cousin, their mother and their daughter all rolled into one. Inbreeding?" He growled a laugh. "I blame it on the parents."

He stalked off, down the hill, and Saark turned to the young women. "Who rattled his chain and collar?"

"He rattled it himself," said Nienna, stepping forward, touching Saark's arm. "Don't be too offended; back in Jalder, he made few friends."

"How many friends?"

"None," admitted Nienna, and laughed. "But he was a wonderful cook!"

"So wonderful he poisoned them all?"

"You are full of charm," said Nienna, breathing a sigh as Saark took her arm. They started down the hill, leaving Kat with two horses, and she scowled after them, eyes narrowing, watching the sway of Saark's noble swagger as he walked, one hand on his hip. He was going home; or at least, to a place of modest civility.

"We'll see who's full of charm," she muttered.

Darkness had fallen as they entered the outskirts of the town, which Saark identified as Jajor Falls. Six cobbled roads ran out from a central square which acted as a hub and market, and there was an ornate stone bridge containing six small gargoyles over a narrow, churning, river. A fresh fall of snow began, as if heralding the travellers' arrival, and they walked tired horses up the snow-laden street, hoof-strikes muffled, looking left and right in the darkness. Some houses showed lantern light in windows; but most were black.

"A sombre place," remarked Kell.

"The inn's livelier."

"What's it called?"

"The Slaughtered Piglet."

"You have to be joking?"

"Apparently, there is a long archaic story of magick and mayhem behind the title. They'll tell us over a tankard of ale." He winked. "You have to admire these peasant types; they tell it like it is."

"Sounds grand."

They heard music before they saw the inn; it came into view, a long, low, black-stone building. Smoke pumped from a stubby chimney, and light showed from behind slatted shutters. Kell led the horses to stables behind the inn, handing them over to a skinny old man who introduced himself as Tom the Ostler. He wore nothing but a thin shirt against the snow, and his limbs were narrow, wiry, his biceps like buds on a branch. He grinned at Kell in a friendly manner, taking the horses, stroking muzzles, staring into eyes, blowing into nostrils. "Come with me, my beauties," he said, and Kell could sense the old man's love for the beasts.

Kell strode back to the inn's door, entered slowly, eyes scanning the busy main room. Tables were crammed in, and full, mainly, of men drinking tankards of ale and talking Falanor politics. A few women sat around the outskirts of the main room, mostly in groups, talking and laughing. Some wore bright dresses, but most wore thick woollen market skirts. Smoke filled the inn, and a general hubbub of noise made Kell gradually relax. Sometimes, it was nice to be anonymous amidst strangers. He looped a long leather thong through the haft of his axe, then over his shoulder, drawing the weapon to his back. Then, he strode to the bar, searching for Saark, Nienna and Kat.

The barman waved at Kell. "What'll it be, squire?" he asked.

"My friend's booked three rooms for the night."

"Ach yes, I just gave him the keys. Up the stairs," he pointed, "rooms twelve, thirteen and fourteen."

Kell grunted thanks, strode up the stairs, and turned on the landing to survey the common room. He made out the gambling table in the corner. Near it were three women, dressed in high stockings, their lips rouged with ink, feathers in their hair. Whores. Kell grunted, eyes narrowing, thinking of Saark and his eagerness. He moved into a smoke-filled corridor and searched for the rooms. Floorboards squeaked under his boots, and this was good. It would be hard to creep down such a passageway.

Locating the first room, he tapped. "Grandfather?" came Nienna's voice, and Kell pushed open the portal, stepping inside, scanning the sparse furnished space. There was a large bed, with ancient carved headboard depicting a raging battle. Thick rugs covered dusty boards, and drawers and two stools lined the far wall. The windows were shuttered. A lantern burned on a table with honey light.

"Cosy," he said, setting down a pack he'd taken from the albino soldier's horse. Then he removed his axe, and stretched broad shoulders. "I hope there's a bath in this place, because I stink, and I hate it when I stink."

"You look like you've had a beating," said Nienna, moving over to him. "I could ask the landlord for some cold cream, to take down the swellings." She reached out, tenderly touched his bruised cheek.

Kell cursed.

"Does it hurt?" said Nienna, concern in her eyes.

"No. It's just people remember a beaten face. I stand out. That's not good."

Nienna nodded. "Shall I go and see if the bathing room is free?"

Kell looked around, then. He frowned. "Where's Kat?"

Nienna shrugged. "I don't know."

Kell moved back to the corridor, walked to the next door with a surprisingly light step, and opened it. Both Saark and Kat were sat on the bed, side by side, just a little bit too close. Kat's laughter tinkled like falling crystals.

Saark looked around, up into Kell's face, and the smile dropped from his features.

"Saark. A word, if you please."

Saark coughed, stood up; Kell saw he had removed his boots. He stepped out. "There a problem, old horse?"

Kell reached past, closed the door, smiling at Kat, then grabbed Saark by the throat and rammed him up against the wall with a thud. Saark's feet kicked for a moment, and Kell lowered him until their faces were inches apart.

"She's not to be touched," growled Kell.

"I don't know what you mean!"

"The girl, Saark. Kat. And my granddaughter, as well, whilst we're having this little man-to-man discussion. Both are not to be… *molested* by you. Do you understand, boy?"

"They're grown women, Kell. They are intelligent, and intuitive. They make their own choices." Saark's smile was stiff.

"And I'm a grown man, telling another grown man that they're little more than children, and if you touch them, I'll break every fucking bone in your spine." His voice was low, but deadly, deathly serious. Saark met his stare with a neutral expression.

"You need to open your eyes, old man. They're far from children. They are roses, blossoming into beauty. They are river currents, flowing out to sea."

Kell snorted, and dropped Saark to the floorboards. "Save your pretty words for the whores downstairs," said Kell. "There was enough good coin in the soldiers' saddlebags to entertain you for a week; take it. But I warn you. Keep away from the girls."

Saark nodded, and brushed down his roughed clothing. He coughed. Stared at Kell, tilting his head. "You finished now, Grandfather? Can I go and get some ale, and a bite to eat? Or would you like to offer a sermon on further corruption and impurity in the world?"

Kell nodded, and Saark moved back to the room. Kell stood, waiting, and Kat emerged, eyes lowered, and hurried into Nienna's room. Kell followed her, retrieving his pack and axe. "I'll meet you down in the common room for food, in about twenty minutes. Aye?"

"Yes, Grandfather," said Nienna. Kat said nothing. Kell grunted and left.

* * *

"How dare he!" raged Kat, a few moments later.

"Shh, he might hear!"

"Damn him, damn him to hell, I don't care! I don't need his protection! I don't need him treating me like his granddaughter, because I'm not, and I've looked after myself far too long to begin adopting an over-zealous guardian now!"

"He... only means well," said Nienna.

"Rubbish! He's jealous! He sees my young limbs, my hips, my ripe breasts, and he wishes he could have a slice of my rich fruit pie. Well, he can't."

Nienna stared at Kat, then. She shook her head. "That's horse-shit, Katrina."

"Maybe so. But Saark says I'm beautiful, and I could take my pick of Jevaiden, Salakarr, Yuill or Anvaresh; and I could make money, lots of money, with my beauty."

"By doing what?"

"I could be a dancer, or escort rich men to the theatre. Saark said they pay a lot of good money to have a beautiful young woman on their arm."

"And in their bed," snapped Nienna. "Are you really that foolish? You'd be little more than a whore!"

"Maybe that's what I want!" stormed Kat, her temper escalating, her fists clenching. "At least it'd be my choice!"

At that moment Saark entered, and stood, smiling at the two women. He was transformed. He wore a fine silk shirt of yellow, with ruffled collar and cuffs of white cotton; he wore rich green trousers made from panels of velvet, high black leather boots, and his long curled hair had been oiled and was scraped back into a loose ponytail. He looked every inch the ravishing dandy, the court noble fop, the friend of royalty. He smiled, and a rich perfume invaded the room, a musky scent of flowers and herbs.

Kat whirled, and her temper died. She smiled at Saark. "You look… ravishing!" she said.

"Where did you get the clothes?" asked Nienna.

"I bought them. From a clothes merchant. I make contacts fast, especially when I enter a new town looking like a diseased cesspit cleaner."

"Kell said for us to keep a low profile."

Saark grinned. "This *is* me keeping a low profile."

"But," said Nienna, choosing her words tactfully, "you look extremely, um, wealthy. And the smell! What is that smell?"

"The perfume of gentry," said Saark. "Popinjay's Musk. It's expensive. Well, ladies, I'm waiting to eat."

"We need to change," said Nienna. "Or at least, to beat the dust from our clothes."

"Wait there," said Saark.

He disappeared, with Nienna and Kat frowning at one another. When he returned, he carried two dresses, one of yellow, one of blue. Both were silk, richly embroidered, and Nienna and Kat clasped their hands together in wonder.

"Saark!" said Nienna. "I don't believe it!"

"They're beautiful," beamed Kat, walking around Saark, her hand reaching out, almost timidly, to touch the silk.

"Only the finest clothes, for such beauty," he said, grinning, his eyes shining, lips moist.

"But we can't wear them," said Nienna, suddenly, smile dropping, lip coming out a little. "Kell wouldn't approve."

"To hell with the old goat. You've been to the Pits of Daragan and back; you deserve a little pampering. I surely couldn't let you go downstairs to eat wearing those tattered rags. It would be... indecent!"

"Thank you, thank you," said Kat, eyes shining.

"Get dressed. I'll meet you down there."

"Did you get anything for Kell?"

"No. If he wishes to look like a beggar in a sack, so be it. He wishes to blend in? Let the old sourpuss blend in. I'm going to have a fine time. We nearly died back there, in Jalder, and on the journey. And I may be dead tomorrow. But tonight! Tonight, ladies, we dance!"

Kat giggled, and Nienna swirled, holding the dress to herself. Saark turned to leave, then whirled about suddenly. He peered out, down the corridor, checking Kell wasn't about to inflict damage on his body again. Then he pulled a vial from his cuff, and handed it to Kat.

"What is it?"

"Perfume. To make you smell as good as you look."

Kat uncorked the vial, and sniffed, and her eyes widened. "But," she said, shrugging, "where do I put it? I've never had perfume before. Old Gran used to say it was the trademark of the whore."

"Pah! Sour words uttered by every damn woman who couldn't afford it. It's called Flowers of Winter Sunset. I once knew a queen who wore it... so trust me, it's special."

"It must have cost a fortune," said Nienna, eyes narrowing. "Or you're full of horse-dung."

"No, it cost a pretty penny," said Saark. "Let's just say the horse I took from the soldier had enough gold coin to sink one of Leanoric's Titan Battleships. So, I cannot take full credit. But enjoy, ladies! Enjoy! I will go and see what paltry food is served on these premises." He stepped forward, took the vial from Kat, tipped the vial to the cork, then dabbed some behind her ears. "Here, princess," he said, smiling into her face. He repeated the action, reached forward, and drew a vertical line down her breastbone, to the dip in her cleavage. "And here," he said, eyes locked to hers. She took the vial from him, then he was gone with a swirl of oiled hair, his rapier flat by his side.

Kat turned to Nienna. Her face was flushed.

"Kell is going to be pissed," said Nienna.

"Saark was right. We've been through *hell* the past couple of days. We deserve a good time."

Nienna shrugged, and sighed. Then she nodded. "Yes," she agreed, and took the perfume bottle from Kat. Mimicking Saark, she dabbed it between her breasts, "And let's put lots here, *you sexy little vixen.*"

Both girls erupted into laughter at her mimicry, and felt tension lift from their shoulders. It was good to laugh. It was good to joke. And for a few hours, at least, ever since the invasion of Jalder, it was good to relax in a safe and secure environment.

Saark caused a stir as he entered the main room, mainly because of his dress, but then because in a loud bellow he announced a round of free drinks for everyone in the room. A cheer went up, and Saark found himself a corner table, the oak planks warped with age. Around the walls were a variety of stuffed creatures, from weasels and foxes to a particularly annoyed looking polecat. Saark sat, sinking a long draught of snow-chilled ale, and allowing his mind to ease.

The second stir occurred when Nienna and Kat entered, in their fine silk dresses, and drew the attention of every man and woman in the room. They moved to Saark, seated themselves, and Saark ordered them each a small glass of port from a bustling server.

"Kell doesn't let me drink," said Nienna, as the server returned holding two glasses. Saark shrugged.

"Well, you're old enough to do what you like."

"What do you think of the dresses?" asked Kat.

Saark gave her a broad smile. "I was stunned upon your entry to the premises; for it was as if two angels, holidaying from the gods, had stowed their wings and glided through gilded windows of pure crystal. The room was diffused with light and effervescence, my nostrils incarcerated by perfume – not just the ravishing scent of wild flowers under moonlight, but the sweet and heady aroma of gorgeous ladies acquiring a friend. You stunned me, ladies. Truly, you stunned me."

Kat was left speechless, whilst Nienna tilted her head, searching Saark's face for traces of mockery. He met her stare with an honest smile, and she realised then he had switched, reverted to a former self, like an actor on the stage. Here, he was at home; revelling in his natural environment. He was a chameleon, he shifted depending on his surroundings. Now he was playing Lord of the Clan, and preening with a perceivable, educated superiority.

Kat laughed out loud, and placed her hand on Saark's knee, leaning forward to say, "You have a beautiful way with words, sir."

"And you have the face of an angel," he replied, voice a little husky.

Kell entered, stalking down the stairs at the far end of the room, and Kat hurriedly removed her hand. Kell eased through the crowded common room, searching, and only spied the group when Saark waved his arm high in the air. Kell strode to them and stood, hands on hips, face full of raw thunder.

"What's this?" he growled.

"A table," said Saark, feigning surprise. "I'm agog with amazement that you failed to recognise such a basic appliance of carpentry."

"The clothes," he raged, "you brightly coloured horse-cock! What do you think you're doing?"

"You would rather the ladies dressed in rags? Showed tits and arses through threadbare holes for every punter to see?"

"No, but… something less… *colourful* would have been appropriate." He lowered his voice, eyes narrowing. "Couldn't you have bought some cotton shirts and trews? We'll be travelling in the snow later; what good are silk dresses then?"

"I have purchased a few normal items, and fur-lined cloaks, Kell, even for you; although I'll wager you'll be as grateful as a rutting dog after a savage castration. Listen, these were all the merchant had. What was I supposed to do? Let them come here with knife rips in their shirts? For I know what would have been the more suspicious."

"Hmph," muttered Kell, slumping to a stool.

Saark turned, and winked at the girls. Kat covered her mouth, and giggled. "Anyway," said Saark, twirling his wrists to allow puffed cotton to flower. "Don't you like my noble attire, good sir? I find it serves when attracting the attention of sophisticated ladies."

"Saark, you're a buffoon, a clown, a macaroni and a peacock! I thought we were travelling to King Leanoric carrying urgent news? Instead, you strut about like a dog with three dicks."

"We are," snapped Saark, "but we can at least have a little fun along the way! Life is shit, Kell, and you have to grasp every moment, every jewel. You go out back and eat with the pigs from their slop-trough if you like; me and the ladies, we are going to dine on meat and sup fine wines."

"No drink," said Kell.

"Why not?"

"We may have to leave fast."

"Bah! You are a killjoy, a grump and a... a damn killjoy! We will drink, the ladies are my guests, and if you have any sense, man, you'll at least have an ale. You look like a horse danced on your face. Admittedly, it improves your savage and ugly looks, but it must hurt a little, surely? A whisky would do no harm, against the pain of injury and winter chill."

"An ale, then," conceded Kell.

The server arrived, a young woman, slightly over-large and with rosy cheeks. Saark ordered the finest

food on the menu – gammon, with eggs and gar-
nished potatoes. He also ordered a flagon of wine, and
two whiskies.

Kell muttered something unheard.

They talked, and Kell surveyed the room. They had
attracted a certain amount of attention with their
fancy clothes, and the act of Saark buying the inn's
population a drink. He was showing he had perhaps
a little too much money; they were certainly marked
as strangers to the Falls.

Little happened before the food arrived. When
plates were delivered, Saark expressed his delight and
tucked in heartily, knife and fork cutting and rising
like a man possessed. The girls ate more sparingly, as
befitted their new image as ladies, and Kell sat, picking
like a buzzard worrying a corpse, despite his hunger,
one eye on the crowd and the door, wondering uneasily at the back of his mind if the albino army was
marching south. And if they were, how far had they
traversed across the Great North Road? Did Leanoric
know of the invasion of Falanor? Did he have intelligence as to the taking of Jalder? Surely he must
know... but only if somebody had escaped the massacre, and managed to get word to him.

Uneasily, Kell ate his eggs and gammon, allowing
juices from the meat to run down his throat. Kell always ate slowly, always savoured his food; there had
been times in his life when he could not afford such
luxuries. Indeed, times in his life when there was no
food to be had, camping in high caves in windy
passes, the snow building outside, no way of making
a fire, no food in his pack... but worst of all, there had

been times far too miserable and brutal to recollect, times

running through dark streets, the only light from fires consuming buildings as citizens cowered indoors screaming flames consuming flesh hot fat running over stone steps and into gutters; charging through streets, blood smeared flesh gleaming in the light of the burning city, axe in hands and blades covered in gore and glory in his mind violence in his soul and dancing along a blade of madness as the Days of Blood consumed him...

Kell snapped out of it. Saark was looking at him. Nienna and Kat were looking at him. He frowned. "What?"

"I said," repeated Saark, rolling his eyes, "are you going to drink that whisky, or stare at it all night?"

Remembering his vision, Kell took the whisky. It was amber, a good half tumbler full – these tiny outpost villages always provided generous measures – and he could see his face distorted in the reflection. He knocked it back in one, then closed his eyes, as if savouring the moment; in reality, he was dreading the moment, for he knew deep down in his heart and deep down in his soul that when the whisky took him, consumed him, he could and would become a very, very bad man...

But not any more, right? He grinned weakly. Those days were dead and gone. Buried, like the burned corpses, the mutilated women, the hacked up pigs...

"Order another," he said, slapping the glass on the oak planks.

"That's my boy!" cheered Saark. He eyed Kell's plate. "Are you going to eat those potatoes?"

"No. Suddenly, I don't feel hungry." He wanted to add, the minute I begin drinking I cannot eat, for all that I want is more whisky. But he did not. Saark reached over and speared a potato, gobbling it down.

"Can't be wasting good food," he said, grinning through mash. "There's village idiots in Falanor starving!"

"You've eaten enough to feed a platoon," said Kell.

Saark pouted. "I'm a growing lad! Need to keep up my strength for tonight, right?"

"Why?" said Kell, as his second whisky arrived. "What's happening tonight?"

"Oh, you know," said Saark, stealing a second unwanted potato. "I feel like a hermit, locked up for a whole month! It's been days since I had a good time. I'm a hedonist at heart, you realise."

"What's a hedonist?" asked Kat.

"A skunk's arsehole," said Kell.

"Funny," snapped Saark, raising his glass. "Here's to getting out of Jalder alive."

Kell lowered his glass. "I don't need to toast that. It's the past. What we should think about is the future."

"No problem," grinned Saark. "Well, let's toast these fine young ravishing women beside us. They are the future!"

Warily, Kell toasted, and Nienna and Kat drank their own glasses of port. Nienna, who had never before experienced alcohol, felt her senses spin. The room was a pond of swimming colours, and warbled sounds and fluctuating smells. Suddenly, her belly flipped, felt queasy, but she fought the sensation for her mind was filled with liquid honey, and Saark was looking surprisingly handsome, now she really thought about it, he was tall and dashing, witty and charming, and when his eyes fell on Nienna she felt her heartbeat quicken and her legs go weak at the knees. She glanced over at Kat, but Kat's topaz eyes were fixed on Saark.

One of the innkeeper's daughters arrived. "You ordered hot water for a bath, sir?" she enquired.

Kell nodded, and stood, feeling the whisky bite him. Damn, he thought. I should never have drunk it so fast! But then, two little whiskies couldn't hurt him, could they? He was a big man, an experienced man, and Saark – damn his fancy ways – was right. It was a miracle they were alive. They deserved at least some normality…

He nodded to Saark. "I need this bath. Don't get in any trouble when I'm away."

"You're right, you do need the bath," agreed Saark. "And don't worry about a thing. I'll look after the ladies. We were considering dessert; some kind of sugared sponge cake, covered in cream. How about it, ladies?"

Kat nodded, licking lips in anticipation. It was rare she got such a treat.

Kell followed the innkeeper's daughter across the crowded room, aware that eyes were on him, curious but somehow… disconcerting. He hated being any centre of attention; the gods only knew, it had happened enough in his life. Usually during combat.

Halting by the stairs, he called the girl back, and checking to see Saark and Nienna weren't watching, told her to bring a bottle of whisky to the bathing room.

"We don't usually…" began the woman.

"I'll pay you double."

"I'm sure it can be arranged, sir," she said, and Kell was gone, stomping up the steps, days of sweat and blood itching him now that a promise of hot water and soap were reality.

After their cake, Saark reclined, patting his belly. "By the gods, I think I've put on a few pounds there."

"Me too," laughed Kat.

"Does port always make you feel like this?" said Nienna.

Saark nodded, and grinned. "How does it feel?"

"I feel like the room is moving. Spinning!"

Saark shrugged. "You'll get used to it. Listen, I have a fancy to go out back to the stables, to check on the horses. Will you two young ladies be fine by yourselves? Feel free to order anything you like to eat or drink."

"We'll be fine," said Nienna, waving her hand.

Saark stood, checked his sword, and left the inn. Nienna missed the meaningful look between him and Kat, and so a minute later, when Kat whispered, "I need to pee, I'm going to the ladies room," Nienna simple smiled, and nodded, and reclined in her own little world of honey and swirling sweet thoughts.

Kat stepped into the snow, but felt no chill. Excitement was fire in her blood, raging in her mind, and she crept around the outer wall of the inn, hearing the noise and banter inside as a muffled backdrop, a blur of sounds rolling into one strange, ululating whole.

She reached the corner, which led to a short opening and the stable-square beyond. She could see nothing.

"Saark?" she whispered. Then louder, "Saark!"

"Yes, princess?" He was behind her, close, and she felt his breath on her neck and a quiver of raw energy rampaged through her veins. She did not turn, instead standing stock still, now she was here, out in the darkness with this beautiful man, and suddenly unsure of what to do.

"I thought you really had gone to see to the horses," she said.

"Maybe I did," he said, and kissed her neck, a gentle tease of lips and tongue, leaving a trail which chilled to ice in the cold air.

Kat shivered. A thrill ran down her spine.

"Did that tickle?"

"It was wonderful."

"Shall I do it again?"

Kat turned, looked up into his eyes. They were wide and pretty and trustworthy. They shone with love. They shone with understanding. She felt her heart melt; again. "Do you really think I'm beautiful?'

"More beautiful than the stars, princess, more beautiful than a snowflake, or a newborn babe." He reached forward, until his lips were a whisper from her own. She felt his hands come to rest lightly on her hips, and again a thrill raged through her, pulsing like energy with every beat of her heart. Her head spun, and she wanted him, wanted him so badly she would risk anything to be with Saark right now, here, in this cold place of snow and ice...

He kissed her.

He was gentle, teasing, his tongue darting into her mouth and she grasped his head in eagerness and pressed her face into his, kissing him with passion, kissing him with a raw ferocity; his arms encircled her waist and she felt his hardness press against the front of her silk dress and it thrilled her like nothing in the world had ever thrilled her before...

He pulled away.

"Don't stop," she panted.

"You're an eager little fox," he said.

"Kiss me," she said. "Kiss me everywhere! Touch me everywhere! *Please...*"

"Oh, my princess," whispered Saark, eyes glinting in the darkness, "believe me, I will."

Kell sank into hot water. It slammed him with a violence he welcomed. He poured a huge glass of whisky, balanced it on the rim of the old, ceramic bath, and allowed the oils in the water to fill his senses with pleasure.

You cannot drink it, said Ilanna.

Go fuck yourself, mused Kell, and sloshed in the bathwater. I'll do what I damn well please. You're not my mother!

You cannot return there!

I can return to whatever piss-hole I like. I am Kell. They wrote poems about me, you know? You were in them as well, but I was the hero, I was the legend.

Kell's Legend they called it – sour crock of deformed and lying shit it really was.

Please don't drink it, Kell.

Why do you care? Because I won't perform? Because I won't kill as efficiently for you? To supply your blood fantasy? Your blood-oil craving?

You misunderstand.

What are you? My gran? Kell was mocking, his laughter slurred. He took the whisky. He drank the large glass in one, felt it swim through him like tiny fishes in vinegar. His mind reeled and he welcomed the feeling; glorified in the abandon.

It had been a long time.

Too long.

Nienna is feeling ill, said Ilanna, playing to the one emotional fulcrum she knew.

Kell cursed, and stood, water and oils dripping from his old, scarred, but mightily impressive frame. Most men grew stringy as they aged, their muscles becoming stretched out, their strength gradually diminishing. Not so Kell. Yes, his joints ached, yes arthritis troubled him, but he knew he was as strong as when he was twenty. Strength was something which had never failed him; he was proud of his prodigy.

Damn you. You lie!

I do not.

What's going on?

Three men are talking to her. They can see she is drunk on the port Saark bought. They seek to bed her, in sobriety, or not.

Kell surged from the bath, knocking the bottle of whisky over. It glugged amber heaven to the rugs and

Kell ignored it. He wrenched on his trews, boots and shirt, grasped his axe, and stormed out and down the stairs.

Ilanna had been right. The inn was even more crowded, now, noisier, rowdier, no longer a place for a genial meal; now this was a pit in which to drink, get drunk, and flirt with whores.

Nienna sat, back to the wall, face a little slack. Three men sat around her in a semi-circle; even as Kell strode down the stairs one pushed a glass to Nienna, feeding her drunken state, and she giggled, throwing back the liquor as she swayed. The men were young, late twenties, in rough labourers clothing and with shadows of stubble.

Kell stopped behind them, and placed his hands on hips. Nienna could barely focus.

"Grappa?" she said, and grinned.

The three men turned.

"I suggest," said Kell, face dark like an approaching storm, "you move away. I wouldn't like to cause a nasty scene in the inn where I sleep; it often increases my lodging bill. And if there's one thing I don't like, it's an extortionate bill for broken furniture."

"Fuck off, grandad, this girl's up for some fun," laughed one young man , turning back to Nienna, and thrusting another drink at her. This meant he'd turned his back on Kell. Later, he would realise his mistake.

Kell's fist struck him on the top of the head so hard his stool broke, and as he keeled over and his head bounced from floorboards, it left a dent. He did not move. Kell glared at the other two men, who half stood, hands on knives.

Kell drew Ilanna, and glared at them. "I dare you," he said, voice little more than a whisper. Both men released knives, and Kell grinned. "I'd like to say this wouldn't hurt. But I'd be lying." He slammed a straight right, which broke the second man's nose, dropping him with a crash, and a powerful left hook broke the third man's cheekbone, rendering him unconscious. It took less than a second.

The innkeeper stepped in, holding a helve, but took one look at Kell and lowered the weapon. "We don't want no trouble," he said.

"I intend to give none. You should allow a better class of scum into your establishment," he said, and gave a sickly smile. "However, I am a fair man, who has not yet lost his temper. Get your daughters to escort my granddaughter to her room, and tend her a while, and I won't seek compensation."

"What do you mean?" asked the innkeeper, touched by fear.

"My name is Kell," he said, eyes glowering coals, "and I kill those who stand in my way. I'm going outside for fresh air. To cool off. To calm down. When I return, I expect these three piglets to have vanished."

At the name, the innkeeper had paled even more. There were few who had not heard of Kell; or indeed, the bad things he had done.

"Whatever you say, sir," muttered the innkeeper.

Still furious, more with himself than anybody else, and especially at invoking the vile magick of his own name, Kell strode to the door and out, away from the smoke and noise now rumbling back into existence after the fight. He took several deep lungfuls, and

cursed the whisky and cursed the snow and cursed
Saark... why hadn't the damn dandy kept an eye on
Nienna as he'd promised? And where was Kat?

"The useless, feckless bastard."

Kell glanced up and down the street, then moved
to the corner of the inn. Snow fell thickly, muffling
the world. Kell stepped towards the stables and
thought he heard a soft moan, little more than a whisper, but carrying vaguely across the quiet stillness and
reminding him of one thing, and one thing only...

Sex.

With rising fury and a clinical intuition, Kell
stomped through the snow towards the nearest stall.
He stopped. Saark was lying back on a pile of hay, fully
clothed, his face in rapture. Kat stood, naked before
him, stepping from her dress even as he watched. Kell
was treated to a full view of her powerful, round but-
tocks.

"You fucking scum," snarled Kell, and slapped open
the stable door.

"Wait!" said Saark.

Kell lurched forward, kicking Saark in the head,
stunning the man who fell back to the hay. He turned
to Kat, face sour. "Get your clothes on, bitch. You'll
be having no fun tonight."

"Oh yes? Why? Haven't you a hard enough cock
yourself?"

Kell raised his hand to strike her, then stared hard,
glancing at his huge splayed fingers; like the claws of
a rabid bear. He lowered his hand, instead grabbing
Saark by the collar and dragging him through the hay,
back out onto the street and throwing him down.

"What did I tell you?" he snarled, and kicked Saark in the ribs. Saark rolled through the snow, grunting, to lie still, staring at snowfall. He gave a deep, wracking cough.

"Wait," Saark managed, lifting his hand.

Kell strode forward, rage rushing through him, an uncontrollable drug. Deep down, he knew it was fuelled by whisky. Whisky was the product of the devil, and it made him behave in savage, evil ways, ways he could not control...

"You would abuse a young, innocent girl?" he screamed, and swung a boot at Saark's face. Saark rolled, catching Kell's leg and twisting it; Kell stumbled back, and Saark crawled to his feet, still stunned by the blows, his face twisted as he spat out blood.

"Kell, what are you doing?" he shouted.

"You went too far," raged Kell, squaring up to Saark. "I'm going to give you a thrashing you'll never forget."

"Don't be ridiculous, old man."

"Don't call me *old man*!" Kell charged, and Saark side-stepped but a whirring fist cracked the side of his head. He spun, and returned two punches which Kell blocked easily, as if fending off a child. Kell charged again, and the men clashed violently, punches hammering at one another in a blur of pounding. They staggered apart, both with bloodied faces, and every atom of Saark's good humour disintegrated.

"This is crazy," he yelled, dabbing at his broken lips. "She's eighteen years old! She knows what she wants!"

"No. She knows what you tell her! You're a womaniser and a cur, and I swear I'm going to beat it out of you."

They clashed again, and Kell clubbed a right hook to Saark's head, stunning him. Saark ducked a second blow, smashed a straight to Kell's jaw, a second to his nose, a hook to his temple, and a straight to his chin. Kell took a step back, eyes narrowed, and Saark realised a lesser man would have fallen. In fact, a great man would have been out in the mud. Saark may have come across as an effeminate dandy, with a poison tongue and love of female sport and hedonism, but once, long ago, he had been a warrior; he knew he could punch harder than most men. Kell should have gone down. Kell should have been out.

Kell coughed, spat on the snow with a splatter of blood, and lifted his fists, eyes raging. "Come on, you dandy bastard. Is that all you've got?" He grinned, and Saark suddenly realised Kell was playing with him. He had allowed Saark the advantage. But Kell's face turned dark. "Let's see what you're fucking made of," he said.

Saark started to retreat, his head pounding, his face numb from the blows, but Kell charged, was on him and he ducked a punch, spun away from a second, leapt back from a third. He held out his hands. "I apologise!" he said, eyes pleading.

"Too late," growled Kell, and slammed a hook that twisted Saark into the air, spinning him up and over, to land with a grunt on the snow, tangled. He coughed, and decided it was wise to stay down for a few moments.

"Get up," said Kell.

"I'm fine just here," said Saark.

"Grandfather!" Nienna was standing in the inn's doorway, sobered by the spectacle, and surrounded by others from the inn who jostled to watch. She ran down the steps, silk shoes flapping, and placed herself before the fallen Saark and the enraged figure of Kell.

"What are you doing?" she shrieked.

"He was trying to rape Kat," said Kell, eyes refusing to meet his granddaughter's.

"I was doing no such thing," snapped Saark, crawling to his knees, then climbing to his feet. "She needed no persuasion, Kell, you old fool. Have you no eyes in your head? She was lusting after me, even back in the tannery. You just can't stand the thought of a young woman desiring a man like me..."

Kell growled something, not words, just primal sounds of anger, and a continually rising rage, and Nienna stepped forward, slapping both hands against his chest. "No!" she yelled, voice strong, eyes boring into her grandfather. "I said NO!"

Viciously, Kell grabbed Nienna and threw her to one side. She stumbled, went down in the snow with a gasp, then rolled over to stare in disbelief at the man she had known for seventeen years, from babe to womanhood, a man she irrefutably knew would never lay a hand on her, would never pluck a hair from her head.

"That's it!" laughed Saark, voice rising a little as he saw the inevitability of battle, of destruction, of death rising towards him like a tidal wave. "Take it out on a young girl, go on Kell, what a fucking man you are." His voice rose in volume, tinged by panic. "Is this really the hero of Jangir Field? Is this truly the mighty

warrior who battled Dake the Axeman, for two days
and two nights and took his decapitated head back to
the king? Go on Kell, why don't you just kick the girl
whilst she's on the ground... after all, you wouldn't
like her to fight back now, would you, bloody coward?
You're a fucking lie, old man... the Black Axeman of
Drennach?" Saark laughed, blood drooling down his
chin as Kell stopped, and unloosed his axe from his
back. The old man's eyes were hard, harder than
granite Saark realised as a terrifying certainty flooded
his heart. "I spit on you! I bet you cowered in the cellars during the Siege of Drennach, listened to the War
Lions raging above tearing men limb from limb...
whilst the real men did the fighting."

Kell lifted his axe. His face was terror. His eyes black
holes. His visage the bleakness of corpse-strewn bat-
tlefields. He was no longer an aged, retired warrior
with arthritis. He was Kell. The Legend.

"Go on," snarled Saark, hatred fuelling him now,
spittle riming his lips, "do it, kill me, end my fucking
suffering, you think I don't hate myself a thousand
times more than you ever could? Go on, bastard... kill
me, you spineless gutless cowering heap of horse-
cock."

"No!" screamed Nienna.

"You speak too much," said Kell, his voice terribly,
dangerously low. "Here, let me help you." He hefted
Ilanna, huge muscles bunching, and only then did
Saark glimpse, from the corner of his eye, a tendril of
white mist drifting across the street. His head
twitched, turned, and he watched ice-smoke pour
from a narrow alleyway, to be joined by another from

a different alley, and yet another from a third... like questing tendrils, wavering tentacles of some great, solidifying mist-monster...

"The albino soldiers!" hissed Nienna, eyes wide as Kat skidded around the corner, face flustered, dress hitched up in her hands. "They're here! Kell, they're *here*!"

Kell lifted Ilanna, face impassive. His body flexed, and twisted, and the mighty axe sang as she slammed in a glittering arc towards Saark's head.

ELEVEN
A Secret Rage

Anu revelled in the cold air gusting from mountain passes as Vashell led her on her chain through the town. As they walked down metal cobbles towards the Engineer's Docks, many vachine stopped to stare, eyes wide at this utterly humiliating and degrading treatment. Anu grinned at them, sometimes hissed, and once, when a young man protruded his fangs she snarled, "Stare as much as you like, bastard, I'll be back to rip out your throat!"

Vashell tugged her tight, then, and she fought the chain for a few moments until Vashell back-handed her across the face, and she hit the ground. She looked up, eyes narrowed in hatred, and Vashell lifted his fist to strike another blow...

"Stop!" It was a little girl, a baby vachine, who ran across the metal cobbles, clogs clattering, long blonde hair fluttering, and she placed herself between Anu and the enraged Engineer. "Have you no shame, Engineer Priest?" she said in her tiny child's voice.

Vashell glowered at the girl, no more than eight or nine years old, in a rage born of arrogance. She turned her back on him, reached down, and took Anukis's hand. She smiled, a sweet smile, and her eyes were full of love. Inside her, Anu heard the *tick tick* of clockwork. Inside the girl, the vampire machine was growing.

"Thank you." Anu stood. She reached out, ruffled the girl's hair. "Thank you for being the only one in the whole valley to show me kindness."

"Everybody is scared of you," said the girl. "They're scared you'll bring down the wrath of the Engineers."

"And we call this a free society?" mocked Anu, casting a sideways glance at Vashell. He snarled something, tugged her lead, and Anu followed obediently... but strange thoughts of her father flowed through her blood and flashed in her mind, and she felt, deep inside her own twisted and failed clockwork, the very thing which made her impure, the very thing which made her different to the vachine around her and unable to take in the gift of blood-oil which kept them alive and fed their cravings and lubricated their clockwork... she felt a tiny, subtle *twist*. Something clicked in her breast, and she felt nauseous, the world spinning violently, and she glanced back and saw the little girl watching her, a curious look on her face, and Anu tilted her head unable to place that look, unable to decipher what it actually meant...

A cold wind blew, peppered with snow.

Huge, perfectly sculpted buildings flowed past, and the vachine population continued to stare as Vashell strode proudly down the centre of the street with his dominated, subdued prize. Above, beyond, to either side, the devastatingly huge Black Pike Mountains reared, black and grey and capped with white, and splashed down low on their mighty flanks with occasional scatterings of colourful green pine forest.

I know what that look meant, realised Anu. Snow whipped her, and she shivered.

It was a look of friendship, of memory, of a link. She knows me, thought Anu, but I do not know her. How is this possible? What does it mean? Where does she come from?

The cobbled street was immensely steep, down to the Engineer's Docks. Distantly, she heard the Silva River slapping the dockside, and Vashell unconsciously accelerated due to the gradient. Anu moved faster, to keep up with the cruel Engineer's long stride, still puzzling over the golden haired child and her curious recognition…

Another puzzle, she thought.

Another conundrum.

Inside her, her clockwork continued to do strange things. She felt odd whirring sensations, the spinning and stepping of gears, like nothing she had ever before felt. Maybe I'm dying, she laughed to herself. Maybe I've been booby-trapped? Whatever, the process made her sick to her vachine core.

They reached the dockside, which was bustling with activity. Brass barges were being loaded and unloaded up and down the river, and Vashell led Anu to a long, sleek vessel. They climbed a narrow plank, went aboard, stood on deck for a moment and then dropped into a plush cabin as befit an Engineer. Vashell tied Anu's lead to a hook, and locked a clasp in place with a *click*. Anu felt a bubble of rage flood her; she felt like a dog.

"Don't want you attempting escape," said Vashell, voice low.

"Go to hell."

Vashell shrugged, and moved away, into the front of the brass barge. After a few moments Anu felt the rhythmical, pendulous hum of the clockwork engine and the barge slid away from the Engineer's Docks, away onto the smooth platform of the Silva River.

Anu sighed, and looked out of a circular portal, watching the Silva River drift by, glinting with ice as Vashell guided them through chunks and small, choppy waves. The noises of the docks drifted away behind them, until only the hum of the engine could be heard and the barge turned north, then northeast, past the opening for the Deshi Caves which seemed to tug at them with unseen currents, with honeyed promises. Come to me, the caves seemed to call. Come and explore my long, winding tunnels. I promise you riches, and glory, and immortality. That, and death, thought Anu.

Vashell picked up a narrow tributary, and guided the barge between silent mountain sentinels. Sheer walls of rock scrolled past, black and rugged grey, with a few sparse and twisted trees clinging for survival. It seemed cold, and gloomy, and snow whipped through the air. The barge hummed on, rocking, and Anu, exhausted with pain, fear, humiliation, and the still-present nagging sensation in her body core, felt sleep creep upon her and she leaned to the side, eyes closing, and for once she truly welcomed the deep dark oblivion of sleep.

* * *

"Wake up."

Vashell was shaking her. Anu yawned, and sat up. Her mouth tasted of metal, of copper, and brass, and something else.

"Where are we?"

"We've stopped at the Ranger Barracks. I've been waved ashore; you will come with me, but no trouble, Anu – or I'll cut the head from your body. Understand?"

"Why don't you leave me here? I am exhausted."

Vashell grinned, eyes twinkling. "What? And have you pull some clever trick, and the next moment the barge is cruising into the Black Pikes without me? No. You never leave my sight… not until the day I die."

Anu was too tired to argue. Conversely, she was more weary than before her sleep, and checking the barge's clock, she saw she'd had six hours. What was the matter with her? Again, she tasted metal… almost a liquid metal, and her tongue explored the weird interior of her mouth. She was not right. Something was changing inside her.

Vashell unlocked her chain, took it in his fist and climbed the steps into cold, bleak sunlight. A bitter wind blew scattered snow from surrounding cliffs, causing the weird effect of sunlight filtering through a snowstorm. Anu followed, shading her eyes, and saw a rough wooden jetty and barracks beyond, with enough accommodation for perhaps two hundred soldiers. The barracks seemed deserted, although she could have been wrong. There was a long, low building, also constructed from rough timber, and a door opened and three albino warriors stepped out, their matt black armour gleaming in the sunlight as they shaded eyes. They hated sunlight, she knew; as did the vachine. It caused them a certain amount of pain, and in really strong light caused their clockwork to slow down, overheat, and in some extreme cases even kill the host through mechanical failure. No. Vachine preferred the cold, and the dark; their albino slaves even more so.

Anu stared at the warriors, and behind them saw a woman, tousled and battered, blood dried on her face and arms, her clothing rimed in filth. She looked little more than a vagabond and Anu's heart went out to her immediately; here was somebody mistreated, beaten, abused, as was she. There was a common link: the humiliation of the victim.

Anu studied the woman carefully, and her gaze was met by a proud, green-eyed stare, returned with a ferocity and attitude which had no doubt earned her endless pain. And, despite her recent beating, and old beatings by the look of her; despite torn clothing, naked feet covered in scabs and sores, despite her matted mane of hair, Anu saw through the agony and attitude, saw a strong woman, tall, elegant, it was in her bearing, in her manner, in her very spirit. And that had not been broken.

"The bitch is a hard one to crack," laughed one of the albino soldiers, gesturing to the woman.

"You have been instructed to treat her thus?" Vashell seemed… vexed. Anu considered his deviated sense of righteousness.

"Yes," replied a second soldier. "By Graal himself. He told us the more we beat and raped her, the more we abused her, the more we broke her – as long as we didn't kill the royal bitch, then it would be a good tool in subjugating her husband."

"Any news on Leanoric's military progress?"

"I will leave those matters for discussion between you and General Graal," said the soldier, who Anu realised was a captain of some sort, although she didn't understand the complexities of the Army of Iron's ranking system. "I was simply instructed to bring her here and await an Engineer's Barge. We thought that was why you had come."

"Coincidence," said Vashel. "I have... another mission."

Vashell tugged the chain, and Anu stumbled, and uttered a guttural growl. The three albino soldiers looked on, amused, laughter smiles touching their lips.

"A wild one, is she?"

Vashell looked back. "One of the wildest," he said, licking his lips, and smiling with narrowed eyes.

"Isn't she Anukis, Kradek-ka's daughter?" said one soldier, peering a little closer, his humour evaporating.

Vashell changed, his manner becoming more professional – more superior – in an instant. "Mind your own business, captain. We are on direct orders from the Watchmakers; I suggest you return to your... little lady, there, and continue with your petty sport. She's looking at you with the longing eyes of a bitch on heat... and trust me well when I say my business does not concern you."

Anu and Alloria's eyes met. Understanding flowed between. This was the Queen of Falanor. A bartering tool for the Engineers, and for The Army of Iron in the fast escalating conflict, the accelerating invasion. "Help me," mouthed Alloria, and Anu saw then, saw the swirl of madness deep at Alloria's core. She was putting on a proud front; but they had nearly destroyed her. There was only so much a human mind could endure.

Anu coughed, and again something *changed* inside her. She felt as if about to vomit, and instead, heard a heavy thunk. Part of her machinery changed. What was wrong with her? What had the bastards *done* to her?

She looked up. The world seemed... different. Almost black and white, and diffused, as if seen through a fine shattered mirror. She felt strength flood her system, like nothing she had felt before. She felt iron wires merge through her muscles, felt her heart swell, felt new claws springs from her fingertips, delicate and gleaming with silver. Silver fangs flowed through her hollow jaws, molten at first but solidifying, and new vampire fangs sprouted from her teeth, replacing the holes where her fake vachine fangs had been forcibly removed. Everything became acute; she could hear the snowfall, the distant flutter of birds in pine, the creak of rock in the Black Pike Mountains, distant avalanche falls, and she could smell the albinos, a certain metallic stink like that of insects, and Vashell reeked of sweat and shit and piss, and Queen Alloria even more so, and she could smell the resin in the timber jetty and the oil on the albino soldier's swords, she could see the hairs in their nostrils, taste their sweat oils in the air... and Anu *smiled*.

She lifted herself to her full height, and took a deep breath, aware her new vachine fangs gleamed silver... an impossibility, for pure silver was a poison to vachine. But now she knew. She knew her father had made her different, created something... unique, when compared to every other vachine in Silva Valley. He had been experimenting with advanced vachine technology. And she had been the template, the upgrade, using the finest clockwork in a non-parasitic fashion... and that's why she could not imbibe the blood-oil narcotic; she did not need it. All Anukis needed to survive was...

Blood. Pure blood.

Ironically, the sign of the impure.

But in this context, a technological advancement.

Her eyes glowed, and she sensed Vashell move and he gathered the chain, his movements slow and bulky, lethargic almost, and Anu lifted her own end of the chain and she pulled. Vashell was jerked from his feet and Anu leapt, a blur of speed, her claws slamming through the chain with a tinkling like ice chimes. Vashell stumbled back, going for his sword, but Anu whirled the length of chain around her head and it slammed Vashell's face, knocking him from his feet with a grunt. She took the collar in her hands and wrenched it apart, bolts pinging across snow.

The albinos tensed, drew their own swords and Anu walked towards them. She heard Vashell lift his weapon, could smell his bloodlust rising and mission or no mission, instructions or no instructions, he was going to kill her and to hell with the consequences.

The soldiers, elite warriors of the Army of Iron, charged.

Anu leapt amongst them, swayed back as a blade hummed over her, and her fist lashed out, talons smashing *through* black iron breast plate and through the albino's chest, exiting with his heart in her fist. She tugged him in close, as her claws shredded his heart in a blur, and she withdrew her fist with a *schlup* sound. Even as he fell, she flicked sideways, rolling in snow, grabbing the second albino by the head and twisting violently. His neck snapped with a crunch, and she took his sword, hurling it across the clearing where it speared the third albino through the throat, pinning him to the barrack wall. He struggled, gurgling, refusing to die, his hands scrabbling at the blood-slippery blade.

Anu turned, ignoring the cowering blood-spattered form of Alloria. She stared at Vashell, who was approaching with the fluid grace of a perfect vachine warrior. She smiled, and ejected claws and fangs.

"You're going to taste death, bitch."

"After you," invited Anu, with a smile, and they leapt at one another, clashing in mid-air, bouncing from each other as Anu twisted, avoiding Vashell's claws and her own cut a line down his flank, through armour and clothing and flesh, and a bloody spray spattered across the snow. They landed ten feet apart, crouched like animals.

Vashell touched his own wounded side. His eyes narrowed. "You'll pay for that."

"Too long I have heard your pretty words," said Anu, her voice quiet, eyes lowered. "You don't understand, do you, poor Vashell? That which alienated me from the rest of the vachine, that which made you call me impure, outcast, illegal, is twisted, reversed, for I was bred by my father to be a superior vachine, an advanced vachine lifeform... not addicted to your blood-oil concoctions... but independent of your controlling Watchmaker and Engineer pseudo-religious culture. Is that why you fear me so? Because you know I am special?"

"Kradek-ka is Heretic!" spat Vashell. "That is why he must help us; and then die."

"He seeks to improve our race using clockwork science," said Anu.

"He seeks to overthrow the Engineers," snapped Vashell, the edge of pain making his words come out fast.

"And the irony! Your Blood Refineries are breaking down; without him, you cannot fix them. You will revert to old savagery; old ways."

"Shut up and die." He snarled and leapt, and this time Anu stood rock still, eyes fixed on him, sunlight glinting from her silver fangs... at the last, split second, she twisted, and his claws slashed past her throat; his fangs slammed for her artery but she was moving, rolling away, to come up with her own claws extended, a curious calm on her face as Vashell growled, and they circled, and he leapt again with a scream of anger and Anu swayed, faster than a blur, and slammed a blow which removed Vashell's face. The skin came off in Anu's claws, removed like a mask, to leave him stood, muscle-masked skull gaping at her in utter disbelief. His face was now a red, pulsing orb from hairline to jaw, and Anu stood up straight, holding his face in her hands, watching his blood drip to the floor and he glanced up, eyes full of pain, eyes full of staggered understanding...

"That's for betraying me," she whispered.

With a growl, he launched at her and she delivered a side-kick to his chest, knocking him back, then leapt high, coming down with both claws extended to slam Vashell to the ground. She landed, kneeling atop his chest, claws locked around his throat.

"Don't kill me," he said, and she looked down at his new, bloody, destroyed face.

"Why not?"

His claws flexed behind her, and without moving her own vachine claws slammed out, cutting them from his fingers, then again to his other hand. Vashell howled in fresh agony, blood-oil spurting from all ten mangled stumps, and Anu leant close to him, mastery flooding her, along with a cold metallic hate. She leaned forward, and her fangs sank into his throat, and he writhed for a while, legs kicking, clawless hands slapping at her in an attempt to dislodge this vachine parasite from feeding. She appreciated the irony of reversal as he screamed and struggled, flapping uselessly, weakly, and Anu finally pulled away, her mouth wearing a beard of blood-oil, and she smiled down at him, reached down, and with a savage wrench, plucked out his fangs.

Anu sat on the jetty, kicking her legs, as Alloria approached to crouch beside her. Tentatively, the woman's hand touched Anu's shoulder and she turned, their eyes meeting, Anu's face coated in slick blood. Some way off, Vashell lay, curled into a ball, weeping salt tears onto the open muscles of his face.

"Are you in pain?"

"No." Anu shook her head, forced a smile. "Come. We must leave this place. It will attract more soldiers like moths to a lantern." She stood, stretched, and her fangs slid away. She walked over to Vashell with Alloria trailing her, uncertain, her green eyes filled with a curious mix of fear and wonder.

"Wait," said Queen Alloria.

"Yes?"

"Where am I? What am I doing here?"

"This is the Silva Valley – where the vachine live."

"I have never… heard of such a place. And yet we are in the mountains, yes? The Black Pike Mountains?"

"Yes. In their heart."

"I thought the Black Pikes were impassable. That is what the people of Falanor believe."

Anu shook her head. "Many of your, shall we say respectable citizens, think like that. But there is a roaring blood trade by Blacklippers. They have no morals. They have no… empathy. No fear."

"What is a Blacklipper?"

"The Halfway People. Illegal to the vachine of Silva Valley, and ostracised by the good men and women of Falanor. They are your illegals, your freaks and vagabonds, the army deserters destined to die, the deformed left to perish in low mountain passes. That is your tradition, isn't it? With the babes who have no arms? Those of twisted limb? Those are the

Blacklippers, they are not the pretty people of a good, noble society. They are the weak. The cripples. The diseased. The underlings who you would rather imagine did not exist." Anu took a deep breath, then looked away up the cold, flowing river. Like me, she thought. And smiled. "I'm sorry. I'm bitter. I have recently been... abused, as an outcast, something different. It's not a pleasant feeling to be hated by those who once accepted you." She met Alloria's gaze. "Once, your outcasts ran to us; but the vachine, also, are filled with a primitive superiority and they turned on the Blacklippers. Now, illegally, the Blacklippers gradually feed your nation to ours. They think of it as a kind of justice. Of payback."

"Feed?"

Anu smiled. "We have a currency in blood," she said, and Alloria gasped, hands coming to her mouth.

"Is that why your army invaded?"

Anu nodded. "Our civilisation expands, and our needs multiply. We are losing the war in an ability to satiate our own needs. And so..." her voice trailed off, as her eyes alighted on the now silent form of Vashell. "So we must spread out, move south; to where there are many ripe, succulent pickings."

"You talk about my people, the good people of Falanor, as if they are cattle!" snapped Alloria, eyes hard.

"They soon will be," said Anu, her head tilting to one side. "Once the vachine roll in the Blood Refineries."

"I don't understand. My husband, the king, is a great warrior. He has thousands of soldiers at his disposal; an army of unconquerable might! He will oppose any invasion with savage force, and chase your vachine people back to the mountains like the savages you undoubtedly are. Either that, or slaughter them without mercy."

Across the clearing, Vashell started to laugh. He sat, bloody face leering at them, mangled hands in his lap, laughing in an obscene gurgle.

Anu strode to him. "Something funny, you faceless bastard?"

Vashell reclined a little, looking up at her. "My Kradek-ka really did a fine job on you, my twisted, sweet little deformity. His technology, I admit, is superb, for never have I been bested in battle. Not by human, not by vachine." He took a deep breath, and Anu could see the pain in his eyes; not just a physical pain, but a mental scarring. He was trying to mask this with bravado; but she knew him too well.

"I threw your face in the river," she said, leaning close. "I didn't think you'd be needing it again."

Vashell shrugged. "You may do what you wish to me; but you do know they will come."

"Who?"

"The Harvesters. I am linked. They have sensed my pain. As you sit there, on your arse, squabbling with prime succulent Falanor Queen-meat, they have already decided your fate. No longer is Kradek-ka to be brought back. I'd wager they simply need your extermination, for your threat is great; your threat, now, is terrible. If you are lucky, little Anu, you little twisted vachine experiment Anu, they will send the cankers. But if you are unlucky…"

"They will never catch us," said Anu, and there was a tinge of panic to her voice. She feared the Harvesters. Everybody feared the Harvesters.

"If you're unlucky, they will come themselves."

Anu's claws slid free. She glared down at Vashell, and even in his pain, now over the sudden shock of his ripped-off face, he mocked her. His arrogance, and loathing, had returned. "I will kill you," she growled, her own hatred swelling.

"No," said Alloria, grasping Anu's arm. Anu threw Alloria to the ground, where she lay, staring up at these two alien creatures.

"I will kill you," repeated Anu, and moved in close...

"That would be foolish. How, then, would you find your father?"

Snow was falling, and the rearing mountains were diffused. Light had started to fail, and the sky held that curious grey brightness, a cold tranquillity, only found in the mountains. A slow unrolling of mist eased in from around the barracks, and Anu caught the silent approach from the corner of her eye. Ice prickled up and down her spine.

"Where is he?" she snapped.

"You need me," said Vashell, his eyes burning. "Only I know where he was last seen. I have my reports. If you kill me, and believe me, I am willing to die, then he will be gone from you forever." He snarled at her, through torn and ragged lips, from a face of rancid horror, from a face that was no longer a face.

"I will cut out your eyes," said Anu.

"Then do it! And stop yapping like a clockwork
puppy."

The mist, cold and brilliantly white, spread across
the ground, rolling out onto the river and masking the
currents. It covered the corpses of the slain albino soldiers, and Vashell pushed himself up onto elbows as
it rolled around him, and he sighed, and his eyes
alighted on Anu and there was a glint of triumph
there…

"The Harvesters move quickly," he said, voice a lullaby, and filled with the honey of blood-oil narcotic;
his system was overloading on the substance, in lieu
of his savage beating. "There must have been one
close by."

Anu felt panic slam her breast. "No," she said
whirling around, eyes scanning the open spaces. She
pointed at Alloria. "Get into the barge!" she snapped,
and then turned back to Vashell, her claws and vam-
piric fangs emerging. "It is simply mountain mist!"
she hissed, but her voice was cracked, there was a
splinter in her heart. They both knew how savage the
Harvesters were; and how strange, even to the vachine whom they deigned to help. They were
creatures of the Black Pike Mountains, creatures from
far beneath the stone; and they had their own eso-
teric agenda.

When the Harvesters drained corpses for Blood Refinement, it was suspected that they themselves
received something by way of a bonus. When they
husked a human, they took a little part of the soul.
But no vachine ever voiced these theories; not if they
valued their own life. The Harvesters were above the

gods, as far as the vachine society were concerned;
and even though Anu would never voice this sentiment, she felt they were the Puppet Masters, and the
vachine simply actors on another creature's stage.

Vashell shrugged, and watched Anu closely.

"You have grown strong," he said, voice slurring a
little, so infused was his damaged system with blood-
oil. "But do you think you have grown strong
enough?"

There came a hiss, like snow on a forest canopy,
and from the swirled ice-smoke came the Harvester.
The oval face stared at Anu as it seemed to glide over
the ground, and it stopped for a moment by the slain
albino warriors.

"Sacrilege?" it said, voice high-pitched, merging
in an odd way with its fast-paced breathing. Then it
looked at Vashell, who shrugged, almost dreamily,
and returned its gaze to Anu. "So. The daughter of
Kradek-ka. You have discovered your gift, I see."

"He would have killed me," said Anu, pointing to
Vashell, her finger shaking.

The Harvester drifted a little closer, head bobbing,
tiny black eyes without emotion fixing hard on
Anu's soul. She felt like she was being eaten, from
the inside out, by a tiny swarm of parasites. She
shivered, as a feeling passed through her, and she
was sure the Harvester could read her thoughts.

"I see," said the Harvester, and she could not read
the black eyes. Fear tasted copper on her tongue.
She felt urine dribble between her legs. She pictured
the husks of the slaughtered; men, women, vachine,
children, dogs. The Harvester had no empathy, no

remorse, no understanding. It could not be negotiated with. It would do what it wanted, protected by vachine law, and practically indestructible...

"I am going to look for my father," she said, voice trembling.

"You are going nowhere, child."

Anu hardened her resolve, through her blanket of fear. More ice-smoke swirled around her ankles, with a biting, icy chill. This fuelled her strength. The Harvesters controlled everything...

"I will find my father," she said, again.

"You disobey me?" said the Harvester.

She considered this, and knew she had embarked upon a path of mystery, a journey she could never have foreseen, understood, nor prophesied. She had stepped sideways from the vachine of Silva Valley; she was an outlaw, yes, and she was totally alone. She realised in a flash of understanding that things would never, could never, be the same. And if she defied this Harvester, she broke every law of the Mountain. Of the Valley. Of the Oak Testament.

"Yes," she said, meeting the Harvester's gaze and holding it.

Long bony fingers emerged from the robe, and the Harvester lifted its arms in a gesture at the same time a little bizarre, a little ridiculous, but containing a thrill of raw terror.

"Then you must die," it said, voice a monotone.

Anu felt strength flood her. Confidence bit through fear. Pride and necessity ate her horror. She smiled at the Harvester, and flexed her claws, and lowered her head, and snarled, "Come and take me, then, you bone-headed freak," as she leapt to the attack.

TWELVE
The Jailers

Saark watched the axe, Ilanna, in Kell's mighty hands; watched her sing in dark prophecy as she rushed towards his skull. And as he observed that crescent razor approach, an utter calm descended on him and he reflected on his life, his early goals, his mistakes, and on his current self-loathing; and he knew, knew life was unfair and the world took no prisoners, but that ultimately he had made his own choices, and he deserved death. He deserved the cold dark earth, the sombre tomb, worms eating his organs. He deserved to be forgotten, for in his life he had done bad things, *terrible things*, and for these he had never been punished. With his death, his end, then the world would be a cleaner place. His scourge would be removed. He smiled. It was a fitting end to be slain by a hero such as Kell; poetic, almost. Despite the irony.

The blade sliced frozen earth a hair's-breadth from his ear, scraped the ice with a metallic shriek, then lifted into the air again and for a horrible moment Saark thought to himself, the old bastard missed! He's pissed on whisky, and he damn well fucking *missed*!

But Kell glared at him, face sour, eyes raging, and held out his hand. "Up, lad. It's not your time. We have a job to do."

Saark turned, rolled, and sprang lightly to his feet, his injuries pushed aside as he watched, with Kell, Nienna, Kat and the others; watched the albino soldiers drifting from wreaths of ice-smoke.

Kell whirled on the gathered crowd. "You must run!" he bellowed. "The ice-smoke will freeze you where you stand, then they will drain you of blood. Stop standing like village idiots, run for your lives!"

A knife flashed from the darkness, and Ilanna leapt up, clattering the blade aside in a show of such consummate skill Saark found his mouth once again dry. The old boy hadn't missed with his strike; nobody that good missed, despite half a bottle of whisky. If Kell wanted Saark dead, by the gods, he'd be dead.

Saark sidled to Kell. The advancing albinos had halted. They seemed to be waiting for something. The mist swirled, huge coils like ghostly snakes, as if gathering strength.

"What do we do, old horse?"

"We run," said Kell. "Tell Nienna and Kat to get the horses."

Kell stood, huge and impassable in the street as the albinos arrayed themselves before him; yet more drifted from the shadows between cottages. They wore black armour, and their crimson eyes were emotionless, insectile.

Like ants, thought Kell. Simply following their programmed instructions…

There were fifty of them, now. Off to the right a platoon of soldiers emerged, and a group of villagers attacked with swords and pitchforks. Their screams sang through the night to a musical accompaniment of steel on steel; they were butchered in less than a minute.

"Come on, come on," muttered Kell, aware that some spell was at work here, and he growled at the albino warriors and then, realised with a jump, that they watched his axe, eyes, as one, fixed on Ilanna. He lifted the great weapon, and their eyes followed it, tracking the terrible butterfly blades.

So, he thought. You understand her, now.

"Come and enjoy her gift," he snarled, and from their midst emerged a Harvester, and Kell nodded to himself. So. That was why they waited. For the hardcore magick to arrive...

Iron-shod hooves clattered on ice and cobbles, and Nienna and Kat rode free of the stables, the geldings sliding as they cornered and Saark whirled, leapt up behind Kat, taking the reins from her shaking fingers.

"Kell!" he bellowed.

Kell, staring at the Harvester, snarled something incomprehensible, then turned and vaulted into the saddle behind Nienna – hardly the action of an old man with rheumatism. "Yah!" he snarled and the horses galloped through the streets, churning snow and frozen mud, slamming through milling people and over the bridge and away...

Behind, the screams began.

"Soldiers ahead!" yelled Saark as they charged down a narrow street of two-storey cottages with

well-tended gardens, and there were ten albino warriors standing in the road, swords free, heads lowered,
and as Saark dragged violently on reins the gelding
whinnied in protest. Kell did not slow, charging his
own horse forward, Nienna gasping between his
mighty arms as Ilanna sang, a high pitched song of
desolation as she cleaved left, then right, leaving two
carved and collapsing corpses in sprays of iridescent
white blood. Kell wheeled the horse, and it reared,
hooves smashing the lower jaw from the face of an albino who shrieked, grabbing at where his mouth had
been. Behind, Saark cursed, and urging his own gelding forward, charged in with his sword drawn. Steel
rang upon steel as he clashed, and to his right Kell
leapt from the saddle as Nienna drew her own sword
from its saddle-sheath. Kell carved a route through
the soldiers, his face grim, eyes glowing, whisky on
his breath and axe moving as if possessed; which it
surely was.

Nienna sat atop the horse, stunned by events; from
fine dresses and heady drinks to sitting in the street,
sword in hand, petrified to her core. Again. She shook
her head, feeling groggy and slow, mouth tasting bad,
head light, and watched almost detached as a soldier
stepped from his comrades, focused on her, and
charged with sword raised…

Panic tore through Nienna. The soldier was there in
the blink of an eye, crimson eyes fixed, sword
whistling towards her in a high horizontal slash; she
stabbed out with her own short blade, and the swords
clashed, noise ringing out. Kell's head slammed left,
as Ilanna cut the head from a warrior's shoulders. Kell

sprinted, then knelt in the snow, sliding, as Ilanna slammed end over end to smash through the albino's spine, curved blade appearing before Nienna's startled gaze on a spray of blood.

Saark finished the last of the soldiers, slitting a man's throat with a dazzling pirouette and shower of horizontal blood droplets. The corpse crumpled, blood settled like rain, and behind them, on the road, ice-smoke crept out and curled like questing fingers.

"We need to get out of Jajor Falls," panted Saark.

"Yes. Let's go."

"How do you do that?"

"Do what?" Kell took the reins, smiling grimly up at Nienna who rubbed her tired face.

"You're not even out of breath, old boy."

"Economy of movement," said Kell, and forced a smile. "I'll teach you, one day."

There came an awkward hiatus. Saark gazed into Kell's eyes.

"I thought you were going to kill me, back there."

"No, laddie. I like you. I wouldn't do that."

Saark let the lie go, and they mounted the geldings. As they rode from Jajor Falls, out into the gloom under heavy falling snow, down a narrow winding lane which led to thick woodland and ten different tracks they could choose at random, behind them, in the now frozen village, the Harvesters moved through the rigid population with a slow, cold, frightening efficiency.

As day broke, so the trail they followed joined with the cobbled splendour of the Great North Road, winding and black, shining under frost and the pink daubs of a low-slung newly-risen sun. The horses cantered, steam ejecting from nostrils, and all four travellers were exhausted in saddles, not just from lack of sleep, but from emotional distress.

"How far to the king?" said Kell, as they rode.

"It's hard to say; depends with which Eagle Division he's camped, or if we have to travel all the damn way to Vor. Best thing is stop the first soldier we see and ask; the army has good communications. The squads should be informed."

"You know a lot about King Leanoric," said Kat, turning to gaze up at Saark. She was aware of his powerful arms around her, his body pressed close to her through silk and furs, which he'd wrapped around her shoulders in the middle of the night to keep her warm. It had been a touching moment.

"I... used to be a soldier," said Saark, slowly.

"Which regiment, laddie?"

"The Swords," said Saark, eyes watching Kell.

"The King's Own, eh?" Kell grinned at him, and rubbed his weary face. The smell of whisky still hung about him like a toxic shawl.

"Yes."

"But you left?"

"Aye."

Kell caught the tension in Saark's voice, and let it go. Kat, however, did not.

"So you fought with the King's Men? The Sword-Champions?"

Saark nodded, squirming uneasily in the saddle. To their left, in the trees, a burst of bird song caught his attention. It seemed at odds with the frost, and the recent slaughter. He shivered as a premonition overtook him.

"Listen, Kell, it occurs to me the Army of Iron is moving south."

"Occurred to me as well, laddie."

"And they're moving fast."

"Fast for an army, aye. They're taking every village as they go, sweeping down through Falanor and leaving nobody behind to oppose them. If the king already knows, he will be mustering his divisions. If he does not…"

"Then Falanor lies wide open."

Kell nodded.

"He must know," said Saark, considering, eyes observing the road ahead. They were moving between rolling hills now, low and rimed with a light scattering of snow, patches of green peeping through patches of white like a winter forest patchwork.

"Why must he?"

"Falanor is riddled with his troops, sergeants, scouts, spies. Even now, Leanoric will be summoning divisions, and they will march on this upstart aggressor. We can be of no further use."

Kell looked sideways at Saark. "You think so, do you?" he murmured.

Saark looked at him. "Don't you?"

"What do you have in mind?"

"We could head west, for the Salarl Ocean. Book passage on a ship, head across the waves to a new land. We are both adept with weapons; we'll find work, there's no question of that."

"Or you could steal a few Dog Gemdog gems, that'd keep you in bread, cheese and fine perfume."

Saark paused. He sighed. "You despise me, don't you? You hate my puking guts."

"Not at all," said Kell, and reined in his mount. "We need to make camp. The girls are freezing. We've put a good twelve leagues between us and the bastards. If we don't get some warmth we'll freeze to death; and my arse feels like a blacksmith's anvil."

"Here's a spot," said Kat, and they dismounted. Kell sent the young women to a nearby woodland to gather fallen branches, as he rummaged in the mount's saddlebags, pulling free two onions, salt and a few strips of jerked beef. "Hell's teeth. Is this all there is? I suppose we left in a hurry."

"We were brawling in the street," said Saark. "We had little warning to gather provisions."

Kell looked at Saark, then placed a hand on his shoulder. "I'm sorry. About that." His face twisted. He was unused to apology. "I… listen, I over-reacted. Kat is a beautiful young woman, but I know your sort, out to take what you want, then you'd leave her behind, weeping and broken, heart smashed into ice fragments."

"Your opinion of me is pure flattery," said Saark, coldly.

"Listen. I lost my temper. There. I said it." He looked into Saark's eyes. "I wouldn't have killed you, lad."

"I think you would," said Saark, carefully. "I've seen that look before."

Kell grinned. "Damn. You're right. I would have killed you."

"What stopped you?"

"The arrival of the soldiers," said Kell, hissing in honesty. "You were the one who brought up this poem, right? This Saga of Kell's Legend. But have you heard the last verse? It's rare the bards remember it; either that, or they choose easily to forget, lest it ruin their night of entertainment."

"The one about Moonlake and Skulkra? Kell fought with the best?"

"No. There is another verse."

"I did not realise."

Kell's voice was a low rumble as he recited, un-evenly, more poetry than song; he would be the first to admit he was no bard. Kell quoted:

"*And Kell now stood with axe in hand,*
The sea raged before him, time torn into strands,
He pondered his legend and screamed at the stars,
Death open beneath him to heal all the scars
Of the hatred he'd felt, and the murders he'd done
And the people he'd killed all the pleasure and life
He'd destroyed.

"*Kell stared melancholy into great rolling waves of*
a Dark Green World,
And knew he could blame no other but himself for
The long Days of Blood, the long Days of Shame,
The worst times flowing through evil years of pain,
And the Legend dispersed and the honour was gone
And all savagery fucked in a world ripped undone
And the answer was clear as the stars in the sky
All the bright stars the white stars the time was to die,

Kell took up Ilanna and bade world farewell,
The demons tore through him as he ended the spell
And closed his eyes."

Kell glanced at Saark. There were tears in his eyes. "I was a bad man, Saark. An evil man. I blame the whisky, for so long I blamed the whisky, but one day I came to realise that it simply masked that which I was. I eventually married, reared two daughters... who came to hate me. Only Nienna has time for me, and for her love I am eternally grateful. Do you know why?"

"Why?" said Saark, voice barely more than a croak.

"Because she is the only thing that calms the savage beast in my soul," said Kell, grasping Ilanna tight. "I try, Saark. I try so hard to be a good man. I try so hard to do the right thing. But it doesn't always work. Deep down inside, at a basic level, I'm simply not a good person."

"Why so glum?" said Nienna, dumping a pile of wood on the ground. She glanced from Saark to Kell, and back, and Kat came up behind with her arms also laden with firewood. "Have you two been arguing again?"

"No," said Saark, and gave a broad, beaming smile. "We were just... going over a few things. Here, let me build a fire, Nienna. You help your grandfather with the soup. I think he needs a few warm words from the granddaughter he loves so dearly."

Kell threw him a dark look, then smiled down at Nienna, and ruffled her hair. "Hello monkey. You did well with the wood."

"Come on, we're both starving." And in torn silk dresses and ragged furs and blankets salvaged from dead soldiers' saddlebags, the group worked together to make a pan of broth.

It was an hour later as they came across a straggled line of refugees, who turned, fear on faces at the sound of striking hoof-beats. Several ran across the fields to the side of the Great North Road, until they saw the young girls who rode with Kell and Saark. They rode to the head of the column, and Kell dismounted beside a burly, gruff-looking man with massive arms and shoulders like a bull.

"Where are you riding?" asked Kell.

"Who wants to know?"

"I am Kell. I ride to warn the king of the invading army."

The man relaxed a little, and eyed Kell's axe and Svian nervously. "I am Brall, I was the smithy back at Tell's Fold. Not any more. The bastard albinos took us in the night, two nights back, magick freezing people in the street. I can still hear their screams. A group of us," he gestured with his eyes, "ran through the woods. And we'll keep on running. Right to the sea if we have to."

A woman approached. "It was horrible," she said, and her eyes were haunted. "They killed everybody. Men, women, little ones. Then these... ghosts, they drifted through the streets and drank the blood of the children." She shuddered, and for a moment Kell thought she was going to be sick. "Turned them into sacks of skin and bone. You'll kill me, won't you,

Brall? Before you let that happen?"

"Aye, lass," he said, and his thick arm encircled her shoulder.

"Have you seen any Falanor men on the road?" asked Saark, dismounting.

"No." Brall shook his head. "Not for the last two weeks. Most of the battalions are south."

"Do you know where King Leanoric camps?"

Brall shrugged. "I am only a smithy," he said. "I would not be entrusted with such things."

"Thank you." Saark turned to Kell. "I know what's happening."

"What's that?"

"More than half of Leanoric's men are paid volunteers; summer men. They go home for the winter. The Black Pike Mountains, much of Leanoric's past angst, are now impassable with snow. So as winter heightens, spreads south, so he stands down most of the volunteers and they return to families. He's been travelling through his divisions, reorganising command structures, deciding who can go home for the winter, that sort of thing."

"So as we stand here, he might even now be disbanding the very army he's going to need?"

"Precisely."

"That's not good," said Kell. "Let's move out."

They cantered on, leaving behind the straggling line of survivors from Tell's Fold.

They rode all day, and as more snow fell and the light failed, so they headed away from the Great North Road, searching for a road shelter, as they were known. In previous decades, following work begun by his father, Leanoric had had shelters built at intervals up and down the huge highway to aid travellers and soldiers in times of need. The snow fell, heavier now, and Saark pointed to the distance where a long, low, timber building nestled in the lee of a hill, surrounded by a thick stand of pine.

"Hard to defend," muttered Kell.

"We need to recharge," said Saark, his cloak pulled tight, his eyes weary. "You might be as strong as an ox, but me and the girls… we need to eat, to sleep. And the horses are dead on their feet."

"Lead the way," said Kell, and they walked through the ankle-deep fall.

Saark opened the door on creaking hinges, allowing snow to blow in, and Kell led the horses behind the road shelter and tied them up in a lean-to stable, at least secluded from the worst of the weather. He found a couple of old, dusty horse blankets and covered the beasts, and filled their nose-bags with oats from the dwindling remains of their saddlebag stores. Saark was right. They needed to rest and recharge; but more, they needed supplies, or soon the wilderness of Falanor would kill them.

"It's bare," said Nienna, moving over and sitting on the first bed. The room had a low roof, and was long, containing perhaps sixteen beds. It was like a small barracks, and was chilled, smelling of damp. A fire had been laid at the far end, but the logs were damp.

"It'll save our life," shivered Saark, and struggled from his cloak. In the gloomy light, his frilled clothes, splattered with dried blood, no longer looked so fine. "How are you two?"

"Exhausted," said Kat, and flashed Saark a smile. "It's been… a strange few days, hasn't it?"

"We need to get a fire going. Nienna, will you go and find some wood?"

Sensing they needed to be alone, Nienna left and the door slammed shut. Saark approached Kat.

"What happened back there…"

"It's all right," she said, smiling and placing a finger against his lips. "We both got carried away in the moment…"

"No. What I meant to say was, I think you're special. I am trying to be different. A reformed character." His smile was twisted, self-mocking. "In my past life, I have been a bad man; in many ways. But I feel for you, Katrina." He stared into her topaz eyes, and ran his hands through her short, red hair, still stuck with bits of straw from back at the village stables.

She reached up, and kissed him, and for a long moment their lips lingered. "Let's take it one step at a time. Let's reach the king. Let's save Falanor. Then we can play at holding hands."

Saark grinned. "You're a wicked wench, that's for sure."

She stroked his moustache, winked, then turned her back on him. "You better believe it, mister."

Nienna returned with firewood, followed by Kell, shivering and brushing snow from the shoulders of his mighty bear-skin jerkin. "Let's get a fire lit," he rumbled, "I could do with a pan of soup."

"You and your soup," said Saark.

"It's good for the ancient teeth," said Kell, but whereas once Saark would have bantered, now a gloomy silence fell on the group and they worked quietly, their humour a thing of the past.

Once the fire was lit, and a little warmth built inside the road shelter, Kell used the last of their supplies to make a thin, watery soup. He also discovered he'd used the last of the salt. He cursed. What was life without a little salt?

Outside, darkness fell, and the snowfall increased in intensity.

"Winter's finally come," said Saark, gesturing out of the small windows.

"Good," grunted Kell. "It'll slow the invading army."

"Don't you find it odd," said Saark, playing with his dagger on the thick-planks of the table.

"What do you mean?"

"The Army of Iron, invading at the start of winter. Guaranteed a slow advance, men freezing to death, supply problems, lowered morale. There's nothing like standing all night in the damn snow to sap a man's morale; it's like spreading syphilis. I know, I've done it. I thought my feet would never get warm again. It was two whole days before I felt life in my little toes! So, a strange choice then, yes?"

"Yes," grunted Kell, finishing the last of his broth. He had made better, but the girls didn't complain. He'd expected a few jibes from Saark, along the lines of his soup being the watery consistency of old goat piss; but Saark had remained silent, moody. Since their fight in the street, Saark had retreated into himself, into his shell, and whilst a part of Kell was glad of the change in character, another part of him, a part he did not recognise, actually missed the banter. With a jolt like a shock of lightning, Kell realised he liked the dandy; although he was damned if he could figure out why.

Nienna and Kat moved away to sort out the sleeping arrangements, and check for extra blankets. They'd found some, which they laid out on the floor before the fire to banish vestiges of damp. Now they searched the cupboards and drawers at the back of the shelter.

"Look," said Kell, staring at Saark across the table. "I... I wanted to apologise. Again. For what happened back at the tavern. It rests uneasy with me, laddie. It shouldn't have happened. I am ashamed of what I did."

"Don't worry about it."

"No," said Kell. "I feel bad. And it wasn't totally your fault; when I drink whisky, it twists my brain. Turns me into the bad man from the poem." He smiled wryly. "Yes, the stanza they never repeat, lest it sour my legend. Ha!" He turned, stared into the fire for a while. Then he reached across the table. "Take my hand."

"Why? You want to read my palm?"

"No, I want to crush your fingers, idiot. Take my damn hand."

Saark took the old man's grizzled paws, felt the massive strength contained therein. He looked up into Kell's eyes, and swallowed. There was power there, true power, charisma, strength and an awesome resolve.

"That will never happen again, Saark, I promise you. I count you as a friend. You have saved my granddaughter's life, and you have fought with great courage on my behalf. If you ever see me touch a whisky bottle to my lips, please, smash me over the head with the fucking bottle. I will understand. And… I owe you, my friend. I owe you with my life. I will give my life to protect you."

Saark blinked, as Kell released him, and sat back a little. He grinned. "You could have just blown me a kiss."

"Don't get smart."

"Or sent some flowers."

"I might not kill you," snarled Kell, "but I'll slap your arse, for sure. Now be a good lad, and go and find some candles… the dark outside, well, it's getting kind of eerie; what with these Harvesters and cankers and damned albino bastards roaming the land."

"Candles won't stop the horrors of the dark, my friend."

"*I know that*! Just find some."

As Saark was rummaging around in the bottom of an old cupboard, the door to the road shelter opened and three figures were illuminated by firelight. They stood for a moment, surveying the interior, and then stepped in, leading another four refugees, presumably from recent slaughter in a local village.

Kell stood, taking up his axe, and stared at the newcomers. The villagers he dismissed immediately from his mind, for they were obviously refugees in tatters, half dead with cold. But the first three; they were warriors, vagabonds, and very, very dangerous. Kell could tell from the glint in their eyes, the wary way they moved, the cynical snarls ingrained on weary, stone-carved expressions.

"We saw your fire," said one of the newcomers, stepping forward. She was tall, taller than Kell even, her limbs wiry and strong, her fingers long, tapered, the nails of her right hand blackened from constant use of the longbow strapped to her back. She had short black hair, cropped rough, and gaunt features, her eyes sunken, her flesh stretched and almost yellow. "My name is Myriam."

"Welcome, Myriam," said Kell, watching as the other newcomers spread out. The four villagers cowered behind them, staring longingly at the fire. "Do you bring any supplies?"

"We have potatoes, meat, a little salt. The villagers here also have food between them. Are those your horses out back?"

"So what if they are?" said Saark, smoothly, standing beside Kell. "They are not for sale."

"I didn't say I wanted to buy them," said Myriam, and stalked forward, taking up a chair, reversing it, and sitting down, her arms leaning over the solid back. The two men approached, standing behind her; she was obviously the leader.

Kell eyed the men carefully. One was of average height, squat, and inexorably ugly. He had pock-marked skin, narrow dark eyes, or eye, as the left was a lifeless socket, red and inflamed, and his cubic head sported tufts of hair as if shaved with a blunt razor. Worst of all, his lips were black, the black of the smuggler, the black of the outlawed Blacklipper, and it gave his countenance a brooding, menacing air. Kell instinctively decided never to turn his back on the man.

"This is Styx," said Myriam, following Kell's gaze. She gave a narrow smile. "Don't lend him any money."

The second man was small and angry-looking, as so often small men were. He wore a thin vest, bloodstained and tattered, and scant protection against the cold. He was heavily muscled in chest, arm and shoulder, but what set him apart more than anything were his tattoos which writhed up hands, arms and shoulders, onto his neck and scampered across his face. His heavy tattooing denoted him as a tribesman from the eastern New Model Tribes, weeks of travel over treacherous swamps and land-pits, as the quicksand plains were known; even past Drennach.

"This is Jex," said Myriam, and Kell nodded to both men, who grunted at him, eyes appraising, noting his manner and his axe. They were gauging him for battle, and it made Kell uneasy. This was not the time, nor place.

"I am Kell. This is Saark. The two girls are Nienna and Kat."

Myriam nodded, and seemed to relax a little now introductions had been made. Styx and Jex pulled up chairs, scraping them across the boards, and sat behind Myriam as if deferring to her to speak.

"I've heard of you, Saark."

"You have?" he said, eyes glittering.

"You were the King's Sword-Champion. I saw you fight, in Vor, about five years ago. You were stunning, if a little arrogant."

"Well, I'll, admit I'm ever more arrogant now," he said, hand on hilt, "and happy to give a display of violence to any who beg."

"Styx here, despite being a Blacklipper and getting the shakes, is adept with a blade. Maybe in the morning we could have a tourney; spin a little coin?"

"I'd feel he was disadvantaged, having only one eye. It makes a devil of defence on that side. But you, my pretty, I'm sure you're adept with your little metal prick…"

Myriam flushed red, frowning, and started to rise.

"Enough!" boomed Kell, and Myriam settled back. Kell glared at Saark, then returned to the woman. "There are enough of the enemy out there to satisfy your bloodlust for a century. So let's just roast that nice bacon joint the villagers brought in, boil a few potatoes, and enjoy a bit of civilised company."

"I'm going to check on the horses," said Saark, and left the cabin, allowing cold air to swirl in.

Myriam shivered, and started to cough. The cough was harsh, savage, and Kell watched as the two men attended her, almost tenderly, despite their vagabond appearances. She coughed for a while, and Kell thought he saw blood. He looked again at her gaunt face, the sunken eyes, the shape of her skull beneath parched skin. He had seen such afflictions before; men, and women, riddled with cancers. He would wager Myriam was getting perilously close to death. It spooked him with a sense of his own mortality.

Give me an enemy to fight with my axe any day, he thought sourly, rather than some nasty sneaky little bastard growing deep down inside. Kell's eyes burned.

He felt a stab of pity for the woman. Nobody should die like that.

Kell stood, poured a cup of water and carried it to Myriam. She drank, and smiled her thanks. Through her pain, and gaunt features, and harsh cropped hair, Kell saw a glimmer of prettiness. Once, she would have been beautiful, he thought. But not just cancer had eaten her; bitterness and a world-weary cynicism had removed what beauty lines remained.

"I suggest you sit nearer the fire."

"She'll sit where she damn well pleases," snarled Jex, voice heavy with an eastern burr.

"As you wish."

"Wait," said Myriam, and met Kell's gaze. "Can I speak with you?"

"You're speaking with me."

"In private."

"There is no privacy." He smiled, coldly.

"Outside. In the snow."

"If you like."

They walked from the long cabin, boots crunching snow, Kell following Myriam a good distance until she stopped, leaning against a tree, wheezing a little. She gazed up at the falling snow, then turned, smiling at Kell. "It's the cold. It affects my lungs."

"I thought it was the cancer."

"That as well. What pains me most are the things I can no longer do, actions I remember performing with ease. Like running. Gods! Once I could run like the wind, all bloody day, up and down mountains. Nothing stopped me. Now, I'm lucky to run to the privy."

"You wanted to speak?" Kell stared at her, and felt a strange twinge of recognition. He leaned close, and she leaned away. "Do I know you?" he said, finally, his memory tugging at him.

"No. But I know of you. The Saga of Kell's Legend, a tale to frighten and inspire, a tale to breed heroes and soldiers, don't let the little ones leave the safety of the fire." She laughed, but Kell did not. "You're a hero through these parts," she said.

"According to some, aye," he sighed, and leant his own back against a pine. The wind howled mournfully through the trees, a low song, a desolate song. Somewhere, an owl hooted. "What's it to you?"

"I just... I heard stories of you. From my father. When I was a child."

"A child?" said Kell, disbelieving. "How old are you, girl?"

"Twenty-nine winters, round about now." She blushed. "I know. I look a lot older. It's because I'm dying, Kell. And... I know some of your past. Some of your history."

"Oh yes?" He did not sound thrilled.

"You could help me."

"I'm busy. There's an invasion going on, or hadn't you noticed?"

"You could save me from dying," she said, and her eyes were pleading. "You've been through the Black Pike Mountains. I know this. I've talked to an old soldier who swears he went there with you. He said you know all the secret trails, the hidden passes; and ways past the deadly Deep Song Valley, the Wall of Kraktos, and the Passage of Dragons. Well," she took a deep breath, "I need to go there; I need to walk the high passes. I need to reach…"

"Where do you need to reach?" said Kell, voice impossibly soft.

"The hidden valley," breathed Myriam, looking Kell straight in the eye. "Silva Valley."

"And what would you do there, lady?"

"You can see what is happening to me," said Myriam. Tears shone in her eyes. "For the past three years I have grown steadily weaker. Meat has fallen from my bones. I get terrible pains, in my sides, in my hips, in my head. I spent a fortune in gold on fat physicians in Vor; they told me I had tumours, parasitical growths inside, each the size of a fist. The physicians said I would die within the year, that there was nothing I could do… damn them all! But, three years later, I am still here, hanging on by a thread, still searching for a cure. But sometimes, Kell, sometimes the pain is so bad I wish I were dead." She started to cough again, and covered her mouth, turning away, staring into the night-blackened trees. Snow swirled on eddies of breeze. Kell could smell ice.

"You didn't answer the question," he said, when the fit had passed.

"What would I do in Silva Valley? They have… machines there. Machines that could heal me."

"They would change you," said Kell. "I have seen the result of their experiments. It was not good."

Myriam was closer, now, had edged closer so that Kell could smell the musk of her body. She pressed herself in to him, and he felt something he had not felt for a long time; a rising lust, surging from a deep dark pool he had thought long vanished with age. It had been a long time. Perhaps too long.

Kell's eyes shone, and he licked his lips, which gleamed, and calmed his breathing.

"I would make it worth your while. I would do anything to live," she said, her gaunt face inches from Kell's, her arms lifting to drape over his shoulders. Her body was lean against his, her small breasts hard, nipples pressing against him.

"You don't understand," Kell said, voice low, arms unconsciously circling her waist. "They are called the vachine. They would change you. They would… kill every part of you that is human. It is better, I think, to die like you are, than to suffer their clockwork indignities."

Myriam was silent for a while. She was crying.

"I'm sorry," said Kell. "The answer is no."

Myriam kissed him.

Back in the cabin, Saark sat back, aloof, watching the two men with open distaste. They were exactly the opposite of Saark; whereas he was beautiful, they were ugly; whereas he was elegant, they were clumsy. He dressed like a noble, Styx and Jex dressed like walking shit.

"Can I get you a drink?" said Kat, approaching the two men.

"You can sit on my lap, pretty one," said Jex, grinning through his tattoos.

"Ahh, no, just…"

"She's with me," said Saark, eyes cold.

"Is that so, dandy man?" Jex smiled at Saark, and he knew, then, knew violence was impending. These were dangerous, rough outlaws. They knew no rules, no laws, and yet by the scars on their arms they had survived battle and war for a considerable time. They were good, despite their savage looks and lack of dress-code. If they weren't good, they'd be long dead.

"It's simply a fact," said Saark, eyes flicking left to where the four refugees were unpacking meagre belongings. There were two men, two women, the youngest woman only sixteen or seventeen years old, hair braided in pigtails, pink skirts soiled from her forest escape. His eyes flickered to the two men. They were plump, hands ink-stained: town workers and bureaucrats, not warriors.

Styx leant forward a little, and drummed his fingers on the table. Saark saw they were near to Kell's Svian, and he blinked. It was unlike Kell to leave behind this weapon; it was his last blade, what he used when parted from his axe. A Svian, so the unwritten rule went, was also used in times of desperation for suicide. For Kell to have left it was… foolish, and meant that something had touched him; had rattled his cage. Did he know these people?

"You're a pretty little man, aren't you?" said Styx. He smiled through blackened stumps of teeth, which merged nauseatingly with the stained lips of the Blacklipper. I bet his breath stinks like a skunk, thought Saark.

"What, you mean in contrast to your own obviously handsome facial properties?"

Anger flared in Styx's good eye, but he controlled it with skill. Saark became wary. There was something more at stake here than a simple trading of insults. This was too controlled, too planned. What did they want?

"What I meant to say," said Styx, tongue moistening his black lips, "is that you're a pretty boy."

"Meaning?"

"Well, it's like this. I love fucking pretty boys, so I do. In more ways than one."

Jex laughed, and Saark caught a glimpse of steel beneath clothing. A hidden blade. Saark's hand strayed towards his own sword, a tentative crawl of edging fingers, eyes never leaving the two men exuding hate and arrogance and dark violent energy.

"I like to hear them squeal, you understand," smiled Styx, "only because pretty boys take so much better to the knives, to the scars. They scream, high and long, like a woman, and when you fuck them, later on as they're bent over a log or table, oh that feeling, so tight, so much resistance," he laughed, a low grumble of mirth, "what I like to call a good tight virgin-fuck, well man, that brings tears to old Styx's eye. But not as much as flowing tears to the weeping eyes of a pretty boy."

Saark smiled easily. "Well then, gentlemen, you seem to have me mixed up with somebody else. Because I fuck women, I fuck men, I fuck anything that moves. I'm used to taking it, so would offer little sport as your... how do you say? Virgin-fuck? But what I will offer..." He launched up, sword out, a movement so quick it brought the room to a sudden standstill and caught Styx and Jex with their mouths open... "Well, if it's a little sword-sport you want, I'm all yours, gentlemen."

Slowly, Jex pulled a weapon from beneath his clothing and pointed it at Saark. It was small, little bigger than his hand, and made from polished oak. Saark tilted his head, frowning. He had never seen such a weapon. There came a tiny *click*.

"You are familiar, of course," said Jex, "with the workings of a crossbow? This is similar. It can punch a fist sized-hole through a man at a hundred metres. It works on clockwork, was created by the very enemy who now advance through our land." He stood, chair scraping, and Saark licked suddenly dry lips. Styx stood as well, beside Jex, and pulled free a similar weapon.

"We call it a Widowmaker," said Styx, single eye gleaming. "But rather than cause unnecessary bloodshed, I see you need a demonstration." His arm moved, there came a *click* and a *whump* as the clockwork-powered mini-crossbow discharged. The sixteen year-old villager was picked up and slammed across her bed, an impact of red at her breast, a funnel of flesh exploding from her back and splattering up the wooden wall with strips of torn heart and tiny shards of bone shrapnel.

"No!" screamed the older woman, and ran to the dead teenager, sobbing, mauling at her corpse which rolled, slack and useless and dead, to the floor. The room fell still; cold and terrifying.

"Damn you, you could have fired at a target!" raged Saark.

Styx nodded, gaze fixed to Saark. "Aye, I did. I find the horrors of the flesh have more immediate impact."

Kat stalked forward, eyes furious, hands clenching and unclenching. "You cheap dirty stinking bastards! She was an innocent villager, she meant no harm to you; why the hell would you do that? Why the hell would you kill an unarmed girl?"

Styx smiled, showing blackened stumps. "Because," he said, eye narrowing, all humour leaving his face to be replaced by an innate cruelty, the natural evil of the predator, the natural amorality of the shark, "I am a Jailer," he said, "and I thrive on the pleasure of killing sport."

"The Jailers," said Saark, voice barely above a whisper, sword still poised.

Styx nodded. "I see you have heard of us."

"What the hell are Jailers?" snapped Kat, eyes moving fast between Jex, Styx and Saark. She willed Saark to attack. She had seen him in battle, seen him kill with his pretty little rapier; she knew he could get to them in time, could slaughter them like the walking offal they were...

"They spent five years in Yelket Jail," said Saark, speaking to Kat but not moving his eyes from the two men with their clockwork crossbows. "They are very, very dangerous. They were put inside because of Kell. And six months ago, they escaped, and have been terrorising travellers on the Great North Road, killing Leanoric's soldiers and innocent people up and down the land... they are destined to be hanged."

"See, you do know us," smiled Styx, and his weapon settled on Kat. "Now, Saark, my queer little friend, I want you to place your sword *very slowly* on the ground. One wrong move, and I blow a ragged hole through Kat's pretty, pouting face."

Saark tensed... and from outside, heard a shout—

Myriam kissed Kell, and he allowed himself to be kissed, but his thoughts flowed back to his long dead wife, so long ago, so distant and yet so real and images flickered through his mind... getting married under the Crooked Oak, Ehlana with flowers in her hair and she kissed him and it was sweet and they were young and carefree, not knowing what troubles would face them over the coming years... and here, and now, this kiss felt like a betrayal even though she was dead, and so long ago gone, and cold, and dust under the ground. Kell pulled away. "No," he said.

"Help me," breathed Myriam.

"I cannot."

"You *will* not."

"Yes." He looked into her torture-riddled eyes. "I will not."

"I think you will," she said, and pushed the brass needle into his neck. Kell grunted in pain, taking a step back as he slammed a right hook to Myriam's head, making her yell out as she was punched into a roll, coming up fast, athletically, on her feet with a dagger out, eyes gleaming, triumphant, a sneer on her lips.

Kell staggered back, fingers touching at the brass needle poking from his flesh like a tiny dagger. "Bitch. What have you done to me?"

"It's a poison," said Myriam, licking her lips, her eyes wide and triumphant. "Very slow acting. Comes from a brace of Trickla flowers, from way across the Salarl Ocean." She tilted her head. "I'm sure you've heard of it?"

Kell nodded, and with a hiss, pulled the needle free, stared down at it, glinting in his palm, covered in his blood.

"You have killed me, then," he said, eyes narrow, face filled with a dark controlled fury.

"Wait!" Myriam snapped, and seemed to be listening for something. Then she stared up at the night sky. "There is an antidote." She grinned at him, head like a skull by starlight. "I have hidden it. Far to the north. Take me to the Black Pike Mountains, Kell, and you will live!"

"How long do I have?"

"A few weeks, at most. But you will grow weak, Kell. You will suffer, even as I suffer. We will be linked, lovers in pain, suffering together in dark throes of an accelerating agony, both searching for a cure."

"I could kill you now, bitch, and take my chances."

Myriam stood up straight, and sheathed her dagger. She held her head high. Her hair was peppered with snow. "Then do it," she said, eyes locked to Kell, "and let's be finished with this fucking business."

Kell took his axe from his back, loosened his shoulder with a rolling motion, and strode towards Myriam with a look of pure and focused evil.

Inside the cabin, Saark leapt, sword slashing down. Styx and Jex moved fast, slamming apart in a heartbeat and Styx's Widowmaker gave another click and whump and something unseen blurred across the open space hitting Katrina in the throat and smacking her back against the wall, pinned her to the boards as her legs kicked and her topaz eyes grew impossibly bright with collected tears and she gurgled and choked and spewed blood, and her fingers scrabbled at her chest and neck and the huge open wound and the dark glinting coil of brass and copper at her throat and quite suddenly...

She died.

Kat slumped, hung there, limp and bloodied, a pinned ragdoll, her legs twisted at odd angles.

"No!" screamed Nienna, dragging free her own sword in a clumsy, obstructed action. "No!" She charged.

THIRTEEN
Insanity Engine

General Graal, Engineer and Watchmaker of the vachine, stood on the hilltop and surveyed the two divisions below him, each comprising 4,800 albino soldiers, mainly infantry; they glittered like dark insects in the moonlight, nearly ten thousand armoured men, one half of the Army of Iron, standing silent and disciplined in ranks awaiting his command. The second half of his army were north, pitched to the southwest of Jalder, different battalions guarding northern passes and other routes leading through the Black Pike Mountains; in effect, guarding the route back to the Silva Valley, home of the vachine. Graal did not want the enemy, despite their apparent ignorance, mounting a counter-attack on his homeland whilst he invaded. But... was Graal making a mistake, taking only half his army south? He smiled, knowing in his heart it was not arrogance that fuelled his decision, but a trust in technology. With the Harvesters, and the power of blood-oil magick, the Army of Iron were... invincible! Even against a foe of far greater numbers; and Falanor barely had that.

Invincible!

And he also had his cankers.

A noise echoed across the valley, and Graal turned, and with acute eyesight aided by clockwork picked out the many canker cages used for more volatile beasts. The less insane were tied up like horses; seemingly docile for the moment. Until they smelt blood. Until they felt the thrill of the kill. Graal watched, licking thin lips, eyes fixing on the huge, stocky beasts which he knew linked so very closely to the vachine soul...

Occasionally, claws would eject and slash at the belly of another canker with snarls and hisses; but other than this, they could be safely tethered. Graal was in possession of just over a thousand cankers; the rejects of vachine society. But more were coming. Many more. Graal went cold inside, as he considered their tenuous position with the Blood Refineries. He thought of Kradek-ka, and his heart went colder still, the gears in his heart stepping up, cogs *whirring* as he grimaced and in a moment of rare anger bared his teeth and swept his gaze over the land before him. Moonlight glittered on armour. Beyond, lay Vorgeth Forest, and angling down he would march on Vor.

Mine! he snarled, an internal diatribe of hate. These people would suffer, they would fall, and his army would *feed!*

Graal calmed himself, for it was not seemly to show temper – an effective loss of control. And especially not before the inferior albino clans from under the mountain. No. Graal took a deep breath. No. A Watchmaker should have charm, and stability, cold logic and

control. They were the superior race. Superior by
birth, genetics and ultimately, superior by clockwork.

Frangeth was a platoon lieutenant, and with sword
drawn he led his twenty men through the trees under
moonlight. An entire battalion had divided, spread
out, and from different points north were advancing
as scouting parties, ahead of the great General Graal
himself. Frangeth was proud to be a part of this oper-
ation, and would happily give his life. For too long he
had felt the hate of the southerners, their irrational
ill-educated fear, and how their culture and art de-
picted his albino race as monsters, little more than
insect workers worthy of nothing more than a swift
execution. He had read many Falanor texts, with titles
like *Northern Ethics*, *On Execution*, and the hate-fuelled
Black Pike Diaries about a group of hardcore mercenaries who had travelled the aforementioned mountains,
searching out "rogue albino scum" and slaughtering
them without mercy.

Frangeth had been part of an elite squad under the
command of the legendary Darius Deall, and they had
infiltrated Falanor – a decade gone, now – to the far
western city of Gollothrim. There, under cover of
darkness, they had found the remains of the mercenary squad, and in particular, the authors of the *Black
Pike Diaries*. Drunk, and rutting in whorehouses on the
proceeds of their hateful tome, the five men had been
captured, harshly beaten, and driven by ox-cart to the
outskirts of Vorgeth Forest where lawlessness was a
given. Here, in an abandoned barn previously scouted,
old, deserted, with cracked timbers and wild rats, the

authors of the *Black Pike Diaries* had been pegged out, cut and sliced and diced, and then left for the rats whilst the albino squad watched from a balcony, eating, drinking, talking quietly. The wild rats, free from a fear of man, took their time with their feast. The authors of the *Black Pike Diaries* had died a horrible but fitting death for their crime.

Frangeth shook his head, smiling at the memories. Ten years. Ten long years! He had raised a family back in his tunnel since then: two daughters, one of them only three years old and even more pretty than her mother, her eyes a deeper red, her skin so perfectly translucent veins stood out like a river map.

Frangeth pushed the images away. No. Not now. This was a time of invasion, a time of war. And here he was, back in the province of the southerners, with their hate and unrivalled prejudice; here he was, travelling the darkest reaches of Vorgeth Forest, searching for the enemy. Any enemy. He smiled. All southern blood tasted the same.

Frangeth and the soldiers were angling south-east, at the same time as a similar battalion crossed Valantrium Moor to the east and angled south-west, the idea being they would link as a forward host to the main force of Graal's army on the Great North Road. That way, it would be difficult for Leanoric's battalions to circle and hit them from behind. That way, it would be a straight fight, with the blood-oil magick chilling ice from the earth, and chilling the enemy... to their very bones.

Frangeth halted, and held up his hand, which gleamed, pale and waxen in the moonlight filtering through firs. Behind, the other nineteen members of the platoon dropped to one knee and waited his instruction. Frangeth heard several whispers of iron on leather, and his eyes narrowed. Such noise was unprofessional.

He focused. It had been a shout, of surprise, more than pain, that alerted him. He took in the scene with an experienced glance, watched the huge man, bear-like in his stance, pluck something from his neck and stare at his great paws. He spoke with... a woman, but a woman who appeared as nothing Frangeth had ever seen. She was skeletal, and quite obviously close to death. Frangeth watched the huge man un-sling a battle-axe from his back and march on the woman and a thrill coursed his veins, for the warrior's demeanour was quite obvious, his intention to kill...

The woman's head snapped right, and her eyes fixed on the darkness where Frangeth and his albino soldiers crouched. Impossible! They were shrouded by blood-oil magick; they were invisible! She drew a small weapon and her arm extended towards the group, she snarled something at the huge warrior as suddenly, there came an explosion of glass and through the window of the timber building accelerated a small, powerful man, to land with a grunt on the snow.

Frangeth glanced back. He blinked. They were waiting.

"Take them," he said, and from the close nigritude of the forest streamed twenty albino warriors...

* * *

Myriam fired her Widowmaker with a *whump*, and
one of the charging albino soldiers was smacked from
his feet with a gurgle and wide spray of blood. Kell
loosened his shoulder and lifted his axe, waiting coolly
for the rush of men. Saark leapt from the window of
the building, landed lightly in the snow behind the
stunned figure of Styx, and lifted his rapier to deliver
a killing blow – as his eyes focused on the stream of
albino soldiers and Kell bellowed, "Saark, to me!" and
the albino soldiers were on them, swords slamming
down, flashing with moonlight. Steel rang on steel as
Myriam dragged free her own sword, the Widowmaker useless at such close quarters. Kell's axe
whirred, decapitating a soldier then twisted, huge
blades cleaving another's arm from his body. Kell
ducked a whistling sword, but a boot struck his chest
and he staggered back. Saark leapt into battle, and as
the forest clearing was filled with savage fighting, the
clash of steel on steel, grunts of combat, a shout from
Myriam echoed.

"Styx! Jex! To me! I need you!"

Styx rolled from the snow, and came up fighting.
Jex staggered from the building with a sword-wound
to his upper arm, face grim, and lifting his blade he
leapt into battle. At the doorway appeared Nienna,
face drawn grey in fear, her short-sword clasped in
one hand, the blade edged with Jex's blood. With a
gasp, she turned and ran back to check on Kat…

Almost unconsciously, Kell, Saark, Myriam, Jex and
Styx formed a fighting unit, a battle square upon
which the albinos hurled themselves. Swords and
Kell's axe rose and fell, and they covered one

another's backs, pushing forward deeper into the forest as the albinos swarmed at them, and were cut down with a savagery not just of desperation, but born from a need to live.

Eight albinos lay dead, and the rest backed away a little, then split without word, six men moving off to each side for an attack against both flanks.

"Kell, what the hell's going on?" snarled Saark.

"Long story," growled Kell. "I'll tell you when we've killed these bastards."

"When?"

"Listen, just don't trust this bunch of cut-throats!"

"I already discovered that," snarled Saark. "Styx killed Katrina."

"What?"

In eerie silence the albinos attacked, and again the clearing was filled with steel on steel. Then a sword-blow cleaved Styx's shoulder with a crunch, and shower of blood. Styx drew out a short knife, and rammed it into the albino's belly, just under the edge of his black breast-plate. He pushed again, harder, and the albino slumped forward onto him. Myriam broke from the group, whirling and dancing, dazzlingly fast as she took up a second sword from a fallen soldier and leapt amongst the men, blades clashing and whirring, then in quick succession killing three albino soldiers who hit the ground in a burst. Saark killed two, and Kell waded into the remaining group with a roar that shook the forest, Ilanna slamming left, then right, a glittering figure of eight which impacted with jarring force leaving body-parts littering the clearing. Kell ducked a sword-strike, front kicked the soldier who stumbled, falling back onto his rump. Kell's axe glittered high, and came down as if chopping a log to cut the albino soldier straight through, from the crown of his head down to his arsehole. His body split in two, peeling away like parted sides of pork revealing brain and skull and fat and meat, and a slither of departing internal organs and bowel. A stench filled the clearing, and Kell turned, face a bloody mask, chest heaving, rage rampant in his eyes and frame. He realised the soldiers were all dead, and he lifted his axe, staring hard at Myriam. Styx sat on the floor, nursing his injured shoulder as Jex tried to stem the flow of blood. Nienna ran out from the barracks, crying, and fell into Kell despite his coating of gore.

"Styx killed Katrina!" she wailed, then looked up into her grandfather's eyes. "Kill him, please, for me," she turned and pointed at Styx and wailed, "Kill him! Kill him now!"

Kell nodded, pushed Nienna aside, and started forward hefting his axe. Myriam leapt between them, head high, eyes bright, and she lifted a hand. "Wait. To kill him, you must go through me. And if you do that, you'll never find the antidote."

"A chance I'm willing to take," growled Kell. "Move, or I'll cut you in half."

"Nienna has also been poisoned."

Kell stopped, then, and his head lowered. When he lifted his face, his eyes were dark pools of evil in a face so contorted with rage it was inhuman; a writhing demon. Myriam took a step back.

Kell turned to Nienna. "Did he stick a needle in you?"

Nienna nodded, pointing at Jex. "That's why I was able to hit him. With my sword. He was too busy playing with his little brass dagger… his needle? What have they done to me?"

"They've poisoned us," snarled Kell.

"But there's an antidote?" said Saark.

"Yes. To the north. If I take this whore to the Black Pike Mountains. She wishes," he gave a nasty grin, "to explore the vachine technology. She wishes to live."

Saark stood alongside Kell, and Nienna. "We should kill them now. We will find this antidote."

"You do not have time," said Myriam, voice soft. "It takes between two and three weeks for the poison to kill. It would be more than that to sail across the Great Salarl." She transferred her gaze to Nienna, and gave a narrow, cruel smile. Without looking at Kell, she said, "I understand your willingness to condemn yourself, old man. But what of this sweet child? So young, pretty, and with so much to look forward to. So much to *live* for."

"We need to warn Leanoric," said Saark, hand on Kell's arm.

Kell felt himself fold, internally; but outside he kept his iron glare, and turned to Nienna. "Do you understand what is happening?"

Nienna nodded, and wiped away her tears. "I understand there are many evil people in the world," she said, voice little more than a whisper. "But we must warn King Leanoric that the enemy approach. Or thousands more will die!"

Kell nodded, glancing at Myriam. "You hear that,

bitch? I will take you to the mountains. But first, we ride south."

"You would gamble with your life? And that of the girl?" Myriam looked aghast, and she shook her head, staring down at Styx and Jex. Styx had his shoulder bound tight, and stood, flexing the limb.

Kell scowled at him. "Know this, Blacklipper. When we are done, I will come looking for you."

"I will be waiting," said Styx.

Ilanna beat a tattoo of warning in Kell's mind, and he gazed off between the trees. "I think there are more," he said, voice low. "We need to get the horses. We need to ride south now."

Saark and Jex went for the mounts, as snow tumbled from bleak dark skies above the edges of Vorgeth Forest. Within a few minutes they had mounted, Nienna behind Saark, and as the forest whispered with ancient leaves and branches and needles, so more platoons of albino soldiers, drawn by distant sounds of battle, emerged warily from the foliage. There were two platoons – forty soldiers, and their cautious advance turned swiftly into a run with weapons drawn as they spotted fallen comrades...

"Ride!" shouted Saark, and his horse reared. Myriam led the way, thundering out of the clearing down a narrow dark path, her sword in her fist, head lowered over her mount. The rest of the group followed, with Jex bringing up the rear firing bolts from his Widowmaker with metallic winding *thumps*, and smashing several soldiers from their feet.

Then they were gone, lost to the sinister forest.

* * *

King Leanoric calmed his horse, a magnificent eighteen-hand stallion, and peered off through the gloom. A curious mist had risen, giving the moorland plateau a curious, cut-off feeling, a sidestep from reality, a different level of existence.

He had left his personal guard behind, a mile hence, aware that the Graverobber would never agree to meet him with soldiers present. The Graverobber was a fickle creature at the best of times, but add in a heady mix of weapons, armour and soldierly sarcasm... well, claws were ejected and the Graverobber would begin to kill without question.

Leanoric walked over springy heather, and stopped by the towering circle of stones. *Le'annath Moorkelth*, they were called in the Old Tongue. Or simply the Passing Place in every contemporary Falanor lexicon. Whatever the origins of the stones, it was said they were over ten thousand years old, and evidence of an earlier race wiped from existence by an angry god. Leanoric peered into the space between the stones, where the Graverobber dwelled, and again felt that curious sensation of light-headedness, as if colours were twisting into something... else. Leanoric rubbed his beard, then stepped into the circle and heard a hiss, a growl, and the patter of fast footfalls on heather...

The Graverobber leapt at him, and Leanoric forced his eyes to remain open, forced himself to stare at the twisted, corrugated body of the deformed creature, once human but deviated by toxins, poisons, its skin a shiny, ceramic black, tinkling as it moved, tinkling as if it might shatter. It, or he, was thin-limbed, his head perfectly round and bald with narrow-slitted eyes and a face not a thousand miles from that of a feline. He had whiskers, and sharp black teeth, and a small red tongue, and as he leapt for Leanoric with claws extending and powerful, corded muscles bunched for the kill, so Leanoric spoke his name, and in doing so, tamed the savage beast–

"Jageraw!"

The Graverobber hit the ground lightly, and turned, spinning around on himself on all fours before rearing into an upright walking position. Leanoric heard the crinkle of ceramic spine, and pretended he hadn't.

"What want you here, human?"

"I have questions."

"What makes you think I answer?"

"I have a gift."

"A gift? For me? How pretty. What is it?" Jageraw's demeanour changed, and he dropped to all fours again, black skin gleaming unnaturally. Leanoric opened the sack he was carrying, and steeling himself, put in his hand. He pulled out a raw liver. It glistened in the gloom, and the muscles on Leanoric's jaw went tight.

Jageraw sniffed, and edged closer, eyes watching Leanoric suspiciously. He swayed, peering past Leanoric into the gloom, then focused on the liver. "Human or animal?"

"Human," said Leanoric, voice little more than a whisper. "Just the way you like it."

Jageraw lashed out, taking the liver, then went through an elaborate sequence where he sniffed, and licked, and tasted, and sampled. When finally happy, the shiny black creature, glistening as if coated with oil, moved to the centre of the stone circle, dug up a little earth and buried the organ.

"You bring me more, human man?"

"Answers."

"To questions? Ask questions. You bring me more?"

"I have two hearts, two kidneys and another liver."

Jageraw's eyes went wide, as if offered the finest feast of his life. He licked his thin shiny lips, and his sharp teeth clattered for a moment as if in unadulterated excitement.

"Ask your questions."

"There is an army advancing on my land. It is said they use blood-oil magick." Jageraw twitched, as if stung, and a crafty look stole over his face. "I want to know if it is true."

"Who leads the army?"

"General Graal. He is a… vachine."

Jageraw hunkered down, and hissed. "They are not good. They are bad. They are not pretty. They are far from pretty. You want to avoid these men, they have blood-oil magick. Yes."

"How do I fight them?"

"Hmm. The food smells nice. Smells pretty. Smells succulent. Jageraw would like another sample."

Leanoric threw the bag, which thudded as it hit the ground. Jageraw leapt forward, excitement thrumming through his taut muscled body, and Leanoric watched the Graverobber chewing and tasting, head in the bag, then emerging, blood dribbling down his chin as his dark eyes surveyed King Leanoric.

"You are very generous, *sire.*" He chuckled, as if at some great jest. His head tilted, and not for the first time Leanoric thought to himself, what the hell kind of creature are you? What happened to you? Why do you eat human remains – hence earning the title of Graverobber, from earlier days? Days when you robbed graves for your food. And, ultimately, why can you no longer leave this ancient circle of stones? Others had asked such questions, and several eminent professors from Jalder University had been sent to research the Old Ways and the Blood-oil Magick Legacy for purposes of scholarly study. All were dead. Jageraw might seem an oddity, but he was powerful beyond belief, and had the ability to… fade away when threatened.

Once, three mercenaries had been hired to bring back the Graverobber's carcass, with or without a head. One entered the circle with a bag of goodies, and enticed Jageraw out as his comrades waited in the gloom of falling night with powerful longbows. They peppered Jageraw with savage, barbed, poisoned arrows, six or seven of which thudded home to sprays of bubbling blood in slick black flesh. In squealing agony, Jageraw grabbed the first mercenary within the circle and they… vanished. Or so the story went. The man's companions waited for three nights for their friend, and one evening emerged to discover him lying in the circle, his body peeled but still, incredibly, alive. He'd whimpered pitifully, pleading and begging for help. His companions on impulse rushed into the circle, and Jageraw pounced from nowhere, his body perfectly healed, his claws cutting through swords and shields to sever heads from bodies. That night, Jageraw ate well.

Now, people left the Graverobber to himself.

"You want to fight Army of Iron, you say? Yes. Their blood-oil magick is powerful, very powerful, and they walk the Old Ways with Harvesters of Legend. That is where their power comes from. Freeze your men with horror," he chuckled, "they will."

"I never said it was the Army of Iron," said Leanoric, eyes narrowing.

"That is who Graal commands. Kill him, you must." Jageraw took a bite from a human heart, and chewed thoughtfully, staring down at his food. "Their magick takes time to cast, that is your strength. They attack at night, yes, pretty pretty night. You must think of a way to circle them, or draw them out. Once they unleash their magick, for a little while, it is out of their control. Now I must go. Now I must eat. Told you too much, I have."

Jageraw grinned, dark eyes glinting malevolently.

"Thank you… Jageraw."

"Come back any time," said the slick black creature, backing away from King Leanoric with ceramic tinklings. "Bring gifts, bring feast, pretty meat from still warm human bodies is what I prefer." His eyes blinked, and he started to fade. "If you survive, little king," he chuckled, and was gone.

Leanoric realised he was kneeling, and stood up. He backed hurriedly from the ancient circle of stones, and realised his sword was half drawn. He shivered, aware there were some things he would never understand; and acknowledging there were things he did not want to understand. Jageraw could rot, for all he now cared.

Leanoric turned, mounted his horse, and set off across the mist-laden moors as fast as he dared.

Behind, at the edge of the circle, unseen and rocking rhythmically sat Jageraw, gnawing on fresh liver, and waving with crinkled, blood-stained claws.

Kell, Saark, Nienna, Myriam, Styx and Jex rode hard through the rest of the night, exhausting their horses and breaking out onto the Great North Road just north of Old Skulkra, a deserted ghost-city which sat three leagues north of the relatively new, modern, and relocated city of Skulkra.

They reined in mounts on a low hill, gazing down the old, overgrown, frost-crusted road which led from the Great North Road to distant, crumbling spires, smashed domes, detonated towers, fragmented buildings and fractured defensive walls. On the flat plain before Old Skulkra Leanoric had two divisions camped after moving north from Valantrium Moor, 9,600 men plus a few cavalry, lancers and archers stationed to the north of the infantry to provide covering fire in case of surprise attack. In the dawn light their fires had burned low, but there was activity.

"Remember," said Myriam, leaning forward over the pommel of her saddle. "Any tricks or signals, and the girl dies in two weeks time. A terrible, painful death."

"How could I forget?" said Kell, and went as if to ride for Leanoric's camp.

"Wait," said Saark, and Kell turned on him. There was pain there, in Saark's face, in his eyes, and he smiled a diluted smile at Kell, then gazed off, towards the camp. "I cannot come," he said.

"Why the hell not?" snapped Kell. "It was your damn fool idea to warn the king in the first place!"

"To travel to that camp would mean death," said Saark, voice gentle.

"What are you muttering about, lad? Come on, we need to warn Leanoric. Those bastards might only be a few hours behind us. What if they hit the army now, like this, camped and scratching its arse? It will be a rout, and they'll flood into the south like a plague."

"If I go down there," said Saark, quietly, "King Leanoric will have me executed."

"Why the hell would he do that, lad?"

Saark looked down, and when he looked up, there were tears in his eyes. "I... betrayed him. Betrayed his trust. And he sentenced me to death. I... ran. Yes. I stand before you filled with shame."

"And still you have come back to warn him?" sneered Styx. "What a fucking fool you are, Saark. As I said. A pretty boy."

"If you do not close your stinking, horse-arse mouth, I'll shove my sword so far up your belly it'll come out the top of your head! Understand, *Blacklipper*?"

Kell held up his hand, glaring at Myriam. "What did you do, Saark?" His voice was soft, eyes understanding.

Saark took a deep breath. "I was Leanoric's Sword-Champion. I was entrusted with guarding the queen. Alloria. We... I, fell in love with her. We committed a great sin, both of us betraying the great King Leanoric." He fell silent, unable to look at Kell. Finally, he glanced up. He met Kell's gaze. "I have been running away ever since. I have been a coward. I knew, when the army invaded Jalder, that even though I might die I had to come here. I had to try and help, even though they would slaughter me as a base criminal, a rapist, a murderer. Now… I cannot face it. Although I should."

Kell nudged his horse forward, and patted Saark on the back. "Don't worry lad. You stay here. I'll go and speak to the king. I know him from… way back. I'll let him know what is happening to his realm."

Saark nodded, and Kell gestured to Nienna. "Come with me, girl. It is important to meet nobility, even in times such as these. I will teach you how to speak with a king."

"I am coming with you," said Myriam.

"No," said Kell.

"I don't trust you."

Kell laughed, then waved his hand. "So be it. You think I would risk my only chance of beating your pathetic little poison for my granddaughter? Come, then, Myriam; come and frighten the little children with your skull face." Myriam flushed crimson with fury, but bit her tongue and said nothing, eyes narrowed, hand on sword-hilt. If Kell had to endure her poison, he reasoned, then she, too, would have to endure his. They were symbiotic, now; but that didn't mean Kell had to enjoy it.

"You see the stand of trees? Over yonder?"

"Aye," said Kell.

"We'll wait for you there," said Saark, eyes hooded, face filled with melancholy.

Kell nodded, reading Saark's face. "Play nice, now," he said, and kicked his horse forward alongside Nienna. A moment later, Myriam followed leaving the three men on the low hill. They watched the small group descend, where they were quickly intercepted by scouts and a small, armoured cavalry squad. Weapons were taken from them, and they were escorted towards the shadowy, crumbling walls of a leering, eerie Old Skulkra.

"You leading the way, pretty boy?" grinned Styx. Saark glanced at him, and saw the Widowmaker held casual in one fist, wound and giving an occasional tick. Saark nodded, and guided his horse south, down the hill and towards nearby woodland. As he rode, his thoughts turned violent.

"Kell! By all the gods, it is good to see you!"

King Leanoric's tent was filled with incense, rich silks and furs, and he was seated in full armour around a narrow table containing maps, alongside Terrakon and Lazaluth, his Division Generals. They had cups of water clasped in gnarled hands, and Lazaluth smoked a pipe, dark eyes narrowed, ancient white whiskers yellowed from the pipe smoke he so loved.

The men stood, and Kell grinned, embracing first Leanoric, then Terrakon and Lazaluth, both of whom Kell knew well, for they had fought alongside one another in ancient, half-forgotten campaigns. The four men stood apart, smiling sombrely.

"I hope, by all that's holy, you've come to fight," said Leanoric.

"So my journey is wasted? You know of the events in Jalder?"

"Only that is has been taken. We have no specifics. It would seem," Leanoric's face turned dark, brooding, "that few survived."

Myriam and Nienna were taken outside, and seated with a group of women awaiting a meal of stew and bread. They accepted this food thankfully, and Myriam found Nienna watching her strangely; there was a hint of hate, there, but also a deep thread of needful revenge. Myriam smiled. Nienna's bitterness, growing cynicism and fast rise to adulthood started to remind her of herself.

Inside the war-tent, Kell hurriedly outlined his recent exploits in Jalder, from the ice-smoke invasion and the incursion of heartless, slaughtering albino soldiers, murdering men, women and children without mercy, down to accounts of the cankers and Harvesters, and the subsequent battles as they travelled south.

"Have you seen this Army of Iron?" said Lazaluth, puffing on his pipe and churning out a cloud of blue smoke.

Kell shook his head. "Only platoons of albino soldiers. But they fight like bastards, and use the ice-smoke blood-oil magick – freezing everybody in their path. And they have the cankers. I know in my heart they have more of these beasts; they are savage indeed."

"How far behind you lies this albino army?"

"The vanguard? No more than a few hours."

"Really," said Leanoric, voice low. His eyes narrowed. "My scouts, to a man, tell me three days. We have another two divisions on the march; they will arrive tomorrow, just ahead of the enemy."

"No," said Kell, shaking his head. "Your scouts are... lying. Or misinformed. Graal is closer than you believe, I swear this by every bone in my body."

"That's impossible!" roared Terrakon. "I have known Angerak since he was a pup! He is a fine scout, and would never betray his king, nor his country! Get the lad in here, we'll question him. You must be mistaken, Kell. It is not in this boy's nature."

Kell waited uneasily as Angerak was summoned, and he felt the eyes of the old Division Generals on him. He grinned at them, a broad-teeth grin. "You can cut out that shit, gentlemen; I no longer serve under your iron principles. You can stick your polished breastplates up your arse!"

"You always were a cheeky young bear," growled Terrakon. "But fight! Gods, I have never seen a man fight like you. It's good to have you here, Kell. It is a good omen. We're going to give this Graal a kicking he won't forget, send him running back to the Black Pikes squeaking with his shitty piglet tail between his legs. Aye?"

Angerak was shown in, and he bowed before Leanoric. He cast a sideways glance at Kell, displaying a narrowed frown, then returned his eyes to the king. "Majesty, you sent for me?"

"Tell me again what you saw of the enemy on your journey north."

"I filed a full report already, sire. I–"

"Again, Angerak."

Angerak looked left and right, at the old Division Generals, then coughed behind the back of his hand.

"I travelled up over Corleth Moor; it was bathed in a heavy mist, and I dismounted, moved further in on foot. There, in the Valley of Crakken Fell, I saw the Army of Iron, camped out with perhaps three to four thousand soldiers. They were disorganised, like children playing at war; like idiots in a village carnival. We will slaughter them with ease, sire. Do not worry."

"So," Leanoric chose his words with infinite care, "there is… no chance they could be closer?"

"No, sire. I would have passed them on my journey. I have been a scout for many years; I do not make mistakes. There were no other battalions nearby, and their skills at subterfuge were, shall we say, lacking."

"It's funny, laddie," interjected Kell, drawing all eyes in the war-tent to him, "but, you know, I've just been chased here through Vorgeth Forest with at least sixty albino soldiers right behind me. Their army is close behind, I'd wager. What would you say to that?"

Angerak placed his hand on his sword-hilt. "I would say you are mistaken, sir." A cool and frosted silence descended on those in the tent. Terrakon and Lazaluth exchanged meaningful glances. Angerak looked around, eyes hooded. "I would also suggest I do not like your tone."

"What are they paying you, boy? What did General Graal offer?"

Angerak said nothing. His eyes remained fixed on Leanoric. He shook his head. Finally, he said, "You are mistaken in your beliefs. I have been a faithful scout for the past–" The dagger appeared from nowhere, and in a quick lunge he leapt at Leanoric… but never made the strike. In his back appeared Ilanna, with a

sickening *thutch*, and Angerak crashed to floor on his
face. Kell stepped forward, placed his boot on
Angerak's arse and wrenched free the weapon, dripping molten flesh. He looked around at those present.

"Get your scouts in here," he said. "It would seem
Graal has already infiltrated your army." Kell threw
Leanoric a thunderous frown. "I hope your strategy is
in place, gentlemen."

"We have two divisions coming from the northeast," said Leanoric. "They will be here by the
morning."

Kell rubbed his beard. "So you have just under ten
thousand men? Let us hope the enemy is weak…"

"We must draw the Army of Iron back, into the city
wasteland of Old Skulkra. I will have archers placed
in ancient towers – a thousand archers! If we can do
this, fake a retreat, draw them in, then we will slaughter them." Leanoric stepped forward, sighing. "Kell,
will you stay? Will you help us?"

"You have your generals here," said Kell, voice
grave, looking to Terrakon and Lazaluth. "I have my
granddaughter to consider… but I will help, where I
can." He stepped swiftly from the tent… just as a
scream rent the air…

"Attack! We're under attack!"

The camp exploded into action, with men
scrambling into armour and strapping on weapons.
Fires flared. Distant over the plain, before Old Skulkra,
the enemy could be seen: the Army of Iron, formed
into squares, a huge and terrifying, perfectly organised
mass. They marched down from the hills in clockwork
unity, boots stomping frozen grass and snow, the

gentle rattle of accoutrements the only indication they
were marching into battle. Leanoric strode out behind
Kell, his strong face lined with anxiety. Quickly, he
surveyed the enemy, and something went dead inside
as he realised the two armies were equally matched.
This was not to be his finely trained troops routing
invading, poorly fed brigands from the mountains.
This was two advanced armies meeting on a flat plain
for a tactical battle...

Draw them back into the city.

*Break away from the ice-smoke, from the blood-oil
magick...*

His troops had been warned; they knew what to do
if General Graal attempted underhand tactics. But
would this be enough? With a skilled eye Leanoric
read the albino discipline like a text. They were tight.
Impossibly so.

Over the horizon, dawn light crept like a frightened
child.

"Generals!" bellowed Leanoric, taking a deep breath
and stepping forward. "To me! Captains – organise
your companies, now!" Leanoric's men quickly fell
into ranks, reorganised into battle squares, as they had
done so many times on the training field. Leanoric felt
pride swell his chest in the freezing dawn chill, for the
men of Falanor showed no fear, and moved with a
practised agility and professionalism.

Then his eyes fell to the enemy.

The Army of Iron had halted, weapons bristling.
They looked formidable, and eerily silent, pale faces
hazy through distance, and through a light mist that
curled across the ground.

"They look invincible," said Leanoric, voice quiet.

"They die like any other bastard," growled Kell. "I have seen this. I have done this." He turned, and grasped Leanoric's arm. "So you're going to draw them back into the city? That is your strategy?"

"If it starts to go badly, aye," said Leanoric. He gave a crooked smile. "If they try to use blood-oil magick. I have a few surprises in store in Old Skulkra."

The enemy ranks across the virgin battlefield parted, and several figures drifted forward between heavily armoured troops, even as Leanoric's captains organised battle squares before the fragmented walls of Old Skulkra. The figures were impossibly tall for men, and wore white robes embroidered in fine gold. They had flat, oval, hairless faces, small black eyes, and slits where the nose should have been. As they advanced before the Army of Iron, they stopped and surveyed Leanoric's divisions.

"Harvesters," said Kell, his voice soft, eyes hard.

And then a howling rent the air, followed by snarls and growls and the enemy ranks parted further as cankers were brought forward, devoid of protective cages, all now on leashes and many held by five, or even ten soldiers. They pulled at their leashes, twisted open faces drawn back, saliva and blood pooling around savage fangs as they snapped and growled, whined and roared, slashing at one another and squabbling as they arraigned their mighty, heavily-muscled, leonine bodies before the infantry squares in a huge, ragged, barely-controlled line.

Leanoric paled, and swallowed. He felt a chill fear sweep his soldiers. "Angerak never spoke of these beasts," he said, voice impossibly low, eyes fixed on the living nightmare cohort of the snarling, thrashing cankers…

They heard a distant command echo over the brittle, chill plain.

The cankers were suddenly unleashed with a jerk of chains, and with cacophonous howls of unbidden joy and bloodlust, a thousand heavily muscled beasts, of deviated flesh and perverted clockwork, charged and surged and galloped forward with snarls and rampant glee… towards the fear-filled ranks of Leanoric's barely organised army.

FOURTEEN
Inner Sanctum

Anu snarled, leaping at the Harvester which made an almost lazy, slow-motion gesture which nevertheless swept Anu aside with an invisible blow. She rolled fast, came up snarling, and circled the Harvester with more care. The Harvester flexed bone fingers, and lowered its head, black eyes glowing, as behind the creature, Alloria backed away, towards the crumpled figure of Vashell and some strangely perceived safety.

More ice-smoke swirled.

Anu attacked, and the Harvester moved fast, arms coming up as Anu's claws slashed down. The Harvester swiped at her, but she ducked, rolled fast, and her claws cut its robe and the pale flesh within. Skin and muscle parted, but no blood emerged.

Anu rolled free, and her eyes were gleaming, feral now, all humanity, even vachine intelligence gone as something else took over her soul and she reverted to the primitive.

"She cut it," whispered Vashell, his eyes wide. Never had he seen such a thing.

The Harvester shrugged off its robe, to reveal a naked, sexless, pale white body sporting occasional clumps of thick black hairs, like a spider's. Its legs were long and jointed the wrong way, like a goat's, and narrow taut muscles writhed under translucent flesh.

The Harvester moved fast, attacking Anu in loping strides, bone fingers slashing the air with a whistle. Anu rolled back, came up with her fangs hissing, then leapt again to be punched from her feet, sliding along frozen grass and almost pitching into the sluggish flow of the Silva River. Immediately she was up, charging, and rolled under swiping bone fingers, reversing her charge to leap on the Harvester's back. It swung around, trying to dislodge her, and savagely Anu's claws gouged the Harvester's throat, ripping free a handful of flesh, of windpipe, of muscle. She landed lightly, back-flipping away as the Harvester staggered.

It turned, and glared at her, eyes glowing, face now snarling. It did not speak. It could not speak. Anu held its windpipe in her fist. Amazingly, instead of dying, the Harvester attacked and Anu deflected a quick succession of blows with her forearms, and bone fingers clattered against her claws and the Harvester looked surprised... Anu's vachine claws should have been cut free. They were not. It snarled at her with a curious hissing gurgle, launched forward and grabbed her, picking her up above its head and moving as if to throw her... but Anu twisted, and there came a savage crack. The Harvester's arm broke, bone poking free through pale skin, again with no blood, just torn straggles of fish-flesh. Anu landed, and her claws slashed the Harvester's belly, then she leapt and her fangs fastened on its head, bearing it to the ground like a dwarf riding a giant. She savaged the Harvester's eyes, biting them out and spitting them free, then staggered back, strips of pale flesh hanging from her fangs, her face stunned as the mangled form of the Harvester rose and orientated on her. The mangled face smiled, and with a scream Anu ran at the creature, both feet slamming its head and driving it staggering backwards. It toppled, into the river, went under, and was immediately swept away. *Gone.*

Anu knelt, panting, staring at the cold surging waters, which calmed, flowing back into position with chunks of bobbing ice. She stood, smoothed her clothing, then turned on Vashell. His eyes were wide in his bloodied mask.

"That is... impossible," he said, softly.

"I killed it!" snarled Anu, face writhing with hatred and a strange light of triumph, of victory, conquering her fear.

"No," said Vashell, shaking his head. "You *hurt* it. And now, it simply needs a little time to..." He gave a soft smile, a caricature of the vachine in his demonic, faceless face. "Regenerate."

Anu stared at him, then back to the river. "Get on the boat."

Vashell eased himself to his feet, huge frame towering over Alloria. Unconsciously, Alloria reached out to help him, to steady him, and he stared at her, surprise in his eyes. She said nothing, but aided him hobbling to the jetty, and then down onto the long Engineer's Barge. Vashell slumped to a seat, blood tears running down his neck, and Alloria stared at

her hands – also gore-stained – and then into
Vashell's eyes.

"Thank… you," he managed. He licked at the broken stumps of his vachine fangs. They leaked precious
blood-oil. He was growing weak. He laughed at this,
a musical sound. Maybe he would die, after all.

Anu leapt into the boat, and as they moved away
from the jetty, the frozen ground sliding away, five
more Harvesters emerged from the mist. They drifted
to the edge of the river, staring silently at the boat.

Anu stared back, unspeaking.

"We will hunt you to the ends of the earth," said
one, voice a sibilant whisper, and then they were
gone, swallowed by towering walls of black rock, the
Engineer's Barge sucked further away and further
into the desolate, brutal realm of the Black Pike
Mountains.

The brass barge journeyed up the river, clockwork engine humming, nose pushing through chunks of ice.
A cold wind howled, desolate and mournful like a lost
spirit, and eventually they came to a river junction,
where two wide fast flowing sections split, each heading off up a particular steep canyon of leering
mountains. Anu's eyes followed each route, then she
turned to Vashell who was sat, head resting on the
barge rail, clawless fingers flexing.

"Which way?" she said.

"You really want to know?"

"Yes." She scowled. "Take me to my father."

"You won't like what you find."

"I will be the judge of that, vachine."

Vashell chuckled, and sighed. His fingers touched his ruined face, tenderly, and he glanced up, and over, at the raging waters, pointing. "That way."

"Are you sure?"

"Of course I am sure, girl!"

"Where does it lead?"

"Why," Vashell smiled, a demonic vision on his tortured face. "It leads to the Vrekken. And to Nonterrazake beyond."

Anu stared at him for a while, holding the brass barge steady in a gentle equilibrium against the current. "That cannot be," she said, finally.

"Why not?"

"Nonterrazake is a myth."

"It is a reality," said Vashell, smugly.

"You have been there?"

"It is something I do not wish to discuss, child." His eyes became hooded.

"I can cause you much pain, and bring you a savage death," said Anu, face ugly with anger in the snow-laden gloom.

Vashell shrugged. "There are some things far worse than death, Anu. That, you will learn. You want me to take you to Kradek-ka, then I will take you to Kradek-ka, although I promise you, you will not thank me for it, nor like the things you learn. But such is the nature of humanity, is it not?" He laughed, then, at his own private joke. "And that of the twisted vampire machines."

Anu guided the Engineer's Barge up the river, and as night fell, and the raging torrents grew calm again, she moored the craft in the centre of the wide river in order to gain a few hours' sleep.

She moved to central chambers below deck, and watched as Alloria made herself comfortable on a narrow bunk. "How do you feel?" asked Anu, and saw the way Alloria looked at her. As if she was a lethal, unpredictable, uncontrollable wild animal. Anu sighed.

"I will be fine once I leave this country," said Alloria, voice gentle, eyes red-rimmed. Only then did Anu realise she had been crying. "Once I travel home."

"You are upset?"

"My country is besieged by a savage clockwork race, and my husband must risk his life in battle. Yes, I am upset. I fear my children will be slaughtered. I fear my husband will have his throat cut. But most of all," she stared hard at Anu, "I fear your people will conquer."

"I am not part of their war," said Anu.

"You are one of them."

"They cast me aside!"

Alloria shrugged, her fear a tangible thing, and Anu realised with great sadness that she had lost Alloria. Alloria had seen the beast raging in Anu's soul; it had shocked her to the core.

"You are still vachine," said Alloria, and turned her back on Anu, snuggling under a heavy blanket.

Anu moved back to the upper deck, and checked the bindings on Vashell. With his vachine claws, he would have easily escaped; but now, neutered as he was, a machine vampire gelding, he could do little harm.

"You should let me go," said Vashell, looking into Anu's eyes.

"No."

"I will tell you the way. Draw you a map… in my own blood." He laughed, and Anu met his gaze. "I do love you, Anu. You know that?"

"You would kill me! You saw me disgraced. You revelled in your power and violent abuse."

"I have many faults," said Vashell. Then he gestured to his face, and chuckled again. "You have taught me humility." His voice grew more serious, emerging as a low growl. "But I do love you. I will always love you. Until the day I die. Until the day you kill me. You thought, back in Silva Valley, I was full of arrogance and hatred and superiority. You were right. I was despicable, and I understand why you spurned my offers of marriage; it wasn't just your fear at being different, Anu, it was deeper, in your soul, under lock and key." He sighed, and looked up at the heavy, cloud-filled sky. More snow began to tumble, and it drifted like ash. "We are destined, you and I. To live in a world of mixed love and hate, each strand intertwining around our hearts, our cores."

He gazed at Anu, eyes filled with tears.

"I will still kill you," said Anu, with tombstone voice.

"Good! I would not have it any other way. Go to sleep now. I will try nothing, do nothing. Trust me. After all… you took away my claws, you took away my fangs. Don't you realise? I am like you, Anu. I am neutered. I am an outcast. You turned me into yourself. I can never go back."

Anu walked down to her cabin, a narrow affair with nothing more than a bunk and brass walls. She locked the door, and realised with horror that Vashell was right. By removing his vachine tools, she had destroyed his rank, his standing, his nobility. She had deformed him from a beautiful vachine. There would be no repair by the Engineers; only terminal condemnation for his very great weakness.

So where would he go? What would he do?

No. Anu had attached Vashell to herself, to her mission, with chains much stronger than love. She had condemned him with a force of exile; an extradition of country, but more importantly, also of race.

The morning was bright and crisp, and snow had fallen lightly during the night, covering the brass barge with a light peppering of white. Vashell uncurled from slumber as Anu crept up the steps, and he stared at her with a bleak smile. Already, his face was healing, skin growing back over his destroyed features; but he would never look the same again. Despite his advanced vachine healing powers, he would be savagely scarred. Anu had, effectively, taken away his handsomeness. Removed his nobility.

Within a few minutes the brass barge was nosing up river, and for the course of the day they came upon more and more tributaries where a decision had to be made on which path to follow. Unfalteringly, Vashell would point, sometimes with a smart comment, other times in brooding silence as his moods swung from savage brutality to almost joyous abandon, as if high on a natural heady cocktail, where he would joke about his ruined features, and mock Anu, saying she was now the only girl for him, and they could breed twisted canker babies together.

As night fell, Anu sat on the deck for a while, huddled in a cloak. Vashell revelled in the cold. Alloria, who had been brooding and silent for the day, returned to her small brass room and huddled under blankets, crying softly to herself. Anu attempted to comfort her, but Alloria had taken to ignoring the young vachine.

"Tell me about Nonterrazake," said Anu.

"No."

"Tell me!"

"No!" He laughed. "There are some secrets a man must keep. Some dark truths he must hold to his heart, like spirals of soul; I could tell you, but it would melt your sweet little mind, curl the edges of your heart into blackened wisps of hatred, burn your soul with an eternity of hell-fire."

Anu shrugged. "Will the Harvesters really come?"

"Yes." Vashell's tone turned serious. "You should not have done what you did; you have angered the Harvesters beyond reprise. They will never, ever, stop the hunt."

"Then I will kill them!" Anu snapped, annoyed at Vashell's negativity.

Vashell shrugged. "When they send five? Ten? A hundred?"

"There are that many?"

"You do not understand what they are," he said, voice gentle.

"Well, they will have to catch me, first," snapped Anu, eyes narrowed.

"That shouldn't be a problem," said Vashell, scratching at his wounded face and the itching, repairing skin.

"Meaning?"

"You travel to Nonterrazake. For your father. Well, that is their homeland. It is the Harvesters who hold Kradek-ka."

Anu sat in stunned silence, unable to speak, unable to think. She had assumed they were fleeing the Harvesters. Now, it seemed, to rescue her father she would have to travel into the belly of the beast.

She gazed up at the stars. They twinkled, impossibly distant. And for a long time, Anu felt her soul melt, felt all hope vanish, and realised that her strength had gone.

In despondency, she went below deck for an endless, troubled, twisting sleep.

Anu slept late, and Alloria awoke her.

"He's gone."

"What? Who?"

"Vashell. The man whose face you removed with your claws."

Groggy, and feeling as if she'd been drugged, Anu stumbled on deck and stared hopelessly at the place where Vashell had been tied. His bonds lay, broken on the deck. He was nowhere to be seen.

Anu ran to the barge's rail. "Vashell!" she shouted. "Vashell!" Her words echoed out across mountain stone, and bounced back wreathed in early morning mist. There came no reply.

"What do we do now?" asked Alloria, softly.

"We continue without him."

* * *

For the morning they travelled, clockwork engine humming, up the ice-filled river. Deep into the maze of the Black Pike Mountains they navigated, were *absorbed*, and Anu realised that there was no life this far in. No animals, no birds; nothing. It was desolate, barren, as bleak as another world. Even the vegetation was dreary, white and pale green, grey and black. There were few, or no trees, the heady rich evergreens had vanished leagues behind. Only tufted grass remained, mostly ensnared by snow and ice. And yet the mountains... spoke to Anu. Rock-falls boomed. Ice cracked. Rock walls shifted. Boulders fell, crackling with menace to be swallowed by the Silva River. High up, occasionally, out of sight, they heard the terrifying roar of avalanche.

With every sound, the Black Pike Mountains screamed their dominance.

After a short break for a lunch of dried meat from the brass barge's hold, they continued, until Alloria, who was leaning at the craft's prow allowing breeze to stream through her hair, gasped.

"What is it?"

"There! That narrow river. To the left. Follow it!"

"What did you see?"

"Just follow it! Maybe I am going insane."

Anu nudged the brass barge up the narrow river, and they travelled for maybe a quarter of a league; the water grew deep, channelled between two towering four thousand feet walls of sheer black granite, polished and gleaming with ice, and they emerged into...

Into a lush, green clearing.

The water ended in a circular flat pool, and beyond
the water's edge stood a proliferation of trees, plants
and flowers. Colours and perfumes raged through the
clearing, and Anu brought the barge to a halt, bump-
ing against a natural sloped jetty of rock.

Alloria jumped out onto the jetty, and stood with
hands on hips, smiling. The sun was shining, beaming
down, warming her face, and she turned back to Anu
and laughed. "What is this place?"

Anu climbed from the boat, wary, aware that when
on the boat she had some small sanctuary from the
Harvesters. She shook her head. "I do not know."

"Vashell talked of such a place," said Alloria.

"He did?"

"Yes, he said it led to… the Vrekken? Whatever that
is. He said there would be green trees and flowers; and
there would be a tunnel. Follow the tunnel, and the
foolish traveller would find the Vrekken."

Anu turned, and her eyes narrowed. In the far wall
there indeed was a tunnel opening. It was too perfect,
so obviously man-made as opposed to a natural oc-
currence. This made Anu even more suspicious.

"Did he say anything else?"

"No. Look! Fruit!" Alloria ran to a tree and pulled
down an apple. She took a bite, and laughed through
juice. "It's wonderful! Fresh and clean. I can't believe
this little… garden exists amongst the mountains. And
can you smell the flowers?"

"I can."

Alloria tossed Anu an apple, which she caught and
bit. Juice ran down her chin, and she felt her mood
lighten a little. Alloria was right; this place, with the

winter sun shining down between towering walls of rock, was a serious uplift to the soul.

"We cannot stay. We must stock up with supplies. We must continue."

Alloria sighed, and waded through flowers to look deep into Anu's eyes. "What are you searching for, Anu?"

"My father. You know this."

"Truly? And to what end?"

Anu opened her mouth to reply, then closed it again. What she wanted more than anything was to be accepted in the Silva Valley; to be accepted as pure vachine. But that had gone, now. Denied her from an early age by the very same father she sought to save; but he'd had his reasons, hadn't he? For forcing her to become outcast? And, she realised suddenly, what she wanted more than anything was for Kradek-ka, the great inventor, to make her whole again. To put right that which he had twisted. But it was too late for that. Her chance had gone.

"I would seek acceptance," she said, finally.

Alloria nodded, and gazed off through the trees. Birds sang in the distance. It was an uplifting sound. "Vashell said there was a path, here; a path that leads south, away, out from the embrace of the Black Pike Mountains."

Anu stared at her. She licked her lips. "You wish to leave?"

"Yes. I would return to my husband. I would return to my children. You understand this, surely?"

Anu sighed. "Yes. I understand you. But it will be a harsh and terrible journey. I believe the paths are... treacherous."

Alloria nodded. "I would suffer anything to see my family again."

"Then go. With my blessing."

"You could come with me," said Alloria. "I heard what Vashell said; about this place, this Nonterrazake. And the Harvesters who reside there. You don't even know if your father still lives! It is insanity to go on."

"You listen well," said Anu, a little stiffly. "No. I will travel there. If nothing else, I will discover the truth."

Queen Alloria moved forward, and gazed into Anu's eyes. "I know I have been… distant." She licked her lips. "but… thank you, for saving me, from the soldiers. I find it hard to comprehend your ways, but hopefully, one day, if you arrive at my lands in Falanor, I will be able to extend you some form of courtesy; some help." She paused, awkward, not really sure what she wanted to say, her mind awash with conflicting thoughts.

Anu smiled, leant forward and hugged Alloria.

"It will be as you say."

Anu stepped back onto the Engineer's Barge, the scents of rich flowers in her nostrils, in her golden curls, and she nosed the boat away from this inner sanctum, this temporary Eden, and towards the ominous cave which seemed to beckon her with a tiny, sibilant whisper.

Come to me, the cave seemed to say.

Come to the Vrekken.

The brass barge glided across still waters, and entered the darkness of the tunnel.

Within seconds, Anu was swallowed. Was gone.

* * *

For hours the brass barge eased through blackness. Occasionally, it would bump against jagged rock walls, and Anukis found herself praying. She did not want to drown. Even worse, she did not want to drown in a tomb-world beneath the Black Pike Mountains!

The wind whistled eerily down tunnels, and it was with a start Anu realised she was in a maze. The tenebrosity obscured the nature of the labyrinth, and it only came with time, with context, as Anu realised she was being drawn along by powerful currents, and no longer the hum of the clockwork engine. For a while she set the engine to full power, heard it clonking, gears stepping, straining against the pull. Then she realised it was futile; whatever pulled the brass barge seemed almost sentient, and she would simply burn out the engine if she continued.

Anu cut the power, and sat in eerie silence made more deafening by the stillness of the barge. She realised, then, she had grown used to the sound of the clockwork engine; it had been a comfort, like mother's heartbeat in the womb.

Now, only the wind sang her to sleep.

Minutes passed into hours passed into days, and Anu lost all concept of time. She slept when she was tired, and ate what meagre rations remained in the hold of the barge, mainly hard bread, salted fish and a little dried pork. Or at least, animal flesh of some kind.

Eventually, veins of crystal ran through the black rock over Anu's head; faintly at first, no more than occasional threads, strands of orange and green to break up the monotony of the terminal black. Then the threads grew more proliferous and thicker in banding, and it provided an eerie, underground light of sorts. Anu could make out the backs of her hands, and a vague outline of the barge. That was all.

The noise came after… she did not know. It could have been two days, could have been five. It was a blur, a blur of time, of memory, of identity. The noise began as a tiny crackling sound, which had Anu scampering down to the engine to see if there was a fault. But the clockwork engine was dead; killed by her own pretty, vachine-clawed hands.

Then, after hours, the noise increased and Anu realised it was the sound of gushing water, like that of a waterfall, or fast rapids over rocks. It echoed through the tunnels, strange acoustics summoned and distributed by the very nature of the environment.

More hours passed, and Anu grew increasingly agitated as she realised the source of the increasingly raging noise. It was the Vrekken, a natural whirlpool talked about with reverence in adventurer circles, around camp fires in the middle of the night, by hushed bards in rush-strewn taverns; and by the Blacklippers, who were said to have some unholy alliance with the great whirlpool. Nowhere, however, had Anu ever heard tales that the Vrekken was beneath the Black Pike Mountains – effectively entombed.

She shivered, now, and was drawn along in the darkness.

She realised that forces beyond her controlled her fate.

And she accepted this fate with a great, heartfelt sigh.

It was said her father, Kradek-ka, was down there, in the mythical land of Nonterrazake, down through the Vrekken, down through the mingled salt and fresh waters of the curious rivers which joined and flowed between savage towers of rock. Either that, or a simple death awaited.

The noise grew with every passing minute, and Anu realised the brass barge was moving subtly faster. The noise increased until it was no longer a noise, but a roar, a roar of anger and bestial hatred, a roar to be feared, a roar to instil pure hot terror. Anu grabbed the barge rail, knuckles white, as it began to rock and she wished, for a fleeting moment, that she had stayed with Alloria, travelled the high mountain passes, faced the threat of the hunting Harvesters. But then her jaw muscles tightened, her eyes narrowed, and she conjured a single word.

No.

She would not fear death. She would search out her father. Or she would die in the process.

The roaring grew and grew until it was so loud Anu could have screamed at full pitch and not heard herself. The river was dangerously agitated, rocking the barge from left to right, and slapping it abusively against rock walls.

And then...

A world opened before Anu, at once incredibly beautiful, and awesomely dangerous. It was stunning like a shark up close is stunning, dazzling like black-magick fire, and it held her gaze and she knew, if she survived this ordeal, nothing, ever, would compare to this moment...

The Vrekken was nearly half a league across, and filling a cavern of such incredible scale she never would have believed it could fit inside a mountain. The arena was lit by wrist-thick skeins of mineral deposits in rock walls, swirling, twining bands of orange and green that put Anu in mind of a carnival or festival; only here, there was very little to celebrate. Unless one wanted to celebrate death.

The Vrekken roared, a mammoth circular portal, a frothing juggernaut of churning river water all spiralling down, down, down into huge sweeping circles and further, into a savage cone depth. Anu's eyes were fixed. Her mouth so dry she could not eject her tongue to moisten lips. The Engineer's Barge was tugged, then flung into the Vrekken and caught like the tiniest of toys, powering along on surges of current, nose in the air leaving a wide wake through circular waters and Anu spun down, and down, and round and down and she realised the mighty whirlpool consisted of layers and she passed down, through layer after layer of this oceanic macrocosm, of whirling dark energy, of raw power and screaming detonation and mighty primordial compression, and she thought...

There is no fabled Nonterrazake.

I am going to die, here.

I am going to die.

And the Vrekken roared in terrible appreciation.

FIFTEEN
Endgame

The cankers charged, howling, and the brave soldiers of Falanor marched in armoured squares to meet the attack head on. In ranks, they advanced across the plain, shields locked, a full division of 4,800 men arranged in twelve battalions of four hundred, with six in the centre two battalions deep, and three battalion squares to either side of the main square, like horns, the intention being to sweep round and enclose the enemy on three sides.

As the two forces closed, so the soldiers let out war cries and increased their pace, and the cankers accelerated to crash into shields with terrifying force, snarling and biting and clawing, a thousand feral clockwork twisted deviants slamming the battalions with rage... for a moment there was deadlock, then the Falanor soldiers were forced back, their swords hammering out, hacking at heads and claws, at shoulders and bellies, but the cankers were resilient, awesomely tough, incredibly powerful, and their claws raked shields bending steel. With screams of metal, they leapt, fastening on heads and ripping them

free of bodies and the armoured shield wall broke
within only a few short minutes, panic sweeping
through Falanor ranks like rampant wildfire...

Kell crouched beside Nienna, whose face was
ghostly pale, watching the carnage below. Terrakon
and Lazaluth had rushed away to command their
troops, now only Leanoric remained, eyes fixed on the
battle, face ashen, nausea pounding him.

"Find a horse," said Kell, softly, forcing Nienna to
tear her gaze from the battle. He took her chin in his
hand, made her look at him. "Steal one if you have
to. Ride for Saark. You understand?"

"No, I can't leave you... what will you do?"

"I must help Leanoric."

"No, Kell! You'll die!"

He smiled, a grim smile. "I have my Legend to uphold!" he said, and pushed Nienna away. "Now go!
You hear me?" She shook her head. "Go!" he roared,
and saw Myriam there beside her, and Myriam locked
eyes with Kell and a silent exchange, an understanding, passed between them. Myriam placed a hand on
Nienna's shoulder, and nodded. Then they took off
through the camp, towards the towering, fractured
walls of Old Skulkra, and tethered horses beyond.

Kell strode to Leanoric. "Sire. It's time we went into
battle." He lifted his axe and began to loosen his
shoulder. He turned, and saw the main block of infantry being forced back yet again. The battalion horns
had swung around to enclose the cankers, on Terrakon and Lazaluth's command, and cankers were
falling under sword blows... but they were slaughtering the soldiers of Falanor in their hundreds.

Below came the snarl and thud of canker carnage. Claws through flesh. Swords through muscle. Kell mounted his horse, and clicked his tongue. In silence, Leanoric followed and the two men rode down from the camp and onto the flat plain, hooves drumming the icy grassland as they both broke into a gallop and readied weapons, and the armoured ranks flowed past and Kell felt the thrill of adrenaline course his blood, and it was like the old times, like the best times and Ilanna spoke to him, her voice metallic and cool...

I can help you.

I can help you win this. No ties. No conditions.

Just let me in.

Kell flowed past the infantry, could see pale faces peering at him as he screamed an ancient war cry and in his calm internal monologue he said, "Do it, Ilanna" and he felt the surge of new power new blood-oil magick flood through him and his mind seemed to accelerate, to run in stop-motion, those around him slow and weak and pitiful flesh and meat and bone and he connected with Ilanna, connected with a force more ancient than feeble vachine clockwork deviation – Kell slammed into the cankers, his axe cleaving left and cutting a beast clean in half, and in the same sweep cutting right to remove a head, the blades thudded and sparkled with drops of blood as Kell's mount pushed gamely on, the axe returning to complete a figure of eight, each blow crunching through bone and muscle and twisted clockwork, and the cankers fell beneath him, crushed before him, and he was laughing, face demonic and splattered with their blood, and a huge canker reared, a massive

black-skinned twisted beast twice the height of a man
and heavily muscled. Its first swipe broke the horse's
neck, and Kell's mount went down and he leapt free,
the huge canker rearing above him screaming and the
whole battle seemed to pause, held in a timeless moment with thousands of eyes fixed on this crazy old
man who'd ridden deep into canker ranks ahead of
the retreating units of infantry and the canker
screamed and howled and lunged and Kell's axe glittered in a tiny black arc and cut the canker from skull
to quivering groin in one massive blow that seemed
to shake the battlefield. Thunder rumbled. The canker
peeled in two parts and a roar went up from the
Falanor men and their armoured squares heaved forward, with vigour renewed, swords rising and falling
and cankers were cut down left and right, bludgeoned into the churned mud of the battlefield, arms
and legs cut from torsos, heads cut from weeping
clockwork necks. The main body of infantry found
new hope in Kell, and they surged forward hacking
and cutting, smashing blades into skulls and Kell
roared from the centre of the battlefield, his axe slamming left and right with consummate ease, every
single mighty blow killing with engineered precision,
every single strike removing a canker from the battlefield and they converged on him, roaring and
snarling, rearing above him and dwarfing him from
sight and Kell laughed like a maniac, drenched in
blood, his entire visage one of gory crimson with bits
of torn clockwork in his hair and beard and he spun
like a demon, Ilanna lashing out, cutting legs from
bodies, and a pulse emanated from the axe and he

held it above his head and the cankers, squealing and limping and blood-shod fell back for a moment, stumbling away in hurried leaps from this bloodied gore-strewn man, and a roar went up from the Falanor men and the cankers covered their ears which pissed blood and tiny mechanical units, whirring clockwork devices that seemed to be trying to get away from unheard noise and the Falanor soldiers charged, breaking ranks and hammering into the disabled cankers as blood pissed from ears and throats and eyes and they writhed in agony, and swords and axes smashed down without mercy. The rest of the cankers fled, stumbling back towards the waiting, silent Army of Iron, almost blind in their pain and panic and Kell stood in the midst of the final butchery, Ilanna in one hand, hair soaked with blood, his entire visage one of butcher in the midst of a murder frenzy, and when the killing was done a cheer went up and soldiers crowded around Kell, chanting his name, "Kell Kell Kell Kell KELL KELL KELL KELL!" and someone shouted, "The Legend, he lives!" and the chant changed, roaring across the battlefield to the silent, motionless albino ranks, "Legend Legend Legend Legend LEGEND LEGEND LEGEND LEGEND!" before the captains, command sergeants and division generals managed to restore order and the soldiers of Falanor reassembled in their units and ranks.

Kell strode back to Terrakon and Lazaluth. Terrakon had a nasty slash from his temple to his chin, his whole face sliced in half, but he was grinning. "That was incredible, man! I have never seen anything like it! You turned the entire tide of the battle!"

Kell grinned at him, face a savage demon mask. "Horse-shit, man! I did no such thing. I simply gave the cankers something nasty to think about; the infantry charged in and did the rest."

"Such modesty should never be trusted."

"Such bitterness should never be concealed."

"You're a vile, moaning goat, Kell."

Kell rolled his shoulders. "That's a nasty gash to your face, Kon. Might need a few stitches." He grinned again.

"Fuck you, you old bastard."

"Old? I'm ten years younger than you!"

"Ha, well it's all about condition, Kell, and I look ten years younger than you."

Around the two men soldiers were chuckling, but the sounds soon dissipated.

"Here come the infantry," said Terrakon, humour dropping like a stone down a well. He switched his blade from one hand to the other, rolling his wrist to loosen it. "Damn arthritis to hell!"

"Now's a good time to bring in those archers," said Kell, prodding Lazaluth. "Go and tell the king."

The albinos marched out, in perfect formation. Their black armour gleamed. It began to snow from towering iron-bruise clouds, and the battlefield became a slurry of blurred men. A pall of fear seemed to fall across the soldiers of Falanor; they realised they had lost hundreds due to slaughter at the claws of the cankers; they were now at the disadvantage. It would be a hard fight.

"Chins up, lads!" roared Kell, striding forward to the head of the centre battalions. They had reformed, most with shields, all grasping their short swords in powerful hands. These were the veterans, the skilled soldiers, the hardcore. Hard to kill, thought Kell with a grim smile, and he bared his teeth at the men.

"Who's going to kill some bastard albinos with me?" he roared, and a noise went up from the Falanor men.

"WE!" screamed the soldiers, blood-lust rising, and slammed swords on shields as behind Kell the albino battalions spread out into a straight line. Kell turned, and laughed at their advancing ranks.

"BRING IT ON, YOU HORSE-FUCKING NORTH-ERNERS!" he roared, and behind him the Falanor men cheered and roared and banged their swords, as Kell moved back and slipped neatly into the front ranks at the centre, taking up his position alongside other hardy men. He looked left, then looked right, and grinned at the soldiers. "Let's kill us some albino," he said, as the enemy broke into a charge in perfectly formed squares, their boots pounding across churned mud. They did not carry shields, only short black swords, and each had white hair, many wearing it long and tied back. None wore helmets, only ancient black armour inscribed with swirling runes.

The snow increased, filling the battlefield with thick flurries. I hope them extra divisions arrive soon, thought Kell sourly to himself; the snow would be superb cover to hit the enemy from behind, to crush them between sea and mountains, hammer and anvil. But then, nothing in life was ever that easy, or convenient; was it?

The albinos charged in eerie silence, and Kell again felt fear washing through the ranks. This was no normal battle, and every man could sense a swirling essence of underlying magick; as if the very ground was cursed.

Distant drums slammed out a complicated beat. Kell tried to remember his old military training, but realised it would be useless. They would change the codes before any battle in order to confuse the enemy, and hopefully negate any information passed on by spies. But Kell realised what was going to happen; Leanoric had explained. They were going to fight, then retreat; draw the albino army back into the ruined city of Old Skulkra, fake a panicked break of ranks and charge through the ancient abandoned streets where nearly a thousand archers waited, hidden in high buildings and towers to rain down slaughter from above.

Kell smiled, dark eyes locked to the charging albinos.

It was a good plan. It could work. At first, it had been a plan nearly devastated by the unexpected cankers and their attack. The panicked breaking of ranks had very nearly been a reality; if that had happened too early, before archers took their positions, the battle would have been lost...

Kell could see the charging men, now, and picked out his first four targets. His butterfly blades would soon taste blood, and he licked his lips, adrenaline and... something else pulsing through his veins. It was Ilanna, like an old drug, a bad disease, her essence flowing through his veins and mingling in his brain and heart and his sister of the soul, his bloodbond axe strengthened him beyond mortality and he laughed out loud, at the savage irony, for he would suffer for this betrayal of his own code.

A roar went up from the Falanor men, but still the Army of Iron charged in silence. Kell could see their eyes now, could see their bared teeth, the jewelled rings they wore on pale-flesh fingers, the shine of their boots, the gleam of their dark swords and he tensed, ready for the awesome massive impact which came from any slam of charging armies…

The albinos suddenly stopped, to a man, and dropped to one knee. The charging ranks of soldiers, in their entirety and with perfect clockwork precision, halted. A surge of warning sluiced through Kell's system, and he realised with a sudden fast-rising horror that it was a trick; they had no intention of infantry attack, it was a stalling tactic to allow…

The ice-smoke.

It poured from the Harvesters in the midst of the albino ranks, and within seconds flooded out towards the Falanor army. "Back!" screamed Kell, "Back!" but the battalions were too tightly packed, their lack of understanding a hindrance, and they began to stumble, to turn and retreat but ice-smoke poured over the men, slowing them instantly, making many fall to knees choking as lungs froze and Kell roared, unable to retreat, and surged forward alone cleaving into the albino ranks who remained, immobile, eyes fixed with glowing red hate on the soldiers of Falanor as Kell's axe thumped left and right, scattering bodies and limbs and heads, and he screamed at the albino soldiers, screamed at the Harvesters but ice-smoke flowed and froze swords to hands, shields to arms, sent crackling ice-hair in shards to the ground, and men toppled over in agony, many dying, but most locked in a dark magick embrace...

Kell's axe slammed left, embedding in a soldier's eyes. He tugged it free, sent another head rolling, and saw the Harvesters converging on him. "Come on, you bastards," he roared with the surge of Ilanna through his veins and he realised, realised that Ilanna kept him pure from the dark magick, as she had done all those days ago during the attack on Jalder, and he revelled in the freedom and whirled, beard-flecked with crimson, blood-soaked snow, and stared in horror at the falling ranks of Falanor men. The ice-smoke had spread, through the main division and the reserves before the walls of Old Skulkra. Even as he watched, tendrils crept like oiled tentacles into the city. And Kell thought about Nienna. And his face curled into a snarl. He turned back as the Harvesters, heads tilted to one side, surrounded him and he blinked, saw General Graal marching towards him to smile, a knowing smile, as his eyes locked to Kell.

Kell placed the blades of his axe on the ground, surrounded by dismembered corpses, and leant on the haft, his dark eyes fixing on Graal. Graal stopped, and smiled a narrow smile without humour.

"We should stop meeting like this, Kell."

Kell laughed, a brittle hollow sound. "Well well, Graal the Coward, Graal the Whoremaster, using his petty little magick to win the day. It's nice to see some things will never change."

"This is a means to an end," said Graal, eyes locked.

"Remember what I said to you, laddie? Back in Jalder?" Graal said nothing, but his eyes glittered. "I told you to remember my name, because I was going to carve it on your arse. Well, it seems now's a good time–"

He leapt into action so fast he was a blur and Graal stumbled back as Harvesters closed in, and a blast of concentrated ice-smoke smashed Kell and he was blinded in an instant and chill magick soaked his flesh and heart and bones and everything went bright white and he was stunned and falling, and he fell down an amazing sparkling white tunnel which seemed to go on...

Forever.

Nienna urged the horse on, hooves galloping across snow, steam rising from the beast's flanks as it laboured uphill towards the woods where Saark, Styx and Jex waited. Myriam was close behind, her own horse lathered with sweat, and the two women flashed through early morning mist as snow swirled about them, obscuring the world.

Nienna reined her horse into a canter as she neared the woods, then stopped, stooping to stare under the trees. She could see nothing. "Saark?" she hissed, then louder, "Saark?"

A little way up, Styx emerged, smiled and waved. Nienna cantered over to him and dismounted, her eyes never leaving the mark of the Blacklipper, his stained dark lips.

"Where's Saark?"

"Further in the woods. We've set up camp. Come on, before enemy scouts see you."

Myriam dismounted behind, and they led their horses into the gloom of the Silver Fir forest. Pigeons cooed in the distance, then all was silent, their footfalls muffled by fallen pine needles.

"Up here." Styx led them along an old deer trail, and they emerged in a small clearing where an ancient, fallen pine acted as a natural bench. Jex was cooking stew over a small fire, and Nienna looked around.

"Where is he?"

The blow slammed the back of Nienna's head, and she felt her face pushed into needles and loam, and there was no pain. She remembered scents, pine resin, soil, old mud and woodland mould. When she blinked, groggy, and came back into a world of gloomy consciousness, she realised she was tied, her back leant against the fallen pine. She groaned.

"We have a live one," grinned Styx, crouching before her. Nienna spat in his face, and his grin fell, his hand lifting to strike her.

"Enough," snapped Myriam, voice harsh. "Go and help Jex pack the horses." Styx departed in silence, and Nienna ran her tongue around a mouth more stale than woodland debris.

"Why?" said Nienna, eventually, looking up at Myriam.

"You are my best bartering tool. When Kell has finished playing battleground hero, he will come looking for you. By taking you north, I guarantee he will follow."

"Is it not enough to poison us?" snapped Nienna, eyes narrowed and full of hate.

"It is not enough," said Myriam, gaunt face hollow, eyes hard.

Nienna's gaze transferred to Saark, seated, slumped forward, face heavily beaten. He lifted himself up a little, drool and blood spilling from his mouth, and smiled at her through the massive swellings on his face. One eye was swollen shut, and blood glistened in his dark curls. His hands were tied behind his back, but even as he shifted he winced, in great pain.

"Saark, what happened to you?"

"Bastards jumped me." He grinned at her, though it looked wrong through his battered features. "Hey, Nienna, fancy a kiss?"

She snorted a laugh, then shook her head. "How can you joke, Saark?"

"It's either that or let them break me." His eyes went serious. "And I'd rather die. Or at least, rather die than be ugly." He glanced up at Myriam, and winked at her with his one good eye. "Like this distorted bitch."

Myriam said nothing, and Styx and Jex returned with their horses. Styx grabbed Nienna roughly, and she kicked and struggled. He punched her, hard, in the face and she went down on her knees gasping, blinded. He dragged her back up again. "We can do this awake, or unconscious. I know which one I'd rather choose," growled the Blacklipper.

Nienna was helped into the saddle, and Styx mounted behind her. His hands rested on her hips, and he grinned, leaning close to her ear. "This is intimate, my sweet. The first of many adventures between us, I think."

"You wave your maggot near me, and I'll bite it off," she snarled.

Styx's grin widened, and he squeezed her flesh with strong fingers. "Like I said. We can do this awake, or unconscious."

Myriam crossed to Saark, and crouched before him. "Look at me."

"I'd rather not. The cancer has eaten your face. There's nothing the vachine can do for you now, my love."

"Bastard! Listen, and listen good. We're taking Nienna north, to the Cailleach Pass. The poison will take three weeks to kill Kell. The ride is around fifteen days. He can meet us by the Cailleach Pass northwest of Jalder; there, I have a partial antidote that will extend his – and Nienna's – lives. Enough to get us through the mountains at least. You understand all this?"

"I understand, bitch."

"Good." She smiled with tombstone teeth. "And here's a little present to remember me by." She pulled free a dagger, and slammed it between Saark's ribs. He grunted, feeling warm blood spread from the embedded blade, and as Myriam pulled it free he gasped, toppling onto his side where he lay, winded, as if struck by a sledge hammer. "Nothing fatal, I assure you. Unless you choose not to move your arse, and lie there like a stuck pig. It'll be a while before you use that pretty sword again, dandy man; Sword-Champion." She knelt and cut Saark's bonds, then turned and leapt with agility into her horse's saddle.

The group wheeled, and galloped from the forest clearing.

Silence fell like ash.

Saark lay, panting, bleeding. There was no pain, and that scared him. Then the lights went out.

King Leanoric knelt in the mud, heavily chained. Beside him were his Division Generals and various captains who hadn't died in either the battle, or from the savage effects of the invasive ice-smoke. Despair slammed through Leanoric, and he looked up, tears in his eyes, across the battlefield of the frozen, the ranks of the dead. His army had been annihilated, as if they were stalks of wheat under the scythes of bad men.

Distantly, the remaining cankers growled and snarled, but the albinos were curiously silent despite their easy victory. There were no battle songs, no drunken revelry; they went about building their camp in total silence, like androgynous workers; like insects.

Tears rolled down Leanoric's cheeks. He had failed, unless his divisions further north surprised Graal's Army of Iron and destroyed them in the night; they were commanded by Retger and Strauz, two wily old Division Generals, strategic experts, and Strauz had never lost a battle. Leanoric's heart lifted a little. If their scouts realised what had happened, that the king's men had been routed, frozen, and slaughtered like cattle…

Maybe then he would see his sweet Alloria again.

His tears returned, and he cast away feelings of shame. There was nothing wrong with a man crying. He was on the brink of losing his wife, his realm, his army, his people. How then did simple tears pale into comparison when so much was at stake?

King Leanoric needed a miracle.

Instead, he got General Graal.

Graal walked through the camp and stopped before the group of men. He drew a short black sword, gazed lovingly at the ornate rune-worked blade for a moment, then cut the head from Terrakon's shoulders. The old Division General's head lay there on frozen mud, grey whiskers tainted by droplets of blood, and Leanoric looked up with hate in his eyes. "My people will kill you," he snarled. "That's a promise."

"Really?" said Graal, almost idly, wandering over to Lazaluth and throwing Leanoric a cold, narrow-lipped smile. He reached up, ran a hand through his white hair, then fixed his eyes on the king. "So often I hear these threats, from the Blacklippers I slaughter, from the smugglers of Dog Gemdog gems, from the kings of conquered peoples."

His sword lashed out, and Lazaluth's head rolled to the mud, a look of shock on the death-impact expression. The body slumped down, blood pumping sluggishly from chilled neck arteries, and Leanoric watched with fury and cold detachment and he knew, he realised, he would be next but at least death would be swift... but hell, it wasn't about death, it was about his people, and their impending slavery. And it was a bad thing to die, knowing you had utterly failed.

Leanoric prayed then. He prayed for a miracle. For surely only a god could stop General Graal?

Graal moved to him, and hunkered down, slamming the black blade into the frozen mud. "How does it feel?" he asked, voice almost nonchalant. "Your army is destroyed, your queen sent north to my

Engineers, your people about to become..." he laughed, a tinkling of wind chimes, "our supper."

"You will burn in Hell," said Leanoric, voice a flat-line. He tried to estimate how long it would be before his returning battalions marched over the hill; for example, now would be a most opportune moment. A surprise attack? Rescued at the final second? Just like in a bard's tale.

Graal watched the king's eyes. Finally, their gazes locked.

"You are thinking of your army, your divisions, your battalions, your cavalry and archers who at this very moment march south, towards this very location in order to hook up with your army and smash the enemy invaders."

Leanoric said nothing.

Graal stood, and stretched his back. He glanced down at King Leanoric, as one would a naughty child. "They are dead, Leanoric. They are all dead. Frozen by the Harvesters blood-oil magick; slaughtered and sucked dry as they knelt. You have no army left, King Leanoric. Face facts. You are a conquered, and an enslaved race."

"No!" screamed Leanoric, surging to his feet despite the weight of chains and around him unseen albino soldiers in the mist drew swords as one, the hiss of metal on oiled scabbard, but Graal lifted one hand, smiled, then stepped in close, lifting Leanoric from his feet, and Leanoric kicked and saw a mad light in the General's eyes and he dragged Leanoric into an embrace and fangs ejected with a crunch and he bit down deep, pushing his fangs into Leanoric's neck, into his flesh, feeling the skin part, the muscle tear, rooting out that precious pump of blood, injecting the meat the vein the artery, closing his eyes as he sucked, and drained, and drew in the king's royal blood.

Leanoric screamed, and kicked, and fought but Graal was strong, so much stronger than he looked; chains jangled and Graal held Leanoric almost horizontal, mouth fastened over his neck, eyes closed in a final revelation; a final gratification.

Graal grunted, and allowed a limp and bloodied Leanoric to topple to the soil. Blood streaked his mouth and armour, and he lifted his open fangs to the sky, to the mist, to the magick, and he exhaled a soft howl which rose on high through clouds and spread out across the Valantrium Moor beyond Old Skulkra, across the Great North Road, across Vorgeth Forest and that howl said, This country is mine, that howl said, These people are mine, that guttural primal noise from a creature older than Falanor itself said, This world is mine.

Saark awoke. He was terribly cold.

He stared up at towering Silver Firs with his one good eye, and tried to remember what had happened in the world, tried to focus on recent events. Then reality and events flooded in and cracked him on the jaw, and he blinked rapidly, and his hand dropped to his ribs – and came away sticky.

"Bastards."

With a grunt, he levered himself up. He was incredibly thirsty. The world swayed, as if he was drunk, his brain caught in a grasp of vertigo. Saark crawled to his knees, and saw his horse, the tall chestnut gelding, still tied where he'd left him. Saark crawled slowly to the gelding, feeling fresh blood pump from the dagger wound and flow down his flank, soaking into his groin. It was warm, and wet, and frightening.

"Hey, boy, how the hell are you?" Saark use the stirrups to lever himself up, and grasping the saddle, he pulled himself to his feet with gritted teeth. Pain washed over him, and he yelped, dizziness swamping him, and he nearly toppled back.

"No," he said, and the gelding turned a little, nuzzling at his hand. "No oats today, boy." Saark struggled with the straps of his saddlebags, his fumbling fingers refusing to work properly, and finally he found his canteen and drank, he drank greedily, water soaking his moustache and flowing down his battered chin. He winced. He face felt like a sack of shit. He probed tenderly at his split lip, cracked nose, cracked cheekbone, swollen eye. He shook his head. When I catch up with them, he thought. When I catch up with them…

Saark laughed, then. Ridiculous! When he caught them? Gods, he could hardly stand.

He stood for a while holding the saddle, swaying, watching the falling snow, listening to the rustle of firs. The air, the world outside, seemed muffled, gloomy, a perpetual dawn or dusk.

Focus. Find Kell. Rescue Nienna. Kill bad people.

He smiled, grabbed the pommel of the saddle, and with a grunt heaved himself up on the third attempt. He slouched forward, and realised he hadn't untethered the gelding. He muttered, drew his rapier from behind the saddle, and slashed at the rope, missing.

He blinked. He slashed down again, and the rope parted.

"Come on, boy." He clicked his tongue, turned the horse, and set off at a gentle canter through the trees.

The whole world spun around him, and he felt sick. He was rocking, an unwilling passenger on a galleon in a storm. His felt as if his brain was spinning around inside his skull, and he slowed the horse to a walk, took in deep breaths, but it did not help. His mouth was dry again. Pain came in waves.

After what seemed an eternity of effort, Saark reached the edge of the woodland. He gazed out, over grass now effectively blanketed by snow. Slowly, he rode through the gloom, across several fields and to the top of the nearest hill. He stared out across a decimated battlefield. His eyes searched, and all he could see was the black armour of the Army of Iron.

Cursing, Saark kicked the horse into a canter and removed himself from the skyline. He dismounted, leaning against the horse for support, his mind spinning. What, was the battle over already? But then, how long had he lain unconscious? The Army of Iron had won?

Holy mother of the gods, he thought, and drew his rapier.

That would mean scouts, patrols – and where was Kell? Had he been captured? Worse. Was he dead?

Saark turned his horse and slapped the gelding's rump; with a whinny, he trotted off down the hill and Saark crawled back to the top on his belly, leaving a smear of blood on the snow, but thankful at least that from this position the world wasn't rolling, his eyes spinning, the ground lurching as if he was drunk on a bottle of thirty year-old whisky. Saark peered out over the enemy camp, spread out now before the battered city walls of Old Skulkra. To Saark's right, the ancient deserted city spread away as far as the eye could see, with crumbling towers, leaning spires, and many buildings having crumbled to the ground after... Saark smiled, sardonically. After the troubles. He fixed his gaze on what was, effectively, a merging of two war camps. The corpses of Falanor's soldiers had been laid out in neat lines away from the new camp and, with a bitter, grim, experienced eye, Saark looked along row after row after row of bodies.

What are they doing? he thought, idly. Why aren't they burning the bodies? Or burying them? What are they waiting for? Why risk disease and vermin? The image sat uneasy with Saark, and he changed tactic, moving his gaze back to the camp. If Kell was alive, and with a sinking feeling Saark realised it was improbable, then he was down there.

Saark scanned the tents, and eventually his gaze was drawn to a group of men, mist curling between them. They were a group of albino soldiers with swords unsheathed, and Saark squinted, trying to make out detail through the haze of distance, gloom and patches of mist. There came some violent activity, and Saark watched a man picked up kicking, struggling, then dropped back to the frozen mud. Saark's mouth formed a narrow line. He recognised Graal, more by his arrogant stance than armour or looks. There was something about the way the general moved; an ancient agility; an age-old arrogance, deeper than royalty, as if the world and all its wonders should move aside when he approached.

Saark watched Graal walk away from the small hill, walking down towards... Saark's breath caught in his throat. There were cages. Lots of cages. *Cankers*. Shit. Saark's good eye moved left, and he saw a huge pile of canker bodies – a huge pile. His heart swelled in pride. At least we got some of the fuckers, he thought bitterly. He tried to spot Graal again, but the general had disappeared in the maze of cages and tents. Where had he gone? Damn. Saark searched, methodically, up and down the rows where cankers snarled and hissed and slept; eventually, he caught sight of Graal. The general was observing... a man. A man, in a cage. Saark grinned. It had to be! Who else needed caging like a canker? There was only one grumpy sour old goat he could think of. Then Saark's heart sank. What else had they done to Kell? Was he tortured? Maimed? Dismembered? Saark knew all too well, and from first-hand experience, the horrors of battle; the insanity of war.

At least he is alive, thought Saark.

He lay back. Closed his eyes against the spinning world, although even then the feeling did not leave him. He moved a little down the hill, then searched in his pockets, finding his tiny medical kit, and as he waited the long, long hours until nightfall, he busied himself with a tiny brass needle and a length of thread made from pig-gut. He sewed himself back together again. And afterwards, after vomiting, he slept.

* * *

Kell came back into a world of consciousness slowly, as if swimming through a sea of black honey. He was lying on a metal floor, and a cold wind caressed him. He was deeply cold, and his eyes opened, staring at the old pitted metal, at the floor, and at the mud beyond streaked with swirls of snow. He coughed, and placed both hands beneath him, heaving himself up, then slumping back, head spinning, senses reeling. And he felt… loss. The loss of Ilanna. The loss of his bloodbond axe.

Kell flexed his fingers, and gazed around. He was in a cage with thick metal bars, and outside, all around him, were similar cages containing twisted, desecrated cankers. Most slept, but a few sat back on their haunches, evil yellow eyes watching him, their hearts ticking unevenly with bent clockwork.

Kell rolled his shoulders, then crawled to his knees and to the corner of the cage, peering out. He was back in Leanoric's camp, only now there were no soldiers of Falanor to be seen; only albino guards, eyes watchful, hands on sword-hilts. Kell frowned, and searched, and realised that the two camps had been made to blend, just like a canker and its clockwork. The Army of Iron had usurped the Falanor camp.

Darkness had fallen, and Kell realised he must have been out of the game for at least a day. He peered out from behind his bars, could just make out the edges of Old Skulkra, with her toothed domes and crumbling walls. Beyond lay Valantrium Moor, and a cold wind blew down from high moorland passes carrying a fresh promise of snow.

Kell shivered. What now? He was a prisoner. Caged, like the barely controllable cankers around him. "Hey?" growled Kell to the nearest canker. "Can you hear me?" The beast gave no response, just stared with the baleful eyes of a lion. "Do you realise you have a face like a horse's arse?" he said. The canker blinked, and its long tongue protruded, licking at lips pulled back over half its head. Inside, tiny gears made click click click noises. Kell shivered again, and this time it was nothing to do with the cold.

"Kell." The voice was low, barely above a whisper. Kell squinted into the darkness.

"Yeah?"

"It's Saark. Wait there."

"I'm not going anywhere, laddie."

There came several grunting sounds, and a squeal of rusted metal. The side of the cage opened, and Saark, skin pale, sweat on his brow, leant against the opened door.

Kell strode out, stood with his hands on his hips, looking around, then turned to Saark. "I thought you would have come sooner."

Saark gave a nasty grin. "A 'thank you' would have sufficed."

"Thank you. I thought you would have come sooner. And by the way, you look like a horse trampled your face."

"I ran into a bit of trouble, with Myriam and her friends."

Kell's brows darkened; his eyes dropped to the bloodstains on Saark's clothing. He softened. "Are you injured?"

"Myriam stabbed me."

"She had Nienna with her."

"She still does. I'm sorry, Kell. She's taken Nienna north, to the Black Pike Mountains. She said to tell you she will wait at the Cailleach Pass. She knows you will come. I'm sorry, Kell; I could do nothing."

The huge warrior remained silent, but rolled his neck and shoulders. His hand leapt to where his Svian was sheathed; to find the weapon gone. "Bastards," he muttered, looked around, then turned and started off between the cages.

"Wait," said Saark, hobbling after him. "You're going the wrong way. We can head out through Old Skulkra; I think even the albinos won't travel there. It's still a poisoned hellhole; stinks like a pig's entrails."

"I'm going to find Graal."

"What?" snapped Saark. He grabbed Kell, stopping him. "What are you talking about, man?" he hissed. "We're surrounded by ten thousand bloody soldiers! You want to march in there and kill him?"

"I don't want to kill him," snapped Kell, eyes glittering. "I want Ilanna."

Saark gave a brittle laugh. "We can buy you another axe, old man," he said.

"She's… not just an axe. She is my bloodbond. I cannot leave her. It is hard to explain."

"You're damn right it's hard to explain. You'd risk your life now? We can escape, Kell. We can go after Nienna."

Kell paused, then, his back to Saark. When his words came, they were low, tainted by uncertainty.

"No. I must have Ilanna; then I find Nienna. Then I kill Myriam and her twisted scum-bastard friends."

"You're insane," said Saark.

"Maybe. You wait here if you like. I'll be back."

"No." Saark caught him up, his rapier glittering in the darkness. "I may be stuck like a pig, but I can still fight. And if we split up now, we're sure to be caught and tortured. Damn you and your stupid fool quest!"

"Be quiet."

They eased through the nightshade.

It watched them. It crept low along the ground, and watched them. When they looked towards it, it hid its face, in shame, great tears rolling down its tortured cheeks as it hunkered to the ground, and its body shook in spasms of grief. Then they were gone, and it rose again, jaws crunching, and paced them through the army of tents…

Only once did Kell meet two albino guards, and the old man moved so fast they didn't see him coming. He broke a jaw, then a neck, then knelt on the first fallen guard, took his face between great paws, and wrenched the guard's head sideways with a sickening crunch. Kell stood, took one of the albino's short black swords, and looked over at Saark.

"Help me hide the bodies."

Saark nodded, and realised Kell danced along a line of brittle madness. He had changed. Something had changed inside the old warrior. He had… hardened. Become far more savage, more brutal; infinitely merciless.

They eased along through black tents, past the glowing embers of fires, and Kell pointed. It had been Leanoric's tent, in which Kell had stood only a few short hours before. Now, Kell knew, Graal's arrogance would make him take residence there. It was something about generals Kell had learned in his early days as a soldier. Most thought they were gods.

Kell stopped, and held up a blood-encrusted hand. Saark paused, crouched, glancing behind him. Slowly, Kell eased into the tent and was gone. Saark felt goose-bumps crawl up and down his arms and neck and went to follow Kell into the tent but froze. He glanced back again, and as if through ice-smoke General Graal materialised. Behind him marched a squad of albino soldiers, heavily armed and armoured, this time wearing black helmets decorated with swirling runes. Graal stopped, and smiled at Saark, and a chill fear ran through the dandy's heart like a splinter.

"Kell?" he whispered. Then, louder, eyes never leaving Graal, "Kell!"

"What is it?" snapped Kell, emerging, and looking at Graal with glittering eyes. "Oh, it's you, laddie."

"Looking for this?" said Graal, lifting Ilanna so moonlight shimmered from her black butterfly blades.

"Give her to me."

Graal rammed the axe into the ground. Behind him, the albino soldiers drew their blades. "Tell me how to make her mine, and you will live. Tell me how to talk with the bloodbond."

"No," snapped Kell.

Graal stepped forward, head lowered for a moment, then glanced up at Kell, blue eyes glittering. "I will grow unhappy," he said, voice low.

"I have been pondering a strange puzzle for some time," said Kell, placing his hands on his hips and meeting Graal's gaze. "How is it, lad, that you have the face and skin and hair of these albino bastards around you... and yet your eyes are blue?" Kell scratched at his whiskers. "I see you have the fangs of the vachine, and yet the vachine are tall, most dark haired, not like these effeminate soldiers behind you. What are you, Graal? Some kind of half-breed?"

"On the contrary," said Graal, taking another step closer. His eyes had gone hard, the mocking humour dropped from his face, and Saark realised Kell had touched some deep nerve with his words. "I am pure-blood," said Graal. "I am Engineer. I am Watchmaker. But more than this—" He leapt, arms smashing down, but Kell moved fast and blocked the blow, taking a step back. "I am one of the first vachine; the three from which all others stem."

Kell grinned. "I thought I could smell something rotten."

Graal snarled, and lashed out again, but Kell ducked the blow, moving inhumanly fast, and delivered a right hook that shook Graal. The general whirled, rolling with the blow, taking Kell's arm and slamming him over to smash the ground. Kell rolled, as Graal's boots hit the frozen earth where his face had been. Kell rose into a crouch and launched himself, grappling Graal around the waist and powering him to the soil. Atop Graal, Kell slammed his fists down with power, speed, accuracy, three blows, four five six seven, his knuckles lacerated and bleeding and Graal twisted, suddenly, throwing Kell to the ground where he grunted, and came up. They leapt at one another with a *crunch*, and suddenly locked, heaving, a match for one another in strength, heads clashing, and Saark who had been eyeing the five albino soldiers uneasily saw long fangs eject from Graal's mouth and screamed, "Kell, his teeth!" and Kell twisted, following Graal's head with a mighty blow that sent Graal reeling to the ground. Kell stood, chest heaving, blood on his face and his fists.

Graal climbed to his feet and stood, and smiled through his blood. "Your strength is prodigious," he said, eyes narrowing. "Too prodigious. Nothing human can stand before me; and yet you have done so."

"I've had lots of practise," said Kell, fists clenching, head lowering. "Once, I worked in the Black Pike Mountains. I was part of a squad sent there by King Searlan to hunt down the vachine; to kill your kind. We did well. We were there for four years... four long, bitter, hard years... it was hard learning, Graal, but we learnt well. I think, even now, I am referred to as Legend by your perverse kind."

"You!" snarled Graal, eyes widening. "The Vachine Hunter! It cannot be! He was slaughtered in the Fires of Karrakesh!"

"It is I," said Kell, "and that is why you could never speak with my bloodbond axe, my Ilanna... for she is anathema to your kind; she is poison to your blood: she is the sworn vachine nemesis."

There came a snarl, high-pitched and terrible, and
something cannoned from the darkness, hitting Graal
in a flurry of slashing claws and frothing fangs. It was
big, a cross between human and lion, obviously a
canker and yet twisted strangely, different from the
other cankers under Graal's command. The head was
long and narrow, and wrapped around with hundreds
of strands of fine golden wire so that only glimpses of
eyes and nose and mouth could be seen. Slashes covered the tufted, half-furred muscular body, but again
muscles, biceps and thighs and abdomen were all
wound about with tight golden wire, and sections of
clockwork could be seen outside the flesh, half embedded, clicking and whirring furiously, as if this body,
this canker, was having some kind of furious internal
battle with the very machinery which now, undoubtedly, kept it alive...

They fought in the gloom of the usurped camp,
Graal and this twisted canker nightmare, a flurry of
insane blows, writhing and wrestling and twisting in
the mud, thumps echoing out, claws and teeth slashing. Graal had exposed his full vachine toolset; was
biting and rending, face lost in a mask of raw primal
savagery that had nothing to do with the human.
They spun and punched and slashed in the mud, both
opening huge wounds down the other's flanks, sparks
flying from crumpled clockwork, grunting and growling and the canker's fist punched Graal's face,
slamming his head back into the mud and the canker
glanced up, eyes masked by the wires circling its head
but they fixed, fixed on Saark with recognition, then
on Kell, and the canker seemed to smile, a lop-sided

stringing of tattered lips and saliva and blood-oil drool...

Saark gasped. "Elias?" he hissed, in disbelief.

"Go – now," forced the canker between corrupted flesh, and Graal's hands grasped Elias's arm, twisted savagely with a popping of tendons and the canker was flung to one side, where it rolled fast and reversed the trajectory with a savage snarl, leaping on Graal's back and burying him and slamming the general into the mud.

Kell walked to his axe, Ilanna, and took her in his great hands. His head came up, eyeing the albino soldiers, who stood uncertainly, swords drawn. He attacked in a blur, each strike cutting bodies in half, and stood back with a grunt, covered in fresh gore, bits of intestines, slivers of heart, chunks of albino bone, to stare bitterly at the ten chunks of corpse.

Saark grabbed his arm. His voice was low. 'We have to move! Now, soldier!' Saark pointed. More enemy were gathering down in the main camp. They were strapping on swords and armour. Kell nodded, and then started to run with Saark beside him.

Saark suddenly stopped. Turned. He wanted to thank the twisted, corrupted shell of Elias; thank him for their lives. But the battle was a savagery of blows and scattered flesh.

They ran.

Through tents and paddocks of horses. Saark motioned, and they unlatched a gate, grabbing two tall chestnut geldings and leaping across them bareback. They kicked heels, and grabbing manes trotted from the paddock, then galloped through

the rest of the camp towards the teetering walls of
Old Skulkra... which loomed before them, vast, ancient, foreboding.

Old Skulkra was haunted, it was said. One of the
oldest cities in Falanor, it had been built over a thousand years before, a majestic and towering series of
vast architectural wonders, immense towers and
bridges, spires and temples, domes and parapets,
many in black marble shipped from the far east over
treacherous marshes. It had been a fortified city, with
towering walls easily defendable against enemies,
each wall forty feet thick. It had vast engine-houses
and factories, once home to massive machines which,
scholars claimed, were able to carry out complex tasks
but were now huge, silent, rusted iron hulks full of
evil black oil and arms and pistons and levers that
would never move again. Now, the city was century-
deserted, its secrets lost in time, its reputation harsh
enough to keep any but the most fearless of adven-
turers away. It was said the city carried plague close
to its heart, and that to walk there killed a man within
days. It was said ghosts drifted through the mist-filled
streets, and that dark blood-oil creatures lived in the
abandoned machinery, awaiting fresh prey.

Kell and Saark had little option. Either ride through
a camp of ten thousand soldiers intent on their anni-
hilation; or brave the deserted streets of Old Skulkra.
It was hardly a choice.

They passed the forty-foot defensive walls, corners
and carved pillars crumbling under the ravages of
time. Huge green and grey stains ran down what had
once been elegantly carved pillars. Despite their flight,

Saark looked around in wonder. "By the gods, this place is huge."

"And dangerous," growled Kell.

"You've been here before?"

"Not by choice," said Kell, and left it at that.

They swept down a wide central avenue, lined by blackened, twisted trees, arms skeletal and vast. Beyond were enormous palaces and huge temples, every wall cracked and jigged and displaced. Even the flagstones were cracked and buckled, as if the city of Old Skulkra had been victim of violent earth upheavals and storms.

The horses' hooves rang on black steel cobbles. The world seemed to drift down into silence. Mist coagulated on street corners. Saark shivered, and turned to look back at the broken gates through which they'd entered. The mist made the vision hazy, obscure. But he could have sworn he saw at least a hundred albino soldiers, clustering there, swords drawn but… refusing to step past the threshold.

They're frightened, he thought.

Or they know something we don't.

"They won't follow us here," said Saark, and his voice rang out, echoing around the ancient, damp place. It echoed back from crumbling buildings, from towers once majestic, now decayed.

"Good," snapped Kell. "Listen. If we can get through the city, we can head northeast, up through Stone Lion Woods. Then we can follow the Selenau River up to Jalder, then further up towards the Black Pike Mountains…"

"She's safe," said Saark, staring at Kell. "They won't harm her. Myriam has too much to lose by angering you further. She knows Nienna is the only bartering tool she has."

Kell nodded, but his eyes were dark, hooded, brooding. He could feel the sluggish pulse of poison in his system, running alongside the bloodbond of Ilanna. It was a curious feeling, and even now made his head clouded, his thoughts unclear. Weakness swept over him. Kell gritted his teeth, and pushed on.

They rode for a half hour at speed, the horses nervous, ears laid back against skulls, eyes rolling. It took great horsemanship to calm them; especially without reins.

And then, they heard the growls.

Kell cursed.

Saark frowned. "What is it?"

"The bastards wouldn't come in on their own. Oh no."

"So what is it?" urged Saark.

"The cankers. They've unleashed the cankers."

Saark paled, and he allowed a breath to ease from his panicked, pain-wracked frame. "That's not good, my friend," he said, finally.

Kell urged his horse on, and they galloped down wide streets, angling north and east. The mist thickened, and the streets became more narrow, more industrial. The buildings changed to factories and stone tower blocks, vast and cold, all windows gone, all doors rotted and vanished an age past. The horses became increasingly agitated, and the occasional growls and snarls of pursuing cankers grew louder, echoing, more pronounced.

"We're not going to make it," said Saark, eyes wide, his tension building.

"Shut up."

They slowed the horses, which were verging on the uncontrollable, until Kell's mount reared, whinnying in terror, and threw him. He landed with a *thud*, rolling on steel cobbles, and came up with his axe in huge hands, eyes glowering, but there was nothing there. Darkness seemed to creep in. Mist swirled. The horse galloped off, and was lost in shadows.

There came a distant *slunch*, a whinny of agony; then silence.

Kell spun around, looking up at the towering stone walls surrounding him. It was cold. His breath streamed. Icicles mixed with the old blood of battle frozen in his beard.

"Get up behind me," said Saark, reaching forward to take Kell's arm. But his own horse reared at that moment, and he somersaulted backwards from the creature, landing in a crouch, rapier drawn, face white with pain. The horse bolted, was gone in seconds between the towering walls of ancient stone.

"Neat trick," growled Kell, rubbing at his own bruised elbow and shoulder.

"I'll show you sometime," Saark grimaced.

The sounds of pursuing cankers grew louder.

"This is bad," said Saark, battered face full of fear, eyes haunted.

"We need somewhere to defend. A stairwell, somewhere narrow." Kell pointed with Ilanna. "There. That tower block."

The edifice was huge, the walls jigged and displaced, full of cracks and mis-aligned stones. A cold wind howled through the block, bringing with it a sour, sulphuric stench.

"I'm not going in there," said Saark.

"Well die out here, then," snapped Kell and started forward.

The cankers rounded a corner. There were a hundred of them, snarling, slashing at one another with claws, and they came in a horde down the narrow street, pushing and jostling, fighting to be first to feed on fresh, sweet meat. Kell ran for the tower, beneath an empty doorway and through a sweeping entrance hall littered with debris, old fires, stones and twisted sections of iron rusted out of shape and purpose; he stopped, looking hurriedly about. "There," he snapped. Saark was close behind him. Too close.

"We're going to die," said Saark, ever the voice of doom.

"Shut up, laddie, or I'll kill you myself."

They ran, skidding to a halt by a narrow sweep of steps. Kell looked up, and could see the sky far far above, perhaps twenty storeys, straight up. The tower block had no roof, and snow-clouds swirled. The steps spiralled up, wide enough for two men, and with a shaky, flaked, mostly rotted iron handrail the only barrier between the steps and a long fall to hard impact. Kell started up, thankful the stairwell was built from stone. Saark followed. They powered up in grim silence, followed by cackles and growls. It was only when Kell ventured too close to the edge that there came a crack, and stones tumbled away taking a quarter section of the staircase with it. Kell leapt back, almost sucked away in the sudden fall.

Saark stared at Kell, sweat on his swollen face, but said nothing.

"Keep to the wall," advised Kell.

"I'd already worked that one out, old horse."

Below, the cankers found the stairwell. They started up, jostling and snarling. Saark glanced down, but Kell powered ahead, face grim, beard frozen with ice-blood, eyes dark, mind working furiously.

The cankers ascended fast, claws scrabbling on icy steps. Panting and drenched with sweat, the two men reached a landing halfway up – ten storeys in height, halfway to the tower block's summit – before the first canker appeared, a huge shaggy beast with tufts of reddish fur and green eyes. Kell's axe clove into its head and Saark's rapier sliced into its belly, and the beast fell back, spitting lumps of clockwork and spewing blood. The two men ran across the landing and onto the next set of steps, as a crowd of cankers surged onto the narrow platform and Kell screamed, 'Run!' to Saark, and stopped on the steps, turning with his axe, the snarling heaving mass only a few feet away as cracks and booms filled the tower. Kell lifted his axe, and struck at the landing, again and again, and the whole floor was shaking under the weight of the cankers and the impact from the axe, and they were there, in his face, fetid breath in his throat as a huge crack echoed through the tower block and the landing fell away, with a whole storey section of steps, fell and tumbled away carrying twenty cankers scrabbling and clawing down the centre of the spiralling stairwell and leaving Kell teetering on the edge of oblivion. He swayed for a moment, and something grabbed him, pulled him back and he fell to his arse, turned, and grinned at Saark.

"Thanks, lad."

"No problem, Kell. Shall we ascend?"

"After you."

They started up, hearing growls and snarls fall away behind as two cankers attempted to leap the chasm, and bounced from walls, dropping away clawing and snarling to be lost in dust and ice and debris. There were *booms* as they impacted with the floor far below, and merged component limbs with ancient lengths of rusted iron.

The two men ran, muscles screaming, sweat staining their skin, limbs burning, fatigue eating them like acid. Eventually, they reached the final set of steps, and burst out into snowy daylight, great iron-bruise clouds filling the sky. A cold wind slammed them. Old Skulkra spread out in all directions, vast, decaying, frightening.

The top of the tower block was a treacherous rat-run of stone beams and channels. Ancient woodwork had long gone, meaning the entire floor was a criss-cross network where one incorrect step meant a long fall to unwelcome stone beneath. The whole tower block seemed to sway in violent gusts of wind. The wind gave long, mournful groans. Kell stepped across various beams to the low wall encircling the top floor of this vast tower. He stared off, across the ancient city, to the Valantrium Moor beyond, distant, enticing, ensconced in a snow shroud.

Saark came up beside him. He peered at another, nearby structure. "Can we make the jump?"

"I'll let you try first," said Kell.

"We can't go back."

Kell nodded. "You can see the Stone Lion Woods from here," he said, pointing.

"We need a plan," said Saark, eyes narrowing. "How do we get down from this shit-hole? Come on Kell, you're the man with all the answers!"

"I have no answers!" he thundered, rage in his face for a moment; then he calmed himself. "I'm just trying to keep us alive long enough to think." He rubbed at his beard, fingers rimed in filth and old blood. Only then did he look down at himself, and he gave a bitter laugh. "Look at the state of me, Saark." His eyes were dark, glittering, feral. "Just like the old days. The Days of Blood."

Saark said nothing. His mind worked fast. Kell was losing it. Kell was going slowly… insane.

"There must be a way off here," said Saark, voice calm. "You wait here, guard the steps. I'll see if I can find a ramp, or gantry, or some other way to the roof of another building."

Saark moved around the outside wall of the tower block, each footstep chosen with care, with precision; below, the tower interior was like a huge, soursmelling throat. Growls echoed up to meet him.

Saark stopped. He looked across the vast, rotting decadence of Old Skulkra. Beyond the walls he could see the enemy: the Army of Iron. A great sorrow took his heart, then, and crushed it in his fist. He realised with bitterness that General Graal had won. He had crushed Falanor's armies as if they were children. He had obliterated their soldiers, and,,, now what?

Saark frowned. From this vantage point he could see the Great North Road, snaking north and south, a meandering black ribbon through hills and woodland, all peppered with snow. To the west he could make out the sprawl of Vorgeth Forest, stretching off for as far as the eye could see. But there, on the road, he could see…

Saark rubbed his eyes. His swollen eye had opened a little, but still he could not understand what he witnessed. Huge, black, angular objects seemed to fill the Great North Road; from the ancient connecting roads of Old Skulkra heading north, for as far as the eye could see. Saark stroked his moustache, mouth dry, fear an ever-present and unwelcome friend.

"The Blood Refineries," said Kell, making Saark jump.

"What?"

"On the road. That's what you can see. The vachine need them to refine blood; and they need blood-oil to survive."

Saark considered this. "They have brought their machinery with them?"

"Yes." Kell nodded. He was sombre. Below, they heard a fresh growl, a snarl, and the scrabble of slashing claws. The cankers had found a way past the collapsed stairwell. They were on their way up.

"So they've won?" said Saark.

"No!" snarled Kell. "We will fight them. We will fight them to the bitter end!"

"They will massacre our people," said Saark, tears in his eyes.

"Aye, lad."

"The men, the women, the children of Falanor."

"Aye. Now take out your sword. There's work to be done." Kell strode to the opening leading to the stairwell. The cankers were growing louder. There were many, and their snarls were terrifying.

Saark stood beside Kell, his rapier out, his eyes fixed on the black maw of the opening.

"Kell?"

"Yes, Saark?"

"We're going to die up here, aren't we?"

Kell laughed, and it contained genuine humour, genuine warmth. He slapped Saark on the back, then rubbed thoughtfully at his bloodied beard, and with glittering eyes said, "We all die sometime, laddie," as the first of the cankers burst from the opening in a flurry of claws and fangs and screwed up faces of pure hatred.

With a roar, Kell leapt to meet them.

THE SAGA OF KELL'S LEGEND

The mighty Kell stood proud upon sandy shores,
He'd willingly cast out a palace of bores,
He pondered on glory of merciless days,
As lounged by his feet decadent poets sang praise,
But now his axe of old lay down by his side,
A weapon of terror and worthy genocide,
As the sea sweet her whisper carried o'er to him,
Her voice a bright loving invitation to swim,
Eternal bed, quoth she, I bring long soothing sleep,
Come to me my darling, now please don't you
    weep;

Our hero of old, he felt not the dread,
Of the battles gone by, of the children now dead,
He dreamt of the slaughter at Valantrium Moor,
A thousand dead foes, there could not be a cure
Of low evil ways and bright terrible deeds,
Of men turned bad, he'd harvest the weeds,
His mighty axe hummed, Ilanna by name,
Twin sharp blades of steel, without any shame
For the deeds she did do, the men she did slay,

Every living bright-eyed creature was legitimate
    prey;
Kell waded through life on a river of blood,
His axe in his hands, dreams misunderstood,
In Moonlake and Skulkra he fought with the best
This hero of old, this hero obsessed,
This hero turned champion of King Searlan
Defiant and worthy a merciless man,
Through Jangir and Black Pike Kell slaughtered
    the foe,
Each battle was empty, each moment gone slow,
And with each bloody murder Kell felt more the
    pain,
Reversal and angst brought home his heart bane.

[Rarely sung final verse:]
And Kell now stood with axe in hand,
The sea raged before him time torn into strands,
He pondered his legend and screamed at the stars,
Death open beneath him to heal all the scars
Of the hatred he'd felt, and the murders he'd done
And the people he'd killed all the pleasure and life
He'd destroyed.

Kell stared melancholy into great rolling waves of
    a Dark Green World,
And knew he could blame no other but himself
    for
The long Days of Blood, the long Days of Shame,
The worst times flowing through evil years of
    pain,

And the Legend dispersed and the honour was gone
And all savagery fucked in a world ripped undone
And the answer was clear as the stars in the sky
All the bright stars the white stars the time was to
   die,
Kell took up Ilanna and bade the world farewell,
The demons tore through him as he ended the spell
And closed his eyes.

ACKNOWLEDGMENTS

Many thanks must go to various people for advice and encouragement along the way, especially when the road glittered dark. Thanks to Ian Graham, author of *Monument*, for hardcore test reading, insightful advice and hallucinating the cankers. Cool!

Thanks to Green Sonia the Savage, for encouraging me to write for insane periods of time in order to hit those deadlines, and never moaning.

Thanks to Joe Blade and Olly Axe, for making me smile when the forest seemed dark.

And thanks to Marc Gascoigne, head of Angry Robot, for giving me a fresh crossbow-shot at scribing fantasy. I owe a few tankards of honey-mead!

Finally, a big thank you to Claire and Natalie Ralph, for their original inspiration and for being such good little vampires.

ABOUT THE AUTHOR

Andy Remic is a British writer with a love of ancient warfare, mountain climbing and sword fighting. Once a member of the Army of Iron, he has since retired from a savage world of blood-oil magick and gnashing vachine, and works as an underworld smuggler of rare Dog Gemdog gems in the seedy districts of Falanor. *Kell's Legend* is his sixth novel, and he's now hard at work on sequels *Soul Stealers* and *Vampire Warlords*.

www.andyremic.com

20 MINUTES INSIDE THE MIND OF
Andy Remic

As part of getting to truly know our authors, we sometimes like to throw a bunch of quickfire questions their way, see if we can get a glimpse of what they really think. And then, well, we lobbed some of those questions at Rem…

One book

Legend by David Gemmell. I read it when I was 15 years old, and it was extremely influential. I later struck up a friendship with Dave, and he never forgave me for a critique I once did (circa 1990) in which I said one of his novels had elements of the "turkey" in it. He said his book had never been described as fowl before, and I was lucky not to receive a right hook.

One book to burn

I don't really criticise other writers' works if I can help it. Authors, without exception, work incredibly hard, even if a book is perceived as "ready to burn", so I leave the acid to "professional critics".

One film

This would have to be *Blade Runner*, extremely influential and dark, moody, violent, intelligent, and based on a superb Phil Dick source text! Although I do have a secret passion which will guarantee small children point at me and laugh – I love those old Conan films. "Conan, what is best in life…"

One film to burn

What do I hate? Hmm. I think it's got to be *The Wizard of Oz*. Everybody bangs on about how brilliant it is; I thought it was a pile of sputum. Go on, burn it. As an aside, I am pretty good at burning things myself. I set fire to my decking a few weeks back using petrol on a BBQ; dumb, I know, and I nearly died, but on the upside the firemen thought it was pretty funny (especially as my brother is a fireman), and I got an invitation from Keith Flint to his annual summer party. Firestarter? Twisted firestarter? Surely not.

One song/record

"Green and Grey" by New Model Army, from the album *Thunder and Consolation*. Just perfect. But it's closely followed by Cypress Hill's "Tequilas Sunrise" from *IV*. That's more than one, right? Hot damn, I wish I could count.

One record to smash

Showwadaawaddywaddy, or however the bastard you spell it. Hell! It's hell, I tell you. I bought an album when I was 10 years old. The shame. The horror. The horror. Kurtz, kill me now.

One creative person you always wanted to be

J.R.R. Tolkien. Think of those royalty statements!! And of course, he was a genius masquerading as a university lecturer. Or maybe a university lecturer masquerading as a genius.

One book you wish you'd written

Harry Potter. Very well written, and just think of those fat royalty statements!

Who's your hero?

Justin Sullivan, of the band New Model Army, who ironically sang, "There are no heroes anymore".

Ideal dinner party guests

Why, that would be the wonderful people from Angry Robot Books. OK, aided and abetted by New Model Army, and hell, why not, the cast from *Twilight*. Yes, I am getting back in touch with my teen roots. Although it has to be said, if Milla Jovovich popped in, I wouldn't deny her a sausage.

The biggest influence on your writing

David Gemmell, recently departed King of Heroic Fantasy. Sorry. It's just the way it is. Because of Dave, I started writing seriously, and indeed started writing heroic fantasy.

The biggest influence on your life

My dad. A complex one this, so I won't go into it here (it's part of my PhD, it's that complex). He was as close to a hero you could get or hope for. He escaped from two prisoner-of-war camps, and he shot some Nazis. Wish I'd been there.

Got a nickname?

Jappo. It's a long story. Oh yes, and there was one at school – Mugsy, after the old Melbourne House Spectrum game about gangsters. And, I believe, some cheeky monkey scamp kids used to call me Captain Ginger Beard when I was a teacher, bless their little cotton chainsaws.

Tell us a joke

It's a rude one. It's about this fat woman. And her fat husband… No, no, my reputation is already bad enough to kill a skunk at fifty yards, without making it worse. I'm trying to keep my big stupid mouth shut. I'm trying, anyway.

Support a team?

No. I believe football (soccer, haha) has become a pure game of pure money. An absolute business trans-action!! And I do not subscribe to money unless it's buying me a new motorbike.

What do you sing in the shower

I don't sing. I scrub. I am a scrubber.

Any notable pets?

Yes, Samson, my big fat chocolate Labrador who starred in my first three Spiral books. He's dead now, bless him, the stubborn teddy-shagging mongrel, but now I have an insane Border Collie called Fizz (not my choice) who puts me to shame on technical ridge-lines at the top of mountains by bounding around like a mountain goat on mescaline whilst I cling in fear to the edges of high rocks. What a bitch.

Earliest memory?

Being naked in a paddling pool in Yugoslavia in 1976. The humiliation, I tell you! My mother has a photo. The bitch.

First story you told?

I was about 7 or 8. I wrote a novel called *The Four-Headed Monster*. It was about a Four-Headed Monster. I told it to the class. They were suitably impressed (as 7 and 8 year-olds are by a Four-Headed Monster).

First story you sold?

My first novel, *Spiral*, to Orbit Books. Thank you, Tim Holman ;-)

What do you say when people ask "Where do you get your ideas from?"

Ideas come from anywhere and everywhere, from books and films, conversations and sex, whisky and demons. You must mash it all up in a big pan, add a splash of rum, mix it with a Big Spoon™ and cook at 190 for about 1 hour 40 minutes. Then you may have the workings of a story.

Do you have an unusual talent or skill?

I can sword fight (really), am a superb cook (forget that amateur Ramsey bloke), and have been known to wield a chainsaw. You've got to be careful with a chainsaw, though, because it is amoral and can easily cut off your own leg.

Best place you ever visited?

Kenya, Africa. Magical and surreal. Went on safari, and watching elephants coming to the watering hole at sunset has to rank up there with All-Time Great Moments. It was highly amusing when a huge bull elephant took exception to the nearby watering hole dining experience, and charged at the couples enjoying a romantic meal – you've never seen fat people move so damn fast.

Favourite building or structure?

Peel Tower, Ramsbottom. My original cycling haunt. The times I've sat on those steps drinking coffee in the rain/snow/sleet and setting the world to rights with my mate, Jake. Eee. Those wer't days, lad.

What keeps you awake at night?

My three year-old climbing into my bed, snuggling down, then spinning in slow circles, methodically kicking me and my wife in the backs of our heads.

The last time you cried?

When my cat died, the nasty, feral, murdering, evil little torturer. Live by the sword, die by the sword, that's what I say.

If you weren't a writer what would you be?

I probably should have joined the army, but in

reality I cannot just cannot respond to authority. So then. Maybe a doctor? I'm certainly a pharmaceutical expert and I do enjoy seeing people in pain.

Favourite fancy dress costume?
My well-used Halloween zombie costume. It's easy. It's comfortable. It's full of rancid fake blood.

Got an irritating/bad habit?
I *am* a bad habit.

Next book you'll read?
The latest Orcs novel by Stan Nicholls. His stuff is visceral, fast-paced, good fun – a bit like mine :-)

Who plays you in the movie?
Probably Vin Diesel. He certainly has more acting talent than me, but I feel that's probably down to my incredible and awful wooden performance potential.

And what's the pivotal scene?
Probably the bit when Vin pulls out the chainsaw to kill the bad guys/ save the world/ save his poisoned girlfriend, before riding off into a toxic LA sunset on an open-pipe Harley.

We're buying... what're you drinking?
Absolutely fucking everything.

Favourite possession?
My BMW GS1200 motorbike. I have something of a Ewan McGregor/Charlie Boorman *Long Way Round* obsession. Ask my wife.

Last dream of note?

It was actually, and honestly, a dream that I'm going to turn into a novel. A kind of Urban Fantasy for the Shotgun Generation.

Favourite item of clothing?

My clogged para-boots. It has been oft claimed that I am far from the pinnacle of fashion, what with my knife-cut army combats and faded South Park t-shirts, but at least my smart designer shirts are better than those of a certain other editor I worked with in the past, who shopped for his clothes in Asda. Haha.

Would you write full-time if you could?

I do, and whilst sometimes it's totally great, sometimes I get cabin-fever and start to pull out hair, gnash teeth and drag my werewolf claws through the plaster. Then I know it's time for some human interaction.

Do you plan in detail or set off hopefully?

I plan in detail, then see where it takes me. If it shifts, I change the plan. I hate writing blind.

What's the view from your writing window?

My house has "open aspects to rear", as they say, so it's mainly fields and a few trees and hedgerows. There are foxes, rabbits and bats at dusk. It is very euphoric and intoxicating, especially (cough) after a few whiskies.

Where would you like to be right now?

New York City, driving a Ferrari. NYC is my favourite

place on Earth. There's this scurrilous rumour about how I stayed at the Waldorf Astoria wearing British army combats and a hoodie amidst people in tuxedoes, and I have to hang my head in shame and say it was totally true.

When & where were you happiest?

At the birth of my two boys. Without question, the two most intense, frightening and wonderful moments of my life. Obviously my wife was there as well, but she was high on pethadine, the lightweight. Ha ha.

Complete this sentence: Rewriting is...

Superb fun, a necessity, and an integral part of the writing process.

Complete this sentence: I owe it all to...

Myself. I am my own hardest task master, and without my own focus and motivation over so many years when the going was tough, I never would have achieved. So. Pat on the back, Remic. Thanks, mate. Here, have a whisky. Thanks again, buddy.

What advice would you give to an aspiring writer?

Be completely anal about every sentence you write, make sure you get it right, work harder than hard and be as persistent as a terrier on a firm leg. Stephen King gives excellent advice in his *On Writing*, and what I like about King's book is that it's totally down to earth, realistic, and lacking in bullshit. The best piece of advice good old Kingy gives is "omit needless words", so I shall say the same. Omit needless words. Trim the trash. Cut the crap. Make your prose sparkle! And never, ever give up!

What are you going to do right now when you've finished this ordeal?

Take the dog for a walk up to Peel Tower. She is a young Border Collie, mad with energy, and if I don't at least try and burn the bitch out, she'll be jiggling and bouncing all bloody day long – and thus stopping me from writing.

And believe me, the second Clockwork Vampire Chronicles book, *Soul Stealers*, is going so well! It will blow you away.